SELECTED
GHOST
STORIES

D0659238

SELECTED
GHOST
STORIES

M. R. JAMES

SENATE

Selected Ghost Stories

First published as *The Collected Ghost Stories of
M. R. James* in 1931 by Edward Arnold & Company,
London

Copyright © M. R. James 1931

This edition first published in 1995 by Senate,
an imprint of Random House UK Ltd,
Random House, 20 Vauxhall Bridge Road,
London SW1V 2SA

3 5 7 9 10 8 6 4 2

All rights reserved. No part of this publication may be
reproduced, stored in a retrieval system or transmitted,
in any form or by any means, electronic, mechanical,
photocopying, recording or otherwise, without the prior
permission of the copyright owners.

ISBN 1 85958 134 X

Printed and bound in Guernsey by
The Guernsey Press Co. Ltd

CONTENTS

	PAGE
CANON ALBERIC'S SCRAP-BOOK	1
LOST HEARTS	20
THE MEZZOTINT	36
THE ASH-TREE	54
NUMBER 13	75
COUNT MAGNUS	99
"OH, WHISTLE, AND I'LL COME TO YOU, MY LAD"	120
THE TREASURE OF ABBOT THOMAS	151
A SCHOOL STORY	180
THE ROSE GARDEN	191
THE TRACTATE MIDDOTH	209
CASTING THE RUNES	235
THE STALLS OF BARCHESTER CATHEDRAL	268
MARTIN'S CLOSE	289
MR. HUMPHREYS AND HIS INHERITANCE	318
THE RESIDENCE AT WHITMINSTER	359

The
COLLECTED GHOST STORIES
of M. R. JAMES

CANON ALBERIC'S SCRAP-BOOK

St. Bertrand de Comminges is a decayed town on the spurs of the Pyrenees, not very far from Toulouse, and still nearer to Bagnères-de-Luchon. It was the site of a bishopric until the Revolution, and has a cathedral which is visited by a certain number of tourists. In the spring of 1883 an Englishman arrived at this old-world place—I can hardly dignify it with the name of city, for there are not a thousand inhabitants. He was a Cambridge man, who had come specially from Toulouse to see St. Bertrand's Church, and had left two friends, who were less keen archæologists than himself, in their hotel at Toulouse, under promise to join him on the following morning. Half an hour at the church would satisfy *them*, and all three could then pursue their journey in the direction of Auch. But our Englishman had come early on the day in question, and proposed to himself to fill a notebook and to use several dozens of plates in the process of describing and photographing every corner of the wonderful church that dominates the

1

little hill of Comminges. In order to carry out this design satisfactorily, it was necessary to monopolize the verger of the church for the day. The verger or sacristan (I prefer the latter appellation, inaccurate as it may be) was accordingly sent for by the somewhat brusque lady who keeps the inn of the Chapeau Rouge; and when he came, the Englishman found him an unexpectedly interesting object of study. It was not in the personal appearance of the little, dry, wizened old man that the interest lay, for he was precisely like dozens of other church-guardians in France, but in a curious furtive, or rather hunted and oppressed, air which he had. He was perpetually half glancing behind him; the muscles of his back and shoulders seemed to be hunched in a continual nervous contraction, as if he were expecting every moment to find himself in the clutch of an enemy. The Englishman hardly knew whether to put him down as a man haunted by a fixed delusion, or as one oppressed by a guilty conscience, or as an unbearably henpecked husband. The probabilities, when reckoned up, certainly pointed to the last idea; but, still, the impression conveyed was that of a more formidable persecutor even than a termagant wife.

However, the Englishman (let us call him Dennistoun) was soon too deep in his notebook and too busy with his camera to give more than an occasional glance to the sacristan. Whenever he did look at him, he found him at no great distance, either huddling himself back against the wall or crouching in one

2

of the gorgeous stalls. Dennistoun became rather
fidgety after a time. Mingled suspicions that he
was keeping the old man from his *déjeuner*, that he
was regarded as likely to make away with St. Bertrand's ivory crozier, or with the dusty stuffed crocodile
that hangs over the font, began to torment him.

"Won't you go home?" he said at last; "I'm
quite well able to finish my notes alone; you can lock
me in if you like. I shall want at least two hours
more here, and it must be cold for you, isn't it?"

"Good heavens!" said the little man, whom
the suggestion seemed to throw into a state of un-
accountable terror, "such a thing cannot be thought
of for a moment. Leave monsieur alone in the
church? No, no; two hours, three hours, all will
be the same to me. I have breakfasted, I am not
at all cold, with many thanks to monsieur."

"Very well, my little man," quoth Dennistoun to
himself: "you have been warned, and you must
take the consequences."

Before the expiration of the two hours, the stalls,
the enormous dilapidated organ, the choir-screen of
Bishop John de Mauléon, the remnants of glass and
tapestry, and the objects in the treasure-chamber, had
been well and truly examined; the sacristan still
keeping at Dennistoun's heels, and every now and then
whipping round as if he had been stung, when one
or other of the strange noises that trouble a large
empty building fell on his ear. Curious noises they
were sometimes.

"Once," Dennistoun said to me, "I could have sworn I heard a thin metallic voice laughing high up in the tower. I darted an inquiring glance at my sacristan. He was white to the lips. 'It is he— that is—it is no one; the door is locked,' was all he said, and we looked at each other for a full minute."

Another little incident puzzled Dennistoun a good deal. He was examining a large dark picture that hangs behind the altar, one of a series illustrating the miracles of St. Bertrand. The composition of the picture is wellnigh indecipherable, but there is a Latin legend below, which runs thus :

"Qualiter S. Bertrandus liberavit hominem quem diabolus diu volebat strangulare." (How St. Bertrand delivered a man whom the Devil long sought to strangle.)

Dennistoun was turning to the sacristan with a smile and a jocular remark of some sort on his lips, but he was confounded to see the old man on his knees, gazing at the picture with the eye of a suppliant in agony, his hands tightly clasped, and a rain of tears on his cheeks. Dennistoun naturally pretended to have noticed nothing, but the question would not away from him, "Why should a daub of this kind affect anyone so strongly ? " He seemed to himself to be getting some sort of clue to the reason of the strange look that had been puzzling him all the day : the man must be a monomaniac ; but what was his monomania ?

It was nearly five o'clock; the short day was drawing in, and the church began to fill with shadows,

while the curious noises—the muffled footfalls and
distant talking voices that had been perceptible all
day—seemed, no doubt because of the fading light
and the consequently quickened sense of hearing, to
become more frequent and insistent.

The sacristan began for the first time to show signs
of hurry and impatience. He heaved a sigh of relief
when camera and notebook were finally packed up
and stowed away, and hurriedly beckoned Dennistoun
to the western door of the church, under the tower.
It was time to ring the Angelus. A few pulls at the
reluctant rope, and the great bell Bertrande, high in
the tower, began to speak, and swung her voice up
among the pines and down to the valleys, loud with
mountain-streams, calling the dwellers on those lonely
hills to remember and repeat the salutation of the
angel to her whom he called Blessed among women.
With that a profound quiet seemed to fall for the
first time that day upon the little town, and Dennistoun
and the sacristan went out of the church.

On the doorstep they fell into conversation.

"Monsieur seemed to interest himself in the old
choir-books in the sacristy."

"Undoubtedly. I was going to ask you if there
were a library in the town."

"No, monsieur; perhaps there used to be one
belonging to the Chapter, but it is now such a small
place——" Here came a strange pause of irresolution, as it seemed; then, with a sort of plunge, he
went on: "But if monsieur is *amateur des vieux livres*,

I have at home something that might interest him.
It is not a hundred yards."

At once all Dennistoun's cherished dreams of finding
priceless manuscripts in untrodden corners of France
flashed up, to die down again the next moment. It
was probably a stupid missal of Plantin's printing,
about 1580. Where was the likelihood that a place
so near Toulouse would not have been ransacked
long ago by collectors? However, it would be foolish
not to go; he would reproach himself for ever after
if he refused. So they set off. On the way the
curious irresolution and sudden determination of the
sacristan recurred to Dennistoun, and he wondered
in a shamefaced way whether he was being decoyed
into some purlieu to be made away with as a supposed
rich Englishman. He contrived, therefore, to begin
talking with his guide, and to drag in, in a rather
clumsy fashion, the fact that he expected two friends
to join him early the next morning. To his surprise,
the announcement seemed to relieve the sacristan at
once of some of the anxiety that oppressed him.

"That is well," he said quite brightly—"that is
very well. Monsieur will travel in company with
his friends; they will be always near him. It is a
good thing to travel thus in company—sometimes."

The last word appeared to be added as an after-
thought, and to bring with it a relapse into gloom for
the poor little man.

They were soon at the house, which was one
rather larger than its neighbours, stone-built, with a

shield carved over the door, the shield of Alberic de
Mauléon, a collateral descendant, Dennistoun tells
me, of Bishop John de Mauléon. This Alberic was
a Canon of Comminges from 1680 to 1701. The
upper windows of the mansion were boarded up,
and the whole place bore, as does the rest of Comminges, the aspect of decaying age.

Arrived on his doorstep, the sacristan paused a
moment.

" Perhaps," he said, " perhaps, after all, monsieur
has not the time ? "

" Not at all—lots of time—nothing to do till to-
morrow. Let us see what it is you have got."

The door was opened at this point, and a face
looked out, a face far younger than the sacristan's,
but bearing something of the same distressing look :
only here it seemed to be the mark, not so much of
fear for personal safety as of acute anxiety on behalf
of another. Plainly, the owner of the face was the
sacristan's daughter ; and, but for the expression I
have described, she was a handsome girl enough. She
brightened up considerably on seeing her father
accompanied by an able-bodied stranger. A few
remarks passed between father and daughter, of
which Dennistoun only caught these words, said by
the sacristan, " He was laughing in the church,"
words which were answered only by a look of terror
from the girl.

But in another minute they were in the sitting-
room of the house, a small, high chamber with a stone

7

floor, full of moving shadows cast by a wood-fire
that flickered on a great hearth. Something of the
character of an oratory was imparted to it by a tall
crucifix, which reached almost to the ceiling on one
side; the figure was painted of the natural colours,
the cross was black. Under this stood a chest of
some age and solidity, and when a lamp had been
brought, and chairs set, the sacristan went to this
chest, and produced therefrom, with growing excitement and nervousness, as Dennistoun thought, a
large book, wrapped in a white cloth, on which cloth
a cross was rudely embroidered in red thread. Even
before the wrapping had been removed, Dennistoun
began to be interested by the size and shape of the
volume. "Too large for a missal," he thought,
"and not the shape of an antiphoner; perhaps it
may be something good, after all." The next moment
the book was open, and Dennistoun felt that he had
at last lit upon something better than good. Before
him lay a large folio, bound, perhaps, late in the
seventeenth century, with the arms of Canon Alberic
de Mauléon stamped in gold on the sides. There
may have been a hundred and fifty leaves of paper in
the book, and on almost every one of them was
fastened a leaf from an illuminated manuscript.
Such a collection Dennistoun had hardly dreamed of
in his wildest moments. Here were ten leaves from
a copy of Genesis, illustrated with pictures, which
could not be later than A.D. 700. Further on was a
complete set of pictures from a Psalter, of English

execution, of the very finest kind that the thirteenth century could produce; and, perhaps best of all, there were twenty leaves of uncial writing in Latin, which, as a few words seen here and there told him at once, must belong to some very early unknown patristic treatise. Could it possibly be a fragment of the copy of Papias "On the Words of Our Lord," which was known to have existed as late as the twelfth century at Nîmes? [1] In any case, his mind was made up; that book must return to Cambridge with him, even if he had to draw the whole of his balance from the bank and stay at St. Bertrand till the money came. He glanced up at the sacristan to see if his face yielded any hint that the book was for sale. The sacristan was pale, and his lips were working.

"If monsieur will turn on to the end," he said.

So monsieur turned on, meeting new treasures at every rise of a leaf; and at the end of the book he came upon two sheets of paper, of much more recent date than anything he had yet seen, which puzzled him considerably. They must be contemporary, he decided, with the unprincipled Canon Alberic, who had doubtless plundered the Chapter library of St. Bertrand to form this priceless scrap-book. On the first of the paper sheets was a plan, carefully drawn and instantly recognizable by a person who knew the ground, of the south aisle and cloisters of St. Bertrand's. There were curious signs looking like

---

[1] We now know that these leaves did contain a considerable fragment of that work, if not of that actual copy of it.

planetary symbols, and a few Hebrew words, in the corners; and in the north-west angle of the cloister was a cross drawn in gold paint. Below the plan were some lines of writing in Latin, which ran thus:

"Responsa 12^{mi} Dec. 1694. Interrogatum est : Inveniamne ? Responsum est : Invenies. Fiamne dives ? Fies. Vivamne invidendus ? Vives. Moriarne in lecto meo ? Ita." (Answers of the 12th of December, 1694. It was asked: Shall I find it ? Answer: Thou shalt. Shall I become rich ? Thou wilt. Shall I live an object of envy ? Thou wilt. Shall I die in my bed ? Thou wilt.)

"A good specimen of the treasure-hunter's record —quite reminds one of Mr. Minor-Canon Quatremain in 'Old St. Paul's,' " was Dennistoun's comment, and he turned the leaf.

What he then saw impressed him, as he has often told me, more than he could have conceived any drawing or picture capable of impressing him. And, though the drawing he saw is no longer in existence, there is a photograph of it (which I possess) which fully bears out that statement. The picture in question was a sepia drawing at the end of the seventeenth century, representing, one would say at first sight, a Biblical scene; for the architecture (the picture represented an interior) and the figures had that semi-classical flavour about them which the artists of two hundred years ago thought appropriate to illustrations of the Bible. On the right was a King on his throne, the throne elevated on twelve steps, a canopy overhead, lions on either side—evidently King Solomon.

He was bending forward with outstretched sceptre, in attitude of command; his face expressed horror and disgust, yet there was in it also the mark of imperious will and confident power. The left half of the picture was the strangest, however. The interest plainly centred there. On the pavement before the throne were grouped four soldiers, surrounding a crouching figure which must be described in a moment. A fifth soldier lay dead on the pavement, his neck distorted, and his eyeballs starting from his head. The four surrounding guards were looking at the King. In their faces the sentiment of horror was intensified; they seemed, in fact, only restrained from flight by their implicit trust in their master. All this terror was plainly excited by the being that crouched in their midst. I entirely despair of conveying by any words the impression which this figure makes upon anyone who looks at it. I recollect once showing the photograph of the drawing to a lecturer on morphology—a person of, I was going to say, abnormally sane and unimaginative habits of mind. He absolutely refused to be alone for the rest of that evening, and he told me afterwards that for many nights he had not dared to put out his light before going to sleep. However, the main traits of the figure I can at least indicate. At first you saw only a mass of coarse, matted black hair; presently it was seen that this covered a body of fearful thinness, almost a skeleton, but with the muscles standing out like wires. The hands were of a dusky pallor, covered, like the body, with long, coarse hairs, and hideously taloned. The eyes, touched in with a burning yellow, had intensely black pupils, and were fixed upon the throned King with a look of beast-like hate. Imagine one of the awful bird-catching spiders of South America translated into human form, and endowed with intelligence just less than human, and you will have some faint conception of the terror inspired by this appalling effigy. One remark is universally made by those to whom I have shown the picture : " It was drawn from the life."

As soon as the first shock of his irresistible fright had subsided, Dennistoun stole a look at his hosts. The sacristan's hands were pressed upon his eyes; his daughter, looking up at the cross on the wall, was telling her beads feverishly.

At last the question was asked, " Is this book for sale ? "

There was the same hesitation, the same plunge of determination that he had noticed before, and then came the welcome answer, " If monsieur pleases."

" How much do you ask for it ? "

" I will take two hundred and fifty francs."

This was confounding. Even a collector's conscience is sometimes stirred, and Dennistoun's conscience was tenderer than a collector's.

" My good man ! " he said again and again, " your book is worth far more than two hundred and fifty francs, I assure you—far more."

But the answer did not vary: "I will take two hundred and fifty francs, not more."

There was really no possibility of refusing such a chance. The money was paid, the receipt signed, a glass of wine drunk over the transaction, and then the sacristan seemed to become a new man. He stood upright, he ceased to throw those suspicious glances behind him, he actually laughed or tried to laugh. Dennistoun rose to go.

"I shall have the honour of accompanying monsieur to his hotel?" said the sacristan.

"Oh no, thanks! it isn't a hundred yards. I know the way perfectly, and there is a moon."

The offer was pressed three or four times, and refused as often.

"Then, monsieur will summon me if—if he finds occasion; he will keep the middle of the road, the sides are so rough."

"Certainly, certainly," said Dennistoun, who was impatient to examine his prize by himself; and he stepped out into the passage with his book under his arm.

Here he was met by the daughter; she, it appeared, was anxious to do a little business on her own account; perhaps, like Gehazi, to "take somewhat" from the foreigner whom her father had spared.

"A silver crucifix and chain for the neck; monsieur would perhaps be good enough to accept it?"

Well, really, Dennistoun hadn't much use for these things. What did mademoiselle want for it?

"Nothing—nothing in the world. Monsieur is more than welcome to it."

The tone in which this and much more was said was unmistakably genuine, so that Dennistoun was reduced to profuse thanks, and submitted to have the chain put round his neck. It really seemed as if he had rendered the father and daughter some service which they hardly knew how to repay. As he set off with his book they stood at the door looking after him, and they were still looking when he waved them a last good night from the steps of the Chapeau Rouge.

Dinner was over, and Dennistoun was in his bedroom, shut up alone with his acquisition. The landlady had manifested a particular interest in him since he had told her that he had paid a visit to the sacristan and bought an old book from him. He thought, too, that he had heard a hurried dialogue between her and the said sacristan in the passage outside the *salle à manger*; some words to the effect that " Pierre and Bertrand would be sleeping in the house " had closed the conversation.

All this time a growing feeling of discomfort had been creeping over him—nervous reaction, perhaps, after the delight of his discovery. Whatever it was, it resulted in a conviction that there was someone behind him, and that he was far more comfortable with his back to the wall. All this, of course, weighed light in the balance as against the obvious value of the collection he had acquired. And now, as I said, he was alone in his bedroom, taking stock of Canon

Alberic's treasures, in which every moment revealed something more charming.

"Bless Canon Alberic!" said Dennistoun, who had an inveterate habit of talking to himself. "I wonder where he is now? Dear me! I wish that landlady would learn to laugh in a more cheering manner; it makes one feel as if there was someone dead in the house. Half a pipe more, did you say? I think perhaps you are right. I wonder what that crucifix is that the young woman insisted on giving me? Last century, I suppose. Yes, probably. It is rather a nuisance of a thing to have round one's neck—just too heavy. Most likely her father has been wearing it for years. I think I might give it a clean up before I put it away."

He had taken the crucifix off, and laid it on the table, when his attention was caught by an object ₁ying on the red cloth just by his left elbow. Two or three ideas of what it might be flitted through his brain with their own incalculable quickness.

"A penwiper? No, no such thing in the house. A rat? No, too black. A large spider? I trust to goodness not—no. Good God! a hand like the hand in that picture!"

In another infinitesimal flash he had taken it in. Pale, dusky skin, covering nothing but bones and tendons of appalling strength; coarse black hairs, longer than ever grew on a human hand; nails rising from the ends of the fingers and curving sharply down and forward, grey, horny and wrinkled.

He flew out of his chair with deadly, inconceivable terror clutching at his heart. The shape, whose left hand rested on the table, was rising to a standing posture behind his seat, its right hand crooked above his scalp. There was black and tattered drapery about it; the coarse hair covered it as in the drawing. The lower jaw was thin—what can I call it?—shallow, like a beast's; teeth showed behind the black lips; there was no nose; the eyes, of a fiery yellow, against which the pupils showed black and intense, and the exulting hate and thirst to destroy life which shone there, were the most horrifying features in the whole vision. There was intelligence of a kind in them—intelligence beyond that of a beast, below that of a man.

The feelings which this horror stirred in Dennistoun were the intensest physical fear and the most profound mental loathing. What did he do? What could he do? He has never been quite certain what words he said, but he knows that he spoke, that he grasped blindly at the silver crucifix, that he was conscious of a movement towards him on the part of the demon, and that he screamed with the voice of an animal in hideous pain.

Pierre and Bertrand, the two sturdy little serving-men, who rushed in, saw nothing, but felt themselves thrust aside by something that passed out between them, and found Dennistoun in a swoon. They sat up with him that night, and his two friends were at St. Bertrand by nine o'clock next morning. He himself, though still shaken and nervous, was almost himself by that time, and his story found credence

16

with them, though not until they had seen the drawing and talked with the sacristan.

Almost at dawn the little man had come to the inn on some pretence, and had listened with the deepest interest to the story retailed by the landlady. He showed no surprise.

"It is he—it is he! I have seen him myself," was his only comment; and to all questionings but one reply was vouchsafed: "Deux fois je l'ai vu; mille fois je l'ai senti." He would tell them nothing of the provenance of the book, nor any details of his experiences. "I shall soon sleep, and my rest will be sweet. Why should you trouble me?" he said.[1]

We shall never know what he or Canon Alberic de Mauléon suffered. At the back of that fateful drawing were some lines of writing which may be supposed to throw light on the situation:

"Contradictio Salomonis cum demonio nocturno.
Albericus de Mauleone delineavit.
V. Deus in adiutorium. Ps. Qui habitat.
Sancte Bertrande, demoniorum effugator, intercede pro me miserrimo.
Primum uidi nocte 12^{mi} Dec. 1694: uidebo mox ultimum. Peccaui et passus sum, plura adhuc passurus. Dec. 29, 1701."[2]

---

[1] He died that summer; his daughter married, and settled at St. Papoul. She never understood the circumstances of her father's "obsession."

[2] *I.e.*, The Dispute of Solomon with a demon of the night. Drawn by Alberic de Mauléon. *Versicle.* O Lord, make haste to help me. *Psalm.* Whoso dwelleth (xci.). Saint Bertrand, who puttest devils to flight, pray for me

I have never quite understood what was Dennistoun's view of the events I have narrated. He quoted to me once a text from Ecclesiasticus: "Some spirits there be that are created for vengeance, and in their fury lay on sore strokes." On another occasion he said: "Isaiah was a very sensible man; doesn't he say something about night monsters living in the ruins of Babylon? These things are rather beyond us at present."

Another confidence of his impressed me rather, and I sympathized with it. We had been, last year, to Comminges, to see Canon Alberic's tomb. It is a great marble erection with an effigy of the Canon in a large wig and soutane, and an elaborate eulogy of his learning below. I saw Dennistoun talking for some time with the Vicar of St. Bertrand's, and as we drove away he said to me: "I hope it isn't wrong: you know I am a Presbyterian—but I—I believe there will be ' saying of Mass and singing of dirges ' for Alberic de Mauléon's rest." Then he added, with a touch of the Northern British in his tone, "I had no notion they came so dear."

The book is in the Wentworth Collection at

most unhappy. I saw it first on the night of Dec. 12, 1694: soon I shall see it for the last time. I have sinned and suffered, and have more to suffer yet. Dec. 29, 1701.

The "Gallia Christiana" gives the date of the Canon's death as December 31, 1701, "in bed, of a sudden seizure." Details of this kind are not common in the great work of the Sammarthani.

Cambridge. The drawing was photographed and then burnt by Dennistoun on the day when he left Comminges on the occasion of his first visit.

LOST HEARTS

IT was, as far as I can ascertain, in September of the year 1811 that a post-chaise drew up before the door of Aswarby Hall, in the heart of Lincolnshire. The little boy who was the only passenger in the chaise, and who jumped out as soon as it had stopped, looked about him with the keenest curiosity during the short interval that elapsed between the ringing of the bell and the opening of the hall door. He saw a tall, square, red-brick house, built in the reign of Anne; a stone-pillared porch had been added in the purer classical style of 1790; the windows of the house were many, tall and narrow, with small panes and thick white woodwork. A pediment, pierced with a round window, crowned the front. There were wings to right and left, connected by curious glazed galleries, supported by colonnades, with the central block. These wings plainly contained the stables and offices of the house. Each was surmounted by an ornamental cupola with a gilded vane.

An evening light shone on the building, making the window-panes glow like so many fires. Away from the Hall in front stretched a flat park studded with oaks and fringed with firs, which stood out against the sky. The clock in the church-tower, buried in trees on the edge of the park, only its golden weather-cock catching the light, was striking six, and the sound came gently beating down the wind. It was alto-gether a pleasant impression, though tinged with the sort of melancholy appropriate to an evening in early autumn, that was conveyed to the mind of the boy who was standing in the porch waiting for the door to open to him.

The post-chaise had brought him from Warwick-shire, where, some six months before, he had been left an orphan. Now, owing to the generous offer of his elderly cousin, Mr. Abney, he had come to live at Aswarby. The offer was unexpected, because all who knew anything of Mr. Abney looked upon him as a somewhat austere recluse, into whose steady-going household the advent of a small boy would import a new and, it seemed, incongruous element. The truth is that very little was known of Mr. Abney's pursuits or temper. The Professor of Greek at Cambridge had been heard to say that no one knew more of the religious beliefs of the later pagans than did the owner of Aswarby. Certainly his library contained all the then available books bearing on the Mysteries, the Orphic poems, the worship of Mithras, and the Neo-Platonists. In the marble-paved hall stood a fine group of Mithras slaying a bull, which had been imported from the Levant at great expense by the owner. He had contributed a description of it to the *Gentleman's Magazine*, and he had written a remarkable series of articles in the *Critical Museum* on the superstitions of the Romans of the Lower Empire. He was looked upon, in fine, as a man wrapped up in his books, and it was a matter of great surprise among his neighbours that he should even have heard of his orphan cousin, Stephen Elliott, much more that he should have volunteered to make him an inmate of Aswarby Hall.

Whatever may have been expected by his neighbours, it is certain that Mr. Abney—the tall, the thin, the austere—seemed inclined to give his young cousin a kindly reception. The moment the front door was opened he darted out of his study, rubbing his hands with delight.

" How are you, my boy ?—how are you ? How old are you ? " said he—" that is, you are not too much tired, I hope, by your journey to eat your supper ? "

" No, thank you, sir," said Master Elliott ; " I am pretty well."

" That's a good lad," said Mr. Abney. " And how old are you, my boy ? "

It seemed a little odd that he should have asked the question twice in the first two minutes of their acquaintance.

" I'm twelve years old next birthday, sir," said Stephen.

" And when is your birthday, my dear boy ? Eleventh of September, eh ? That's well—that's very well. Nearly a year hence, isn't it ? I like— ha, ha !—I like to get these things down in my book. Sure it's twelve ? Certain ? "

"Yes, quite sure, sir."

"Well, well! Take him to Mrs. Bunch's room, Parkes, and let him have his tea—supper—whatever it is."

"Yes, sir," answered the staid Mr. Parkes; and conducted Stephen to the lower regions.

Mrs. Bunch was the most comfortable and human person whom Stephen had as yet met in Aswarby. She made him completely at home; they were great friends in a quarter of an hour: and great friends they remained. Mrs. Bunch had been born in the neighbourhood some fifty-five years before the date of Stephen's arrival, and her residence at the Hall was of twenty years' standing. Consequently, if anyone knew the ins and outs of the house and the district, Mrs. Bunch knew them; and she was by no means disinclined to communicate her information.

Certainly there were plenty of things about the Hall and the Hall gardens which Stephen, who was of an adventurous and inquiring turn, was anxious to have explained to him. "Who built the temple at the end of the laurel walk? Who was the old man whose picture hung on the staircase, sitting at a table, with a skull under his hand?" These and many similar points were cleared up by the resources of Mrs. Bunch's powerful intellect. There were others, however, of which the explanations furnished were less satisfactory.

One November evening Stephen was sitting by the

fire in the housekeeper's room reflecting on his surroundings.

"Is Mr. Abney a good man, and will he go to heaven?" he suddenly asked, with the peculiar confidence which children possess in the ability of their elders to settle these questions, the decision of which is believed to be reserved for other tribunals.

"Good?—bless the child!" said Mrs. Bunch. "Master's as kind a soul as ever I see! Didn't I never tell you of the little boy as he took in out of the street, as you may say, this seven years back? and the little girl, two years after I first come here?"

"No. Do tell me all about them, Mrs. Bunch —now this minute!"

"Well," said Mrs. Bunch, "the little girl I don't seem to recollect so much about. I know master brought her back with him from his walk one day, and give orders to Mrs. Ellis, as was housekeeper then, as she should be took every care with. And the pore child hadn't no one belonging to her—she told me so her own self—and here she lived with us a matter of three weeks it might be; and then, whether she were somethink of a gipsy in her blood or what not, but one morning she out of her bed afore any of us had opened a eye, and neither track nor yet trace of her have I set eyes on since. Master was wonderful put about, and had all the ponds dragged; but it's my belief she was had away by them gipsies, for there was singing round the house for as much as an hour the night she went, and Parkes, he declare as he heard them a-calling in the woods all that afternoon. Dear, dear! a hodd child she was, so silent in her ways and all, but I was wonderful taken up with her, so domesticated she was—surprising."

" And what about the little boy?" said Stephen.

" Ah, that pore boy!" sighed Mrs. Bunch. " He were a foreigner—Jevanny he called hisself—and he come a-tweaking his 'urdy-gurdy round and about the drive one winter day, and master 'ad him in that minute, and ast all about where he came from, and how old he was, and how he made his way, and where was his relatives, and all as kind as heart could wish. But it went the same way with him. They're a hunruly lot, them foreign nations, I do suppose, and he was off one fine morning just the same as the girl. Why he went and what he done was our question for as much as a year after; for he never took his 'urdy-gurdy, and there it lays on the shelf."

The remainder of the evening was spent by Stephen in miscellaneous cross-examination of Mrs. Bunch and in efforts to extract a tune from the hurdy-gurdy.

That night he had a curious dream. At the end of the passage at the top of the house, in which his bedroom was situated, there was an old disused bath-room. It was kept locked, but the upper half of the door was glazed, and, since the muslin curtains which used to hang there had long been gone, you could look in and see the lead-lined bath affixed to the wall on the right hand, with its head towards the window.

On the night of which I am speaking, Stephen

Elliott found himself, as he thought, looking through the glazed door. The moon was shining through the window, and he was gazing at a figure which lay in the bath.

His description of what he saw reminds me of what I once beheld myself in the famous vaults of St. Michan's Church in Dublin, which possess the horrid property of preserving corpses from decay for centuries. A figure inexpressibly thin and pathetic, of a dusty leaden colour, enveloped in a shroud-like garment, the thin lips crooked into a faint and dreadful smile, the hands pressed tightly over the region of the heart.

As he looked upon it, a distant, almost inaudible moan seemed to issue from its lips, and the arms began to stir. The terror of the sight forced Stephen backwards, and he awoke to the fact that he was indeed standing on the cold boarded floor of the passage in the full light of the moon. With a courage which I do not think can be common among boys of his age, he went to the door of the bathroom to ascertain if the figure of his dream were really there. It was not, and he went back to bed.

Mrs. Bunch was much impressed next morning by his story, and went so far as to replace the muslin curtain over the glazed door of the bathroom. Mr. Abney, moreover, to whom he confided his experiences at breakfast, was greatly interested, and made notes of the matter in what he called " his book."

The spring equinox was approaching, as Mr. Abney frequently reminded his cousin, adding that this had been always considered by the ancients to be a critical time for the young : that Stephen would do well to take care of himself, and to shut his bedroom window at night; and that Censorinus had some valuable remarks on the subject. Two incidents that occurred about this time made an impression upon Stephen's mind.

The first was after an unusually uneasy and oppressed night that he had passed—though he could not recall any particular dream that he had had.

The following evening Mrs. Bunch was occupying herself in mending his nightgown.

" Gracious me, Master Stephen ! " she broke forth rather irritably, " how do you manage to tear your nightdress all to flinders this way ? Look here, sir, what trouble you do give to poor servants that have to darn and mend after you ! "

There was indeed a most destructive and apparently wanton series of slits or scorings in the garment, which would undoubtedly require a skilful needle to make good. They were confined to the left side of the chest—long, parallel slits, about six inches in length, some of them not quite piercing the texture of the linen. Stephen could only express his entire ignorance of their origin : he was sure they were not there the night before.

" But," he said, " Mrs. Bunch, they are just the same as the scratches on the outside of my bedroom door; and I'm sure I never had anything to do with making *them*."

Mrs. Bunch gazed at him open-mouthed, then snatched up a candle, departed hastily from the room, and was heard making her way upstairs. In a few minutes she came down.

" Well," she said, " Master Stephen, it's a funny thing to me how them marks and scratches can 'a' come there—too high up for any cat or dog to 'ave made 'em, much less a rat: for all the world like a Chinaman's finger-nails, as my uncle in the tea-trade used to tell us of when we was girls together. I wouldn't say nothing to master, not if I was you, Master Stephen, my dear; and just turn the key of the door when you go to your bed."

" I always do, Mrs. Bunch, as soon as I've said my prayers."

" Ah, that's a good child: always say your prayers, and then no one can't hurt you."

Herewith Mrs. Bunch addressed herself to mending the injured nightgown, with intervals of meditation, until bed-time. This was on a Friday night in March, 1812.

On the following evening the usual duet of Stephen and Mrs. Bunch was augmented by the sudden arrival of Mr. Parkes, the butler, who as a rule kept himself rather *to* himself in his own pantry. He did not see that Stephen was there: he was, moreover, flustered, and less slow of speech than was his wont.

" Master may get up his own wine, if he likes, of

an evening," was his first remark. " Either I do it in the daytime or not at all, Mrs. Bunch. I don't know what it may be : very like it's the rats, or the wind got into the cellars ; but I'm not so young as I was, and I can't go through with it as I have done."

" Well, Mr. Parkes, you know it is a surprising place for the rats, is the Hall."

" I'm not denying that, Mrs. Bunch ; and, to be sure, many a time I've heard the tale from the men in the shipyards about the rat that could speak. I never laid no confidence in that before ; but to-night, if I'd demeaned myself to lay my ear to the door of the further bin, I could pretty much have heard what they was saying."

" Oh, there, Mr. Parkes, I've no patience with your fancies ! Rats talking in the wine-cellar indeed ! "

" Well, Mrs. Bunch, I've no wish to argue with you : all I say is, if you choose to go to the far bin, and lay your ear to the door, you may prove my words this minute."

" What nonsense you do talk, Mr. Parkes—not fit for children to listen to ! Why, you'll be frightening Master Stephen there out of his wits."

" What ! Master Stephen ? " said Parkes, awaking to the consciousness of the boy's presence. " Master Stephen knows well enough when I'm a-playing a joke with you, Mrs. Bunch."

In fact, Master Stephen knew much too well to suppose that Mr. Parkes had in the first instance intended a joke. He was interested, not altogether pleasantly, in the situation; but all his questions were unsuccessful in inducing the butler to give any more detailed account of his experiences in the wine-cellar.

We have now arrived at March 24, 1812. It was a day of curious experiences for Stephen: a windy, noisy day, which filled the house and the gardens with a restless impression. As Stephen stood by the fence of the grounds, and looked out into the park, he felt as if an endless procession of unseen people were sweeping past him on the wind, borne on resistlessly and aimlessly, vainly striving to stop themselves, to catch at something that might arrest their flight and bring them once again into contact with the living world of which they had formed a part. After luncheon that day Mr. Abney said:

" Stephen, my boy, do you think you could manage to come to me to-night as late as eleven o'clock in my study? I shall be busy until that time, and I wish to show you something connected with your future life which it is most important that you should know. You are not to mention this matter to Mrs. Bunch nor to anyone else in the house; and you had better go to your room at the usual time."

Here was a new excitement added to life: Stephen eagerly grasped at the opportunity of sitting up till eleven o'clock. He looked in at the library door on his way upstairs that evening, and saw a brazier, which he had often noticed in the corner of the room, moved out before the fire; an old silver-gilt cup stood on the table, filled with red wine, and some written sheets of paper lay near it. Mr. Abney was sprinkling some incense on the brazier from a round silver box as Stephen passed, but did not seem to notice his step.

The wind had fallen, and there was a still night and a full moon. At about ten o'clock Stephen was standing at the open window of his bedroom, looking out over the country. Still as the night was, the mysterious population of the distant moonlit woods was not yet lulled to rest. From time to time strange cries as of lost and despairing wanderers sounded from across the mere. They might be the notes of owls or water-birds, yet they did not quite resemble either sound. Were not they coming nearer? Now they sounded from the nearer side of the water, and in a few moments they seemed to be floating about among the shrubberies. Then they ceased; but just as Stephen was thinking of shutting the window and resuming his reading of *Robinson Crusoe*, he caught sight of two figures standing on the gravelled terrace that ran along the garden side of the Hall—the figures of a boy and girl, as it seemed; they stood side by side, looking up at the windows. Something in the form of the girl recalled irresistibly his dream of the figure in the bath. The boy inspired him with more acute fear.

Whilst the girl stood still, half smiling, with her hands clasped over her heart, the boy, a thin shape, with black hair and ragged clothing, raised his arms

31

in the air with an appearance of menace and of un-
appeasable hunger and longing. The moon shone
upon his almost transparent hands, and Stephen saw
that the nails were fearfully long and that the light
shone through them. As he stood with his arms
thus raised, he disclosed a terrifying spectacle. On
the left side of his chest there opened a black and
gaping rent; and there fell upon Stephen's brain,
rather than upon his ear, the impression of one of
those hungry and desolate cries that he had heard
resounding over the woods of Aswarby all that
evening. In another moment this dreadful pair had
moved swiftly and noiselessly over the dry gravel,
and he saw them no more.

Inexpressibly frightened as he was, he determined
to take his candle and go down to Mr. Abney's study,
for the hour appointed for their meeting was near at
hand. The study or library opened out of the front
hall on one side, and Stephen, urged on by his terrors,
did not take long in getting there. To effect an
entrance was not so easy. The door was not locked,
he felt sure, for the key was on the outside of it as
usual. His repeated knocks produced no answer.
Mr. Abney was engaged: he was speaking. What!
why did he try to cry out? and why was the cry
choked in his throat? Had he, too, seen the mysterious children? But now everything was quiet,
and the door yielded to Stephen's terrified and frantic
pushing.

    *   *   *   *   *

On the table in Mr. Abney's study certain papers were found which explained the situation to Stephen Elliott when he was of an age to understand them. The most important sentences were as follows :

" It was a belief very strongly and generally held by the ancients—of whose wisdom in these matters I have had such experience as induces me to place confidence in their assertions—that by enacting certain processes, which to us moderns have something of a barbaric complexion, a very remarkable enlightenment of the spiritual faculties in man may be attained : that, for example, by absorbing the personalities of a certain number of his fellow-creatures, an individual may gain a complete ascendancy over those orders of spiritual beings which control the elemental forces of our universe.

" It is recorded of Simon Magus that he was able to fly in the air, to become invisible, or to assume any form he pleased, by the agency of the soul of a boy whom, to use the libellous phrase employed by the author of the *Clementine Recognitions*, he had ' murdered.' I find it set down, moreover, with considerable detail in the writings of Hermes Trismegistus, that similar happy results may be produced by the absorption of the hearts of not less than three human beings below the age of twenty-one years. To the testing of the truth of this receipt I have devoted the greater part of the last twenty years, selecting as the *corpora vilia* of my experiment such persons as could conveniently be removed without occasioning a sensible gap in society. The first step I effected by the removal of one Phœbe Stanley, a girl of gipsy extraction, on March 24, 1792. The second, by the removal of a wandering Italian lad, named Giovanni Paoli, on the night of March 23, 1805. The final ' victim '—to employ a word repugnant in the highest degree to my feelings—must be my cousin, Stephen Elliott. His day must be this March 24, 1812.

" The best means of effecting the required absorption is to remove the heart from the *living* subject, to reduce it to ashes, and to mingle them with about a pint of some red wine, preferably port. The remains of the first two subjects, at least, it will be well to conceal : a disused bathroom or wine-cellar will be found convenient for such a purpose. Some annoyance may be experienced from the psychic portion of the subjects, which popular language dignifies with the name of ghosts. But the man of philosophic temperament—to whom alone the experiment is appropriate—will be little prone to attach importance to the feeble efforts of these beings to wreak their vengeance on him. I contemplate with the liveliest satisfaction the enlarged and emancipated existence which the experiment, if successful, will confer on me ; not only placing me beyond the reach of human justice (so-called), but eliminating to a great extent the prospect of death itself."

Mr. Abney was found in his chair, his head thrown

back, his face stamped with an expression of rage, fright, and mortal pain. In his left side was a terrible lacerated wound, exposing the heart. There was no blood on his hands, and a long knife that lay on the table was perfectly clean. A savage wild-cat might have inflicted the injuries. The window of the study was open, and it was the opinion of the coroner that Mr. Abney had met his death by the agency of some wild creature. But Stephen Elliott's study of the papers I have quoted led him to a very different conclusion.

THE MEZZOTINT

SOME time ago I believe I had the pleasure of telling you the story of an adventure which happened to a friend of mine by the name of Dennistoun, during his pursuit of objects of art for the museum at Cambridge.

He did not publish his experiences very widely upon his return to England; but they could not fail to become known to a good many of his friends, and among others to the gentleman who at that time presided over an art museum at another University. It was to be expected that the story should make a considerable impression on the mind of a man whose vocation lay in lines similar to Dennistoun's, and that he should be eager to catch at any explanation of the matter which tended to make it seem improbable that he should ever be called upon to deal with so agitating an emergency. It was, indeed, somewhat consoling to him to reflect that he was not expected to acquire ancient MSS. for his institution; that was the business of the Shelburnian Library. The authorities of that might, if they pleased, ransack obscure corners of the Continent for such matters. He was glad to be obliged at the moment to confine his attention to enlarging the already unsurpassed collection of English topographical drawings and engravings possessed by his museum. Yet, as it turned out, even a department so homely and familiar as this may have its dark corners, and to one of these Mr. Williams was unexpectedly introduced.

Those who have taken even the most limited interest in the acquisition of topographical pictures are aware that there is one London dealer whose aid is indispensable to their researches. Mr. J. W. Britnell publishes at short intervals very admirable catalogues of a large and constantly changing stock of engravings, plans, and old sketches of mansions, churches, and towns in England and Wales. These catalogues were, of course, the ABC of his subject to Mr. Williams : but as his museum already contained an enormous accumulation of topographical pictures, he was a regular, rather than a copious, buyer ; and he rather looked to Mr. Britnell to fill up gaps in the rank and file of his collection than to supply him with rarities.

Now, in February of last year there appeared upon Mr. Williams's desk at the museum a catalogue from Mr. Britnell's emporium, and accompanying it was a typewritten communication from the dealer himself. This latter ran as follows :

Dear Sir,—

We beg to call your attention to No. 978 in our accompanying catalogue, which we shall be glad to send on approval. Yours faithfully,

J. W. Britnell.

To turn to No. 978 in the accompanying catalogue was with Mr. Williams (as he observed to himself) the work of a moment, and in the place indicated he found the following entry :

" 978.—*Unknown*. Interesting mezzotint : View of a manor-house, early part of the century. 15 by 10 inches ; black frame. £2 2*s*."

It was not specially exciting, and the price seemed high. However, as Mr. Britnell, who knew his business and his customer, seemed to set store by it, Mr. Williams wrote a postcard asking for the article to be sent on approval, along with some other engravings and sketches which appeared in the same catalogue. And so he passed without much excitement of anticipation to the ordinary labours of the day.

A parcel of any kind always arrives a day later than you expect it, and that of Mr. Britnell proved, as I believe the right phrase goes, no exception to the rule. It was delivered at the museum by the afternoon post of Saturday, after Mr. Williams had left his work, and it was accordingly brought round to his rooms in college by the attendant, in order that he might not have to wait over Sunday before looking through it and returning such of the contents as he did not propose to keep. And here he found it when he came in to tea, with a friend.

The only item with which I am concerned was the rather large, black-framed mezzotint of which I have already quoted the short description given in Mr. Britnell's catalogue. Some more details of it will

have to be given, though I cannot hope to put before
you the look of the picture as clearly as it is present
to my own eye. Very nearly the exact duplicate of
it may be seen in a good many old inn parlours, or
in the passages of undisturbed country mansions at
the present moment. It was a rather indifferent
mezzotint, and an indifferent mezzotint is, perhaps,
the worst form of engraving known. It presented a
full-face view of a not very large manor-house of the
last century, with three rows of plain sashed windows
with rusticated masonry about them, a parapet with
balls or vases at the angles, and a small portico in the
centre. On either side were trees, and in front a
considerable expanse of lawn. The legend " A. W. F.
sculpsit " was engraved on the narrow margin; and
there was no further inscription. The whole thing
gave the impression that it was the work of an amateur.
What in the world Mr. Britnell could mean by affixing
the price of £2 2s. to such an object was more than
Mr. Williams could imagine. He turned it over with
a good deal of contempt; upon the back was a paper
label, the left-hand half of which had been torn off.
All that remained were the ends of two lines of
writing: the first had the letters —*ngley Hall*; the
second, —*ssex*.

It would, perhaps, be just worth while to identify
the place represented, which he could easily do with
the help of a gazetteer, and then he would send it
back to Mr. Britnell, with some remarks reflecting
upon the judgment of that gentleman.

He lighted the candles, for it was now dark, made the tea, and supplied the friend with whom he had been playing golf (for I believe the authorities of the University I write of indulge in that pursuit by way of relaxation); and tea was taken to the accompaniment of a discussion which golfing persons can imagine for themselves, but which the conscientious writer has no right to inflict upon any non-golfing persons.

The conclusion arrived at was that certain strokes might have been better, and that in certain emergencies neither player had experienced that amount of luck which a human being has a right to expect. It was now that the friend—let us call him Professor Binks—took up the framed engraving, and said:

"What's this place, Williams?"

"Just what I am going to try to find out," said Williams, going to the shelf for a gazetteer. "Look at the back. Somethingley Hall, either in Sussex or Essex. Half the name's gone, you see. You don't happen to know it, I suppose?"

"It's from that man Britnell, I suppose, isn't it?" said Binks. "Is it for the museum?"

"Well, I think I should buy it if the price was five shillings," said Williams; "but for some unearthly reason he wants two guineas for it. I can't conceive why. It's a wretched engraving, and there aren't even any figures to give it life."

"It's not worth two guineas, I should think," said Binks; "but I don't think it's so badly done. The

moonlight seems rather good to me; and I should
have thought there *were* figures, or at least a figure,
just on the edge in front."

"Let's look," said Williams. "Well, it's true the
light is rather cleverly given. Where's your figure?
Oh yes! Just the head, in the very front of the
picture."

And indeed there was—hardly more than a black
blot on the extreme edge of the engraving—the head
of a man or woman, a good deal muffled up, the back
turned to the spectator, and looking towards the house.

Williams had not noticed it before.

"Still," he said, "though it's a cleverer thing than
I thought, I can't spend two guineas of museum
money on a picture of a place I don't know."

Professor Binks had his work to do, and soon went;
and very nearly up to Hall time Williams was engaged
in a vain attempt to identify the subject of his picture.
"If the vowel before the *ng* had only been left, it
would have been easy enough," he thought; "but
as it is, the name may be anything from Guestingley
to Langley, and there are many more names ending
like this than I thought; and this rotten book has
no index of terminations."

Hall in Mr. Williams's college was at seven. It
need not be dwelt upon; the less so as he met there
colleagues who had been playing golf during the
afternoon, and words with which we have no concern
were freely bandied across the table—merely golfing
words, I would hasten to explain.

I suppose an hour or more to have been spent in what is called common-room after dinner. Later in the evening some few retired to Williams's rooms, and I have little doubt that whist was played and tobacco smoked. During a lull in these operations Williams picked up the mezzotint from the table without looking at it, and handed it to a person mildly interested in art, telling him where it had come from, and the other particulars which we already know.

The gentleman took it carelessly, looked at it, then said, in a tone of some interest:

"It's really a very good piece of work, Williams; it has quite a feeling of the romantic period. The light is admirably managed, it seems to me, and the figure, though it's rather too grotesque, is somehow very impressive."

"Yes, isn't it?" said Williams, who was just then busy giving whisky-and-soda to others of the company, and was unable to come across the room to look at the view again.

It was by this time rather late in the evening, and the visitors were on the move. After they went Williams was obliged to write a letter or two and clear up some odd bits of work. At last, some time past midnight, he was disposed to turn in, and he put out his lamp after lighting his bedroom candle. The picture lay face upwards on the table where the last man who looked at it had put it, and it caught his eye as he turned the lamp down. What he saw made him very nearly drop the candle on the floor, and he declares now that if he had been left in the dark at that moment he would have had a fit. But, as that did not happen, he was able to put down the light on the table and take a good look at the picture. It was indubitable—rankly impossible, no doubt, but absolutely certain. In the middle of the lawn in front of the unknown house there was a figure where no figure had been at five o'clock that afternoon. It was crawling on all-fours towards the house, and it was muffled in a strange black garment with a white cross on the back.

I do not know what is the ideal course to pursue in a situation of this kind. I can only tell you what Mr. Williams did. He took the picture by one corner and carried it across the passage to a second set of rooms which he possessed. There he locked it up in a drawer, sported the doors of both sets of rooms, and retired to bed; but first he wrote out and signed an account of the extraordinary change which the picture had undergone since it had come into his possession.

Sleep visited him rather late; but it was consoling to reflect that the behaviour of the picture did not depend upon his own unsupported testimony. Evidently the man who had looked at it the night before had seen something of the same kind as he had, otherwise he might have been tempted to think that something gravely wrong was happening either to his eyes or his mind. This possibility being fortunately precluded, two matters awaited him on the morrow. He must take stock of the picture very carefully, and call in a witness for the purpose, and he must make a determined effort to ascertain what house it was that was represented. He would therefore ask his neighbour Nisbet to breakfast with him, and he would subsequently spend a morning over the gazetteer.

Nisbet was disengaged, and arrived about 9.30. His host was not quite dressed, I am sorry to say, even at this late hour. During breakfast nothing was said about the mezzotint by Williams, save that he had a picture on which he wished for Nisbet's opinion. But those who are familiar with University life can picture for themselves the wide and delightful range of subjects over which the conversation of two Fellows of Canterbury College is likely to extend during a Sunday morning breakfast. Hardly a topic was left unchallenged, from golf to lawn-tennis. Yet I am bound to say that Williams was rather distraught; for his interest naturally centred in that very strange picture which was now reposing, face downwards, in the drawer in the room opposite.

The morning pipe was at last lighted, and the moment had arrived for which he looked. With very considerable—almost tremulous—excitement, he ran across, unlocked the drawer, and, extracting the picture—still face downwards—ran back, and put it into Nisbet's hands.

" Now," he said, " Nisbet, I want you to tell me

exactly what you see in that picture. Describe it, if you don't mind, rather minutely. I'll tell you why afterwards."

"Well," said Nisbet, "I have here a view of a country-house — English, I presume — by moonlight."

"Moonlight? You're sure of that?"

"Certainly. The moon appears to be on the wane, if you wish for details, and there are clouds in the sky."

"All right. Go on. I'll swear," added Williams in an aside, "there was no moon when I saw it first."

"Well, there's not much more to be said," Nisbet continued. "The house has one—two—three rows of windows, five in each row, except at the bottom, where there's a porch instead of the middle one, and——"

"But what about figures?" said Williams, with marked interest.

"There aren't any," said Nisbet; "but——"

"What! No figure on the grass in front?"

"Not a thing."

"You'll swear to that?"

"Certainly I will. But there's just one other thing."

"What?"

"Why, one of the windows on the ground-floor —left of the door—is open."

"Is it really? My goodness! he must have got in," said Williams, with great excitement; and he hurried to the back of the sofa on which Nisbet was sitting, and, catching the picture from him, verified the matter for himself.

It was quite true. There was no figure, and there was the open window. Williams, after a moment of speechless surprise, went to the writing-table and scribbled for a short time. Then he brought two papers to Nisbet, and asked him first to sign one—it was his own description of the picture, which you have just heard—and then to read the other which was Williams's statement written the night before.

"What can it all mean?" said Nisbet.

"Exactly," said Williams. "Well, one thing I must do—or three things, now I think of it. I must find out from Garwood "—this was his last night's visitor—" what he saw, and then I must get the thing photographed before it goes further, and then I must find out what the place is."

" I can do the photographing myself," said Nisbet, " and I will. But, you know, it looks very much as if we were assisting at the working out of a tragedy somewhere. The question is, Has it happened already, or is it going to come off? You must find out what the place is. Yes," he said, looking at the picture again, " I expect you're right : he has got in. And if I don't mistake there'll be the devil to pay in one of the rooms upstairs."

" I'll tell you what," said Williams : " I'll take the picture across to old Green " (this was the senior Fellow of the College, who had been Bursar for many years). " It's quite likely he'll know it. We have property in Essex and Sussex, and he must have been over the two counties a lot in his time."

" Quite likely he will," said Nisbet; " but just let me take my photograph first. But look here, I rather think Green isn't up to-day. He wasn't in Hall last night, and I think I heard him say he was going down for the Sunday."

" That's true, too," said Williams; " I know he's gone to Brighton. Well, if you'll photograph it now, I'll go across to Garwood and get his statement, and you keep an eye on it while I'm gone. I'm beginning to think two guineas is not a very exorbitant price for it now."

In a short time he had returned, and brought Mr. Garwood with him. Garwood's statement was to the effect that the figure, when he had seen it, was clear of the edge of the picture, but had not got far across the lawn. He remembered a white mark on the back of its drapery, but could not have been sure it was a cross. A document to this effect was then drawn up and signed, and Nisbet proceeded to photograph the picture.

" Now what do you mean to do ? " he said. " Are you going to sit and watch it all day ? "

" Well, no, I think not," said Williams. " I rather imagine we're meant to see the whole thing. You see, between the time I saw it last night and this morning there was time for lots of things to happen, but the creature only got into the house. It could

47

easily have got through its business in the time and gone to its own place again; but the fact of the window being open, I think, must mean that it's in there now. So I feel quite easy about leaving it. And, besides, I have a kind of idea that it wouldn't change much, if at all, in the daytime. We might go out for a walk this afternoon, and come in to tea, or whenever it gets dark. I shall leave it out on the table here, and sport the door. My skip can get in, but no one else."

The three agreed that this would be a good plan; and, further, that if they spent the afternoon together they would be less likely to talk about the business to other people; for any rumour of such a transaction as was going on would bring the whole of the Phasmatological Society about their ears.

We may give them a respite until five o'clock.

At or near that hour the three were entering Williams's staircase. They were at first slightly annoyed to see that the door of his rooms was unsported; but in a moment it was remembered that on Sunday the skips came for orders an hour or so earlier than on week-days. However, a surprise was awaiting them. The first thing they saw was the picture leaning up against a pile of books on the table, as it had been left, and the next thing was Williams's skip, seated on a chair opposite, gazing at it with undisguised horror. How was this? Mr. Filcher (the name is not my own invention) was a servant of considerable standing, and set the standard of etiquette to all his own college and to several neighbouring ones, and nothing could be more alien to his practice than to be found sitting on his master's chair, or appearing to take any particular notice of his master's furniture or pictures. Indeed, he seemed to feel this himself. He started violently when the three men came into the room, and got up with a marked effort. Then he said:

"I ask your pardon, sir, for taking such a freedom as to set down."

"Not at all, Robert," interposed Mr. Williams. "I was meaning to ask you some time what you thought of that picture."

"Well, sir, of course I don't set up my opinion again yours, but it ain't the pictur I should 'ang where my little girl could see it, sir."

"Wouldn't you, Robert? Why not?"

"No, sir. Why, the pore child, I recollect once she see a Door Bible, with pictures not 'alf what that is, and we 'ad to set up with her three or four nights afterwards, if you'll believe me; and if she was to ketch a sight of this skelinton here, or whatever it is, carrying off the pore baby, she would be in a taking. You know 'ow it is with children; 'ow nervish they git with a little thing and all. But what I should say, it don't seem a right pictur to be laying about, sir, not where anyone that's liable to be startled could come on it. Should you be wanting anything this evening, sir? Thank you, sir."

With these words the excellent man went to continue the round of his masters, and you may be sure the gentlemen whom he left lost no time in gathering round the engraving. There was the house, as before, under the waning moon and the drifting clouds. The window that had been open was shut, and the figure was once more on the lawn : but not this time crawling cautiously on hands and knees. Now it was erect and stepping swiftly, with long strides, towards the front of the picture. The moon was behind it, and the black drapery hung down over its face so that only hints of that could be seen, and what was visible made the spectators profoundly thankful that they could see no more than a white dome-like forehead and a few straggling hairs. The head was bent down, and the arms were tightly clasped over an object which could be dimly seen and identified as a child, whether dead or living it was not possible to say. The legs of the appearance alone could be plainly discerned, and they were horribly thin.

From five to seven the three companions sat and watched the picture by turns. But it never changed. They agreed at last that it would be safe to leave it, and that they would return after Hall and await further developments.

When they assembled again, at the earliest possible moment, the engraving was there, but the figure was gone, and the house was quiet under the moonbeams. There was nothing for it but to spend the evening over gazetteers and guide-books. Williams was the lucky one at last, and perhaps he deserved it. At

11.30 p.m. he read from Murray's *Guide to Essex* the following lines :

"16½ miles, *Anningley*. The church has been an interesting building of Norman date, but was extensively classicized in the last century. It contains the tombs of the family of Francis, whose mansion, Anningley Hall, a solid Queen Anne house, stands immediately beyond the churchyard in a park of about 80 acres. The family is now extinct, the last heir having disappeared mysteriously in infancy in the year 1802. The father, Mr. Arthur Francis, was locally known as a talented amateur engraver in mezzotint. After his son's disappearance he lived in complete retirement at the Hall, and was found dead in his studio on the third anniversary of the disaster, having just completed an engraving of the house, impressions of which are of considerable rarity."

This looked like business, and, indeed, Mr. Green on his return at once identified the house as Anningley Hall.

"Is there any kind of explanation of the figure, Green ? " was the question which Williams naturally asked.

"I don't know, I'm sure, Williams. What used to be said in the place when I first knew it, which was before I came up here, was just this : old Francis was always very much down on these poaching fellows, and whenever he got a chance he used to get a man whom he suspected of it turned off the estate, and by degrees he got rid of them all but one. Squires could do a lot of things then that they daren't think of now. Well, this man that was left was what you find pretty often in that country—the last remains of a very old family. I believe they were Lords of the Manor at one time. I recollect just the same thing in my own parish."

" What, like the man in *Tess of the D'Urbervilles* ? " Williams put in.

" Yes, I dare say ; it's not a book I could ever read myself. But this fellow could show a row of tombs in the church there that belonged to his ancestors, and all that went to sour him a bit ; but Francis, they said, could never get at him—he always kept just on the right side of the law—until one night the keepers found him at it in a wood right at the end of the estate. I could show you the place now ; it marches with some land that used to belong to an uncle of mine. And you can imagine there was a row ; and this man Gawdy (that was the name, to be sure—Gawdy ; I thought I should get it—Gawdy), he was unlucky enough, poor chap ! to shoot a keeper. Well, that was what Francis wanted, and grand juries—you know what they would have been then—and poor Gawdy was strung up in double-quick time ; and I've been shown the place he was buried in, on the north side of the church—you know the way in that part of the world : anyone that's been hanged or made away with themselves, they bury them that side. And the idea was that some friend of Gawdy's—not a relation, because he had none, poor devil! he was the last of his line : kind of *spes ultima gentis*—must have planned to get hold of Francis's boy and put an end to *his* line, too. I don't know—it's rather an out-of-the-way thing for an Essex poacher to think of—but, you know, I should say now it looks more as if old Gawdy had managed the job himself. Booh! I hate to think of it! have some whisky, Williams ! "

The facts were communicated by Williams to Dennistoun, and by him to a mixed company, of which I was one, and the Sadducean Professor of Ophiology another. I am sorry to say that the latter, when asked what he thought of it, only remarked : " Oh, those Bridgeford people will say anything "— a sentiment which met with the reception it deserved.

I have only to add that the picture is now in the Ashleian Museum; that it has been treated with a view to discovering whether sympathetic ink has been used in it, but without effect; that Mr. Britnell knew nothing of it save that he was sure it was uncommon; and that, though carefully watched, it has never been known to change again.

THE ASH-TREE

EVERYONE who has travelled over Eastern England knows the smaller country-houses with which it is studded—the rather dank little buildings, usually in the Italian style, surrounded with parks of some eighty to a hundred acres. For me they have always had a very strong attraction : with the grey paling of split oak, the noble trees, the meres with their reed-beds, and the line of distant woods. Then, I like the pillared portico—perhaps stuck on to a red-brick Queen Anne house which has been faced with stucco to bring it into line with the " Grecian " taste of the end of the eighteenth century ; the hall inside, going up to the roof, which hall ought always to be provided with a gallery and a small organ. I like the library, too, where you may find anything from a Psalter of the thirteenth century to a Shakespeare quarto. I like the pictures, of course ; and perhaps most of all I like fancying what life in such a house was when it was first built, and in the piping times of landlords' prosperity, and not least now, when, if money is not so plentiful, taste is more varied and life quite as interesting. I wish to have one of these houses, and enough money to keep it together and entertain my friends in it modestly.

But this is a digression. I have to tell you of a curious series of events which happened in such a house as I have tried to describe. It is Castringham Hall in Suffolk. I think a good deal has been done to the building since the period of my story, but the essential features I have sketched are still there—Italian portico, square block of white house, older inside than out, park with fringe of woods, and mere. The one feature that marked out the house from a score of others is gone. As you looked at it from the park, you saw on the right a great old ash-tree growing within half a dozen yards of the wall, and almost or quite touching the building with its branches. I suppose it had stood there ever since Castringham ceased to be a fortified place, and since the moat was filled in and the Elizabethan dwelling-house built. At any rate, it had wellnigh attained its full dimensions in the year 1690.

In that year the district in which the Hall is situated was the scene of a number of witch-trials. It will be long, I think, before we arrive at a just estimate of the amount of solid reason—if there was any—which lay at the root of the universal fear of witches in old times. Whether the persons accused of this offence really did imagine that they were possessed of unusual powers of any kind; or whether they had the will at least, if not the power, of doing mischief to their neighbours; or whether all the confessions, of which there are so many, were extorted by the mere cruelty of the witch-finders—these are questions which are not, I fancy, yet solved. And the present narrative gives me pause. I cannot altogether sweep it away as mere invention. The reader must judge for himself.

Castringham contributed a victim to the *auto-da-fé*. Mrs. Mothersole was her name, and she differed from the ordinary run of village witches only in being rather better off and in a more influential position. Efforts were made to save her by several reputable farmers of the parish. They did their best to testify to her character, and showed considerable anxiety as to the verdict of the jury.

But what seems to have been fatal to the woman was the evidence of the then proprietor of Castringham Hall—Sir Matthew Fell. He deposed to having watched her on three different occasions from his window, at the full of the moon, gathering sprigs " from the ash-tree near my house." She had climbed into the branches, clad only in her shift, and was cutting off small twigs with a peculiarly curved knife, and as she did so she seemed to be talking to herself. On each occasion Sir Matthew had done his best to capture the woman, but she had always taken alarm at some accidental noise he had made, and all he could see when he got down to the garden was a hare running across the park in the direction of the village.

On the third night he had been at the pains to follow at his best speed, and had gone straight to Mrs. Mothersole's house ; but he had had to wait a quarter of an hour battering at her door, and then she had come out very cross, and apparently very sleepy, as if just out of bed; and he had no good explanation to offer of his visit.

Mainly on this evidence, though there was much more of a less striking and unusual kind from other parishioners, Mrs. Mothersole was found guilty and condemned to die. She was hanged a week after the trial, with five or six more unhappy creatures, at Bury St. Edmunds.

Sir Matthew Fell, then Deputy-Sheriff, was present at the execution. It was a damp, drizzly March morning when the cart made its way up the rough grass hill outside Northgate, where the gallows stood. The other victims were apathetic or broken down with misery; but Mrs. Mothersole was, as in life so in death, of a very different temper. Her "poysonous Rage," as a reporter of the time puts it, "did so work upon the Bystanders—yea, even upon the Hangman —that it was constantly affirmed of all that saw her that she presented the living Aspect of a mad Divell. Yet she offer'd no Resistance to the Officers of the Law; onely she looked upon those that laid Hands upon her with so direfull and venomous an Aspect that—as one of them afterwards assured me—the meer Thought of it preyed inwardly upon his Mind for six Months after."

However, all that she is reported to have said was the seemingly meaningless words: "There will be guests at the Hall." Which she repeated more than once in an undertone.

Sir Matthew Fell was not unimpressed by the bearing of the woman. He had some talk upon the matter with the Vicar of his parish, with whom he travelled home after the assize business was over. His evidence at the trial had not been very willingly given; he was not specially infected with the witch-finding mania, but he declared, then and afterwards, that he could not give any other account of the matter than that he had given, and that he could not possibly have been mistaken as to what he saw. The whole transaction had been repugnant to him, for he was a man who liked to be on pleasant terms with those about him; but he saw a duty to be done in this business, and he had done it. That seems to have been the gist of his sentiments, and the Vicar applauded it, as any reasonable man must have done.

A few weeks after, when the moon of May was at the full, Vicar and Squire met again in the park, and walked to the Hall together. Lady Fell was with her mother, who was dangerously ill, and Sir Matthew was alone at home; so the Vicar, Mr. Crome, was easily persuaded to take a late supper at the Hall.

Sir Matthew was not very good company this evening. The talk ran chiefly on family and parish matters, and, as luck would have it, Sir Matthew made a memorandum in writing of certain wishes or intentions of his regarding his estates, which afterwards proved exceedingly useful.

When Mr. Crome thought of starting for home, about half-past nine o'clock, Sir Matthew and he took a preliminary turn on the gravelled walk at the back of the house. The only incident that struck Mr. Crome was this : they were in sight of the ash-tree which I described as growing near the windows of the building, when Sir Matthew stopped and said :

"What is that that runs up and down the stem of the ash ? It is never a squirrel ? They will all be in their nests by now."

The Vicar looked and saw the moving creature, but he could make nothing of its colour in the moon-light. The sharp outline, however, seen for an instant, was imprinted on his brain, and he could have sworn, he said, though it sounded foolish, that, squirrel or not, it had more than four legs.

Still, not much was to be made of the momentary vision, and the two men parted. They may have met since then, but it was not for a score of years.

Next day Sir Matthew Fell was not downstairs at six in the morning, as was his custom, nor at seven, nor yet at eight. Hereupon the servants went and knocked at his chamber door. I need not prolong the description of their anxious listenings and renewed batterings on the panels. The door was opened at last from the outside, and they found their master dead and black. So much you have guessed. That there were any marks of violence did not at the moment appear ; but the window was open.

One of the men went to fetch the parson, and then by his directions rode on to give notice to the coroner. Mr. Crome himself went as quick as he might to the

Hall, and was shown to the room where the dead man lay. He has left some notes among his papers which show how genuine a respect and sorrow was felt for Sir Matthew, and there is also this passage, which I transcribe for the sake of the light it throws upon the course of events, and also upon the common beliefs of the time :

" There was not any the least Trace of an Entrance having been forc'd to the Chamber : but the Casement stood open, as my poor Friend would always have it in this Season. He had his Evening Drink of small Ale in a silver vessel of about a pint measure, and to-night had not drunk it out. This Drink was examined by the Physician from Bury, a Mr. Hodgkins, who could not, however, as he afterwards declar'd upon his Oath, before the Coroner's quest, discover that any matter of a venomous kind was present in it. For, as was natural, in the great Swelling and Blackness of the Corpse, there was talk made among the Neighbours of Poyson. The Body was very much Disorder'd as it laid in the Bed, being twisted after so extream a sort as gave too probable Conjecture that my worthy Friend and Patron had expir'd in great Pain and Agony. And what is as yet unexplain'd, and to myself the Argument of some Horrid and Artfull Designe in the Perpetrators of this Barbarous Murther, was this, that the Women which were entrusted with the laying-out of the Corpse and washing it, being both sad Persons and very well Respected in their Mournfull Profession, came to me in a great Pain and Distress both of Mind and Body, saying, what was indeed confirmed upon the first View, that they had no sooner touch'd the Breast of the Corpse with their naked Hands than they were sensible of a more than ordinary violent Smart and Acheing in their Palms, which, with their whole Forearms, in no long time swell'd so immoderately, the Pain still continuing, that, as afterwards proved, during many weeks they were forc'd to lay by the exercise of their Calling; and yet no mark seen on the Skin.

" Upon hearing this, I sent for the Physician, who was still in the House, and we made as carefull a Proof as we were able by the Help of a small Magnifying Lens of Crystal of the condition of the Skinn on this Part of the Body: but could not detect with the Instrument we had any Matter of Importance beyond a couple of small Punctures or Pricks, which we then concluded were the Spotts by which the Poyson might be introduced, remembering that Ring of *Pope Borgia*, with other known Specimens of the Horrid Art of the Italian Poysoners of the last age.

" So much is to be said of the Symptoms seen on the Corpse. As to what I am to add, it is meerly my own Experiment, and to be left to Posterity to judge whether there be anything of Value therein. There was on the Table by the Beddside a Bible of the small size, in which my Friend—punctuall as in Matters of less Moment, so in this more weighty one—used nightly, and upon his First Rising, to read a sett

Portion. And I taking it up—not without a Tear duly paid to him which from the Study of this poorer Adumbration was now pass'd to the contemplation of its great Originall—it came into my Thoughts, as at such moments of Helplessness we are prone to catch at any the least Glimmer that makes promise of Light, to make trial of that old and by many accounted Superstitious Practice of drawing the *Sortes* : of which a Principall Instance, in the case of his late Sacred Majesty the Blessed Martyr King *Charles* and my Lord *Falkland*, was now much talked of. I must needs admit that by my Trial not much Assistance was afforded me : yet, as the Cause and Origin of these Dreadful Events may hereafter be search'd out, I set down the Results, in the case it may be found that they pointed the true Quarter of the Mischief to a quicker Intelligence than my own.

"I made, then, three trials, opening the Book and placing my Finger upon certain Words : which gave in the first these words, from Luke xiii. 7, *Cut it down* ; in the second, Isaiah xiii. 20, *It shall never be inhabited* ; and upon the third Experiment, Job xxxix. 30, *Her young ones also suck up blood.*"

This is all that need be quoted from Mr. Crome's papers. Sir Matthew Fell was duly coffined and laid into the earth, and his funeral sermon, preached by Mr. Crome on the following Sunday, has been printed under the title of " The Unsearchable Way ; or, England's Danger and the Malicious Dealings of Antichrist," it being the Vicar's view, as well as that most commonly held in the neighbourhood, that the Squire was the victim of a recrudescence of the Popish Plot.

His son, Sir Matthew the second, succeeded to the title and estates. And so ends the first act of the Castringham tragedy. It is to be mentioned, though the fact is not surprising, that the new Baronet did not occupy the room in which his father had died. Nor, indeed, was it slept in by anyone but an occasional visitor during the whole of his occupation. He died in 1735, and I do not find that anything particular marked his reign, save a curiously constant mortality among his cattle and live-stock in general, which showed a tendency to increase slightly as time went on.

Those who are interested in the details will find a statistical account in a letter to the *Gentleman's Magazine* of 1772, which draws the facts from the Baronet's own papers. He put an end to it at last by a very simple expedient, that of shutting up all his beasts in sheds at night, and keeping no sheep in his park. For he had noticed that nothing was ever attacked that spent the night indoors. After that the disorder confined itself to wild birds, and beasts of chase. But as we have no good account of the symptoms, and as all-night watching was quite unproductive of any clue, I do not dwell on what the Suffolk farmers called the " Castringham sickness."

The second Sir Matthew died in 1735, as I said, and was duly succeeded by his son, Sir Richard. It was

in his time that the great family pew was built out
on the north side of the parish church. So large were
the Squire's ideas that several of the graves on that
unhallowed side of the building had to be disturbed
to satisfy his requirements. Among them was that
of Mrs. Mothersole, the position of which was
accurately known, thanks to a note on a plan of the
church and yard, both made by Mr. Crome.

A certain amount of interest was excited in the
village when it was known that the famous witch, who
was still remembered by a few, was to be exhumed.
And the feeling of surprise, and indeed disquiet, was
very strong when it was found that, though her coffin
was fairly sound and unbroken, there was no trace
whatever inside it of body, bones, or dust. Indeed,
it is a curious phenomenon, for at the time of her
burying no such things were dreamt of as resurrection-
men, and it is difficult to conceive any rational motive
for stealing a body otherwise than for the uses of the
dissecting-room.

The incident revived for a time all the stories of
witch-trials and of the exploits of the witches, dormant
for forty years, and Sir Richard's orders that the
coffin should be burnt were thought by a good many
to be rather foolhardy, though they were duly carried
out.

Sir Richard was a pestilent innovator, it is certain.
Before his time the Hall had been a fine block of the
mellowest red brick; but Sir Richard had travelled
in Italy and become infected with the Italian taste,

and, having more money than his predecessors, he
determined to leave an Italian palace where he had
found an English house. So stucco and ashlar
masked the brick; some indifferent Roman marbles
were planted about in the entrance-hall and gardens;
a reproduction of the Sibyl's temple at Tivoli was
erected on the opposite bank of the mere; and
Castringham took on an entirely new, and, I must say,
a less engaging, aspect. But it was much admired,
and served as a model to a good many of the neighbouring gentry in after-years.

One morning (it was in 1754) Sir Richard woke
after a night of discomfort. It had been windy, and
his chimney had smoked persistently, and yet it was
so cold that he must keep up a fire. Also something
had so rattled about the window that no man could
get a moment's peace. Further, there was the
prospect of several guests of position arriving in the
course of the day, who would expect sport of some
kind, and the inroads of the distemper (which continued among his game) had been lately so serious
that he was afraid for his reputation as a game-
preserver. But what really touched him most nearly
was the other matter of his sleepless night. He could
certainly not sleep in that room again.

That was the chief subject of his meditations at
breakfast, and after it he began a systematic examination of the rooms to see which would suit his notions
best. It was long before he found one. This had

a window with an eastern aspect and that with a
northern; this door the servants would be always
passing, and he did not like the bedstead in that. No,
he must have a room with a western look-out, so
that the sun could not wake him early, and it must
be out of the way of the business of the house. The
housekeeper was at the end of her resources.

"Well, Sir Richard," she said, "you know that
there is but one room like that in the house."

"Which may that be?" said Sir Richard.

"And that is Sir Matthew's—the West Chamber."

"Well, put me in there, for there I'll lie to-night,"
said her master. "Which way is it? Here, to be
sure"; and he hurried off.

"Oh, Sir Richard, but no one has slept there these
forty years. The air has hardly been changed since
Sir Matthew died there."

Thus she spoke, and rustled after him.

"Come, open the door, Mrs. Chiddock. I'll see
the chamber, at least."

So it was opened, and, indeed, the smell was very
close and earthy. Sir Richard crossed to the window,
and, impatiently, as was his wont, threw the shutters
back, and flung open the casement. For this end of
the house was one which the alterations had barely
touched, grown up as it was with the great ash-tree,
and being otherwise concealed from view.

"Air it, Mrs. Chiddock, all to-day, and move my
bed-furniture in in the afternoon. Put the Bishop
of Kilmore in my old room."

66

" Pray, Sir Richard," said a new voice, breaking in on this speech, " might I have the favour of a moment's interview ? "

Sir Richard turned round and saw a man in black in the doorway, who bowed.

" I must ask your indulgence for this intrusion, Sir Richard. You will, perhaps, hardly remember me. My name is William Crome, and my grandfather was Vicar here in your grandfather's time."

" Well, sir," said Sir Richard, " the name of Crome is always a passport to Castringham. I am glad to renew a friendship of two generations' standing. In what can I serve you ? for your hour of calling— and, if I do not mistake you, your bearing—shows you to be in some haste."

" That is no more than the truth, sir. I am riding from Norwich to Bury St. Edmunds with what haste I can make, and I have called in on my way to leave with you some papers which we have but just come upon in looking over what my grandfather left at his death. It is thought you may find some matters of family interest in them."

" You are mighty obliging, Mr. Crome, and, if you will be so good as to follow me to the parlour, and drink a glass of wine, we will take a first look at these same papers together. And you, Mrs. Chiddock, as I said, be about airing this chamber. . . . Yes, it is here my grandfather died. . . . Yes, the tree, per- haps, does make the place a little dampish. . . . No ; I do not wish to listen to any more. Make no difficulties, I beg. You have your orders—go. Will you follow me, sir?"

They went to the study. The packet which young Mr. Crome had brought—he was then just become a Fellow of Clare Hall in Cambridge, I may say, and subsequently brought out a respectable edition of Polyænus—contained among other things the notes which the old Vicar had made upon the occasion of Sir Matthew Fell's death. And for the first time Sir Richard was confronted with the enigmatical *Sortes Biblicæ* which you have heard. They amused him a good deal.

"Well," he said, "my grandfather's Bible gave one prudent piece of advice—*Cut it down*. If that stands for the ash-tree, he may rest assured I shall not neglect it. Such a nest of catarrhs and agues was never seen."

The parlour contained the family books, which, pending the arrival of a collection which Sir Richard had made in Italy, and the building of a proper room to receive them, were not many in number.

Sir Richard looked up from the paper to the book-case.

"I wonder," says he, "whether the old prophet is there yet? I fancy I see him."

Crossing the room, he took out a dumpy Bible, which, sure enough, bore on the flyleaf the inscription: "To Matthew Fell, from his Loving Godmother, Anne Aldous, 2 September, 1659."

"It would be no bad plan to test him again, Mr.

Crome. I will wager we get a couple of names in the Chronicles. H'm! what have we here? 'Thou shalt seek me in the morning, and I shall not be.' Well, well! Your grandfather would have made a fine omen of that, hey? No more prophets for me! They are all in a tale. And now, Mr. Crome, I am infinitely obliged to you for your packet. You will, I fear, be impatient to get on. Pray allow me—another glass."

So with offers of hospitality, which were genuinely meant (for Sir Richard thought well of the young man's address and manner), they parted.

In the afternoon came the guests—the Bishop of Kilmore, Lady Mary Hervey, Sir William Kentfield, etc. Dinner at five, wine, cards, supper, and dispersal to bed.

Next morning Sir Richard is disinclined to take his gun with the rest. He talks with the Bishop of Kilmore. This prelate, unlike a good many of the Irish Bishops of his day, had visited his see, and, indeed, resided there for some considerable time. This morning, as the two were walking along the terrace and talking over the alterations and improvements in the house, the Bishop said, pointing to the window of the West Room:

"You could never get one of my Irish flock to occupy that room, Sir Richard."

"Why is that, my lord? It is, in fact, my own."

"Well, our Irish peasantry will always have it that it brings the worst of luck to sleep near an ash-tree, and you have a fine growth of ash not two yards from your chamber window. Perhaps," the Bishop went on, with a smile, " it has given you a touch of its quality already, for you do not seem, if I may say it, so much the fresher for your night's rest as your friends would like to see you."

" That, or something else, it is true, cost me my sleep from twelve to four, my lord. But the tree is to come down to-morrow, so I shall not hear much more from it."

" I applaud your determination. It can hardly be wholesome to have the air you breathe strained, as it were, through all that leafage."

" Your lordship is right there, I think. But I had not my window open last night. It was rather the noise that went on—no doubt from the twigs sweeping the glass—that kept me open-eyed."

" I think that can hardly be, Sir Richard. Here— you see it from this point. None of these nearest branches even can touch your casement unless there were a gale, and there was none of that last night. They miss the panes by a foot."

" No, sir, true. What, then, will it be, I wonder, that scratched and rustled so—ay, and covered the dust on my sill with lines and marks ? "

At last they agreed that the rats must have come up through the ivy. That was the Bishop's idea, and Sir Richard jumped at it.

So the day passed quietly, and night came, and the party dispersed to their rooms, and wished Sir Richard a better night.

And now we are in his bedroom, with the light out and the Squire in bed. The room is over the kitchen, and the night outside still and warm, so the window stands open.

There is very little light about the bedstead, but there is a strange movement there; it seems as if Sir Richard were moving his head rapidly to and fro with only the slightest possible sound. And now you would guess, so deceptive is the half-darkness, that he had several heads, round and brownish, which move back and forward, even as low as his chest. It is a horrible illusion. Is it nothing more? There! something drops off the bed with a soft plump, like a kitten, and is out of the window in a flash; another —four—and after that there is quiet again.

" *Thou shalt seek me in the morning, and I shall not be.*"

As with Sir Matthew, so with Sir Richard—dead and black in his bed!

A pale and silent party of guests and servants gathered under the window when the news was known. Italian poisoners, Popish emissaries, infected air—all these and more guesses were hazarded, and the Bishop of Kilmore looked at the tree, in the fork of whose lower boughs a white tom-cat was crouching, looking down the hollow which years had gnawed in the trunk. It was watching something inside the tree with great interest.

Suddenly it got up and craned over the hole. Then

a bit of the edge on which it stood gave way, and it went slithering in. Everyone looked up at the noise of the fall.

It is known to most of us that a cat can cry; but few of us have heard, I hope, such a yell as came out of the trunk of the great ash. Two or three screams there were—the witnesses are not sure which—and then a slight and muffled noise of some commotion or struggling was all that came. But Lady Mary Hervey fainted outright, and the housekeeper stopped her ears and fled till she fell on the terrace.

The Bishop of Kilmore and Sir William Kentfield stayed. Yet even they were daunted, though it was only at the cry of a cat; and Sir William swallowed once or twice before he could say:

"There is something more than we know of in that tree, my lord. I am for an instant search."

And this was agreed upon. A ladder was brought, and one of the gardeners went up, and, looking down the hollow, could detect nothing but a few dim indications of something moving. They got a lantern, and let it down by a rope.

"We must get at the bottom of this. My life upon it, my lord, but the secret of these terrible deaths is there."

Up went the gardener again with the lantern, and let it down the hole cautiously. They saw the yellow light upon his face as he bent over, and saw his face struck with an incredulous terror and loathing before he cried out in a dreadful voice and fell back from

the ladder—where, happily, he was caught by two
of the men—letting the lantern fall inside the tree.

He was in a dead faint, and it was some time before
any word could be got from him.

By then they had something else to look at. The
lantern must have broken at the bottom, and the light
in it caught upon dry leaves and rubbish that lay there,
for in a few minutes a dense smoke began to come
up, and then flame; and, to be short, the tree was
in a blaze.

The bystanders made a ring at some yards' distance,
and Sir William and the Bishop sent men to get what
weapons and tools they could; for, clearly, whatever
might be using the tree as its lair would be forced
out by the fire.

So it was. First, at the fork, they saw a round body
covered with fire—the size of a man's head—appear
very suddenly, then seem to collapse and fall back.
This, five or six times; then a similar ball leapt into
the air and fell on the grass, where after a moment it
lay still. The Bishop went as near as he dared to it,
and saw—what but the remains of an enormous spider,
veinous and seared! And, as the fire burned lower
down, more terrible bodies like this began to break
out from the trunk, and it was seen that these were
covered with greyish hair.

All that day the ash burned, and until it fell to
pieces the men stood about it, and from time to
time killed the brutes as they darted out. At last
there was a long interval when none appeared, and

73

they cautiously closed in and examined the roots of the tree.

"They found," says the Bishop of Kilmore, "below it a rounded hollow place in the earth, wherein were two or three bodies of these creatures that had plainly been smothered by the smoke; and, what is to me more curious, at the side of this den, against the wall, was crouching the anatomy or skeleton of a human being, with the skin dried upon the bones, having some remains of black hair, which was pronounced by those that examined it to be undoubtedly the body of a woman, and clearly dead for a period of fifty years."

NUMBER 13

AMONG the towns of Jutland, Viborg justly holds a high place. It is the seat of a bishopric; it has a handsome but almost entirely new cathedral, a charming garden, a lake of great beauty, and many storks. Near it is Hald, accounted one of the prettiest things in Denmark; and hard by is Finderup, where Marsk Stig murdered King Erik Glipping on St. Cecilia's Day, in the year 1286. Fifty-six blows of square-headed iron maces were traced on Erik's skull when his tomb was opened in the seventeenth century. But I am not writing a guide-book.

There are good hotels in Viborg—Preisler's and the Phœnix are all that can be desired. But my cousin, whose experiences I have to tell you now, went to the Golden Lion the first time that he visited Viborg. He has not been there since, and the following pages will perhaps explain the reason of his abstention.

The Golden Lion is one of the very few houses in the town that were not destroyed in the great fire of 1726, which practically demolished the cathedral, the Sognekirke, the Raadhuus, and so much else that was old and interesting. It is a great red-brick house—that is, the front is of brick, with corbie steps on the gables and a text over the door; but the court-

75

yard into which the omnibus drives is of black and white "cage-work" in wood and plaster.

The sun was declining in the heavens when my cousin walked up to the door, and the light smote full upon the imposing façade of the house. He was delighted with the old-fashioned aspect of the place, and promised himself a thoroughly satisfactory and amusing stay in an inn so typical of old Jutland.

It was not business in the ordinary sense of the word that had brought Mr. Anderson to Viborg. He was engaged upon some researches into the Church history of Denmark, and it had come to his knowledge that in the Rigsarkiv of Viborg there were papers, saved from the fire, relating to the last days of Roman Catholicism in the country. He proposed, therefore, to spend a considerable time—perhaps as much as a fortnight or three weeks—in examining and copying these, and he hoped that the Golden Lion would be able to give him a room of sufficient size to serve alike as a bedroom and a study. His wishes were explained to the landlord, and, after a certain amount of thought, the latter suggested that perhaps it might be the best way for the gentleman to look at one or two of the larger rooms and pick one for himself. It seemed a good idea.

The top floor was soon rejected as entailing too much getting upstairs after the day's work; the second floor contained no room of exactly the dimensions required; but on the first floor there was a

choice of two or three rooms which would, so far
as size went, suit admirably.

The landlord was strongly in favour of Number 17,
but Mr. Anderson pointed out that its windows
commanded only the blank wall of the next house,
and that it would be very dark in the afternoon.
Either Number 12 or Number 14 would be better,
for both of them looked on the street, and the bright
evening light and the pretty view would more than
compensate him for the additional amount of noise.

Eventually Number 12 was selected. Like its
neighbours, it had three windows, all on one side of
the room; it was fairly high and unusually long.
There was, of course, no fireplace, but the stove was
handsome and rather old—a cast-iron erection, on
the side of which was a representation of Abraham
sacrificing Isaac, and the inscription, " 1 Bog Mose,
Cap. 22," above. Nothing else in the room was
remarkable; the only interesting picture was an old
coloured print of the town, date about 1820.

Supper-time was approaching, but when Anderson,
refreshed by the ordinary ablutions, descended the
staircase, there were still a few minutes before the
bell rang. He devoted them to examining the list of
his fellow-lodgers. As is usual in Denmark, their
names were displayed on a large blackboard, divided
into columns and lines, the numbers of the rooms
being painted in at the beginning of each line. The
list was not exciting. There was an advocate, or
Sagförer, a German, and some bagmen from Copen-

hagen. The one and only point which suggested any food for thought was the absence of any Number 13 from the tale of the rooms, and even this was a thing which Anderson had already noticed half a dozen times in his experience of Danish hotels. He could not help wondering whether the objection to that particular number, common as it is, was so widespread and so strong as to make it difficult to let a room so ticketed, and he resolved to ask the landlord if he and his colleagues in the profession had actually met with many clients who refused to be accommodated in the thirteenth room.

He had nothing to tell me (I am giving the story as I heard it from him) about what passed at supper, and the evening, which was spent in unpacking and arranging his clothes, books, and papers, was not more eventful. Towards eleven o'clock he resolved to go to bed, but with him, as with a good many other people nowadays, an almost necessary preliminary to bed, if he meant to sleep, was the reading of a few pages of print, and he now remembered that the particular book which he had been reading in the train, and which alone would satisfy him at that present moment, was in the pocket of his greatcoat, then hanging on a peg outside the dining-room.

To run down and secure it was the work of a moment, and, as the passages were by no means dark, it was not difficult for him to find his way back to his own door. So, at least, he thought; but when he arrived there, and turned the handle, the door entirely refused to open, and he caught the sound of a hasty movement towards it from within. He had tried the wrong door, of course. Was his own room to the right or to the left? He glanced at the number: it was 13. His room would be on the left; and so it was. And not before he had been in bed for some minutes, had read his wonted three or four pages of his book, blown out his light, and turned over to go to sleep, did it occur to him that, whereas on the blackboard of the hotel there had been no Number 13, there was undoubtedly a room numbered 13 in the hotel. He felt rather sorry he had not chosen it for his own. Perhaps he might have done the landlord a little service by occupying it, and given him the chance of saying that a well-born English gentleman had lived in it for three weeks and liked it very much. But probably it was used as a servant's room or something of the kind. After all, it was most likely not so large or good a room as his own. And he looked drowsily about the room, which was fairly perceptible in the half-light from the street-lamp. It was a curious effect, he thought. Rooms usually look larger in a dim light than a full one, but this seemed to have contracted in length and grown proportionately higher. Well, well! sleep was more important than these vague ruminations—and to sleep he went.

On the day after his arrival Anderson attacked the Rigsarkiv of Viborg. He was, as one might expect in Denmark, kindly received, and access to all that he wished to see was made as easy for him as possible.

The documents laid before him were far more numerous and interesting than he had at all anticipated. Besides official papers, there was a large bundle of correspondence relating to Bishop Jörgen Friis, the last Roman Catholic who held the see, and in these there cropped up many amusing and what are called "intimate" details of private life and individual character. There was much talk of a house owned by the Bishop, but not inhabited by him, in the town. Its tenant was apparently somewhat of a scandal and a stumbling-block to the reforming party. He was a disgrace, they wrote, to the city ; he practised secret and wicked arts, and had sold his soul to the enemy. It was of a piece with the gross corruption and superstition of the Babylonish Church that such a viper and blood-sucking *Troldmand* should be patronized and harboured by the Bishop. The Bishop met these reproaches boldly ; he protested his own abhorrence of all such things as secret arts, and required his antagonists to bring the matter before the proper court—of course, the spiritual court—and sift it to the bottom. No one could be more ready and willing than himself to condemn Mag. Nicolas Francken if the evidence showed him to have been guilty of any of the crimes informally alleged against him.

Anderson had not time to do more than glance at the next letter of the Protestant leader, Rasmus Nielsen, before the record office was closed for the day, but he gathered its general tenor, which was to the effect that Christian men were now no longer

bound by the decisions of Bishops of Rome, and that
the Bishop's Court was not, and could not be, a fit
or competent tribunal to judge so grave and weighty
a cause.

On leaving the office, Mr. Anderson was accompanied by the old gentleman who presided over it,
and, as they walked, the conversation very naturally
turned to the papers of which I have just been speaking.

Herr Scavenius, the Archivist of Viborg, though
very well informed as to the general run of the documents under his charge, was not a specialist in those
of the Reformation period. He was much interested
in what Anderson had to tell him about them. He
looked forward with great pleasure, he said, to seeing
the publication in which Mr. Anderson spoke of
embodying their contents. "This house of the
Bishop Friis," he added, "it is a great puzzle to me
where it can have stood. I have studied carefully the
topography of old Viborg, but it is most unlucky—
of the old terrier of the Bishop's property which was
made in 1560, and of which we have the greater part
in the Arkiv, just the piece which had the list of the
town property is missing. Never mind. Perhaps I
shall some day succeed to find him."

After taking some exercise—I forget exactly how
or where—Anderson went back to the Golden Lion,
his supper, his game of patience, and his bed. On the
way to his room it occurred to him that he had forgotten to talk to the landlord about the omission of
Number 13 from the hotel, and also that he might

as well make sure that Number 13 did actually exist before he made any reference to the matter.

The decision was not difficult to arrive at. There was the door with its number as plain as could be, and work of some kind was evidently going on inside it, for as he neared the door he could hear footsteps and voices, or a voice, within. During the few seconds in which he halted to make sure of the number, the footsteps ceased, seemingly very near the door, and he was a little startled at hearing a quick hissing breathing as of a person in strong excitement. He went on to his own room, and again he was surprised to find how much smaller it seemed now than it had when he selected it. It was a slight disappointment, but only slight. If he found it really not large enough, he could very easily shift to another. In the meantime he wanted something—as far as I remember it was a pocket-handkerchief—out of his portmanteau, which had been placed by the porter on a very inadequate trestle or stool against the wall at the farthest end of the room from his bed. Here was a very curious thing : the portmanteau was not to be seen. It had been moved by officious servants ; doubtless the contents had been put in the wardrobe. No, none of them were there. This was vexatious. The idea of a theft he dismissed at once. Such things rarely happen in Denmark, but some piece of stupidity had certainly been performed (which is not so uncommon), and the *stuepige* must be severely spoken to. Whatever it was that he wanted, it was not so necessary to his comfort that he could not wait till the morning for it, and he therefore settled not to ring the bell and disturb the servants. He went to the window—the right-hand window it was—and looked out on the quiet street. There was a tall building opposite, with large spaces of dead wall ; no passers-by ; a dark night ; and very little to be seen of any kind.

The light was behind him, and he could see his own shadow clearly cast on the wall opposite. Also the shadow of the bearded man in Number 11 on the left, who passed to and fro in shirtsleeves once or twice, and was seen first brushing his hair, and later on in a nightgown. Also the shadow of the occupant of Number 13 on the right. This might be more interesting. Number 13 was, like himself, leaning on his elbows on the window-sill looking out into the street. He seemed to be a tall thin man—or was it by any chance a woman ?—at least, it was someone who covered his or her head with some kind of drapery before going to bed, and, he thought, must be possessed of a red lamp-shade—and the lamp must be flickering very much. There was a distinct playing up and down of a dull red light on the opposite wall. He craned out a little to see if he could make any more of the figure, but beyond a fold of some light, perhaps white, material on the window-sill he could see nothing.

Now came a distant step in the street, and its approach seemed to recall Number 13 to a sense of his exposed position, for very swiftly and suddenly he swept aside from the window, and his red light went out. Anderson, who had been smoking a cigarette, laid the end of it on the window-sill and went to bed.

Next morning he was woke by the *stuepige* with hot water, etc. He roused himself, and after thinking out the correct Danish words, said as distinctly as he could :

" You must not move my portmanteau. Where is it ? "

As is not uncommon, the maid laughed, and went away without making any distinct answer.

Anderson, rather irritated, sat up in bed, intending to call her back, but he remained sitting up, staring straight in front of him. There was his portmanteau on its trestle, exactly where he had seen the porter put it when he first arrived. This was a rude shock for a man who prided himself on his accuracy of observation. How it could possibly have escaped him the night before he did not pretend to understand ; at any rate, there it was now.

The daylight showed more than the portmanteau ; it let the true proportions of the room with its three windows appear, and satisfied its tenant that his choice after all had not been a bad one. When he was almost dressed he walked to the middle one of the three windows to look out at the weather. Another shock awaited him. Strangely unobservant he must have been last night. He could have sworn ten times over that he had been smoking at the right-hand window the last thing before he went to bed, and here was his cigarette-end on the sill of the middle window.

He started to go down to breakfast. Rather late, but Number 13 was later : here were his boots still outside his door—a gentleman's boots. So then Number 13 was a man, not a woman. Just then he caught sight of the number on the door. It was 14. He thought he must have passed Number 13 without noticing it. Three stupid mistakes in twelve hours were too much for a methodical, accurate-minded man, so he turned back to make sure. The next number to 14 was number 12, his own room. There was no Number 13 at all.

After some minutes devoted to a careful consideration of everything he had had to eat and drink during the last twenty-four hours, Anderson decided to give the question up. If his sight or his brain were giving way he would have plenty of opportunities for ascertaining that fact ; if not, then he was evidently being treated to a very interesting experience. In either case the development of events would certainly be worth watching.

During the day he continued his examination of the episcopal correspondence which I have already summarized. To his disappointment, it was incomplete. Only one other letter could be found which referred to the affair of Mag. Nicolas Francken. It was from the Bishop Jörgen Friis to Rasmus Nielsen. He said :

" Although we are not in the least degree inclined to assent to your judgment concerning our court, and shall be prepared if need be to withstand you to the uttermost in that behalf, yet forasmuch as our trusty and well-beloved Mag. Nicolas Francken, against whom you have dared to allege certain false and malicious charges, hath been suddenly removed from among us, it is apparent that the question for this time falls. But forasmuch as you further allege that the Apostle and Evangelist St. John in his heavenly Apocalypse describes the Holy Roman Church under the guise and symbol of the Scarlet Woman, be it known to you," etc.

Search as he might, Anderson could find no sequel to this letter nor any clue to the cause or manner of the "removal" of the *casus belli*. He could only suppose that Francken had died suddenly; and as there were only two days between the date of Nielsen's last letter—when Francken was evidently still in being—and that of the Bishop's letter, the death must have been completely unexpected.

In the afternoon he paid a short visit to Hald, and took his tea at Baekkelund; nor could he notice, though he was in a somewhat nervous frame of mind, that there was any indication of such a failure of eye or brain as his experiences of the morning had led him to fear.

At supper he found himself next to the landlord.

" What," he asked him, after some indifferent conversation, "is the reason why in most of the hotels

86

one visits in this country the number thirteen is left out of the list of rooms ? I see you have none here."

The landlord seemed amused.

" To think that you should have noticed a thing like that ! I've thought about it once or twice myself, to tell the truth. An educated man, I've said, has no business with these superstitious notions. I was brought up myself here in the High School of Viborg, and our old master was always a man to set his face against anything of that kind. He's been dead now this many years—a fine upstanding man he was, and ready with his hands as well as his head. I recollect us boys, one snowy day——"

Here he plunged into reminiscence.

" Then you don't think there is any particular objection to having a Number 13 ? " said Anderson.

" Ah ! to be sure. Well, you understand, I was brought up to the business by my poor old father. He kept an hotel in Aarhuus first, and then, when we were born, he moved to Viborg here, which was his native place, and had the Phœnix here until he died. That was in 1876. Then I started business in Silkeborg, and only the year before last I moved into this house."

Then followed more details as to the state of the house and business when first taken over.

"And when you came here, was there a Number 13 ? "

" No, no. I was going to tell you about that. You see, in a place like this, the commercial class —the travellers—are what we have to provide for in

general.   And put them in Number 13 ?   Why, they'd
as soon sleep in the street, or sooner.   As far as I'm
concerned myself, it wouldn't make a penny difference
to me what the number of my room was, and so
I've often said to them ; but they stick to it that it
brings them bad luck.   Quantities of stories they
have among them of men that have slept in a Number
13 and never been the same again, or lost their best
customers, or—one thing and another," said the
landlord, after searching for a more graphic phrase.

"Then, what do you use your Number 13 for ?"
said Anderson, conscious as he said the words of a
curious anxiety quite disproportionate to the importance of the question.

"My Number 13 ?   Why, don't I tell you that
there isn't such a thing in the house ?   I thought you
might have noticed that.   If there was it would be
next door to your own room."

"Well, yes ; only I happened to think—that is, I
fancied last night that I had seen a door numbered
thirteen in that passage ; and, really, I am almost
certain I must have been right, for I saw it the night
before as well."

Of course, Herr Kristensen laughed this notion to
scorn, as Anderson had expected, and emphasized
with much iteration the fact that no Number 13
existed or had existed before him in that hotel.

Anderson was in some ways relieved by his certainty
but still puzzled, and he began to think that the best
way to make sure whether he had indeed been subject

to an illusion or not was to invite the landlord to his room to smoke a cigar later on in the evening. Some photographs of English towns which he had with him formed a sufficiently good excuse.

Herr Kristensen was flattered by the invitation, and most willingly accepted it. At about ten o'clock he was to make his appearance, but before that Anderson had some letters to write, and retired for the purpose of writing them. He almost blushed to himself at confessing it, but he could not deny that it was the fact that he was becoming quite nervous about the question of the existence of Number 13 ; so much so that he approached his room by way of Number 11, in order that he might not be obliged to pass the door, or the place where the door ought to be. He looked quickly and suspiciously about the room when he entered it, but there was nothing, beyond that indefinable air of being smaller than usual, to warrant any misgivings. There was no question of the presence or absence of his portmanteau to-night. He had himself emptied it of its contents and lodged it under his bed. With a certain effort he dismissed the thought of Number 13 from his mind, and sat down to his writing.

His neighbours were quiet enough. Occasionally a door opened in the passage and a pair of boots was thrown out, or a bagman walked past humming to himself, and outside, from time to time a cart thundered over the atrocious cobble-stones, or a quick step hurried along the flags.

Anderson finished his letters, ordered in whisky and soda, and then went to the window and studied the dead wall opposite and the shadows upon it.

As far as he could remember, Number 14 had been occupied by the lawyer, a staid man, who said little at meals, being generally engaged in studying a small bundle of papers beside his plate. Apparently, however, he was in the habit of giving vent to his animal spirits when alone. Why else should he be dancing? The shadow from the next room evidently showed that he was. Again and again his thin form crossed the window, his arms waved, and a gaunt leg was kicked up with surprising agility. He seemed to be barefooted, and the floor must be well laid, for no sound betrayed his movements. Sagförer Herr Anders Jensen, dancing at ten o'clock at night in a hotel bedroom, seemed a fitting subject for a historical painting in the grand style; and Anderson's thoughts, like those of Emily in the *Mysteries of Udolpho*, began to " arrange themselves in the following lines " :

> " When I return to my hotel,
>   At ten o'clock p.m.,
> The waiters think I am unwell;
>   I do not care for them.
> But when I've locked my chamber door,
>   And put my boots outside,
> I dance all night upon the floor.
> And even if my neighbours swore,
> I'd go on dancing all the more,
> For I'm acquainted with the law,
> And in despite of all their jaw,
>   Their protests I deride."

90

Had not the landlord at this moment knocked at the door, it is probable that quite a long poem might have been laid before the reader. To judge from his look of surprise when he found himself in the room, Herr Kristensen was struck, as Anderson had been, by something unusual in its aspect. But he made no remark. Anderson's photographs interested him mightily, and formed the text of many autobiographical discourses. Nor is it quite clear how the conversation could have been diverted into the desired channel of Number 13, had not the lawyer at this moment begun to sing, and to sing in a manner which could leave no doubt in anyone's mind that he was either exceedingly drunk or raving mad. It was a high, thin voice that they heard, and it seemed dry, as if from long disuse. Of words or tune there was no question. It went sailing up to a surprising height, and was carried down with a despairing moan as of a winter wind in a hollow chimney, or an organ whose wind fails suddenly. It was a really horrible sound, and Anderson felt that if he had been alone he must have fled for refuge and society to some neighbour bagman's room.

The landlord sat open-mouthed.

" I don't understand it," he said at last, wiping his forehead. " It is dreadful. I have heard it once before, but I made sure it was a cat."

" Is he mad ? " said Anderson.

" He must be ; and what a sad thing ! Such a good customer, too, and so successful in his business, by what I hear, and a young family to bring up."

Just then came an impatient knock at the door, and the knocker entered, without waiting to be asked. It was the lawyer, in deshabille and very rough-haired; and very angry he looked.

"I beg pardon, sir," he said, "but I should be much obliged if you would kindly desist——"

Here he stopped, for it was evident that neither of the persons before him was responsible for the disturbance; and after a moment's lull it swelled forth again more wildly than before.

"But what in the name of Heaven does it mean?" broke out the lawyer. "Where is it? Who is it? Am I going out of my mind?"

"Surely, Herr Jensen, it comes from your room next door? Isn't there a cat or something stuck in the chimney?"

This was the best that occurred to Anderson to say, and he realized its futility as he spoke; but anything was better than to stand and listen to that horrible voice, and look at the broad, white face of the landlord, all perspiring and quivering as he clutched the arms of his chair.

"Impossible," said the lawyer, "impossible. There is no chimney. I came here because I was convinced the noise was going on here. It was certainly in the next room to mine."

"Was there no door between yours and mine?" said Anderson eagerly.

"No, sir," said Herr Jensen, rather sharply. "At least, not this morning."

" Ah ! " said Anderson. " Nor to-night ? "

" I am not sure," said the lawyer with some hesitation.

Suddenly the crying or singing voice in the next room died away, and the singer was heard seemingly to laugh to himself in a crooning manner. The three men actually shivered at the sound. Then there was a silence.

" Come," said the lawyer, " what have you to say, Herr Kristensen ? What does this mean ? "

" Good Heaven ! " said Kristensen. " How should I tell ! I know no more than you, gentlemen. I pray I may never hear such a noise again."

" So do I," said Herr Jensen, and he added something under his breath. Anderson thought it sounded like the last words of the Psalter, " *omnis spiritus laudet Dominum*," but he could not be sure.

" But we must do something," said Anderson— " the three of us. Shall we go and investigate in the next room ? "

" But that is Herr Jensen's room," wailed the landlord. " It is no use ; he has come from there himself."

" I am not so sure," said Jensen. " I think this gentleman is right : we must go and see."

The only weapons of defence that could be mustered on the spot were a stick and umbrella. The expedition went out into the passage, not without quakings. There was a deadly quiet outside, but a light shone from under the next door. Anderson and Jensen approached it. The latter turned the handle, and gave a sudden vigorous push. No use. The door stood fast.

"Herr Kristensen," said Jensen, "will you go and fetch the strongest servant you have in the place? We must see this through."

The landlord nodded, and hurried off, glad to be away from the scene of action. Jensen and Anderson remained outside looking at the door.

"It *is* Number 13, you see," said the latter.

"Yes ; there is your door, and there is mine," said Jensen.

"My room has three windows in the daytime," said Anderson, with difficulty suppressing a nervous laugh.

"By George, so has mine ! " said the lawyer, turning and looking at Anderson. His back was now to the door. In that moment the door opened, and an arm came out and clawed at his shoulder. It was clad in ragged, yellowish linen, and the bare skin, where it could be seen, had long grey hair upon it.

Anderson was just in time to pull Jensen out of its reach with a cry of disgust and fright, when the door shut again, and a low laugh was heard.

Jensen had seen nothing, but when Anderson hurriedly told him what a risk he had run, he fell into a great state of agitation, and suggested that they should retire from the enterprise and lock themselves up in one or other of their rooms.

However, while he was developing this plan, the landlord and two able-bodied men arrived on the

scene, all looking rather serious and alarmed. Jensen
met them with a torrent of description and explanation,
which did not at all tend to encourage them for the
fray.

The men dropped the crowbars they had brought,
and said flatly that they were not going to risk their
throats in that devil's den. The landlord was miser-
ably nervous and undecided, conscious that if the
danger were not faced his hotel was ruined, and very
loth to face it himself. Luckily Anderson hit upon
a way of rallying the demoralized force.

"Is this," he said, "the Danish courage I have
heard so much of? It isn't a German in there, and
if it was, we are five to one."

The two servants and Jensen were stung into action
by this, and made a dash at the door.

"Stop!" said Anderson. "Don't lose your heads.
You stay out here with the light, landlord, and one
of you two men break in the door, and don't go in
when it gives way."

The men nodded, and the younger stepped forward,
raised his crowbar, and dealt a tremendous blow on
the upper panel. The result was not in the least what
any of them anticipated. There was no cracking or
rending of wood—only a dull sound, as if the solid
wall had been struck. The man dropped his tool
with a shout, and began rubbing his elbow. His
cry drew their eyes upon him for a moment; then
Anderson looked at the door again. It was gone;
the plaster wall of the passage stared him in the face,

with a considerable gash in it where the crowbar had struck it. Number 13 had passed out of existence.

For a brief space they stood perfectly still, gazing at the blank wall. An early cock in the yard beneath was heard to crow ; and as Anderson glanced in the direction of the sound, he saw through the window at the end of the long passage that the eastern sky was paling to the dawn.

*   *   *   *   *

" Perhaps," said the landlord, with hesitation, " you gentlemen would like another room for to-night— a double-bedded one ? "

Neither Jensen nor Anderson was averse to the suggestion. They felt inclined to hunt in couples after their late experience. It was found convenient, when each of them went to his room to collect the articles he wanted for the night, that the other should go with him and hold the candle. They noticed that both Number 12 and Number 14 had *three* windows.

Next morning the same party reassembled in Number 12. The landlord was naturally anxious to avoid engaging outside help, and yet it was imperative that the mystery attaching to that part of the house should be cleared up. Accordingly the two servants had been induced to take upon them the function of carpenters. The furniture was cleared away, and, at the cost of a good many irretrievably damaged planks, that portion of the floor was taken up which lay nearest to Number 14.

You will naturally suppose that a skeleton—say that of Mag. Nicolas Francken—was discovered. That was not so. What they did find lying between the beams which supported the flooring was a small copper box. In it was a neatly-folded vellum document, with about twenty lines of writing. Both Anderson and Jensen (who proved to be something of a palæographer) were much excited by this discovery, which promised to afford the key to these extraordinary phenomena.

*   *   *   *   *

I possess a copy of an astrological work which I have never read. It has, by way of frontispiece, a woodcut by Hans Sebald Beham, representing a number of sages seated round a table. This detail may enable connoisseurs to identify the book. I cannot myself recollect its title, and it is not at this moment within reach; but the fly-leaves of it are covered with writing, and, during the ten years in which I have owned the volume, I have not been able to determine which way up this writing ought to be read, much less in what language it is. Not dissimilar was the position of Anderson and Jensen after the protracted examination to which they submitted the document in the copper box.

After two days' contemplation of it, Jensen, who was the bolder spirit of the two, hazarded the conjecture that the language was either Latin or Old Danish.

Anderson ventured upon no surmises, and was

very willing to surrender the box and the parchment to the Historical Society of Vibörg to be placed in their museum.

I had the whole story from him a few months later, as we sat in a wood near Upsala, after a visit to the library there, where we—or, rather, I—had laughed over the contract by which Daniel Salthenius (in later life Professor of Hebrew at Königsberg) sold himself to Satan. Anderson was not really amused.

"Young idiot!" he said, meaning Salthenius, who was only an undergraduate when he committed that indiscretion, "how did he know what company he was courting?"

And when I suggested the usual considerations he only grunted. That same afternoon he told me what you have read; but he refused to draw any inferences from it, and to assent to any that I drew for him.

COUNT MAGNUS

By what means the papers out of which I have made a connected story came into my hands is the last point which the reader will learn from these pages. But it is necessary to prefix to my extracts from them a statement of the form in which I possess them.

They consist, then, partly of a series of collections for a book of travels, such a volume as was a common product of the forties and fifties. Horace Marryat's *Journal of a Residence in Jutland and the Danish Isles* is a fair specimen of the class to which I allude. These books usually treated of some unfamiliar district on the Continent. They were illustrated with woodcuts or steel plates. They gave details of hotel accommodation, and of means of communication, such as we now expect to find in any well-regulated guide-book, and they dealt largely in reported conversations with intelligent foreigners, racy innkeepers and garrulous peasants. In a word, they were chatty.

Begun with the idea of furnishing material for such a book, my papers as they progressed assumed the character of a record of one single personal experience, and this record was continued up to the very eve, almost, of its termination.

The writer was a Mr. Wraxall. For my knowledge

of him I have to depend entirely on the evidence his writings afford, and from these I deduce that he was a man past middle age, possessed of some private means, and very much alone in the world. He had, it seems, no settled abode in England, but was a denizen of hotels and boarding-houses. It is probable that he entertained the idea of settling down at some future time which never came; and I think it also likely that the Pantechnicon fire in the early seventies must have destroyed a great deal that would have thrown light on his antecedents, for he refers once or twice to property of his that was warehoused at that establishment.

It is further apparent that Mr. Wraxall had published a book, and that it treated of a holiday he had once taken in Brittany. More than this I cannot say about his work, because a diligent search in bibliographical works has convinced me that it must have appeared either anonymously or under a pseudonym.

As to his character, it is not difficult to form some superficial opinion. He must have been an intelligent and cultivated man. It seems that he was near being a Fellow of his college at Oxford—Brasenose, as I judge from the Calendar. His besetting fault was pretty clearly that of over-inquisitiveness, possibly a good fault in a traveller, certainly a fault for which this traveller paid dearly enough in the end.

On what proved to be his last expedition, he was plotting another book. Scandinavia, a region not widely known to Englishmen forty years ago, had struck him as an interesting field. He must have lighted on some old books of Swedish history or memoirs, and the idea had struck him that there was room for a book descriptive of travel in Sweden, interspersed with episodes from the history of some of the great Swedish families. He procured letters of introduction, therefore, to some persons of quality in Sweden, and set out thither in the early summer of 1863.

Of his travels in the North there is no need to speak, nor of his residence of some weeks in Stockholm. I need only mention that some *savant* resident there put him on the track of an important collection of family papers belonging to the proprietors of an ancient manor-house in Vestergothland, and obtained for him permission to examine them.

The manor-house, or *herrgård*, in question is to be called Råbäck (pronounced something like Roebeck), though that is not its name. It is one of the best buildings of its kind in all the country, and the picture of it in Dahlenberg's *Suecia antiqua et moderna*, engraved in 1694, shows it very much as the tourist may see it to-day. It was built soon after 1600, and is, roughly speaking, very much like an English house of that period in respect of material—red-brick with stone facings—and style. The man who built it was a scion of the great house of De la Gardie, and his descendants possess it still. De la Gardie is the name by which I will designate them when mention of them becomes necessary.

They received Mr. Wraxall with great kindness and
courtesy, and pressed him to stay in the house as long
as his researches lasted. But, preferring to be inde-
pendent, and mistrusting his powers of conversing
in Swedish, he settled himself at the village inn, which
turned out quite sufficiently comfortable, at any rate
during the summer months. This arrangement would
entail a short walk daily to and from the manor-house
of something under a mile. The house itself stood
in a park, and was protected—we should say grown
up—with large old timber. Near it you found the
walled garden, and then entered a close wood fringing
one of the small lakes with which the whole country
is pitted. Then came the wall of the demesne, and
you climbed a steep knoll—a knob of rock lightly
covered with soil—and on the top of this stood the
church, fenced in with tall dark trees. It was a curious
building to English eyes. The nave and aisles were
low, and filled with pews and galleries. In the
western gallery stood the handsome old organ, gaily
painted, and with silver pipes. The ceiling was flat,
and had been adorned by a seventeenth-century artist
with a strange and hideous " Last Judgment," full of
lurid flames, falling cities, burning ships, crying souls,
and brown and smiling demons. Handsome brass
coronæ hung from the roof; the pulpit was like a
doll's-house, covered with little painted wooden
cherubs and saints ; a stand with three hour-glasses
was hinged to the preacher's desk. Such sights as
these may be seen in many a church in Sweden now,

but what distinguished this one was an addition to the original building. At the eastern end of the north aisle the builder of the manor-house had erected a mausoleum for himself and his family. It was a largish eight-sided building, lighted by a series of oval windows, and it had a domed roof, topped by a kind of pumpkin-shaped object rising into a spire, a form in which Swedish architects greatly delighted. The roof was of copper externally, and was painted black, while the walls, in common with those of the church, were staringly white. To this mausoleum there was no access from the church. It had a portal and steps of its own on the northern side.

Past the churchyard the path to the village goes, and not more than three or four minutes bring you to the inn door.

On the first day of his stay at Råbäck Mr. Wraxall found the church door open, and made those notes of the interior which I have epitomized. Into the mausoleum, however, he could not make his way. He could by looking through the keyhole just descry that there were fine marble effigies and sarcophagi of copper, and a wealth of armorial ornament, which made him very anxious to spend some time in investigation.

The papers he had come to examine at the manor-house proved to be of just the kind he wanted for his book. There were family correspondence, journals, and account-books of the earliest owners of the estate, very carefully kept and clearly written, full of amusing and picturesque detail. The first De la Gardie appeared in them as a strong and capable man. Shortly after the building of the mansion there had been a period of distress in the district, and the peasants had risen and attacked several châteaux and done some damage. The owner of Råbäck took a leading part in suppressing the trouble, and there was reference to executions of ringleaders and severe punishments inflicted with no sparing hand.

The portrait of this Magnus de la Gardie was one of the best in the house, and Mr. Wraxall studied it with no little interest after his day's work. He gives no detailed description of it, but I gather that the face impressed him rather by its power than by its beauty or goodness; in fact, he writes that Count Magnus was an almost phenomenally ugly man.

On this day Mr. Wraxall took his supper with the family, and walked back in the late but still bright evening.

" I must remember," he writes, " to ask the sexton if he can let me into the mausoleum at the church. He evidently has access to it himself, for I saw him to-night standing on the steps, and, as I thought, locking or unlocking the door."

I find that early on the following day Mr. Wraxall had some conversation with his landlord. His setting it down at such length as he does surprised me at first; but I soon realized that the papers I was reading were, at least in their beginning, the materials for the book he was meditating, and that it was to have been one of those quasi-journalistic productions which admit of the introduction of an admixture of conversational matter.

His object, he says, was to find out whether any traditions of Count Magnus de la Gardie lingered on in the scenes of that gentleman's activity, and whether the popular estimate of him were favourable or not. He found that the Count was decidedly not a favourite. If his tenants came late to their work on the days which they owed to him as Lord of the Manor, they were set on the wooden horse, or flogged and branded in the manor-house yard. One or two cases there were of men who had occupied lands which encroached on the lord's domain, and whose houses had been mysteriously burnt on a winter's night, with the whole family inside. But what seemed to dwell on the innkeeper's mind most— for he returned to the subject more than once—was that the Count had been on the Black Pilgrimage, and had brought something or someone back with him.

You will naturally inquire, as Mr. Wraxall did, what the Black Pilgrimage may have been. But your curiosity on the point must remain unsatisfied for the time being, just as his did. The landlord was evidently unwilling to give a full answer, or indeed any answer, on the point, and, being called out for a moment, trotted off with obvious alacrity, only putting his head in at the door a few minutes afterwards to say that he was called away to Skara, and should not be back till evening.

So Mr. Wraxall had to go unsatisfied to his day's work at the manor-house. The papers on which he was just then engaged soon put his thoughts into another channel, for he had to occupy himself with glancing over the correspondence between Sophia Albertina in Stockholm and her married cousin Ulrica Leonora at Råbäck in the years 1705–1710. The letters were of exceptional interest from the light they threw upon the culture of that period in Sweden, as anyone can testify who has read the full edition of them in the publications of the Swedish Historical Manuscripts Commission.

In the afternoon he had done with these, and after returning the boxes in which they were kept to their places on the shelf, he proceeded, very natur-ally, to take down some of the volumes nearest to them, in order to determine which of them had best be his principal subject of investigation next day. The shelf he had hit upon was occupied mostly by a collection of account-books in the writing of the first Count Magnus. But one among them was not an account-book, but a book of alchemical and other tracts in another sixteenth-century hand. Not being very familiar with alchemical literature, Mr. Wraxall spends much space which he might have spared in setting out the names and beginnings of the various treatises : The book of the Phœnix, book of the Thirty Words, book of the Toad, book of Miriam, Turba philosophorum, and so forth; and then he announces with a good deal of circumstance his

delight at finding, on a leaf originally left blank
near the middle of the book, some writing of Count
Magnus himself headed " Liber nigræ peregrinationis."
It is true that only a few lines were written, but
there was quite enough to show that the landlord had
that morning been referring to a belief at least as old
as the time of Count Magnus, and probably shared
by him. This is the English of what was written :

" If any man desires to obtain a long life, if he
would obtain a faithful messenger and see the blood
of his enemies, it is necessary that he should first
go into the city of Chorazin, and there salute the
prince. . . ." Here there was an erasure of one
word, not very thoroughly done, so that Mr. Wraxall
felt pretty sure that he was right in reading it as
aëris (" of the air "). But there was no more of the
text copied, only a line in Latin : " Quære reliqua
hujus materiei inter secretiora " (See the rest of this
matter among the more private things).

It could not be denied that this threw a rather
lurid light upon the tastes and beliefs of the Count ;
but to Mr. Wraxall, separated from him by nearly
three centuries, the thought that he might have
added to his general forcefulness alchemy, and to
alchemy something like magic, only made him a
more picturesque figure ; and when, after a rather
prolonged contemplation of his picture in the hall,
Mr. Wraxall set out on his homeward way, his mind
was full of the thought of Count Magnus. He had
no eyes for his surroundings, no perception of the

evening scents of the woods or the evening light on the lake; and when all of a sudden he pulled up short, he was astonished to find himself already at the gate of the churchyard, and within a few minutes of his dinner. His eyes fell on the mausoleum.

"Ah," he said, "Count Magnus, there you are. I should dearly like to see you."

"Like many solitary men," he writes, "I have a habit of talking to myself aloud; and, unlike some of the Greek and Latin particles, I do not expect an answer. Certainly, and perhaps fortunately in this case, there was neither voice nor any that regarded: only the woman who, I suppose, was cleaning up the church, dropped some metallic object on the floor, whose clang startled me. Count Magnus, I think, sleeps sound enough."

That same evening the landlord of the inn, who had heard Mr. Wraxall say that he wished to see the clerk or deacon (as he would be called in Sweden) of the parish, introduced him to that official in the inn parlour. A visit to the De la Gardie tombhouse was soon arranged for the next day, and a little general conversation ensued.

Mr. Wraxall, remembering that one function of Scandinavian deacons is to teach candidates for Confirmation, thought he would refresh his own memory on a Biblical point.

"Can you tell me," he said, "anything about Chorazin?"

The deacon seemed startled, but readily reminded him how that village had once been denounced.

"To be sure," said Mr. Wraxall; "it is, I suppose, quite a ruin now?"

"So I expect," replied the deacon. "I have heard some of our old priests say that Antichrist is to be born there; and there are tales——"

"Ah! what tales are those?" Mr. Wraxall put in.

"Tales, I was going to say, which I have forgotten," said the deacon; and soon after that he said good night.

The landlord was now alone, and at Mr. Wraxall's mercy; and that inquirer was not inclined to spare him.

"Herr Nielsen," he said, "I have found out something about the Black Pilgrimage. You may as well tell me what you know. What did the Count bring back with him?"

Swedes are habitually slow, perhaps, in answering, or perhaps the landlord was an exception. I am not sure; but Mr. Wraxall notes that the landlord spent at least one minute in looking at him before he said anything at all. Then he came close up to his guest, and with a good deal of effort he spoke:

"Mr. Wraxall, I can tell you this one little tale, and no more—not any more. You must not ask anything when I have done. In my grandfather's time—that is, ninety-two years ago—there were two men who said: 'The Count is dead; we do not care for him. We will go to-night and have a free

109

hunt in his wood '—the long wood on the hill that you have seen behind Råbäck. Well, those that heard them say this, they said : ' No, do not go ; we are sure you will meet with persons walking who should not be walking. They should be resting, not walking.' These men laughed. There were no forest-men to keep the wood, because no one wished to hunt there. The family were not here at the house. These men could do what they wished.

" Very well, they go to the wood that night. My grandfather was sitting here in this room. It was the summer, and a light night. With the window open, he could see out to the wood, and hear.

" So he sat there, and two or three men with him, and they listened. At first they hear nothing at all ; then they hear someone—you know how far away it is—they hear someone scream, just as if the most inside part of his soul was twisted out of him. All of them in the room caught hold of each other, and they sat so for three-quarters of an hour. Then they hear someone else, only about three hundred ells off. They hear him laugh out loud : it was not one of those two men that laughed, and, indeed, they have all of them said that it was not any man at all. After that they hear a great door shut.

" Then, when it was just light with the sun, they all went to the priest. They said to him :

" ' Father, put on your gown and your ruff, and come to bury these men, Anders Bjornsen and Hans Thorbjorn.'

"You understand that they were sure these men were dead. So they went to the wood—my grandfather never forgot this. He said they were all like so many dead men themselves. The priest, too, he was in a white fear. He said when they came to him :

"'I heard one cry in the night, and I heard one laugh afterwards. If I cannot forget that, I shall not be able to sleep again.'

"So they went to the wood, and they found these men on the edge of the wood. Hans Thorbjorn was standing with his back against a tree, and all the time he was pushing with his hands—pushing something away from him which was not there. So he was not dead. And they led him away, and took him to the house at Nykjoping, and he died before the winter; but he went on pushing with his hands. Also Anders Bjornsen was there; but he was dead. And I tell you this about Anders Bjornsen, that he was once a beautiful man, but now his face was not there, because the flesh of it was sucked away off the bones. You understand that? My grandfather did not forget that. And they laid him on the bier which they brought, and they put a cloth over his head, and the priest walked before; and they began to sing the psalm for the dead as well as they could. So, as they were singing the end of the first verse, one fell down, who was carrying the head of the bier, and the others looked back, and they saw that the cloth had fallen off, and the eyes of Anders Bjornsen were looking up, because there was nothing to close over them. And this they could not bear. Therefore the priest laid the cloth upon him, and sent for a spade, and they buried him in that place."

The next day Mr. Wraxall records that the deacon called for him soon after his breakfast, and took him to the church and mausoleum. He noticed that the key of the latter was hung on a nail just by the pulpit, and it occurred to him that, as the church door seemed to be left unlocked as a rule, it would not be difficult for him to pay a second and more private visit to the monuments if there proved to be more of interest among them than could be digested at first. The building, when he entered it, he found not unimposing. The monuments, mostly large erections of the seventeenth and eighteenth centuries, were dignified if luxuriant, and the epitaphs and heraldry were copious. The central space of the domed room was occupied by three copper sarcophagi, covered with finely-engraved ornament. Two of them had, as is commonly the case in Denmark and Sweden, a large metal crucifix on the lid. The third, that of Count Magnus, as it appeared, had, instead of that, a full-length effigy engraved upon it, and round the edge were several bands of similar ornament representing various scenes. One was a battle, with cannon belching out smoke, and walled towns, and troops of pikemen. Another showed an execution. In a third, among trees, was a man running at full speed, with flying hair and outstretched hands. After him followed a strange form; it would be hard to say whether the artist had intended it for a man, and was unable to give the requisite similitude, or whether it was intentionally made as monstrous as it looked. In view of the skill with which the rest of the drawing was done, Mr. Wraxall felt inclined to adopt the latter idea. The figure was unduly short, and was for the most part muffled in a hooded garment which swept the ground. The only part of the form which projected from that shelter was not shaped like any hand or arm. Mr. Wraxall compares it to the tentacle of a devil-fish, and continues: "On seeing this, I said to myself, 'This, then, which is evidently an allegorical representation of some kind—a fiend pursuing a hunted soul—may be the origin of the story of Count Magnus and his mysterious companion. Let us see how the huntsman is pictured: doubtless it will be a demon blowing his horn.'" But, as it turned out, there was no such sensational figure, only the semblance of a cloaked man on a hillock, who stood leaning on a stick, and watching the hunt with an interest which the engraver had tried to express in his attitude.

Mr. Wraxall noted the finely-worked and massive steel padlocks—three in number—which secured the sarcophagus. One of them, he saw, was detached, and lay on the pavement. And then, unwilling to delay the deacon longer or to waste his own working-time, he made his way onward to the manor-house.

"It is curious," he notes, "how on retracing a familiar path one's thoughts engross one to the absolute exclusion of surrounding objects. To-night, for the second time, I had entirely failed to notice where I was going (I had planned a private visit to the tomb-house to copy the epitaphs), when I suddenly, as it were, awoke to consciousness, and found myself (as before) turning in at the churchyard gate, and, I believe, singing or chanting some such words as, 'Are you awake, Count Magnus? Are you asleep, Count Magnus?' and then something more which I have failed to recollect. It seemed to me that I must have been behaving in this nonsensical way for some time."

He found the key of the mausoleum where he had expected to find it, and copied the greater part of what he wanted; in fact, he stayed until the light began to fail him.

"I must have been wrong," he writes, "in saying that one of the padlocks of my Count's sarcophagus was unfastened; I see to-night that two are loose. I picked both up, and laid them carefully on the window-ledge, after trying unsuccessfully to close them. The remaining one is still firm, and, though I take it to be a spring lock, I cannot guess how it is opened. Had I succeeded in undoing it, I am almost afraid I should have taken the liberty of opening the sarcophagus. It is strange, the interest I feel in the personality of this, I fear, somewhat ferocious and grim old noble."

The day following was, as it turned out, the last
of Mr. Wraxall's stay at Råbäck. He received letters connected with certain investments which made
it desirable that he should return to England; his
work among the papers was practically done, and
travelling was slow. He decided, therefore, to make
his farewells, put some finishing touches to his notes,
and be off.

These finishing touches and farewells, as it turned
out, took more time than he had expected. The
hospitable family insisted on his staying to dine with
them—they dined at three—and it was verging on
half-past six before he was outside the iron gates of
Råbäck. He dwelt on every step of his walk by the
lake, determined to saturate himself, now that he trod
it for the last time, in the sentiment of the place and
hour. And when he reached the summit of the
churchyard knoll, he lingered for many minutes, gazing at the limitless prospect of woods near and
distant, all dark beneath a sky of liquid green. When
at last he turned to go, the thought struck him that
surely he must bid farewell to Count Magnus as well
as the rest of the De la Gardies. The church was but
twenty yards away, and he knew where the key of
the mausoleum hung. It was not long before he
was standing over the great copper coffin, and, as
usual, talking to himself aloud. "You may have
been a bit of a rascal in your time, Magnus," he was
saying, "but for all that I should like to see you, or,
rather——"

" Just at that instant," he says, " I felt a blow on my foot. Hastily enough I drew it back, and something fell on the pavement with a clash. It was the third, the last of the three padlocks which had fastened the sarcophagus. I stooped to pick it up, and —Heaven is my witness that I am writing only the bare truth—before I had raised myself there was a sound of metal hinges creaking, and I distinctly saw the lid shifting upwards. I may have behaved like a coward, but I could not for my life stay for one moment. I was outside that dreadful building in less time than I can write—almost as quickly as I could have said—the words ; and what frightens me yet more, I could not turn the key in the lock. As I sit here in my room noting these facts, I ask myself (it was not twenty minutes ago) whether that noise of creaking metal continued, and I cannot tell whether it did or not. I only know that there was something more than I have written that alarmed me, but whether it was sound or sight I am not able to remember. What is this that I have done ? "

Poor Mr. Wraxall ! He set out on his journey to England on the next day, as he had planned, and he reached England in safety ; and yet, as I gather from his changed hand and inconsequent jottings, a broken man. One of several small notebooks that have come to me with his papers gives, not a key to, but a kind of inkling of, his experiences. Much of his journey was made by canal-boat, and I find not less than six painful attempts to enumerate and describe his fellow-passengers. The entries are of this kind :

" 24. Pastor of village in Skåne. Usual black coat and soft black hat.
" 25. Commercial traveller from Stockholm going to Trollhättan. Black cloak, brown hat.
" 26. Man in long black cloak, broad-leafed hat, very old-fashioned."

This entry is lined out, and a note added : " Perhaps identical with No. 13. Have not yet seen his face." On referring to No. 13, I find that he is a Roman priest in a cassock.

The net result of the reckoning is always the same. Twenty-eight people appear in the enumeration, one being always a man in a long black cloak and broad hat, and the other a " short figure in dark cloak and hood." On the other hand, it is always noted that only twenty-six passengers appear at meals, and that the man in the cloak is perhaps absent, and the short figure is certainly absent.

On reaching England, it appears that Mr. Wraxall landed at Harwich, and that he resolved at once to put himself out of the reach of some person or persons whom he never specifies, but whom he had evidently come to regard as his pursuers. Accordingly he took a vehicle—it was a closed fly—not trusting the railway, and drove across country to the village of Belchamp St. Paul. It was about

nine o'clock on a moonlight August night when he
neared the place. He was sitting forward, and
looking out of the window at the fields and thickets
—there was little else to be seen—racing past him.
Suddenly he came to a cross-road. At the corner
two figures were standing motionless ; both were
in dark cloaks ; the taller one wore a hat, the shorter
a hood. He had no time to see their faces, nor did
they make any motion that he could discern. Yet
the horse shied violently and broke into a gallop,
and Mr. Wraxall sank back into his seat in something like desperation. He had seen them before.

Arrived at Belchamp St. Paul, he was fortunate
enough to find a decent furnished lodging, and for
the next twenty-four hours he lived, comparatively
speaking, in peace. His last notes were written on
this day. They are too disjointed and ejaculatory to
be given here in full, but the substance of them is
clear enough. He is expecting a visit from his
pursuers—how or when he knows not—and his
constant cry is " What has he done ? " and " Is
there no hope ? " Doctors, he knows, would call
him mad, policemen would laugh at him. The parson is away. What can he do but lock his door and
cry to God ?

People still remembered last year at Belchamp St.
Paul how a strange gentleman came one evening in
August years back ; and how the next morning but
one he was found dead, and there was an inquest ;

and the jury that viewed the body fainted, seven of 'em did, and none of 'em wouldn't speak to what they see, and the verdict was visitation of God; and how the people as kep' the 'ouse moved out that same week, and went away from that part. But they do not, I think, know that any glimmer of light has ever been thrown, or could be thrown, on the mystery. It so happened that last year the little house came into my hands as part of a legacy. It had stood empty since 1863, and there seemed no prospect of letting it; so I had it pulled down, and the papers of which I have given you an abstract were found in a forgotten cupboard under the window in the best bedroom.

"OH, WHISTLE, AND I'LL COME TO YOU, MY LAD"

"I SUPPOSE you will be getting away pretty soon, now Full term is over, Professor," said a person not in the story to the Professor of Ontography, soon after they had sat down next to each other at a feast in the hospitable hall of St. James's College.

The Professor was young, neat, and precise in speech.

"Yes," he said; "my friends have been making me take up golf this term, and I mean to go to the East Coast—in point of fact to Burnstow—(I dare say you know it) for a week or ten days, to improve my game. I hope to get off to-morrow."

"Oh, Parkins," said his neighbour on the other side, "if you are going to Burnstow, I wish you would look at the site of the Templars' preceptory, and let me know if you think it would be any good to have a dig there in the summer."

It was, as you might suppose, a person of antiquarian pursuits who said this, but, since he merely appears in this prologue, there is no need to give his entitlements.

"Certainly," said Parkins, the Professor: "if you will describe to me whereabouts the site is, I will do my best to give you an idea of the lie of the land when I get back; or I could write to you about it, if you would tell me where you are likely to be."

"Don't trouble to do that, thanks. It's only that I'm thinking of taking my family in that direction in the Long, and it occurred to me that, as very few of the English preceptories have ever been properly planned, I might have an opportunity of doing something useful on off-days."

The Professor rather sniffed at the idea that planning out a preceptory could be described as useful. His neighbour continued:

"The site—I doubt if there is anything showing above ground—must be down quite close to the beach now. The sea has encroached tremendously, as you know, all along that bit of coast. I should think, from the map, that it must be about three-quarters of a mile from the Globe Inn, at the north end of the town. Where are you going to stay?"

"Well, *at* the Globe Inn, as a matter of fact," said Parkins; "I have engaged a room there. I couldn't get in anywhere else; most of the lodging-houses are shut up in winter, it seems; and, as it is, they tell me that the only room of any size I can have is really a double-bedded one, and that they haven't a corner in which to store the other bed, and so on. But I must have a fairly large room, for I am taking some books down, and mean to do a bit of work; and though I don't quite fancy having an empty bed—not to speak of two—in what I may call for the time being my study, I suppose I can manage to rough it for the short time I shall be there."

"Do you call having an extra bed in your room roughing it, Parkins?" said a bluff person opposite. "Look here, I shall come down and occupy it for a bit; it'll be company for you."

The Professor quivered, but managed to laugh in a courteous manner.

"By all means, Rogers; there's nothing I should like better. But I'm afraid you would find it rather dull; you don't play golf, do you?"

"No, thank Heaven!" said rude Mr. Rogers.

"Well, you see, when I'm not writing I shall most likely be out on the links, and that, as I say, would be rather dull for you, I'm afraid."

"Oh, I don't know! There's certain to be somebody I know in the place; but, of course, if you don't want me, speak the word, Parkins; I shan't be offended. Truth, as you always tell us, is never offensive."

Parkins was, indeed, scrupulously polite and strictly truthful. It is to be feared that Mr. Rogers sometimes practised upon his knowledge of these characteristics. In Parkins's breast there was a conflict now raging, which for a moment or two did not allow him to answer. That interval being over, he said :

"Well, if you want the exact truth, Rogers, I was considering whether the room I speak of would really be large enough to accommodate us both comfortably; and also whether (mind, I shouldn't have said this if you hadn't pressed me) you would not constitute something in the nature of a hindrance to my work."

Rogers laughed loudly.

"Well done, Parkins!" he said. "It's all right. I promise not to interrupt your work; don't you disturb yourself about that. No, I won't come if you don't want me; but I thought I should do so nicely to keep the ghosts off." Here he might have been seen to wink and to nudge his next neighbour. Parkins might also have been seen to become pink. "I beg pardon, Parkins," Rogers continued; "I oughtn't to have said that. I forgot you didn't like levity on these topics."

"Well," Parkins said, "as you have mentioned the matter, I freely own that I do *not* like careless talk about what you call ghosts. A man in my position," he went on, raising his voice a little, "cannot, I find, be too careful about appearing to sanction the current beliefs on such subjects. As you know, Rogers, or as you ought to know; for I think I have never concealed my views——"

"No, you certainly have not, old man," put in Rogers *sotto voce*.

"——I hold that any semblance, any appearance of concession to the view that such things might exist is equivalent to a renunciation of all that I hold most sacred. But I'm afraid I have not succeeded in securing your attention."

"Your *undivided* attention, was what Dr. Blimber actually *said*,"[1] Rogers interrupted, with every appearance of an earnest desire for accuracy. "But I beg your pardon, Parkins : I'm stopping you."

"No, not at all," said Parkins. "I don't remember Blimber; perhaps he was before my time. But I needn't go on. I'm sure you know what I mean."

"Yes, yes," said Rogers, rather hastily—"just so. We'll go into it fully at Burnstow, or somewhere."

In repeating the above dialogue I have tried to give the impression which it made on me, that Parkins was something of an old woman—rather hen-like, perhaps, in his little ways ; totally destitute, alas ! of the sense of humour, but at the same time dauntless and sincere in his convictions, and a man deserving of the greatest respect. Whether or not the reader has gathered so much, that was the character which Parkins had.

On the following day Parkins did, as he had hoped, succeed in getting away from his college, and in arriving at Burnstow. He was made welcome at the Globe Inn, was safely installed in the large double-bedded room of which we have heard, and was able before retiring to rest to arrange his materials for work in apple-pie order upon a commodious table which occupied the outer end of the room, and was surrounded on three sides by windows looking out seaward ; that is to say, the central window looked

[1] Mr. Rogers was wrong, *vide Dombey and Son*, chapter xii.

straight out to sea, and those on the left and right commanded prospects along the shore to the north and south respectively. On the south you saw the village of Burnstow. On the north no houses were to be seen, but only the beach and the low cliff backing it. Immediately in front was a strip—not considerable —of rough grass, dotted with old anchors, capstans, and so forth; then a broad path; then the beach. Whatever may have been the original distance between the Globe Inn and the sea, not more than sixty yards now separated them.

The rest of the population of the inn was, of course, a golfing one, and included few elements that call for a special description. The most conspicuous figure was, perhaps, that of an *ancien militaire*, secretary of a London club, and possessed of a voice of incredible strength, and of views of a pronouncedly Protestant type. These were apt to find utterance after his attendance upon the ministrations of the Vicar, an estimable man with inclinations towards a picturesque ritual, which he gallantly kept down as far as he could out of deference to East Anglian tradition.

Professor Parkins, one of whose principal characteristics was pluck, spent the greater part of the day following his arrival at Burnstow in what he had called improving his game, in company with this Colonel Wilson: and during the afternoon— whether the process of improvement were to blame or not, I am not sure—the Colonel's demeanour assumed a colouring so lurid that even Parkins jibbed at the thought of walking home with him from the links. He determined, after a short and furtive look at that bristling moustache and those incarnadined features, that it would be wiser to allow the influences of tea and tobacco to do what they could with the Colonel before the dinner-hour should render a meeting inevitable.

"I might walk home to-night along the beach," he reflected—"yes, and take a look—there will be light enough for that—at the ruins of which Disney was talking. I don't exactly know where they are, by the way; but I expect I can hardly help stumbling on them."

This he accomplished, I may say, in the most literal sense, for in picking his way from the links to the shingle beach his foot caught, partly in a gorse-root and partly in a biggish stone, and over he went. When he got up and surveyed his surroundings, he found himself in a patch of somewhat broken ground covered with small depressions and mounds. These latter, when he came to examine them, proved to be simply masses of flints embedded in mortar and grown over with turf. He must, he quite rightly concluded, be on the site of the preceptory he had promised to look at. It seemed not unlikely to reward the spade of the explorer; enough of the foundations was probably left at no great depth to throw a good deal of light on the general plan. He remembered vaguely that the Templars,

to whom this site had belonged, were in the habit
of building round churches, and he thought a particular series of the humps or mounds near him did
appear to be arranged in something of a circular
form. Few people can resist the temptation to try
a little amateur research in a department quite outside their own, if only for the satisfaction of showing
how successful they would have been had they only
taken it up seriously. Our Professor, however, if
he felt something of this mean desire, was also truly
anxious to oblige Mr. Disney. So he paced with
care the circular area he had noticed, and wrote
down its rough dimensions in his pocket-book.
Then he proceeded to examine an oblong eminence
which lay east of the centre of the circle, and seemed
to his thinking likely to be the base of a platform
or altar. At one end of it, the northern, a patch of
the turf was gone—removed by some boy or other
creature *feræ naturæ*. It might, he thought, be as
well to probe the soil here for evidences of masonry,
and he took out his knife and began scraping away
the earth. And now followed another little discovery : a portion of soil fell inward as he scraped,
and disclosed a small cavity. He lighted one match
after another to help him to see of what nature the
hole was, but the wind was too strong for them all.
By tapping and scratching the sides with his knife,
however, he was able to make out that it must be
an artificial hole in masonry. It was rectangular,
and the sides, top, and bottom, if not actually plastered,

were smooth and regular. Of course it was empty.
No ! As he withdrew the knife he heard a metallic
clink, and when he introduced his hand it met with
a cylindrical object lying on the floor of the hole.
Naturally enough, he picked it up, and when he
brought it into the light, now fast fading, he could
see that it, too, was of man's making—a metal tube
about four inches long, and evidently of some considerable age.

By the time Parkins had made sure that there was
nothing else in this odd receptacle, it was too late
and too dark for him to think of undertaking any
further search. What he had done had proved so
unexpectedly interesting that he determined to sacrifice
a little more of the daylight on the morrow to archæ-
ology. The object which he now had safe in his
pocket was bound to be of some slight value at least,
he felt sure.

Bleak and solemn was the view on which he took
a last look before starting homeward. A faint yellow
light in the west showed the links, on which a few
figures moving towards the club-house were still
visible, the squat martello tower, the lights of Aldsey
village, the pale ribbon of sands intersected at intervals
by black wooden groynes, the dim and murmuring
sea. The wind was bitter from the north, but was
at his back when he set out for the Globe. He
quickly rattled and clashed through the shingle and
gained the sand, upon which, but for the groynes
which had to be got over every few yards, the going

was both good and quiet. One last look behind, to measure the distance he had made since leaving the ruined Templars' church, showed him a prospect of company on his walk, in the shape of a rather indistinct personage, who seemed to be making great efforts to catch up with him, but made little, if any, progress. I mean that there was an appearance of running about his movements, but that the distance between him and Parkins did not seem materially to lessen. So, at least, Parkins thought, and decided that he almost certainly did not know him, and that it would be absurd to wait until he came up. For all that, company, he began to think, would really be very welcome on that lonely shore, if only you could choose your companion. In his unenlightened days he had read of meetings in such places which even now would hardly bear thinking of. He went on thinking of them, however, until he reached home, and particularly of one which catches most people's fancy at some time of their childhood. "Now I saw in my dream that Christian had gone but a very little way when he saw a foul fiend coming over the field to meet him." "What should I do now," he thought, "if I looked back and caught sight of a black figure sharply defined against the yellow sky, and saw that it had horns and wings? I wonder whether I should stand or run for it. Luckily, the gentleman behind is not of that kind, and he seems to be about as far off now as when I saw him first. Well, at this rate he won't get his dinner as soon as I shall; and, dear me! it's within a quarter of an hour of the time now. I must run!"

Parkins had, in fact, very little time for dressing. When he met the Colonel at dinner, Peace—or as much of her as that gentleman could manage—reigned once more in the military bosom; nor was she put to flight in the hours of bridge that followed dinner, for Parkins was a more than respectable player. When, therefore, he retired towards twelve o'clock, he felt that he had spent his evening in quite a satisfactory way, and that, even for so long as a fortnight or three weeks, life at the Globe would be supportable under similar conditions—"especially," thought he, "if I go on improving my game."

As he went along the passages he met the boots of the Globe, who stopped and said:

"Beg your pardon, sir, but as I was a-brushing your coat just now there was somethink fell out of the pocket. I put it on your chest of drawers, sir, in your room, sir—a piece of a pipe or somethink of that, sir. Thank you, sir. You'll find it on your chest of drawers, sir—yes, sir. Good night, sir."

The speech served to remind Parkins of his little discovery of that afternoon. It was with some considerable curiosity that he turned it over by the light of his candles. It was of bronze, he now saw, and was shaped very much after the manner of the modern dog-whistle; in fact it was—yes, certainly it was—actually no more nor less than a whistle.

He put it to his lips, but it was quite full of a fine, caked-up sand or earth, which would not yield to knocking, but must be loosened with a knife. Tidy as ever in his habits, Parkins cleared out the earth on to a piece of paper, and took the latter to the window to empty it out. The night was clear and bright, as he saw when he had opened the casement, and he stopped for an instant to look at the sea and note a belated wanderer stationed on the shore in front of the inn. Then he shut the window, a little surprised at the late hours people kept at Burnstow, and took his whistle to the light again. Why, surely there were marks on it, and not merely marks, but letters! A very little rubbing rendered the deeply-cut inscription quite legible, but the Professor had to confess, after some earnest thought, that the meaning of it was as obscure to him as the writing on the wall to Belshazzar. There were legends both on the front and on the back of the whistle. The one read thus :

FLA

FUR   BIS

FLE

The other :

✠ QUIS EST ISTE QUI UENIT ✠

" I ought to be able to make it out," he thought ; " but I suppose I am a little rusty in my Latin. When I come to think of it, I don't believe I even know the word for a whistle. The long one does seem simple enough. It ought to mean, ' Who is this

who is coming?' Well, the best way to find out
is evidently to whistle for him."

He blew tentatively and stopped suddenly, startled
and yet pleased at the note he had elicited. It had
a quality of infinite distance in it, and, soft as it was,
he somehow felt it must be audible for miles round.
It was a sound, too, that seemed to have the power
(which many scents possess) of forming pictures in
the brain. He saw quite clearly for a moment a
vision of a wide, dark expanse at night, with a fresh
wind blowing, and in the midst a lonely figure—
how employed, he could not tell. Perhaps he would
have seen more had not the picture been broken by
the sudden surge of a gust of wind against his casement, so sudden that it made him look up, just in
time to see the white glint of a sea-bird's wing somewhere outside the dark panes.

The sound of the whistle had so fascinated him
that he could not help trying it once more, this
time more boldly. The note was little, if at all,
louder than before, and repetition broke the illusion
—no picture followed, as he had half hoped it might.
"But what is this? Goodness! what force the wind
can get up in a few minutes! What a tremendous
gust! There! I knew that window-fastening was
no use! Ah! I thought so—both candles out. It's
enough to tear the room to pieces."

The first thing was to get the window shut. While
you might count twenty Parkins was struggling with
the small casement, and felt almost as if he were

pushing back a sturdy burglar, so strong was the pressure. It slackened all at once, and the window banged to and latched itself. Now to relight the candles and see what damage, if any, had been done. No, nothing seemed amiss ; no glass even was broken in the casement. But the noise had evidently roused at least one member of the household : the Colonel was to be heard stumping in his stockinged feet on the floor above, and growling.

Quickly as it had risen, the wind did not fall at once. On it went, moaning and rushing past the house, at times rising to a cry so desolate that, as Parkins disinterestedly said, it might have made fanciful people feel quite uncomfortable ; even the unimaginative, he thought after a quarter of an hour, might be happier without it.

Whether it was the wind, or the excitement of golf, or of the researches in the preceptory that kept Parkins awake, he was not sure. Awake he remained, in any case, long enough to fancy (as I am afraid I often do myself under such conditions) that he was the victim of all manner of fatal disorders : he would lie counting the beats of his heart, convinced that it was going to stop work every moment, and would entertain grave suspicions of his lungs, brain, liver, etc.—suspicions which he was sure would be dispelled by the return of daylight, but which until then refused to be put aside. He found a little vicarious comfort in the idea that someone else was in the same boat. A near neighbour (in the darkness it was not easy to tell his direction) was tossing and rustling in his bed, too.

The next stage was that Parkins shut his eyes and determined to give sleep every chance. Here again over-excitement asserted itself in another form—that of making pictures. *Experto crede*, pictures do come to the closed eyes of one trying to sleep, and are often so little to his taste that he must open his eyes and disperse them.

Parkins's experience on this occasion was a very distressing one. He found that the picture which presented itself to him was continuous. When he opened his eyes, of course, it went; but when he shut them once more it framed itself afresh, and acted itself out again, neither quicker nor slower than before. What he saw was this:

A long stretch of shore—shingle edged by sand, and intersected at short intervals with black groynes running down to the water—a scene, in fact, so like that of his afternoon's walk that, in the absence of any landmark, it could not be distinguished therefrom. The light was obscure, conveying an impression of gathering storm, late winter evening, and slight cold rain. On this bleak stage at first no actor was visible. Then, in the distance, a bobbing black object appeared; a moment more, and it was a man running, jumping, clambering over the groynes, and every few seconds looking eagerly back. The nearer he came the more obvious it was that he was not only anxious, but even terribly frightened, though

his face was not to be distinguished. He was, moreover, almost at the end of his strength. On he
came; each successive obstacle seemed to cause him
more difficulty than the last. "Will he get over
this next one?" thought Parkins; "it seems a little
higher than the others." Yes; half climbing, half
throwing himself, he did get over, and fell all in a
heap on the other side (the side nearest to the spectator). There, as if really unable to get up again, he
remained crouching under the groyne, looking up
in an attitude of painful anxiety.

So far no cause whatever for the fear of the runner
had been shown; but now there began to be seen,
far up the shore, a little flicker of something light-
coloured moving to and fro with great swiftness and
irregularity. Rapidly growing larger, it, too, declared
itself as a figure in pale, fluttering draperies, ill-
defined. There was something about its motion
which made Parkins very unwilling to see it at close
quarters. It would stop, raise arms, bow itself to-
ward the sand, then run stooping across the beach
to the water-edge and back again; and then, rising
upright, once more continue its course forward at
a speed that was startling and terrifying. The moment
came when the pursuer was hovering about from
left to right only a few yards beyond the groyne
where the runner lay in hiding. After two or three
ineffectual castings hither and thither it came to a
stop, stood upright, with arms raised high, and then
darted straight forward towards the groyne.

It was at this point that Parkins always failed in his resolution to keep his eyes shut. With many misgivings as to incipient failure of eyesight, over-worked brain, excessive smoking, and so on, he finally resigned himself to light his candle, get out a book, and pass the night waking, rather than be tormented by this persistent panorama, which he saw clearly enough could only be a morbid reflection of his walk and his thoughts on that very day.

The scraping of match on box and the glare of light must have startled some creatures of the night —rats or what not—which he heard scurry across the floor from the side of his bed with much rustling. Dear, dear! the match is out! Fool that it is! But the second one burnt better, and a candle and book were duly procured, over which Parkins pored till sleep of a wholesome kind came upon him, and that in no long space. For about the first time in his orderly and prudent life he forgot to blow out the candle, and when he was called next morning at eight there was still a flicker in the socket and a sad mess of guttered grease on the top of the little table.

After breakfast he was in his room, putting the finishing touches to his golfing costume—fortune had again allotted the Colonel to him for a partner —when one of the maids came in.

" Oh, if you please," she said, " would you like any extra blankets on your bed, sir ? "

" Ah! thank you," said Parkins. " Yes, I think

I should like one. It seems likely to turn rather colder."

In a very short time the maid was back with the blanket.

"Which bed should I put it on, sir?" she asked.

"What? Why, that one—the one I slept in last night," he said, pointing to it.

"Oh yes! I beg your pardon, sir, but you seemed to have tried both of 'em; leastways, we had to make 'em both up this morning."

"Really? How very absurd!" said Parkins. "I certainly never touched the other, except to lay some things on it. Did it actually seem to have been slept in?"

"Oh yes, sir!" said the maid. "Why, all the things was crumpled and throwed about all ways, if you'll excuse me, sir—quite as if anyone 'adn't passed but a very poor night, sir."

"Dear me," said Parkins. "Well, I may have disordered it more than I thought when I unpacked my things. I'm very sorry to have given you the extra trouble, I'm sure. I expect a friend of mine soon, by the way—a gentleman from Cambridge—to come and occupy it for a night or two. That will be all right, I suppose, won't it?"

"Oh yes, to be sure, sir. Thank you, sir. It's no trouble, I'm sure," said the maid, and departed to giggle with her colleagues.

Parkins set forth, with a stern determination to improve his game.

I am glad to be able to report that he succeeded so far in this enterprise that the Colonel, who had been rather repining at the prospect of a second day's play in his company, became quite chatty as the morning advanced; and his voice boomed out over the flats, as certain also of our own minor poets have said, "like some great bourdon in a minster tower."

"Extraordinary wind, that, we had last night," he said. "In my old home we should have said someone had been whistling for it."

"Should you, indeed!" said Parkins. "Is there a superstition of that kind still current in your part of the country?"

"I don't know about superstition," said the Colonel. "They believe in it all over Denmark and Norway, as well as on the Yorkshire coast; and my experience is, mind you, that there's generally something at the bottom of what these country-folk hold to, and have held to for generations. But it's your drive" (or whatever it might have been: the golfing reader will have to imagine appropriate digressions at the proper intervals).

When conversation was resumed, Parkins said, with a slight hesitancy:

"Apropos of what you were saying just now, Colonel, I think I ought to tell you that my own views on such subjects are very strong. I am, in fact, a convinced disbeliever in what is called the 'supernatural.'"

"What!" said the Colonel, "do you mean to tell me you don't believe in second-sight, or ghosts, or anything of that kind?"

"In nothing whatever of that kind," returned Parkins firmly.

"Well," said the Colonel, "but it appears to me at that rate, sir, that you must be little better than a Sadducee."

Parkins was on the point of answering that, in his opinion, the Sadducees were the most sensible persons he had ever read of in the Old Testament; but, feeling some doubt as to whether much mention of them was to be found in that work, he preferred to laugh the accusation off.

"Perhaps I am," he said; "but—— Here, give me my cleek, boy!—Excuse me one moment, Colonel." A short interval. "Now, as to whistling for the wind, let me give you my theory about it. The laws which govern winds are really not at all perfectly known—to fisher-folk and such, of course, not known at all. A man or woman of eccentric habits, perhaps, or a stranger, is seen repeatedly on the beach at some unusual hour, and is heard whistling. Soon afterwards a violent wind rises; a man who could read the sky perfectly or who possessed a barometer could have foretold that it would. The simple people of a fishing-village have no barometers, and only a few rough rules for prophesying weather. What more natural than that the eccentric personage I postulated should be regarded as having raised the wind, or that he or she should clutch eagerly at the reputation of being able to do so? Now, take last night's wind: as it happens, I myself was whistling. I blew a whistle twice, and the wind seemed to come absolutely in answer to my call. If anyone had seen me——"

The audience had been a little restive under this harangue, and Parkins had, I fear, fallen somewhat into the tone of a lecturer; but at the last sentence the Colonel stopped.

"Whistling, were you?" he said. "And what sort of whistle did you use? Play this stroke first." Interval.

"About that whistle you were asking, Colonel. It's rather a curious one. I have it in my—— No; I see I've left it in my room. As a matter of fact, I found it yesterday."

And then Parkins narrated the manner of his discovery of the whistle, upon hearing which the Colonel grunted, and opined that, in Parkins's place, he should himself be careful about using a thing that had belonged to a set of Papists, of whom, speaking generally, it might be affirmed that you never knew what they might not have been up to. From this topic he diverged to the enormities of the Vicar, who had given notice on the previous Sunday that Friday would be the Feast of St. Thomas the Apostle, and that there would be service at eleven o'clock in the church. This and other similar proceedings constituted in the Colonel's view a strong presumption

that the Vicar was a concealed Papist, if not a Jesuit;
and Parkins, who could not very readily follow the
Colonel in this region, did not disagree with him.
In fact, they got on so well together in the morning
that there was no talk on either side of their separating
after lunch.

Both continued to play well during the afternoon,
or, at least, well enough to make them forget everything else until the light began to fail them. Not
until then did Parkins remember that he had meant
to do some more investigating at the preceptory;
but it was of no great importance, he reflected. One
day was as good as another; he might as well go
home with the Colonel.

As they turned the corner of the house, the Colonel
was almost knocked down by a boy who rushed into
him at the very top of his speed, and then, instead
of running away, remained hanging on to him and
panting. The first words of the warrior were
naturally those of reproof and objurgation, but he
very quickly discerned that the boy was almost
speechless with fright. Inquiries were useless at
first. When the boy got his breath he began to
howl, and still clung to the Colonel's legs. He was
at last detached, but continued to howl.

"What in the world *is* the matter with you?
What have you been up to? What have you seen?"
said the two men.

"Ow, I seen it wive at me out of the winder,"
wailed the boy, "and I don't like it."

"What window?" said the irritated Colonel.
"Come, pull yourself together, my boy."

"The front winder it was, at the 'otel," said the boy.

At this point Parkins was in favour of sending the
boy home, but the Colonel refused; he wanted to get
to the bottom of it, he said; it was most dangerous
to give a boy such a fright as this one had had, and
if it turned out that people had been playing jokes,
they should suffer for it in some way. And by a
series of questions he made out this story: The boy
had been playing about on the grass in front of the
Globe with some others; then they had gone home
to their teas, and he was just going, when he happened
to look up at the front winder and see it a-wiving at
him. *It* seemed to be a figure of some sort, in white
as far as he knew—couldn't see its face; but it wived
at him, and it warn't a right thing—not to say not a
right person. Was there a light in the room? No,
he didn't think to look if there was a light. Which
was the window? Was it the top one or the second
one? The seckind one it was—the big winder
what got two little uns at the sides.

"Very well, my boy," said the Colonel, after a
few more questions. "You run away home now.
I expect it was some person trying to give you a
start. Another time, like a brave English boy, you
just throw a stone—well, no, not that exactly, but
you go and speak to the waiter, or to Mr. Simpson,
the landlord, and—yes—and say that I advised you
to do so."

142

The boy's face expressed some of the doubt he felt as to the likelihood of Mr. Simpson's lending a favourable ear to his complaint, but the Colonel did not appear to perceive this, and went on:

"And here's a sixpence—no, I see it's a shilling —and you be off home, and don't think any more about it."

The youth hurried off with agitated thanks, and the Colonel and Parkins went round to the front of the Globe and reconnoitred. There was only one window answering to the description they had been hearing.

"Well, that's curious," said Parkins; "it's evidently my window the lad was talking about. Will you come up for a moment, Colonel Wilson? We ought to be able to see if anyone has been taking liberties in my room."

They were soon in the passage, and Parkins made as if to open the door. Then he stopped and felt in his pockets.

"This is more serious than I thought," was his next remark. "I remember now that before I started this morning I locked the door. It is locked now, and, what is more, here is the key." And he held it up. "Now," he went on, "if the servants are in the habit of going into one's room during the day when one is away, I can only say that—well, that I don't approve of it at all." Conscious of a somewhat weak climax, he busied himself in opening the door (which was indeed locked) and in lighting candles. "No," he said, "nothing seems disturbed."

"Except your bed," put in the Colonel.

"Excuse me, that isn't my bed," said Parkins. "I don't use that one. But it does look as if someone had been playing tricks with it."

It certainly did : the clothes were bundled up and twisted together in a most tortuous confusion. Parkins pondered.

"That must be it," he said at last : "I disordered the clothes last night in unpacking, and they haven't made it since. Perhaps they came in to make it, and that boy saw them through the window; and then they were called away and locked the door after them. Yes, I think that must be it."

"Well, ring and ask," said the Colonel, and this appealed to Parkins as practical.

The maid appeared, and, to make a long story short, deposed that she had made the bed in the morning when the gentleman was in the room, and hadn't been there since. No, she hadn't no other key. Mr. Simpson he kep' the keys; he'd be able to tell the gentleman if anyone had been up.

This was a puzzle. Investigation showed that nothing of value had been taken, and Parkins remembered the disposition of the small objects on tables and so forth well enough to be pretty sure that no pranks had been played with them. Mr. and Mrs. Simpson furthermore agreed that neither of them had given the duplicate key of the room to any person whatever during the day. Nor could Parkins, fair-

minded man as he was, detect anything in the
demeanour of master, mistress, or maid that indicated
guilt. He was much more inclined to think that
the boy had been imposing on the Colonel.

The latter was unwontedly silent and pensive at
dinner and throughout the evening. When he bade
good night to Parkins, he murmured in a gruff undertone :

" You know where I am if you want me during
the night."

" Why, yes, thank you, Colonel Wilson, I think I
do ; but there isn't much prospect of my disturbing
you, I hope. By the way," he added, " did I show
you that old whistle I spoke of ? I think not. Well,
here it is."

The Colonel turned it over gingerly in the light
of the candle.

" Can you make anything of the inscription ? "
asked Parkins, as he took it back.

" No, not in this light. What do you mean to
do with it ? "

" Oh, well, when I get back to Cambridge I shall
submit it to some of the archæologists there, and see
what they think of it ; and very likely, if they consider it worth having, I may present it to one of the
museums."

" 'M ! " said the Colonel. " Well, you may be
right. All I know is that, if it were mine, I should
chuck it straight into the sea. It's no use talking,
I'm well aware, but I expect that with you it's a case

145

of live and learn. I hope so, I'm sure, and I wish
you a good night."

He turned away, leaving Parkins in act to speak
at the bottom of the stair, and soon each was in his
own bedroom.

By some unfortunate accident, there were neither
blinds nor curtains to the windows of the Professor's
room. The previous night he had thought little of
this, but to-night there seemed every prospect of a
bright moon rising to shine directly on his bed, and
probably wake him later on. When he noticed this
he was a good deal annoyed, but, with an ingenuity
which I can only envy, he succeeded in rigging up,
with the help of a railway-rug, some safety-pins, and
a stick and umbrella, a screen which, if it only held
together, would completely keep the moonlight off
his bed. And shortly afterwards he was comfortably
in that bed. When he had read a somewhat solid
work long enough to produce a decided wish for
sleep, he cast a drowsy glance round the room, blew
out the candle, and fell back upon the pillow.

He must have slept soundly for an hour or more,
when a sudden clatter shook him up in a most un-
welcome manner. In a moment he realized what
had happened : his carefully-constructed screen had
given way, and a very bright frosty moon was shining
directly on his face. This was highly annoying.
Could he possibly get up and reconstruct the screen ?
or could he manage to sleep if he did not ?

For some minutes he lay and pondered over the

possibilities; then he turned over sharply, and with all his eyes open lay breathlessly listening. There had been a movement, he was sure, in the empty bed on the opposite side of the room. To-morrow he would have it moved, for there must be rats or something playing about in it. It was quiet now. No! the commotion began again. There was a rustling and shaking: surely more than any rat could cause.

I can figure to myself something of the Professor's bewilderment and horror, for I have in a dream thirty years back seen the same thing happen; but the reader will hardly, perhaps, imagine how dreadful it was to him to see a figure suddenly sit up in what he had known was an empty bed. He was out of his own bed in one bound, and made a dash towards the window, where lay his only weapon, the stick with which he had propped his screen. This was, as it turned out, the worst thing he could have done, because the personage in the empty bed, with a sudden smooth motion, slipped from the bed and took up a position, with outspread arms, between the two beds, and in front of the door. Parkins watched it in a horrid perplexity. Somehow, the idea of getting past it and escaping through the door was intolerable to him; he could not have borne—he didn't know why—to touch it; and as for its touching him, he would sooner dash himself through the window than have that happen. It stood for the moment in a band of dark shadow, and he had not seen what its face was like. Now it began to move, in a stooping posture, and all at once the spectator realized, with some horror and some relief, that it must be blind, for it seemed to feel about it with its muffled arms in a groping and random fashion. Turning half away from him, it became suddenly conscious of the bed he had just left, and darted towards it, and bent over and felt the pillows in a way which made Parkins shudder as he had never in his life thought it possible. In a very few moments it seemed to know that the bed was empty, and then, moving forward into the area of light and facing the window, it showed for the first time what manner of thing it was.

Parkins, who very much dislikes being questioned about it, did once describe something of it in my hearing, and I gathered that what he chiefly remembers about it is a horrible, an intensely horrible, face *of crumpled linen*. What expression he read upon it he could not or would not tell, but that the fear of it went nigh to maddening him is certain.

But he was not at leisure to watch it for long. With formidable quickness it moved into the middle of the room, and, as it groped and waved, one corner of its draperies swept across Parkins's face. He could not—though he knew how perilous a sound was—he could not keep back a cry of disgust, and this gave the searcher an instant clue. It leapt towards him upon the instant, and the next moment he was half-way through the window backwards, uttering cry upon cry at the utmost pitch of his voice, and the linen face was thrust close into his own. At this, almost the last possible second, deliverance came, as you will have guessed: the Colonel burst the door open, and was just in time to see the dreadful group at the window. When he reached the figures only one was left. Parkins sank forward into the room in a faint, and before him on the floor lay a tumbled heap of bed-clothes.

Colonel Wilson asked no questions, but busied himself in keeping everyone else out of the room and in getting Parkins back to his bed; and himself, wrapped in a rug, occupied the other bed for the rest of the night. Early on the next day Rogers arrived, more welcome than he would have been a day before, and the three of them held a very long consultation in the Professor's room. At the end of it the Colonel left the hotel door carrying a small object between his finger and thumb, which he cast as far into the sea as a very brawny arm could send it. Later on the smoke of a burning ascended from the back premises of the Globe.

Exactly what explanation was patched up for the staff and visitors at the hotel I must confess I do not recollect. The Professor was somehow cleared of the ready suspicion of delirium tremens, and the hotel of the reputation of a troubled house.

There is not much question as to what would have happened to Parkins if the Colonel had not intervened when he did. He would either have fallen out of the window or else lost his wits. But it is not so evident what more the creature that came in answer

149

to the whistle could have done than frighten. There seemed to be absolutely nothing material about it save the bed-clothes of which it had made itself a body. The Colonel, who remembered a not very dissimilar occurrence in India, was of opinion that if Parkins had closed with it it could really have done very little, and that its one power was that of frightening. The whole thing, he said, served to confirm his opinion of the Church of Rome.

There is really nothing more to tell, but, as you may imagine, the Professor's views on certain points are less clear cut than they used to be. His nerves, too, have suffered : he cannot even now see a surplice hanging on a door quite unmoved, and the spectacle of a scarecrow in a field late on a winter afternoon has cost him more than one sleepless night.

THE TREASURE OF ABBOT THOMAS

I

" VERUM usque in præsentem diem multa garriunt inter se Canonici de abscondito quodam istius Abbatis Thomæ thesauro, quem sæpe, quanquam adhuc incassum, quæsiverunt Steinfeldenses. Ipsum enim Thomam adhuc florida in ætate existentem ingentem auri massam circa monasterium defodisse perhibent; de quo multoties interrogatus ubi esset, cum risu respondere solitus erat : ' Job, Johannes, et Zacharias vel vobis vel posteris indicabunt '; idemque aliquando adiicere se inventuris minime invisurum. Inter alia huius Abbatis opera, hoc memoria præcipue dignum iudico quod fenestram magnam in orientali parte alæ australis in ecclesia sua imaginibus optime in vitro depictis impleverit : id quod et ipsius effigies et insignia ibidem posita demonstrant. Domum quoque Abbatialem fere totam restauravit : puteo in atrio ipsius effosso et lapidibus marmoreis pulchre cælatis exornato. Decessit autem, morte aliquantulum subitanea perculsus, ætatis suæ anno lxxii^{do}, incarnationis vero Dominicæ mdxxix°."

" I suppose I shall have to translate this," said the antiquary to himself, as he finished copying the above lines from that rather rare and exceedingly

diffuse book, the " *Sertum Steinfeldense Norbertinum.*" [1]
" Well, it may as well be done first as last," and
accordingly the following rendering was very quickly
produced :

" Up to the present day there is much gossip among
the Canons about a certain hidden treasure of this
Abbot Thomas, for which those of Steinfeld have
often made search, though hitherto in vain. The
story is that Thomas, while yet in the vigour of life,
concealed a very large quantity of gold somewhere
in the monastery. He was often asked where it was,
and always answered, with a laugh : ' Job, John, and
Zechariah will tell either you or your successors.'
He sometimes added that he should feel no grudge
against those who might find it. Among other
works carried out by this Abbot I may specially
mention his filling the great window at the east end
of the south aisle of the church with figures admirably
painted on glass, as his effigy and arms in the window
attest. He also restored almost the whole of the
Abbot's lodging, and dug a well in the court of it,
which he adorned with beautiful carvings in marble.
He died rather suddenly in the seventy-second year
of his age, A.D. 1529."

The object which the antiquary had before him at

---

[1] An account of the Premonstratensian abbey of Steinfeld,
in the Eiffel, with lives of the Abbots, published at Cologne
in 1712 by Christian Albert Erhard, a resident in the district.
The epithet *Norbertinum* is due to the fact that St. Norbert was
founder of the Premonstratensian Order.

the moment was that of tracing the whereabouts of the painted windows of the Abbey Church of Stein-feld. Shortly after the Revolution, a very large quantity of painted glass made its way from the dissolved abbeys of Germany and Belgium to this country, and may now be seen adorning various of our parish churches, cathedrals, and private chapels. Steinfeld Abbey was among the most considerable of these involuntary contributors to our artistic possessions (I am quoting the somewhat ponderous preamble of the book which the antiquary wrote), and the greater part of the glass from that institution can be identified without much difficulty by the help, either of the numerous inscriptions in which the place is mentioned, or of the subjects of the windows, in which several well-defined cycles or narratives were represented.

The passage with which I began my story had set the antiquary on the track of another identification. In a private chapel—no matter where—he had seen three large figures, each occupying a whole light in a window, and evidently the work of one artist. Their style made it plain that that artist had been a German of the sixteenth century; but hitherto the more exact localizing of them had been a puzzle. They represented—will you be surprised to hear it?—JOB PATRIARCHA, JOHANNES EVANGELISTA, ZACHARIAS PROPHETA, and each of them held a book or scroll, inscribed with a sentence from his writings. These, as a matter of course, the antiquary had noted, and had been struck by the curious way in which they differed from any text of the Vulgate that he had been able to examine. Thus the scroll in Job's hand was inscribed : " Auro est locus in quo absconditur " (for " conflatur ") ;[1] on the book of John was : " Habent in vestimentis suis scripturam quam nemo novit "[2] (for "in vestimento scriptum," the following words being taken from another verse) ; and Zacharias had : " Super lapidem unum septem oculi sunt "[3] (which alone of the three presents an unaltered text).

A sad perplexity it had been to our investigator to think why these three personages should have been placed together in one window. There was no bond of connection between them, either historic, symbolic, or doctrinal, and he could only suppose that they must have formed part of a very large series of Prophets and Apostles, which might have filled, say, all the clerestory windows of some capacious church. But the passage from the " *Sertum* " had altered the situation by showing that the names of the actual personages represented in the glass now in Lord D——'s chapel had been constantly on the lips of Abbot Thomas von Eschenhausen of Steinfeld, and that this Abbot had put up a painted window, probably about the year 1520, in the south aisle of his abbey church. It was no very wild conjecture that the three figures might have formed part of

[1] There is a place for gold where it is hidden.
[2] They have on their raiment a writing which no man knoweth.
[3] Upon one stone are seven eyes.

Abbot Thomas's offering; it was one which, more-over, could probably be confirmed or set aside by another careful examination of the glass. And, as Mr. Somerton was a man of leisure, he set out on pilgrimage to the private chapel with very little delay. His conjecture was confirmed to the full. Not only did the style and technique of the glass suit perfectly with the date and place required, but in another window of the chapel he found some glass, known to have been bought along with the figures, which contained the arms of Abbot Thomas von Eschenhausen.

At intervals during his researches Mr. Somerton had been haunted by the recollection of the gossip about the hidden treasure, and, as he thought the matter over, it became more and more obvious to him that if the Abbot meant anything by the enigmatical answer which he gave to his questioners, he must have meant that the secret was to be found somewhere in the window he had placed in the abbey church. It was undeniable, furthermore, that the first of the curiously-selected texts on the scrolls in the window might be taken to have a reference to hidden treasure.

Every feature, therefore, or mark which could possibly assist in elucidating the riddle which, he felt sure, the Abbot had set to posterity he noted with scrupulous care, and, returning to his Berkshire manor-house, consumed many a pint of the midnight oil over his tracings and sketches. After two or three weeks, a day came when Mr. Somerton announced to his man that he must pack his own and his master's things for a short journey abroad, whither for the moment we will not follow him.

II

Mr. Gregory, the Rector of Parsbury, had strolled out before breakfast, it being a fine autumn morning, as far as the gate of his carriage-drive, with intent to meet the postman and sniff the cool air. Nor was he disappointed of either purpose. Before he had had time to answer more than ten or eleven of the miscellaneous questions propounded to him in the lightness of their hearts by his young offspring, who had accompanied him, the postman was seen approaching; and among the morning's budget was one letter bearing a foreign postmark and stamp (which became at once the objects of an eager competition among the youthful Gregorys), and was addressed in an uneducated, but plainly an English hand.

When the Rector opened it, and turned to the signature, he realized that it came from the confidential valet of his friend and squire, Mr. Somerton. Thus it ran:

HONOURD SIR,—

Has I am in a great anxeity about Master I write at is Wish to Beg you Sir if you could be so good as Step over. Master Has add a Nastey Shock and keeps His Bedd. I never Have known Him like this but No wonder and Nothing will serve but you Sir. Master says would I mintion the Short Way Here is Drive to Cobblince and take a Trap. Hopeing I Have maid all Plain, but am much Confused in Myself what with Anxiatey and Weakfulness at Night. If I might be so Bold Sir it will be a Pleasure to see a Honnest Brish Face among all These Forig ones.

I am Sir
Your obed^t Servt
WILLIAM BROWN.'

P.S.—The Villiage for Town I will not Turm It is name Steenfeld.'

The reader must be left to picture to himself in detail the surprise, confusion, and hurry of preparation into which the receipt of such a letter would be likely to plunge a quiet Berkshire parsonage in the year of grace 1859. It is enough for me to say that a train to town was caught in the course of the day, and that Mr. Gregory was able to secure a cabin in the Antwerp boat and a place in the Coblentz train. Nor was it difficult to manage the transit from that centre to Steinfeld.

I labour under a grave disadvantage as narrator of this story in that I have never visited Steinfeld myself, and that neither of the principal actors in the episode (from whom I derive my information) was able to give me anything but a vague and rather dismal idea of its appearance. I gather that it is a small place, with a large church despoiled of its ancient fittings; a number of rather ruinous great buildings, mostly of the seventeenth century, surround this church; for the abbey, in common with most of those on the Continent, was rebuilt in a luxurious fashion by its inhabitants at that period. It has not seemed to me worth while to lavish money on a visit to the place, for though it is probably far more attractive than either Mr. Somerton or Mr. Gregory thought it, there is evidently little, if anything, of first-rate interest to be seen—except, perhaps, one thing, which I should not care to see.

The inn where the English gentleman and his servant were lodged is, or was, the only " possible " one in the village. Mr. Gregory was taken to it at once by his driver, and found Mr. Brown waiting at the door. Mr. Brown, a model when in his Berkshire home of the impassive whiskered race who are known as confidential valets, was now egregiously out of his element, in a light tweed suit, anxious, almost irritable, and plainly anything but master of the situation. His relief at the sight of the " honest British face " of his Rector was unmeasured, but words to describe it were denied him. He could only say:

" Well, I ham pleased, I'm sure, sir, to see you. And so I'm sure, sir, will master."

" How *is* your master, Brown? " Mr. Gregory eagerly put in.

" I think he's better, sir, thank you; but he's had

a dreadful time of it. I 'ope he's gettin' some sleep now, but——"

"What has been the matter—I couldn't make out from your letter? Was it an accident of any kind?"

"Well, sir, I 'ardly know whether I'd better speak about it. Master was very partickler he should be the one to tell you. But there's no bones broke—that's one thing I'm sure we ought to be thankful——"

"What does the doctor say?" asked Mr. Gregory. They were by this time outside Mr. Somerton's bedroom door, and speaking in low tones. Mr. Gregory, who happened to be in front, was feeling for the handle, and chanced to run his fingers over the panels. Before Brown could answer, there was a terrible cry from within the room.

"In God's name, who is that?" were the first words they heard. "Brown, is it?"

"Yes, sir—me, sir, and Mr. Gregory," Brown hastened to answer, and there was an audible groan of relief in reply.

They entered the room, which was darkened against the afternoon sun, and Mr. Gregory saw, with a shock of pity, how drawn, how damp with drops of fear, was the usually calm face of his friend, who, sitting up in the curtained bed, stretched out a shaking hand to welcome him.

"Better for seeing you, my dear Gregory," was the reply to the Rector's first question, and it was palpably true.

After five minutes of conversation Mr. Somerton

was more his own man, Brown afterwards reported, than he had been for days. He was able to eat a more than respectable dinner, and talked confidently of being fit to stand a journey to Coblentz within twenty-four hours.

"But there's one thing," he said, with a return of agitation which Mr. Gregory did not like to see, "which I must beg you to do for me, my dear Gregory. Don't," he went on, laying his hand on Gregory's to forestall any interruption—"don't ask me what it is, or why I want it done. I'm not up to explaining it yet; it would throw me back— undo all the good you have done me by coming. The only word I will say about it is that you run no risk whatever by doing it, and that Brown can and will show you to-morrow what it is. It's merely to put back—to keep—something—— No; I can't speak of it yet. Do you mind calling Brown?"

"Well, Somerton," said Mr. Gregory, as he crossed the room to the door, "I won't ask for any explanations till you see fit to give them. And if this bit of business is as easy as you represent it to be, I will very gladly undertake it for you the first thing in the morning."

"Ah, I was sure you would, my dear Gregory; I was certain I could rely on you. I shall owe you more thanks than I can tell. Now, here is Brown. Brown, one word with you."

"Shall I go?" interjected Mr. Gregory.

"Not at all. Dear me, no. Brown, the first

thing to-morrow morning—(you don't mind early hours, I know, Gregory)—you must take the Rector to—*there*, you know" (a nod from Brown, who looked grave and anxious), " and he and you will put that back. You needn't be in the least alarmed; it's *perfectly* safe in the daytime. You know what I mean. It lies on the step, you know, where—where we put it." (Brown swallowed dryly once or twice, and, failing to speak, bowed.) " And—yes, that's all. Only this one other word, my dear Gregory. If you *can* manage to keep from questioning Brown about this matter, I shall be still more bound to you. To-morrow evening, at latest, if all goes well, I shall be able, I believe, to tell you the whole story from start to finish. And now I'll wish you good night. Brown will be with me—he sleeps here—and if I were you, I should lock my door. Yes, be particular to do that. They—they like it, the people here, and it's better. Good night, good night."

They parted upon this, and if Mr. Gregory woke once or twice in the small hours and fancied he heard a fumbling about the lower part of his locked door, it was, perhaps, no more than what a quiet man, suddenly plunged into a strange bed and the heart of a mystery, might reasonably expect. Certainly he thought, to the end of his days, that he had heard such a sound twice or three times between midnight and dawn.

He was up with the sun, and out in company with Brown soon after. Perplexing as was the service he had been asked to perform for Mr. Somerton, it was not a difficult or an alarming one, and within half an hour from his leaving the inn it was over. What it was I shall not as yet divulge.

Later in the morning Mr. Somerton, now almost himself again, was able to make a start from Steinfeld; and that same evening, whether at Coblentz or at some intermediate stage on the journey I am not certain, he settled down to the promised explanation. Brown was present, but how much of the matter was ever really made plain to his comprehension he would never say, and I am unable to conjecture.

III

This was Mr. Somerton's story:

" You know roughly, both of you, that this expedition of mine was undertaken with the object of tracing something in connection with some old painted glass in Lord D——'s private chapel. Well, the starting-point of the whole matter lies in this passage from an old printed book, to which I will ask your attention."

And at this point Mr. Somerton went carefully over some ground with which we are already familiar.

" On my second visit to the chapel," he went on, " my purpose was to take every note I could of figures, lettering, diamond-scratchings on the glass, and even apparently accidental markings. The first point which I tackled was that of the inscribed scrolls. I could not doubt that the first of these, that of Job—

'There is a place for the gold where it is hidden'
—with its intentional alteration, must refer to the
treasure; so I applied myself with some confidence
to the next, that of St. John—' They have on their
vestures a writing which no man knoweth.' The
natural question will have occurred to you: Was
there an inscription on the robes of the figures? I
could see none; each of the three had a broad black
border to his mantle, which made a conspicuous
and rather ugly feature in the window. I was non-
plussed, I will own, and but for a curious bit of luck
I think I should have left the search where the Canons
of Steinfeld had left it before me. But it so happened
that there was a good deal of dust on the surface of
the glass, and Lord D——, happening to come in,
noticed my blackened hands, and kindly insisted on
sending for a Turk's head broom to clean down the
window. There must, I suppose, have been a rough
piece in the broom; anyhow, as it passed over the
border of one of the mantles, I noticed that it left a
long scratch, and that some yellow stain instantly
showed up. I asked the man to stop his work for
a moment, and ran up the ladder to examine the
place. The yellow stain was there, sure enough, and
what had come away was a thick black pigment,
which had evidently been laid on with the brush
after the glass had been burnt, and could therefore
be easily scraped off without doing any harm. I
scraped, accordingly, and you will hardly believe—
no, I do you an injustice; you will have guessed

already—that I found under this black pigment two or three clearly-formed capital letters in yellow stain on a clear ground. Of course, I could hardly contain my delight.

" I told Lord D—— that I had detected an inscription which I thought might be very interesting, and begged to be allowed to uncover the whole of it. He made no difficulty about it whatever, told me to do exactly as I pleased, and then, having an engagement, was obliged—rather to my relief, I must say— to leave me. I set to work at once, and found the task a fairly easy one. The pigment, disintegrated, of course, by time, came off almost at a touch, and I don't think that it took me a couple of hours, all told, to clean the whole of the black borders in all three lights. Each of the figures had, as the inscription said, ' a writing on their vestures which nobody knew.'

" This discovery, of course, made it absolutely certain to my mind that I was on the right track. And, now, what was the inscription ? While I was cleaning the glass I almost took pains not to read the lettering, saving up the treat until I had got the whole thing clear. And when that *was* done, my dear Gregory, I assure you I could almost have cried from sheer disappointment. What I read was only the most hopeless jumble of letters that was ever shaken up in a hat. Here it is :

Job. **DREVICIOPEDMOOMSMVIVLISLCAVI BASBATAOVT**

St. John.   RDIIEAMRLESIPVSPODSEEIRSETTAA
            ESGIAVNNR

Zechariah.   FTEEAILNQDPVAIVMTLEEATTOHIO
            ONVMCAAT.H.Q.E.

" Blank as I felt and must have looked for the first few minutes, my disappointment didn't last long. I realized almost at once that I was dealing with a cipher or cryptogram; and I reflected that it was likely to be of a pretty simple kind, considering its early date. So I copied the letters with the most anxious care. Another little point, I may tell you. turned up in the process which confirmed my belief in the cipher. After copying the letters on Job's robe I counted them, to make sure that I had them right. There were thirty-eight; and, just as I finished going through them, my eye fell on a scratching made with a sharp point on the edge of the border. It was simply the number xxxviii in Roman numerals. To cut the matter short, there was a similar note, as I may call it, in each of the other lights; and that made it plain to me that the glass-painter had had very strict orders from Abbot Thomas about the inscription, and had taken pains to get it correct.

" Well, after that discovery you may imagine how minutely I went over the whole surface of the glass in search of further light. Of course, I did not neglect the inscription on the scroll of Zechariah— ' Upon one stone are seven eyes,' but I very quickly concluded that this must refer to some mark on a stone which could only be found *in situ*, where the

165

treasure was concealed. To be short, I made all possible notes and sketches and tracings, and then came back to Parsbury to work out the cipher at leisure. Oh, the agonies I went through ! I thought myself very clever at first, for I made sure that the key would be found in some of the old books on secret writing. The '*Steganographia*' of Joachim Trithemius, who was an earlier contemporary of Abbot Thomas, seemed particularly promising ; so I got that, and Selenius's ' *Cryptographia* ' and Bacon ' *de Augmentis Scientiarum*,' and some more. But I could hit upon nothing. Then I tried the principle of the ' most frequent letter,' taking first Latin and then German as a basis. That didn't help, either ; whether it ought to have done so, I am not clear. And then I came back to the window itself, and read over my notes, hoping almost against hope that the Abbot might himself have somewhere supplied the key I wanted. I could make nothing out of the colour or pattern of the robes. There were no landscape backgrounds with subsidiary objects ; there was nothing in the canopies. The only resource possible seemed to be in the attitudes of the figures. ' Job,' I read : ' scroll in left hand, forefinger of right hand extended upwards. John : holds inscribed book in left hand ; with right hand blesses, with two fingers. Zechariah : scroll in left hand ; right hand extended upwards, as Job, but with three fingers pointing up.' In other words, I reflected, Job has *one* finger extended, John has *two*, Zechariah has *three*.

May not there be a numeral key concealed in that?
My dear Gregory," said Mr. Somerton, laying his
hand on his friend's knee, " that *was* the key. I
didn't get it to fit at first, but after two or three trials
I saw what was meant. After the first letter of the
inscription you skip *one* letter, after the next you skip
two, and after that skip *three*. Now look at the result
I got. I've underlined the letters which form words :

DREVICIOPEDMOOMSMVIVLISLCAVIBASBA
TAOVT

RDIIEAMRLESIPVSPODSEEIRSETTAAESGIA
VNNR

FTEEAILNQDPVAIVMTLEEATTOHIOONVMC
AAT.H.Q E.

" Do you see it ? ' *Decem millia auri reposita sunt
in puteo in at* . . .' (Ten thousand [pieces] of gold
are laid up in a well in . . .), followed by an incomplete word beginning *at*. So far so good. I tried
the same plan with the remaining letters ; but it
wouldn't work, and I fancied that perhaps the placing
of dots after the three last letters might indicate some
difference of procedure. Then I thought to myself,
' Wasn't there some allusion to a well in the account
of Abbot Thomas in that book the " *Sertum* " ? '
Yes, there was : he built a *puteus in atrio* (a well in
the court). There, of course, was my word *atrio*.
The next step was to copy out the remaining letter

of the inscription, omitting those I had already used. That gave what you will see on this slip:

RVIIOPDOOSMVVISCAVBSBTAOTDIEAMLSIV
SPDEERSETAEGIANRFEEALQDVAIMLEATTH
OOVMCA.H.Q.E.

"Now, I knew what the three first letters I wanted were,—namely, *rio*—to complete the word *atrio* ; and, as you will see, these are all to be found in the first five letters. I was a little confused at first by the occurrence of two *i's*, but very soon I saw that every alternate letter must be taken in the remainder of the inscription. You can work it out for yourself ; the result, continuing where the first ' round ' left off, is this :

' rio domus abbatialis de Steinfeld a me, Thoma, qui posui custodem super ea.   Gare à qui la touche.'

"So the whole secret was out:

' Ten thousand pieces of gold are laid up in the well in the court of the Abbot's house of Steinfeld by me, Thomas, who have set a guardian over them.   *Gare à qui la touche.*'

"The last words, I ought to say, are a device which Abbot Thomas had adopted. I found it with his arms in another piece of glass at Lord D——'s, and he drafted it bodily into his cipher, though it doesn't quite fit in point of grammar.

"Well, what would any human being have been tempted to do, my dear Gregory, in my place ? Could he have helped setting off, as I did, to Steinfeld, and tracing the secret literally to the fountain-head ? I don't believe he could. Anyhow, I couldn't, and, as I needn't tell you, I found myself at Steinfeld as soon as the resources of civilization could put me there, and installed myself in the inn you saw. I must tell you that I was not altogether free from forebodings—on one hand of disappointment, on the other of danger. There was always the possibility that Abbot Thomas's well might have been wholly obliterated, or else that someone, ignorant of crypto-grams, and guided only by luck, might have stumbled on the treasure before me. And then "—there was a very perceptible shaking of the voice here—" I was not entirely easy, I need not mind confessing, as to the meaning of the words about the guardian of the treasure. But, if you don't mind, I'll say no more about that until—until it becomes necessary.

" At the first possible opportunity Brown and I began exploring the place. I had naturally repre-sented myself as being interested in the remains of the abbey, and we could not avoid paying a visit to the church, impatient as I was to be elsewhere. Still, it did interest me to see the windows where the glass had been, and especially that at the east end of the south aisle. In the tracery lights of that I was startled to see some fragments and coats-of-arms remaining —Abbot Thomas's shield was there, and a small figure with a scroll inscribed ' Oculos habent, et non videbunt ' (They have eyes, and shall not see), which, I take it, was a hit of the Abbot at his Canons.

" But, of course, the principal object was to find

the Abbot's house. There is no prescribed place for this, so far as I know, in the plan of a monastery; you can't predict of it, as you can of the chapter-house, that it will be on the eastern side of the cloister, or, as of the dormitory, that it will communicate with a transept of the church. I felt that if I asked many questions I might awaken lingering memories of the treasure, and I thought it best to try first to discover it for myself. It was not a very long or difficult search. That three-sided court south-east of the church, with deserted piles of building round it, and grass-grown pavement, which you saw this morning, was the place. And glad enough I was to see that it was put to no use, and was neither very far from our inn nor overlooked by any inhabited building; there were only orchards and paddocks on the slopes east of the church. I can tell you that fine stone glowed wonderfully in the rather watery yellow sunset that we had on the Tuesday afternoon.

"Next, what about the well? There was not much doubt about that, as you can testify. It is really a very remarkable thing. That curb is, I think, of Italian marble, and the carving I thought must be Italian also. There were reliefs, you will perhaps remember, of Eliezer and Rebekah, and of Jacob opening the well for Rachel, and similar subjects; but, by way of disarming suspicion, I suppose, the Abbot had carefully abstained from any of his cynical and allusive inscriptions.

"I examined the whole structure with the keenest

interest, of course—a square well-head with an opening in one side; an arch over it, with a wheel for the rope to pass over, evidently in very good condition still, for it had been used within sixty years, or perhaps even later, though not quite recently. Then there was the question of depth and access to the interior. I suppose the depth was about sixty to seventy feet; and as to the other point, it really seemed as if the Abbot had wished to lead searchers up to the very door of his treasure-house, for, as you tested for yourself, there were big blocks of stone bonded into the masonry, and leading down in a regular staircase round and round the inside of the well.

"It seemed almost too good to be true. I wondered if there was a trap—if the stones were so contrived as to tip over when a weight was placed on them; but I tried a good many with my own weight and with my stick, and all seemed, and actually were, perfectly firm. Of course, I resolved that Brown and I would make an experiment that very night.

"I was well prepared. Knowing the sort of place I should have to explore, I had brought a sufficiency of good rope and bands of webbing to surround my body, and crossbars to hold to, as well as lanterns and candles and crowbars, all of which would go into a single carpet-bag and excite no suspicion. I satisfied myself that my rope would be long enough, and that the wheel for the bucket was in good working order, and then we went home to dinner.

"I had a little cautious conversation with the landlord, and made out that he would not be over-much surprised if I went out for a stroll with my man about nine o'clock, to make (Heaven forgive me!) a sketch of the abbey by moonlight. I asked no questions about the well, and am not likely to do so now. I fancy I know as much about it as anyone in Steinfeld : at least "—with a strong shudder— "I don't want to know any more.

"Now we come to the crisis, and, though I hate to think of it, I feel sure, Gregory, that it will be better for me in all ways to recall it just as it happened. We started, Brown and I, at about nine with our bag, and attracted no attention; for we managed to slip out at the hinder end of the inn-yard into an alley which brought us quite to the edge of the village. In five minutes we were at the well, and for some little time we sat on the edge of the well-head to make sure that no one was stirring or spying on us. All we heard was some horses cropping grass out of sight farther down the eastern slope. We were perfectly unobserved, and had plenty of light from the gorgeous full moon to allow us to get the rope properly fitted over the wheel. Then I secured the band round my body beneath the arms. We attached the end of the rope very securely to a ring in the stonework. Brown took the lighted lantern and followed me; I had a crowbar. And so we began to descend cautiously, feeling every step before we set foot on it, and scanning the walls in search of any marked stone.

" Half aloud I counted the steps as we went down, and we got as far as the thirty-eighth before I noted anything at all irregular in the surface of the masonry. Even here there was no mark, and I began to feel very blank, and to wonder if the Abbot's cryptogram could possibly be an elaborate hoax. At the forty-ninth step the staircase ceased. It was with a very sinking heart that I began retracing my steps, and when I was back on the thirty-eighth—Brown, with the lantern, being a step or two above me—I scrutinized the little bit of irregularity in the stone-work with all my might; but there was no vestige of a mark.

" Then it struck me that the texture of the surface looked just a little smoother than the rest, or, at least, in some way different. It might possibly be cement and not stone. I gave it a good blow with my iron bar. There was a decidedly hollow sound, though that might be the result of our being in a well. But there was more. A great flake of cement dropped on to my feet, and I saw marks on the stone underneath. I had tracked the Abbot down, my dear Gregory ; even now I think of it with a certain pride. It took but a very few more taps to clear the whole of the cement away, and I saw a slab of stone about two feet square, upon which was engraven a cross. Disappointment again, but only for a moment. It was you, Brown, who reassured me by a casual remark. You said, if I remember right :

" ' It's a funny cross ; looks like a lot of eyes."

" I snatched the lantern out of your hand, and saw with inexpressible pleasure that the cross *was* composed of seven eyes, four in a vertical line, three horizontal. The last of the scrolls in the window was explained in the way I had anticipated. Here was my ' stone with the seven eyes.' So far the Abbot's data had been exact, and, as I thought of this, the anxiety about the ' guardian ' returned upon me with increased force. Still, I wasn't going to retreat now.

" Without giving myself time to think, I knocked away the cement all round the marked stone, and then gave it a prise on the right side with my crow-bar. It moved at once, and I saw that it was but a thin light slab, such as I could easily lift out myself, and that it stopped the entrance to a cavity. I did lift it out unbroken, and set it on the step, for it might be very important to us to be able to replace it. Then I waited for several minutes on the step just above. I don't know why, but I think to see if any dreadful thing would rush out. Nothing happened. Next I lit a candle, and very cautiously I placed it inside the cavity, with some idea of seeing whether there were foul air, and of getting a glimpse of what was inside. There *was* some foulness of air which nearly extinguished the flame, but in no long

All transactions are subject to proof and verification.
CMA CP 00224 (4-95) NH

Acknowledgement

ComeriCARD

Mike J Smith CENTER

Date	Time	Center

Card Number 272 1273

4/11 O
Will born Love

Olansing Mi 48911
MLope2
lope @ @Aol.com

Dreaming of a New Home?

Call the experts at Comerica Mortgage for your home loan needs.

- Fixed and Adjustable
- FHA/VA Loans
- 95% Financing
- Builder/One-time close
- Purchase + Improvements
- Portfolio Products

For more information, please call us:

In Dallas: (214) 890-4388
In Houston: (713) 263-8208
or
1-800-345-2650

Bring this receipt to your appointment and we will cover $125 of your processing fee at closing.

Offer good through 8/31/95.

Comerica

Comerica Mortgage Corporation

EQUAL HOUSING LENDER

time it burned quite steadily. The hole went some little way back, and also on the right and left of the entrance, and I could see some rounded light-coloured objects within which might be bags. There was no use in waiting. I faced the cavity, and looked in. There was nothing immediately in the front of the hole. I put my arm in and felt to the right, very gingerly. . . .

"Just give me a glass of cognac, Brown. I'll go on in a moment, Gregory. . . .

"Well, I felt to the right, and my fingers touched something curved, that felt—yes—more or less like leather; dampish it was, and evidently part of a heavy, full thing. There was nothing, I must say, to alarm one. I grew bolder, and putting both hands in as well as I could, I pulled it to me, and it came. It was heavy, but moved more easily than I had expected. As I pulled it towards the entrance, my left elbow knocked over and extinguished the candle. I got the thing fairly in front of the mouth and began drawing it out. Just then Brown gave a sharp ejaculation and ran quickly up the steps with the lantern. He will tell you why in a moment. Startled as I was, I looked round after him, and saw him stand for a minute at the top and then walk away a few yards. Then I heard him call softly, ' All right, sir,' and went on pulling out the great bag, in complete darkness. It hung for an instant on the edge of the hole, then slipped forward on to my chest, and *put its arms round my neck.*

"My dear Gregory, I am telling you the exact truth. I believe I am now acquainted with the extremity of terror and repulsion which a man can endure without losing his mind. I can only just manage to tell you now the bare outline of the experience. I was conscious of a most horrible smell of mould, and of a cold kind of face pressed against my own, and moving slowly over it, and of several—I don't know how many—legs or arms or tentacles or something clinging to my body. I screamed out, Brown says, like a beast, and fell away backward from the step on which I stood, and the creature slipped downwards, I suppose, on to that same step. Providentially the band round me held firm. Brown did not lose his head, and was strong enough to pull me up to the top and get me over the edge quite promptly. How he managed it exactly I don't know, and I think he would find it hard to tell you. I believe he contrived to hide our implements in the deserted building near by, and with very great difficulty he got me back to the inn. I was in no state to make explanations, and Brown knows no German; but next morning I told the people some tale of having had a bad fall in the abbey ruins, which, I suppose, they believed. And now, before I go further, I should just like you to hear what Brown's experiences during those few minutes were. Tell the Rector, Brown, what you told me."

"Well, sir," said Brown, speaking low and nervously, "it was just this way. Master was busy

down in front of the 'ole, and I was 'olding the
lantern and looking on, when I 'eard somethink
drop in the water from the top, as I thought. So
I looked up, and I see someone's 'ead lookin' over
at us. I s'pose I must ha' said somethink, and I
'eld the light up and run up the steps, and my light
shone right on the face. That was a bad un, sir, if
ever I see one! A holdish man, and the face very
much fell in, and larfin, as I thought. And I got up
the steps as quick pretty nigh as I'm tellin' you, and
when I was out on the ground there warn't a sign
of any person. There 'adn't been the time for anyone to get away, let alone a hold chap, and I made
sure he warn't crouching down by the well, nor
nothink. Next thing I hear master cry out somethink 'orrible, and hall I see was him hanging out
by the rope, and, as master says, 'owever I got him
up I couldn't tell you."

"You hear that, Gregory?" said Mr. Somerton.
"Now, does any explanation of that incident strike
you?"

"The whole thing is so ghastly and abnormal
that I must own it puts me quite off my balance;
but the thought did occur to me that possibly the
—well, the person who set the trap might have
come to see the success of his plan."

"Just so, Gregory, just so. I can think of nothing
else so—*likely*, I should say, if such a word had a
place anywhere in my story. I think it must have
been the Abbot. . . . Well, I haven't much more to

177

tell you. I spent a miserable night, Brown sitting up with me. Next day I was no better; unable to get up; no doctor to be had; and, if one had been available, I doubt if he could have done much for me. I made Brown write off to you, and spent a second terrible night. And, Gregory, of this I am sure, and I think it affected me more than the first shock, for it lasted longer: there was someone or something on the watch outside my door the whole night. I almost fancy there were two. It wasn't only the faint noises I heard from time to time all through the dark hours, but there was the smell—the hideous smell of mould. Every rag I had had on me on that first evening I had stripped off and made Brown take it away. I believe he stuffed the things into the stove in his room; and yet the smell was there, as intense as it had been in the well; and, what is more, it came from outside the door. But with the first glimmer of dawn it faded out, and the sounds ceased, too; and that convinced me that the thing or things were creatures of darkness, and could not stand the daylight; and so I was sure that if anyone could put back the stone, it or they would be powerless until someone else took it away again. I had to wait until you came to get that done. Of course, I couldn't send Brown to do it by himself, and still less could I tell anyone who belonged to the place.

"Well, there is my story; and if you don't believe it, I can't help it. But I think you do."

"Indeed," said Mr. Gregory, "I can find no

alternative. I *must* believe it! I saw the well and the stone myself, and had a glimpse, I thought, of the bags or something else in the hole. And, to be plain with you, Somerton, I believe my door was watched last night, too."

" I dare say it was, Gregory; but, thank goodness, that is over. Have you, by the way, anything to tell about your visit to that dreadful place ? "

" Very little," was the answer. " Brown and I managed easily enough to get the slab into its place, and he fixed it very firmly with the irons and wedges you had desired him to get, and we contrived to smear the surface with mud so that it looks just like the rest of the wall. One thing I did notice in the carving on the well-head, which I think must have escaped you. It was a horrid, grotesque shape— perhaps more like a toad than anything else, and there was a label by it inscribed with the two words, ' Depositum custodi.' " [1]

[1] " Keep that which is committed to thee."

A SCHOOL STORY

Two men in a smoking-room were talking of their private-school days. "At *our* school," said A., "we had a ghost's footmark on the staircase. What was it like? Oh, very unconvincing. Just the shape of a shoe, with a square toe, if I remember right. The staircase was a stone one. I never heard any story about the thing. That seems odd, when you come to think of it. Why didn't somebody invent one, I wonder?"

"You never can tell with little boys. They have a mythology of their own. There's a subject for you, by the way—'The Folklore of Private Schools.'"

"Yes; the crop is rather scanty, though. I imagine, if you were to investigate the cycle of ghost stories, for instance, which the boys at private schools tell each other, they would all turn out to be highly-compressed versions of stories out of books."

"Nowadays the *Strand* and *Pearson's*, and so on, would be extensively drawn upon."

"No doubt: they weren't born or thought of in *my* time. Let's see. I wonder if I can remember the staple ones that I was told. First, there was the house with a room in which a series of people insisted on passing a night; and each of them in the morning was found kneeling in a corner, and had just time to say, 'I've seen it,' and died."

"Wasn't that the house in Berkeley Square?"

"I dare say it was. Then there was the man who heard a noise in the passage at night, opened his door, and saw someone crawling towards him on all fours with his eye hanging out on his cheek. There was besides, let me think—— Yes! the room where a man was found dead in bed with a horseshoe mark on his forehead, and the floor under the bed was covered with marks of horseshoes also ; I don't know why. Also there was the lady who, on locking her bedroom door in a strange house, heard a thin voice among the bed-curtains say, 'Now we're shut in for the night.' None of those had any explanation or sequel. I wonder if they go on still, those stories."

"Oh, likely enough—with additions from the magazines, as I said. You never heard, did you, of a real ghost at a private school? I thought not ; nobody has that ever I came across."

"From the way in which you said that, I gather that *you* have."

"I really don't know ; but this is what was in my mind. It happened at my private school thirty odd years ago, and I haven't any explanation of it.

"The school I mean was near London. It was established in a large and fairly old house—a great white building with very fine grounds about it ; there were large cedars in the garden, as there are in so many of the older gardens in the Thames valley, and ancient elms in the three or four fields which we used for our games. I think probably it was quite an attractive place, but boys seldom allow that their schools possess any tolerable features.

" I came to the school in a September, soon after the year 1870 ; and among the boys who arrived on the same day was one whom I took to : a Highland boy, whom I will call McLeod. I needn't spend time in describing him : the main thing is that I got to know him very well. He was not an exceptional boy in any way—not particularly good at books or games —but he suited me.

" The school was a large one : there must have been from 120 to 130 boys there as a rule, and so a considerable staff of masters was required, and there were rather frequent changes among them.

" One term—perhaps it was my third or fourth— a new master made his appearance. His name was Sampson. He was a tallish, stoutish, pale, black-bearded man. I think we liked him : he had travelled a good deal, and had stories which amused us on our school walks, so that there was some competition among us to get within earshot of him. I remember too—dear me, I have hardly thought of it since then ! —that he had a charm on his watch-chain that attracted my attention one day, and he let me examine it. It was, I now suppose, a gold Byzantine coin ; there was an effigy of some absurd emperor on one side ; the other side had been worn practically smooth, and he had had cut on it—rather barbarously—his own initials, G.W.S., and a date, 24 July, 1865. Yes, I can see it now : he told me he had picked it up in Constantinople : it was about the size of a florin, perhaps rather smaller.

" Well, the first odd thing that happened was this. Sampson was doing Latin grammar with us. One of his favourite methods—perhaps it is rather a good one—was to make us construct sentences out of our own heads to illustrate the rules he was trying to make us learn. Of course that is a thing which gives a silly boy a chance of being impertinent : there are lots of school stories in which that happens—or anyhow there might be. But Sampson was too good a disciplinarian for us to think of trying that on with him. Now, on this occasion he was telling us how to express *remembering* in Latin : and he ordered us each to make a sentence bringing in the verb *memini*, ' I remember.' Well, most of us made up some ordinary sentence such as ' I remember my father,' or ' He remembers his book,' or something equally uninteresting : and I dare say a good many put down *memino librum meum*, and so forth : but the boy I mentioned—McLeod—was evidently thinking of something more elaborate than that. The rest of us wanted to have our sentences passed, and get on to something else, so some kicked him under the desk, and I, who was next to him, poked him and whispered to him to look sharp. But he didn't seem to attend. I looked at his paper and saw he had put down nothing at all. So I jogged him again harder than before

and upbraided him sharply for keeping us all waiting.
That did have some effect. He started and seemed
to wake up, and then very quickly he scribbled about
a couple of lines on his paper, and showed it up with
the rest. As it was the last, or nearly the last, to
come in, and as Sampson had a good deal to say to
the boys who had written *meminiscimus patri meo* and
the rest of it, it turned out that the clock struck
twelve before he had got to McLeod, and McLeod
had to wait afterwards to have his sentence corrected.
There was nothing much going on outside when I
got out, so I waited for him to come. He came very
slowly when he did arrive, and I guessed there had
been some sort of trouble. ' Well,' I said, ' what did
you get ? ' ' Oh, I don't know,' said McLeod,
' nothing much : but I think Sampson's rather sick
with me.' ' Why, did you show him up some rot ? '
' No fear,' he said. ' It was all right as far as I could
see : it was like this : *Memento*—that's right enough
for remember, and it takes a genitive,—*memento putei
inter quatuor taxos.*' ' What silly rot ! ' I said. ' What
made you shove that down ? What does it mean ? '
' That's the funny part,' said McLeod. ' I'm not
quite sure what it does mean. All I know is, it just
came into my head and I corked it down. I know
what I *think* it means, because just before I wrote it
down I had a sort of picture of it in my head : I
believe it means " Remember the well among the
four "—what are those dark sort of trees that have
red berries on them ? ' ' Mountain ashes, I s'pose

184

you mean.' 'I never heard of them,' said McLeod;
'no, *I'll* tell you—yews.' 'Well, and what did
Sampson say?' 'Why, he was jolly odd about it.
When he read it he got up and went to the mantelpiece and stopped quite a long time without saying
anything, with his back to me. And then he said,
without turning round, and rather quiet, "What do
you suppose that means?" I told him what I
thought; only I couldn't remember the name of the
silly tree: and then he wanted to know why I put
it down, and I had to say something or other. And
after that he left off talking about it, and asked me
how long I'd been here, and where my people lived,
and things like that: and then I came away: but he
wasn't looking a bit well.'

"I don't remember any more that was said by
either of us about this. Next day McLeod took to
his bed with a chill or something of the kind, and it
was a week or more before he was in school again.
And as much as a month went by without anything
happening that was noticeable. Whether or not Mr.
Sampson was really startled, as McLeod had thought,
he didn't show it. I am pretty sure, of course, now,
that there was something very curious in his past
history, but I'm not going to pretend that we boys
were sharp enough to guess any such thing.

" There was one other incident of the same kind
as the last which I told you. Several times since that
day we had had to make up examples in school to
illustrate different rules, but there had never been any

row except when we did them wrong. At last there came a day when we were going through those dismal things which people call Conditional Sentences, and we were told to make a conditional sentence, expressing a future consequence. We did it, right or wrong, and showed up our bits of paper, and Sampson began looking through them. All at once he got up, made some odd sort of noise in his throat, and rushed out by a door that was just by his desk. We sat there for a minute or two, and then—I suppose it was incorrect—but we went up, I and one or two others, to look at the papers on his desk. Of course I thought someone must have put down some nonsense or other, and Sampson had gone off to report him. All the same, I noticed that he hadn't taken any of the papers with him when he ran out. Well, the top paper on the desk was written in red ink—which no one used—and it wasn't in anyone's hand who was in the class. They all looked at it—McLeod and all —and took their dying oaths that it wasn't theirs. Then I thought of counting the bits of paper. And of this I made quite certain: that there were seventeen bits of paper on the desk, and sixteen boys in the form. Well, I bagged the extra paper, and kept it, and I believe I have it now. And now you will want to know what was written on it. It was simple enough, and harmless enough, I should have said.

" ' *Si tu non veneris ad me, ego veniam ad te,*' which means, I suppose, ' If you don't come to me, I'll come to you.' "

" Could you show me the paper ? " interrupted the listener.

" Yes, I could : but there's another odd thing about it. That same afternoon I took it out of my locker —I know for certain it was the same bit, for I made a finger-mark on it—and no single trace of writing of any kind was there on it. I kept it, as I said, and since that time I have tried various experiments to see whether sympathetic ink had been used, but absolutely without result.

" So much for that. After about half an hour Sampson looked in again : said he had felt very unwell, and told us we might go. He came rather gingerly to his desk, and gave just one look at the uppermost paper : and I suppose he thought he must have been dreaming : anyhow, he asked no questions.

" That day was a half-holiday, and next day Sampson was in school again, much as usual. That night the third and last incident in my story happened.

" We—McLeod and I—slept in a dormitory at right angles to the main building. Sampson slept in the main building on the first floor. There was a very bright full moon. At an hour which I can't tell exactly, but some time between one and two, I was woken up by somebody shaking me. It was McLeod ; and a nice state of mind he seemed to be in. ' Come,' he said,—' come ! there's a burglar getting in through Sampson's window.' As soon as I could speak, I said, ' Well, why not call out and wake everybody up ? ' ' No, no,' he said, ' I'm not sure who

it is : don't make a row : come and look.' Naturally
I came and looked, and naturally there was no one
there. I was cross enough, and should have called
McLeod plenty of names : only—I couldn't tell why
—it seemed to me that there *was* something wrong
—something that made me very glad I wasn't alone
to face it. We were still at the window looking out,
and as soon as I could, I asked him what he had heard
or seen. ' I didn't *hear* anything at all,' he said, ' but
about five minutes before I woke you, I found myself
looking out of this window here, and there was a
man sitting or kneeling on Sampson's window-sill,
and looking in, and I thought he was beckoning.'
' What sort of man ? ' McLeod wriggled. ' I don't
know,' he said, ' but I can tell you one thing—he was
beastly thin : and he looked as if he was wet all over :
and,' he said, looking round and whispering as if he
hardly liked to hear himself, ' I'm not at all sure that
he was alive.'

" We went on talking in whispers some time longer,
and eventually crept back to bed. No one else in
the room woke or stirred the whole time. I believe
we did sleep a bit afterwards, but we were very cheap
next day.

" And next day Mr. Sampson was gone : not to
be found : and I believe no trace of him has ever
come to light since. In thinking it over, one of the
oddest things about it all has seemed to me to be the
fact that neither McLeod nor I ever mentioned what
we had seen to any third person whatever. Of course

no questions were asked on the subject, and if they had been, I am inclined to believe that we could not have made any answer : we seemed unable to speak about it.

" That is my story," said the narrator. " The only approach to a ghost story connected with a school that I know, but still, I think, an approach to such a thing."

* * * * *

The sequel to this may perhaps be reckoned highly conventional ; but a sequel there is, and so it must be produced. There had been more than one listener to the story, and, in the latter part of that same year, or of the next, one such listener was staying at a country house in Ireland.

One evening his host was turning over a drawer full of odds and ends in the smoking-room. Suddenly he put his hand upon a little box. " Now," he said, " you know about old things ; tell me what that is." My friend opened the little box, and found in it a thin gold chain with an object attached to it. He glanced at the object and then took off his spectacles to examine it more narrowly. " What's the history of this ? " he asked. " Odd enough," was the answer. " You know the yew thicket in the shrubbery : well, a year or two back we were cleaning out the old well that used to be in the clearing here, and what do you suppose we found ? "

" Is it possible that you found a body ? " said the visitor, with an odd feeling of nervousness.

"We did that : but what's more, in every sense of the word, we found two."

"Good Heavens! Two? Was there anything to show how they got there? Was this thing found with them?"

"It was. Amongst the rags of the clothes that were on one of the bodies. A bad business, whatever the story of it may have been. One body had the arms tight round the other. They must have been there thirty years or more—long enough before we came to this place. You may judge we filled the well up fast enough. Do you make anything of what's cut on that gold coin you have there?"

"I think I can," said my friend, holding it to the light (but he read it without much difficulty); "it seems to be G.W.S., 24 July, 1865."

THE ROSE GARDEN

Mr. and Mrs. Anstruther were at breakfast in the parlour of Westfield Hall, in the county of Essex. They were arranging plans for the day.

" George," said Mrs. Anstruther, " I think you had better take the car to Maldon and see if you can get any of those knitted things I was speaking about which would do for my stall at the bazaar."

" Oh well, if you wish it, Mary, of course I can do that, but I had half arranged to play a round with Geoffrey Williamson this morning. The bazaar isn't till Thursday of next week, is it ? "

" What has that to do with it, George ? I should have thought you would have guessed that if I can't get the things I want in Maldon I shall have to write to all manner of shops in town : and they are certain to send something quite unsuitable in price or quality the first time. If you have actually made an appointment with Mr. Williamson, you had better keep it, but I must say I think you might have let me know."

" Oh no, no, it wasn't really an appointment. I quite see what you mean. I'll go. And what shall you do yourself ? "

" Why, when the work of the house is arranged

for, I must see about laying out my new rose garden. By the way, before you start for Maldon I wish you would just take Collins to look at the place I fixed upon. You know it, of course."

"Well, I'm not quite sure that I do, Mary. Is it at the upper end, towards the village?"

"Good gracious no, my dear George; I thought I had made that quite clear. No, it's that small clearing just off the shrubbery path that goes towards the church."

"Oh yes, where we were saying there must have been a summer-house once: the place with the old seat and the posts. But do you think there's enough sun there?"

"My dear George, do allow me *some* common sense, and don't credit me with all your ideas about summer-houses. Yes, there will be plenty of sun when we have got rid of some of those box-bushes. I know what you are going to say, and I have as little wish as you to strip the place bare. All I want Collins to do is to clear away the old seats and the posts and things before I come out in an hour's time. And I hope you will manage to get off fairly soon. After luncheon I think I shall go on with my sketch of the church; and if you please you can go over to the links, or——"

"Ah, a good idea—very good! Yes, you finish that sketch, Mary, and I should be glad of a round."

"I was going to say, you might call on the Bishop; but I suppose it is no use my making *any* suggestion.

And now do be getting ready, or half the morning will be gone."

Mr. Anstruther's face, which had shown symptoms of lengthening, shortened itself again, and he hurried from the room, and was soon heard giving orders in the passage. Mrs. Anstruther, a stately dame of some fifty summers, proceeded, after a second consideration of the morning's letters, to her housekeeping.

Within a few minutes Mr. Anstruther had discovered Collins in the greenhouse, and they were on their way to the site of the projected rose garden. I do not know much about the conditions most suitable to these nurseries, but I am inclined to believe that Mrs. Anstruther, though in the habit of describing herself as "a great gardener," had not been well advised in the selection of a spot for the purpose. It was a small, dank clearing, bounded on one side by a path, and on the other by thick box-bushes, laurels, and other evergreens. The ground was almost bare of grass and dark of aspect. Remains of rustic seats and an old and corrugated oak post somewhere near the middle of the clearing had given rise to Mr. Anstruther's conjecture that a summer-house had once stood there.

Clearly Collins had not been put in possession of his mistress's intentions with regard to this plot of ground : and when he learnt them from Mr. Anstruther he displayed no enthusiasm.

" Of course I could clear them seats away soon

enough," he said. "They aren't no ornament to the place, Mr. Anstruther, and rotten too. Look 'ere, sir "—and he broke off a large piece—" rotten right through. Yes, clear them away, to be sure we can do that."

"And the post," said Mr. Anstruther, "that's got to go too."

Collins advanced, and shook the post with both hands : then he rubbed his chin.

"That's firm in the ground, that post is," he said. "That's been there a number of years, Mr. Anstruther. I doubt I shan't get that up not quite so soon as what I can do with them seats."

"But your mistress specially wishes it to be got out of the way in an hour's time," said Mr. Anstruther.

Collins smiled and shook his head slowly. "You'll excuse me, sir, but you feel of it for yourself. No, sir, no one can't do what's impossible to 'em, can they, sir ? I could git that post up by after tea-time, sir, but that'll want a lot of digging. What you require, you see, sir, if you'll excuse me naming of it, you want the soil loosening round this post 'ere, and me and the boy we shall take a little time doing of that. But now, these 'ere seats," said Collins, appearing to appropriate this portion of the scheme as due to his own resourcefulness, "why, I can get the barrer round and 'ave them cleared away in, why less than an hour's time from now, if you'll permit of it. Only——"

194

" Only what, Collins ? "

" Well now, it ain't for me to go against orders no more than what it is for you yourself—or anyone else " (this was added somewhat hurriedly), " but if you'll pardon me, sir, this ain't the place I should have picked out for no rose garden myself. Why look at them box and laurestinus, 'ow they reg'lar preclude the light from——"

" Ah yes, but we've got to get rid of some of them, of course."

" Oh, indeed, get rid of them ! Yes, to be sure, but—I beg your pardon, Mr. Anstruther——"

" I'm sorry, Collins, but I must be getting on now. I hear the car at the door. Your mistress will explain exactly what she wishes. I'll tell her, then, that you can see your way to clearing away the seats at once, and the post this afternoon. Good morning."

Collins was left rubbing his chin. Mrs. Anstruther received the report with some discontent, but did not insist upon any change of plan.

By four o'clock that afternoon she had dismissed her husband to his golf, had dealt faithfully with Collins and with the other duties of the day, and, having sent a campstool and umbrella to the proper spot, had just settled down to her sketch of the church as seen from the shrubbery, when a maid came hurrying down the path to report that Miss Wilkins had called.

Miss Wilkins was one of the few remaining members of the family from whom the Anstruthers had bought the Westfield estate some few years back. She had been staying in the neighbourhood, and this was probably a farewell visit. "Perhaps you could ask Miss Wilkins to join me here," said Mrs. Anstruther, and soon Miss Wilkins, a person of mature years, approached.

"Yes, I'm leaving the Ashes to-morrow, and I shall be able to tell my brother how tremendously you have improved the place. Of course he can't help regretting the old house just a little—as I do myself—but the garden is really delightful now."

"I am so glad you can say so. But you mustn't think we've finished our improvements. Let me show you where I mean to put a rose garden. It's close by here."

The details of the project were laid before Miss Wilkins at some length; but her thoughts were evidently elsewhere.

"Yes, delightful," she said at last rather absently. "But do you know, Mrs. Anstruther, I'm afraid I was thinking of old times. I'm *very* glad to have seen just this spot again before you altered it. Frank and I had quite a romance about this place."

"Yes?" said Mrs. Anstruther smilingly; "do tell me what it was. Something quaint and charming, I'm sure."

"Not so very charming, but it has always seemed to me curious. Neither of us would ever be here alone when we were children, and I'm not sure that I should care about it now in certain moods. It is

one of those things that can hardly be put into words
—by me at least—and that sound rather foolish if
they are not properly expressed. I can tell you after
a fashion what it was that gave us—well, almost a
horror of the place when we were alone. It was
towards the evening of one very hot autumn day,
when Frank had disappeared mysteriously about the
grounds, and I was looking for him to fetch him to
tea, and going down this path I suddenly saw him,
not hiding in the bushes, as I rather expected, but
sitting on the bench in the old summer-house—there
was a wooden summer-house here, you know—up in
the corner, asleep, but with such a dreadful look on
his face that I really thought he must be ill or even
dead. I rushed at him and shook him, and told him
to wake up; and wake up he did, with a scream. I
assure you the poor boy seemed almost beside himself with fright. He hurried me away to the house,
and was in a terrible state all that night, hardly
sleeping. Someone had to sit up with him, as far
as I remember. He was better very soon, but for
days I couldn't get him to say why he had been in
such a condition. It came out at last that he had
really been asleep and had had a very odd disjointed
sort of dream. He never *saw* much of what was
around him, but he *felt* the scenes most vividly.
First he made out that he was standing in a large
room with a number of people in it, and that someone was opposite to him who was ' very powerful,'
and he was being asked questions which he felt to be

very important, and, whenever he answered them, someone—either the person opposite to him, or someone else in the room—seemed to be, as he said, making something up against him. All the voices sounded to him very distant, but he remembered bits of the things that were said : ' Where were you on the 19th of October ? ' and ' Is this your handwriting ? ' and so on. I can see now, of course, that he was dreaming of some trial : but we were never allowed to see the papers, and it was odd that a boy of eight should have such a vivid idea of what went on in a court. All the time he felt, he said, the most intense anxiety and oppression and hopelessness (though I don't suppose he used such words as that to me). Then, after that, there was an interval in which he remembered being dreadfully restless and miserable, and then there came another sort of picture, when he was aware that he had come out of doors on a dark raw morning with a little snow about. It was in a street, or at any rate among houses, and he felt that there were numbers and numbers of people there too, and that he was taken up some creaking wooden steps and stood on a sort of platform, but the only thing he could actually see was a small fire burning somewhere near him. Someone who had been holding his arm left hold of it and went towards this fire, and then he said the fright he was in was worse than at any other part of his dream, and if I had not wakened him up he didn't know what would have become of him. A curious dream for a child to have, wasn't

it ? Well, so much for that. It must have been later
in the year that Frank and I were here, and I was
sitting in the arbour just about sunset. I noticed the
sun was going down, and told Frank to run in and
see if tea was ready while I finished a chapter in the
book I was reading. Frank was away longer than I
expected, and the light was going so fast that I had
to bend over my book to make it out. All at once
I became conscious that someone was whispering to
me inside the arbour. The only words I could
distinguish, or thought I could, were something like
' Pull, pull. I'll push, you pull.'

" I started up in something of a fright. The voice
—it was little more than a whisper—sounded so
hoarse and angry, and yet as if it came from a long,
long way off—just as it had done in Frank's dream.
But, though I was startled, I had enough courage to
look round and try to make out where the sound
came from. And—this sounds very foolish, I know,
but still it is the fact—I made sure that it was strongest
when I put my ear to an old post which was part of
the end of the seat. I was so certain of this that I
remember making some marks on the post—as deep
as I could with the scissors out of my work-basket.
I don't know why. I wonder, by the way, whether
that isn't the very post itself. . . . Well, yes, it
might be : there *are* marks and scratches on it—but
one can't be sure. Anyhow, it was just like that post
you have there. My father got to know that both
of us had had a fright in the arbour, and he went

down there himself one evening after dinner, and the
arbour was pulled down at very short notice. I
recollect hearing my father talking about it to an old
man who used to do odd jobs in the place, and the
old man saying, ' Don't you fear for that, sir : he's
fast enough in there without no one don't take and
let him out.' But when I asked who it was, I could
get no satisfactory answer. Possibly my father or
mother might have told me more about it when I
grew up, but, as you know, they both died when we
were still quite children. I must say it has always
seemed very odd to me, and I've often asked the older
people in the village whether they knew of anything
strange : but either they knew nothing or they
wouldn't tell me. Dear, dear, how I have been
boring you with my childish remembrances ! but
indeed that arbour did absorb our thoughts quite
remarkably for a time. You can fancy, can't you,
the kind of stories that we made up for ourselves.
Well, dear Mrs. Anstruther, I must be leaving you
now. We shall meet in town this winter, I hope,
shan't we ? " etc., etc.

The seats and the post were cleared away and uprooted respectively by that evening. Late summer
weather is proverbially treacherous, and during dinner-
time Mrs. Collins sent up to ask for a little brandy,
because her husband had took a nasty chill and she
was afraid he would not be able to do much next
day.

Mrs. Anstruther's morning reflections were not

wholly placid. She was sure some roughs had got into the plantation during the night. "And another thing, George: the moment that Collins is about again, you must tell him to do something about the owls. I never heard anything like them, and I'm positive one came and perched somewhere just outside our window. If it had come in I should have been out of my wits: it must have been a very large bird, from its voice. Didn't you hear it? No, of course not, you were sound asleep as usual. Still, I must say, George, you don't look as if your night had done you much good."

"My dear, I feel as if another of the same would turn me silly. You have no idea of the dreams I had. I couldn't speak of them when I woke up, and if this room wasn't so bright and sunny I shouldn't care to think of them even now."

"Well, really, George, that isn't very common with you, I must say. You must have—no, you only had what I had yesterday—unless you had tea at that wretched club house: did you?"

"No, no; nothing but a cup of tea and some bread and butter. I should really like to know how I came to put my dream together—as I suppose one does put one's dreams together from a lot of little things one has been seeing or reading. Look here, Mary, it was like this—if I shan't be boring you——"

"I *wish* to hear what it was, George. I will tell you when I have had enough."

"All right. I must tell you that it wasn't like

other nightmares in one way, because I didn't really
see anyone who spoke to me or touched me, and yet
I was most fearfully impressed with the reality of it
all. First I was sitting, no, moving about, in an old-
fashioned sort of panelled room. I remember there
was a fireplace and a lot of burnt papers in it, and
I was in a great state of anxiety about something.
There was someone else—a servant, I suppose, because I remember saying to him, ' Horses, as quick
as you can,' and then waiting a bit : and next I heard
several people coming upstairs and a noise like spurs
on a boarded floor, and then the door opened and
whatever it was that I was expecting happened."

" Yes, but what was that ? "

" You see, I couldn't tell : it was the sort of shock
that upsets you in a dream. You either wake up or
else everything goes black. That was what happened
to me. Then I was in a big dark-walled room,
panelled, I think, like the other, and a number of
people, and I was evidently——"

" Standing your trial, I suppose, George."

" Goodness ! yes, Mary, I was ; but did you dream
that too ? How very odd ! "

" No, no ; I didn't get enough sleep for that. Go
on, George, and I will tell you afterwards."

" Yes ; well, I *was* being tried, for my life, I've no
doubt, from the state I was in. I had no one speaking for me, and somewhere there was a most fearful
fellow—on the bench ; I should have said, only that
he seemed to be pitching into me most unfairly, and

twisting everything I said, and asking most abominable questions."

" What about ? "

" Why, dates when I was at particular places, and letters I was supposed to have written, and why I had destroyed some papers; and I recollect his laughing at answers I made in a way that quite daunted me. It doesn't sound much, but I can tell you, Mary, it was really appalling at the time. I am quite certain there was such a man once, and a most horrible villain he must have been. The things he said——"

" Thank you, I have no wish to hear them. I can go to the links any day myself. How did it end ? "

" Oh, against me; *he* saw to that. I do wish, Mary, I could give you a notion of the strain that came after that, and seemed to me to last for days : waiting and waiting, and sometimes writing things I knew to be enormously important to me, and waiting for answers and none coming, and after that I came out——"

" Ah ! "

" What makes you say that ? Do you know what sort of thing I saw ? "

" Was it a dark cold day, and snow in the streets, and a fire burning somewhere near you ? "

" By George, it was ! You *have* had the same nightmare ! Really not ? Well, it is the oddest thing ! Yes; I've no doubt it was an execution for high treason. I know I was laid on straw and jolted along most wretchedly, and then had to go up some steps, and someone was holding my arm, and I remember seeing a bit of a ladder and hearing a sound of a lot of people. I really don't think I could bear now to go into a crowd of people and hear the noise they make talking. However, mercifully, I didn't get to the real business. The dream passed off with a sort of thunder inside my head. But, Mary——"

" I know what you are going to ask. I suppose this is an instance of a kind of thought-reading. Miss Wilkins called yesterday and told me of a dream her brother had as a child when they lived here, and something did no doubt make me think of that when I was awake last night listening to those horrible owls and those men talking and laughing in the shrubbery (by the way, I wish you would see if they have done any damage, and speak to the police about it) ; and so, I suppose, from my brain it must have got into yours while you were asleep. Curious, no doubt, and I am sorry it gave you such a bad night. You had better be as much in the fresh air as you can to-day."

" Oh, it's all right now ; but I think I *will* go over to the Lodge and see if I can get a game with any of them. And you ? "

" I have enough to do for this morning ; and this afternoon, if I am not interrupted, there is my drawing."

" To be sure—I want to see that finished very much."

No damage was discoverable in the shrubbery.

Mr. Anstruther surveyed with faint interest the site of the rose garden, where the uprooted post still lay, and the hole it had occupied remained unfilled. Collins, upon inquiry made, proved to be better, but quite unable to come to his work. He expressed, by the mouth of his wife, a hope that he hadn't done nothing wrong clearing away them things. Mrs. Collins added that there was a lot of talking people in Westfield, and the hold ones was the worst: seemed to think everything of them having been in the parish longer than what other people had. But as to what they said no more could then be ascertained than that it had quite upset Collins, and was a lot of nonsense.

Recruited by lunch and a brief period of slumber, Mrs. Anstruther settled herself comfortably upon her sketching chair in the path leading through the shrubbery to the side-gate of the churchyard. Trees and buildings were among her favourite subjects, and here she had good studies of both. She worked hard, and the drawing was becoming a really pleasant thing to look upon by the time that the wooded hills to the west had shut off the sun. Still she would have persevered, but the light changed rapidly, and it became obvious that the last touches must be added on the morrow. She rose and turned towards the house, pausing for a time to take delight in the limpid green western sky. Then she passed on between the dark box-bushes, and, at a point just before the path debouched on the lawn, she stopped once again and considered the quiet evening landscape, and made a mental note that that must be the tower of one of the Roothing churches that one caught on the sky-line. Then a bird (perhaps) rustled in the box-bush on her left, and she turned and started at seeing what at first she took to be a Fifth of November mask peeping out among the branches. She looked closer.

It was not a mask. It was a face—large, smooth, and pink. She remembers the minute drops of perspiration which were starting from its forehead : she remembers how the jaws were clean-shaven and the eyes shut. She remembers also, and with an accuracy which makes the thought intolerable to her, how the mouth was open and a single tooth appeared below the upper lip. As she looked the face receded into the darkness of the bush. The shelter of the house was gained and the door shut before she collapsed.

Mr. and Mrs. Anstruther had been for a week or more recruiting at Brighton before they received a circular from the Essex Archæological Society, and a query as to whether they possessed certain historical portraits which it was desired to include in the forthcoming work on Essex Portraits, to be published under the Society's auspices. There was an accompanying letter from the Secretary which contained the following passage : " We are specially anxious to know whether you possess the original of the engraving of which I enclose a photograph. It represents Sir —— ——, Lord Chief Justice under Charles II, who, as you doubtless know, retired after his disgrace to Westfield, and is supposed to have died there of remorse. It may interest you to hear that a curious entry has recently been found in the registers, not of Westfield but of Priors Roothing, to the effect that the parish was so much troubled after his death that the rector of Westfield summoned the parsons of all the Roothings to come and lay him; which they did. The entry ends by saying: ' The stake is in a field adjoining to the churchyard of Westfield, on the west side.' Perhaps you can let us know if any tradition to this effect is current in your parish."

The incidents which the " enclosed photograph " recalled were productive of a severe shock to Mrs. Anstruther. It was decided that she must spend the winter abroad.

Mr. Anstruther, when he went down to Westfield to make the necessary arrangements, not unnaturally told his story to the rector (an old gentleman), who showed little surprise.

" Really I had managed to piece out for myself very much what must have happened, partly from old people's talk and partly from what I saw in your grounds. Of course we have suffered to some extent also. Yes, it was bad at first: like owls, as you say, and men talking sometimes. One night it was in this garden, and at other times about several of the cottages. But lately there has been very little: I think it will die out. There is nothing in our registers except the entry of the burial, and what I for a long

time took to be the family motto; but last time I
looked at it I noticed that it was added in a later hand
and had the initials of one of our rectors quite late
in the seventeenth century, A. C.—Augustine Cromp-
ton. Here it is, you see—*quieta non movere*. I
suppose—— Well, it is rather hard to say exactly
what I do suppose."

THE TRACTATE MIDDOTH

TOWARDS the end of an autumn afternoon an elderly
man with a thin face and grey Piccadilly weepers
pushed open the swing-door leading into the vestibule
of a certain famous library, and addressing himself to
an attendant, stated that he believed he was entitled
to use the library, and inquired if he might take a
book out. Yes, if he were on the list of those to
whom that privilege was given. He produced his
card—Mr. John Eldred—and, the register being consulted, a favourable answer was given. "Now,
another point," said he. "It is a long time since I
was here, and I do not know my way about your
building; besides, it is near closing-time, and it is
bad for me to hurry up and down stairs. I have here
the title of the book I want : is there anyone at liberty
who could go and find it for me ? " After a moment's
thought the doorkeeper beckoned to a young man
who was passing. "Mr. Garrett," he said, "have
you a minute to assist this gentleman ? " "With
pleasure," was Mr. Garrett's answer. The slip with
the title was handed to him. "I think I can put my
hand on this ; it happens to be in the class I inspected
last quarter, but I'll just look it up in the catalogue
to make sure. I suppose it is that particular edition

that you require, sir?" "Yes, if you please; that, and no other," said Mr. Eldred; "I am exceedingly obliged to you." "Don't mention it I beg, sir," said Mr. Garrett, and hurried off.

"I thought so," he said to himself, when his finger, travelling down the pages of the catalogue, stopped at a particular entry. "Talmud: Tractate Middoth, with the commentary of Nachmanides, Amsterdam, 1707. 11.3.34. Hebrew class, of course. Not a very difficult job this."

Mr. Eldred, accommodated with a chair in the vestibule, awaited anxiously the return of his messenger—and his disappointment at seeing an empty-handed Mr. Garrett running down the staircase was very evident. "I'm sorry to disappoint you, sir," said the young man, "but the book is out." "Oh dear!" said Mr. Eldred, "is that so? You are sure there can be no mistake?" "I don't think there is much chance of it, sir; but it's possible, if you like to wait a minute, that you might meet the very gentleman that's got it. He must be leaving the library soon, and I *think* I saw him take that particular book out of the shelf." "Indeed! You didn't recognize him, I suppose? Would it be one of the professors or one of the students?" "I don't think so: certainly not a professor. I should have known him; but the light isn't very good in that part of the library at this time of day, and I didn't see his face. I should have said he was a shortish old gentleman, perhaps a clergyman, in a cloak. If you could wait, I can easily find out whether he wants the book very particularly."

" No, no," said Mr. Eldred, " I won't—I can't wait now, thank you—no. I must be off. But I'll call again to-morrow if I may, and perhaps you could find out who has it."

" Certainly, sir, and I'll have the book ready for you if we——" But Mr. Eldred was already off, and hurrying more than one would have thought wholesome for him.

Garrett had a few moments to spare ; and, thought he, " I'll go back to that case and see if I can find the old man. Most likely he could put off using the book for a few days. I dare say the other one doesn't want to keep it for long." So off with him to the Hebrew class. But when he got there it was unoccupied, and the volume marked 11.3.34 was in its place on the shelf. It was vexatious to Garrett's self-respect to have disappointed an inquirer with so little reason : and he would have liked, had it not been against library rules, to take the book down to the vestibule then and there, so that it might be ready for Mr. Eldred when he called. However, next morning he would be on the look out for him, and he begged the doorkeeper to send and let him know when the moment came. As a matter of fact, he was himself in the vestibule when Mr. Eldred arrived, very soon after the library opened, and when hardly anyone besides the staff were in the building.

" I'm very sorry," he said ; " it's not often that

I make such a stupid mistake, but I did feel sure that the old gentleman I saw took out that very book and kept it in his hand without opening it, just as people do, you know, sir, when they mean to take a book out of the library and not merely refer to it. But, however, I'll run up now at once and get it for you this time."

And here intervened a pause. Mr. Eldred paced the entry, read all the notices, consulted his watch, sat and gazed up the staircase, did all that a very impatient man could, until some twenty minutes had run out. At last he addressed himself to the door-keeper and inquired if it was a very long way to that part of the library to which Mr. Garrett had gone.

"Well, I was thinking it was funny, sir : he's a quick man as a rule, but to be sure he might have been sent for by the libarian, but even so I think he'd have mentioned to him that you was waiting. I'll just speak him up on the toob and see." And to the tube he addressed himself. As he absorbed the reply to his question his face changed, and he made one or two supplementary inquiries which were shortly answered. Then he came forward to his counter and spoke in a lower tone. " I'm sorry to hear, sir, that something seems to have 'appened a little awkward. Mr. Garrett has been took poorly, it appears, and the libarian sent him 'ome in a cab the other way. Something of an attack, by what I can hear." "What, really? Do you mean that someone has injured him?" "No, sir, not violence 'ere, but, as I should judge, attacted with an attack, what you might term it, of illness. Not a strong constitootion, Mr. Garrett. But as to your book, sir, perhaps you might be able to find it for yourself. It's too bad you should be disappointed this way twice over——" "Er—well, but I'm so sorry that Mr. Garrett should have been taken ill in this way while he was obliging me. I think I must leave the book, and call and inquire after him. You can give me his address, I suppose." That was easily done: Mr. Garrett, it appeared, lodged in rooms not far from the station. "And, one other question. Did you happen to notice if an old gentleman, perhaps a clergyman, in a—yes—in a black cloak, left the library after I did yesterday. I think he may have been a—I think, that is, that he may be staying—or rather that I may have known him."

"Not in a black cloak, sir; no. There were only two gentlemen left later than what you done, sir, both of them youngish men. There was Mr. Carter took out a music-book and one of the prefessors with a couple o' novels. That's the lot, sir; and then I went off to me tea, and glad to get it. Thank you, sir, much obliged."

Mr. Eldred, still a prey to anxiety, betook himself in a cab to Mr. Garrett's address, but the young man was not yet in a condition to receive visitors. He was better, but his landlady considered that he must have had a severe shock. She thought most likely from what the doctor said that he would be able to see Mr. Eldred to-morrow. Mr. Eldred returned to his hotel at dusk and spent, I fear, but a dull evening.

On the next day he was able to see Mr. Garrett. When in health Mr. Garrett was a cheerful and pleasant-looking young man. Now he was a very white and shaky being, propped up in an arm-chair by the fire, and inclined to shiver and keep an eye on the door. If, however, there were visitors whom he was not prepared to welcome, Mr. Eldred was not among them. "It really is I who owe you an apology, and I was despairing of being able to pay it, for I didn't know your address. But I am very glad you have called. I do dislike and regret giving all this trouble, but you know I could not have foreseen this—this attack which I had."

"Of course not; but now, I am something of a doctor. You'll excuse my asking; you have had, I am sure, good advice. Was it a fall you had?"

"No. I did fall on the floor—but not from any height. It was, really, a shock."

"You mean something startled you. Was it anything you thought you saw?"

"Not much *thinking* in the case, I'm afraid. Yes, it was something I saw. You remember when you called the first time at the library?"

"Yes, of course. Well, now, let me beg you not to try to describe it—it will not be good for you to recall it, I'm sure."

"But indeed it would be a relief to me to tell anyone like yourself: you might be able to explain it away. It was just when I was going into the class where your book is——"

"Indeed, Mr. Garrett, I insist; besides, my watch tells me I have but very little time left in which to get my things together and take the train. No —not another word—it would be more distressing to you than you imagine, perhaps. Now there is just one thing I want to say. I feel that I am really indirectly responsible for this illness of yours, and I think I ought to defray the expense which it has —eh?"

But this offer was quite distinctly declined. Mr. Eldred, not pressing it, left almost at once: not, however, before Mr. Garrett had insisted upon his taking a note of the class-mark of the Tractate Middoth, which, as he said, Mr. Eldred could at leisure get for himself. But Mr. Eldred did not reappear at the library.

William Garrett had another visitor that day in the person of a contemporary and colleague from the library, one George Earle. Earle had been one of those who found Garrett lying insensible on the floor just inside the "class" or cubicle (opening upon the central alley of a spacious gallery) in which the Hebrew books were placed, and Earle had naturally been very anxious about his friend's condition. So as soon as library hours were over he appeared at the lodgings. "Well," he said (after other conversation), "I've no notion what it was that put you wrong, but I've got the idea that there's something wrong in the atmosphere of the library. I know this, that just before we found you I was coming along the gallery with Davis, and I said to him, 'Did ever you know such a musty smell anywhere as there is about here? It can't be wholesome.' Well now, if one goes on living a long time with a smell of that kind (I tell you it was worse than I ever knew it) it must get into the system and break out some time, don't you think?"

Garrett shook his head. "That's all very well about the smell—but it isn't always there, though I've noticed it the last day or two—a sort of unnaturally strong smell of dust. But no—that's not what did for me. It was something I *saw*. And I want to tell you about it. I went into that Hebrew class to get a book for a man that was inquiring for it down below. Now that same book I'd made a mistake about the day before. I'd been for it, for the same man, and made sure that I saw an old parson in a cloak taking it out. I told my man it was out: off he went, to call again next day. I went back to see if I could get it out of the parson: no parson there, and the book on the shelf. Well, yesterday, as I say, I went again. This time, if you please—ten o'clock in the morning, remember, and as much light as ever you get in those classes, and there was my parson again, back to me, looking at the books on the shelf I wanted. His hat was on the table,

and he had a bald head. I waited a second or two
looking at him rather particularly. I tell you, he had
a very nasty bald head. It looked to me dry, and it
looked dusty, and the streaks of hair across it were
much less like hair than cobwebs. Well, I made a
bit of a noise on purpose, coughed and moved my
feet. He turned round and let me see his face—which
I hadn't seen before. I tell you again, I'm not mistaken. Though, for one reason or another I didn't
take in the lower part of his face, I did see the upper
part; and it was perfectly dry, and the eyes were
very deep-sunk; and over them, from the eye-
brows to the cheek-bone, there were *cobwebs*—thick.
Now that closed me up, as they say, and I can't tell
you anything more."

What explanations were furnished by Earle of this
phenomenon it does not very much concern us to
inquire; at all events they did not convince Garrett
that he had not seen what he had seen.

Before William Garrett returned to work at the
library, the librarian insisted upon his taking a week's
rest and change of air. Within a few days' time,
therefore, he was at the station with his bag, looking for a desirable smoking compartment in which
to travel to Burnstow-on-Sea, which he had not
previously visited. One compartment and one only
seemed to be suitable. But, just as he approached
it, he saw, standing in front of the door, a figure so
like one bound up with recent unpleasant associations

that, with a sickening qualm, and hardly knowing what he did, he tore open the door of the next compartment and pulled himself into it as quickly as if death were at his heels. The train moved off, and he must have turned quite faint, for he was next conscious of a smelling-bottle being put to his nose. His physician was a nice-looking old lady, who, with her daughter, was the only passenger in the carriage.

But for this incident it is not very likely that he would have made any overtures to his fellow-travellers. As it was, thanks and inquiries and general conversation supervened inevitably; and Garrett found himself provided before the journey's end not only with a physician, but with a landlady: for Mrs. Simpson had apartments to let at Burnstow, which seemed in all ways suitable. The place was empty at that season, so that Garrett was thrown a good deal into the society of the mother and daughter. He found them very acceptable company. On the third evening of his stay he was on such terms with them as to be asked to spend the evening in their private sitting-room.

During their talk it transpired that Garrett's work lay in a library. "Ah, libraries are fine places," said Mrs. Simpson, putting down her work with a sigh; "but for all that, books have played me a sad turn, or rather *a* book has."

"Well, books give me my living, Mrs. Simpson, and I should be sorry to say a word against them: I don't like to hear that they have been bad for you."

"Perhaps Mr. Garrett could help us to solve our puzzle, mother," said Miss Simpson.

"I don't want to set Mr. Garrett off on a hunt that might waste a lifetime, my dear, nor yet to trouble him with our private affairs."

"But if you think it in the least likely that I could be of use, I do beg you to tell me what the puzzle is, Mrs. Simpson. If it is finding out anything about a book, you see, I am in rather a good position to do it."

"Yes, I do see that, but the worst of it is that we don't know the name of the book."

"Nor what it is about?"

"No, nor that either."

"Except that we don't think it's in English, mother —and that is not much of a clue."

"Well, Mr. Garrett," said Mrs. Simpson, who had not yet resumed her work, and was looking at the fire thoughtfully, "I shall tell you the story. You will please keep it to yourself, if you don't mind? Thank you. Now it is just this. I had an old uncle, a Dr. Rant. Perhaps you may have heard of him. Not that he was a distinguished man, but from the odd way he chose to be buried."

"I rather think I have seen the name in some guide-book."

"That would be it," said Miss Simpson. "He left directions—horrid old man!—that he was to be put, sitting at a table in his ordinary clothes, in a brick room that he'd had made underground in a field near his house. Of course the country people say he's been seen about there in his old black cloak."

"Well, dear, I don't know much about such things," Mrs. Simpson went on, "but anyhow he is dead, these twenty years and more. He was a clergyman, though I'm sure I can't imagine how he got to be one : but he did no duty for the last part of his life, which I think was a good thing ; and he lived on his own property : a very nice estate not a great way from here. He had no wife or family ; only one niece, who was myself, and one nephew, and he had no particular liking for either of us—nor for anyone else, as far as that goes. If anything, he liked my cousin better than he did me—for John was much more like him in his temper, and, I'm afraid I must say, his very mean sharp ways. It might have been different if I had not married ; but I did, and that he very much resented. Very well : here he was with this estate and a good deal of money, as it turned out, of which he had the absolute disposal, and it was understood that we—my cousin and I —would share it equally at his death. In a certain winter, over twenty years back, as I said, he was taken ill, and I was sent for to nurse him. My husband was alive then, but the old man would not hear of *his* coming. As I drove up to the house I saw my cousin John driving away from it in an open fly and looking, I noticed, in very good spirits. I went up and did what I could for my uncle, but I was very soon sure that this would be his last illness; and he was convinced of it too. During the day before he died he got me to sit by him all the time, and I could see there was something, and probably something unpleasant, that he was saving up to tell me, and putting it off as long as he felt he could afford the strength—I'm afraid purposely in order to keep me on the stretch. But, at last, out it came. ' Mary,' he said,—' Mary, I've made my will in John's favour: he has everything, Mary.' Well, of course that came as a bitter shock to me, for we —my husband and I—were not rich people, and if he could have managed to live a little easier than he was obliged to do, I felt it might be the prolonging of his life. But I said little or nothing to my uncle, except that he had a right to do what he pleased: partly because I couldn't think of anything to say, and partly because I was sure there was more to come: and so there was. ' But, Mary,' he said, ' I'm not very fond of John, and I've made another will in *your* favour. *You* can have everything. Only you've got to find the will, you see: and I don't mean to tell you where it is.' Then he chuckled to himself, and I waited, for again I was sure he hadn't finished. ' That's a good girl,' he said after a time,—' you wait, and I'll tell you as much as I told John. But just let me remind you, you can't go into court with what I'm saying to you, for *you* won't be able to produce any collateral evidence beyond your own word, and John's a man that can do a little hard swearing if necessary. Very well then, that's understood. Now, I had the fancy that I wouldn't write this will quite in the common way, so I wrote it in a book, Mary, a printed book. And there's several thousand books in this house. But there! you needn't trouble yourself with them, for it isn't one of them. It's in safe keeping elsewhere: in a place where John can go and find it any day, if he only knew, and you can't. A good will it is: properly signed and witnessed, but I don't think you'll find the witnesses in a hurry.'

"Still I said nothing: if I had moved at all I must have taken hold of the old wretch and shaken him. He lay there laughing to himself, and at last he said:

"'Well, well, you've taken it very quietly, and as I want to start you both on equal terms, and John has a bit of a purchase in being able to go where the book is, I'll tell you just two other things which I didn't tell him. The will's in English, but you won't know that if ever you see it. That's one thing, and another is that when I'm gone you'll find an envelope in my desk directed to you, and inside it something that would help you to find it, if only you have the wits to use it.'

"In a few hours from that he was gone, and though I made an appeal to John Eldred about it——"

"John Eldred? I beg your pardon, Mrs. Simpson—I think I've seen a Mr. John Eldred. What is he like to look at?"

"It must be ten years since I saw him: he would be a thin elderly man now, and unless he has shaved them off, he has that sort of whiskers which people used to call Dundreary or Piccadilly something."

" ——weepers. Yes, that *is* the man."

" Where did you come across him, Mr. Garrett ? "

" I don't know if I could tell you," said Garrett mendaciously, " in some public place.   But you hadn't finished."

" Really I had nothing much to add, only that John Eldred, of course, paid no attention whatever to my letters, and has enjoyed the estate ever since, while my daughter and I have had to take to the lodging-house business here, which I must say has not turned out by any means so unpleasant as I feared it might."

" But about the envelope."

" To be sure !   Why, the puzzle turns on that. Give Mr. Garrett the paper out of my desk."

It was a small slip, with nothing whatever on it but five numerals, not divided or punctuated in any way : 11334.

Mr. Garrett pondered, but there was a light in his eye. Suddenly he " made a face," and then asked, " Do you suppose that Mr. Eldred can have any more clue than you have to the title of the book ? "

" I have sometimes thought he must," said Mrs. Simpson, " and in this way : that my uncle must have made the will not very long before he died (that, I think, he said himself), and got rid of the book immediately afterwards. But all his books were very carefully catalogued : and John has the catalogue : and John was most particular that no books whatever should be sold out of the house. And I'm told that he is always journeying about to booksellers and libraries ; so I fancy that he must have found out just which books are missing from my uncle's library of those which are entered in the catalogue, and must be hunting for them."

" Just so, just so," said Mr. Garrett, and relapsed into thought.

No later than next day he received a letter which, as he told Mrs. Simpson with great regret, made it absolutely necessary for him to cut short his stay at Burnstow.

Sorry as he was to leave them (and they were at least as sorry to part with him), he had begun to feel that a crisis, all-important to Mrs. (and shall we add, Miss ?) Simpson, was very possibly supervening.

In the train Garrett was uneasy and excited. He racked his brains to think whether the press mark of the book which Mr. Eldred had been inquiring after was one in any way corresponding to the numbers on Mrs. Simpson's little bit of paper. But he found to his dismay that the shock of the previous week had really so upset him that he could neither remember any vestige of the title or nature of the book, or even of the locality to which he had gone to seek it. And yet all other parts of library topography and work were clear as ever in his mind.

And another thing—he stamped with annoyance

as he thought of it—he had at first hesitated, and then had forgotten, to ask Mrs. Simpson for the name of the place where Eldred lived. That, however, he could write about.

At least he had his clue in the figures on the paper. If they referred to a press mark in his library, they were only susceptible of a limited number of interpretations. They might be divided into 1.13.34, 11.33.4, or 11.3.34. He could try all these in the space of a few minutes, and if any one were missing he had every means of tracing it. He got very quickly to work, though a few minutes had to be spent in explaining his early return to his landlady and his colleagues. 1.13.34. was in place and contained no extraneous writing. As he drew near to Class 11 in the same gallery, its association struck him like a chill. But he *must* go on. After a cursory glance at 11.33.4 (which first confronted him, and was a perfectly new book) he ran his eye along the line of quartos which fills 11.3. The gap he feared was there: 34 was out. A moment was spent in making sure that it had not been misplaced, and then he was off to the vestibule.

"Has 11.3.34 gone out? Do you recollect noticing that number?"

"Notice the number? What do you take me for, Mr. Garrett? There, take and look over the tickets for yourself, if you've got a free day before you."

"Well then, has a Mr. Eldred called again?—the

old gentleman who came the day I was taken ill. Come! you'd remember him."

"What do you suppose? Of course I recollect of him: no, he haven't been in again, not since you went off for your 'oliday. And yet I seem to —there now. Roberts 'll know. Roberts, do you recollect of the name of Heldred?"

"Not arf," said Roberts. "You mean the man that sent a bob over the price for the parcel, and I wish they all did."

"Do you mean to say you've been sending books to Mr. Eldred? Come, do speak up! Have you?"

"Well now, Mr. Garrett, if a gentleman sends the ticket all wrote correct and the secketry says this book may go and the box ready addressed sent with the note, and a sum of money sufficient to deefray the railway charges, what would be *your* action in the matter, Mr. Garrett, if I may take the liberty to ask such a question? Would you or would you not have taken the trouble to oblige, or would you have chucked the 'ole thing under the counter and——"

"You were perfectly right, of course, Hodgson —perfectly right: only, would you kindly oblige me by showing me the ticket Mr. Eldred sent, and letting me know his address?"

"To be sure, Mr. Garrett; so long as I'm not 'ectored about and informed that I don't know my duty, I'm willing to oblige in every way feasible to my power. There is the ticket on the file. J. Eldred, 11.3.34. Title of work: T—a—l—m——

well, there, you can make what you like of it—not a
novel, I should 'azard the guess. And here is Mr.
Heldred's note applying for the book in question,
which I see he terms it a track."

"Thanks, thanks : but the address ? There's
none on the note."

"Ah, indeed ; well, now . . . stay now, Mr.
Garrett, I 'ave it. Why, that note come inside of
the parcel, which was directed very thoughtful to
save all trouble, ready to be sent back with the book
inside ; and if I *have* made any mistake in this 'ole
transaction, it lays just in the one point that I neglected
to enter the address in my little book here what I
keep. Not but what I dare say there was good reasons
for me not entering of it : but there, I haven't the
time, neither have you, I dare say, to go into 'em
just now. And—no, Mr. Garrett, I do *not* carry it
in my 'ed, else what would be the use of me keeping
this little book here—just a ordinary common notebook, you see, which I make a practice of entering
all such names and addresses in it as I see fit to do ? "

"Admirable arrangement, to be sure—but—all
right, thank you. When did the parcel go off ? "

"Half-past ten, this morning."

"Oh, good ; and it's just one now."

Garrett went upstairs in deep thought. How
was he to get the address ? A telegram to Mrs.
Simpson : he might miss a train by waiting for
the answer. Yes, there was one other way. She
had said that Eldred lived on his uncle's estate.

If this were so, he might find that place entered in the donation-book. That he could run through quickly, now that he knew the title of the book. The register was soon before him, and, knowing that the old man had died more than twenty years ago, he gave him a good margin, and turned back to 1870. There was but one entry possible. 1875, August 14th. *Talmud : Tractatus Middoth cum comm. R. Nachmanidæ.* Amstelod. 1707. Given by J. Rant, D.D., of Bretfield Manor."

A gazetteer showed Bretfield to be three miles from a small station on the main line. Now to ask the doorkeeper whether he recollected if the name on the parcel had been anything like Bretfield.

" No, nothing like. It was, now you mention it, Mr. Garrett, either Bredfield or Britfield, but nothing like that other name what you coated."

So far well. Next, a time-table. A train could be got in twenty minutes—taking two hours over the journey. The only chance, but one not to be missed ; and the train was taken.

If he had been fidgety on the journey up, he was almost distracted on the journey down. If he found Eldred, what could he say ? That it had been dis-covered that the book was a rarity and must be recalled ? An obvious untruth. Or that it was believed to contain important manuscript notes ? Eldred would of course show him the book, from which the leaf would already have been removed. He might, perhaps, find traces of the removal—a torn edge of a fly-leaf probably—and who could disprove, what Eldred was certain to say, that he too had noticed and regretted the mutilation? Altogether the chase seemed very hopeless. The one chance was this. The book had left the library at 10.30: it might not have been put into the first possible train, at 11.20. Granted that, then he might be lucky enough to arrive simultaneously with it and patch up some story which would induce Eldred to give it up.

It was drawing towards evening when he got out upon the platform of his station, and, like most country stations, this one seemed unnaturally quiet. He waited about till the one or two passengers who got out with him had drifted off, and then inquired of the stationmaster whether Mr. Eldred was in the neighbourhood.

"Yes, and pretty near too, I believe. I fancy he means calling here for a parcel he expects. Called for it once to-day already, didn't he, Bob?" (to the porter).

"Yes, sir, he did; and appeared to think it was all along of me that it didn't come by the two o'clock. Anyhow, I've got it for him now," and the porter flourished a square parcel, which a glance assured Garrett contained all that was of any importance to him at that particular moment.

"Bretfield, sir? Yes—three miles just about. Short cut across these three fields brings it down by half a mile. There: there's Mr. Eldred's trap."

A dog-cart drove up with two men in it, of whom Garrett, gazing back as he crossed the little station yard, easily recognized one. The fact that Eldred was driving was slightly in his favour—for most likely he would not open the parcel in the presence of his servant. On the other hand, he would get home quickly, and unless Garrett were there within a very few minutes of his arrival, all would be over. He must hurry; and that he did. His short cut took him along one side of a triangle, while the cart had two sides to traverse; and it was delayed a little at the station, so that Garrett was in the third of the three fields when he heard the wheels fairly near. He had made the best progress possible, but the pace at which the cart was coming made him despair. At this rate it *must* reach home ten minutes before him, and ten minutes would more than suffice for the fulfilment of Mr. Eldred's project.

It was just at this time that the luck fairly turned. The evening was still, and sounds came clearly. Seldom has any sound given greater relief than that which he now heard : that of the cart pulling up. A few words were exchanged, and it drove on. Garrett, halting in the utmost anxiety, was able to see as it drove past the stile (near which he now stood) that it contained only the servant and not Eldred ; further, he made out that Eldred was following on foot. From behind the tall hedge by the stile leading into the road he watched the thin wiry figure pass quickly by with the parcel beneath its arm, and

feeling in its pockets. Just as he passed the stile
something fell out of a pocket upon the grass, but
with so little sound that Eldred was not conscious
of it. In a moment more it was safe for Garrett
to cross the stile into the road and pick up—a box of
matches. Eldred went on, and, as he went, his arms
made hasty movements, difficult to interpret in the
shadow of the trees that overhung the road. But, as
Garrett followed cautiously, he found at various
points the key to them—a piece of string, and then
the wrapper of the parcel—meant to be thrown *over*
the hedge, but sticking in it.

Now Eldred was walking slower, and it could
just be made out that he had opened the book and
was turning over the leaves. He stopped, evidently
troubled by the failing light. Garrett slipped into
a gate-opening, but still watched. Eldred, hastily
looking around, sat down on a felled tree-trunk by the
roadside and held the open book up close to his eyes.
Suddenly he laid it, still open, on his knee, and felt
in all his pockets : clearly in vain, and clearly to his
annoyance. " You would be glad of your matches
now," thought Garrett. Then he took hold of a leaf,
and was carefully tearing it out, when two things happened. First, something black seemed to drop upon
the white leaf and run down it, and then as Eldred
started and was turning to look behind him, a little
dark form appeared to rise out of the shadow behind
the tree-trunk and from it two arms enclosing a mass
of blackness came before Eldred's face and covered

his head and neck. His legs and arms were wildly
flourished, but no sound came. Then, there was no
more movement. Eldred was alone. He had fallen
back into the grass behind the tree-trunk. The
book was cast into the roadway. Garrett, his anger
and suspicion gone for the moment at the sight of
this horrid struggle, rushed up with loud cries of
" Help ! " and so too, to his enormous relief, did a
labourer who had just emerged from a field opposite.
Together they bent over and supported Eldred, but
to no purpose. The conclusion that he was dead was
inevitable. " Poor gentleman ! " said Garrett to
the labourer, when they had laid him down, " what
happened to him, do you think ? " " I wasn't two
hundred yards away," said the man, " when I see
Squire Eldred setting reading in his book, and to
my thinking he was took with one of these fits—face
seemed to go all over black." " Just so," said Garrett. " You didn't see anyone near him ? It couldn't
have been an assault ? " " Not possible—no one
couldn't have got away without you or me seeing
them." " So I thought. Well, we must get some
help, and the doctor and the policeman ; and perhaps
I had better give them this book."

It was obviously a case for an inquest, and obvious
also that Garrett must stay at Bretfield and give his
evidence. The medical inspection showed that,
though some black dust was found on the face and
in the mouth of the deceased, the cause of death
was a shock to a weak heart, and not asphyxiation.

The fateful book was produced, a respectable quarto printed wholly in Hebrew, and not of an aspect likely to excite even the most sensitive.

"You say, Mr. Garrett, that the deceased gentleman appeared at the moment before his attack to be tearing a leaf out of this book?"

"Yes; I think one of the fly-leaves."

"There is here a fly-leaf partially torn through. It has Hebrew writing on it. Will you kindly inspect it?"

"There are three names in English, sir, also, and a date. But I am sorry to say I cannot read Hebrew writing."

"Thank you. The names have the appearance of being signatures. They are John Rant, Walter Gibson, and James Frost, and the date is 20 July, 1875. Does anyone here know any of these names?"

The Rector, who was present, volunteered a statement that the uncle of the deceased, from whom he inherited, had been named Rant.

The book being handed to him, he shook a puzzled head. "This is not like any Hebrew I ever learnt."

"You are sure that it is Hebrew?"

"What? Yes—I suppose. . . . No—my dear sir, you are perfectly right—that is, your suggestion is exactly to the point. Of course—it is not Hebrew at all. It is English, and it is a will."

It did not take many minutes to show that here was indeed a will of Dr. John Rant, bequeathing the whole of the property lately held by John Eldred to Mrs. Mary Simpson. Clearly the discovery of such a document would amply justify Mr. Eldred's agitation. As to the partial tearing of the leaf, the coroner pointed out that no useful purpose could be attained by speculations whose correctness it would never be possible to establish.

The Tractate Middoth was naturally taken in charge by the coroner for further investigation, and Mr. Garrett explained privately to him the history of it, and the position of events so far as he knew or guessed them.

He returned to his work next day, and on his walk to the station passed the scene of Mr. Eldred's catastrophe. He could hardly leave it without another look, though the recollection of what he had seen there made him shiver, even on that bright morning. He walked round, with some misgivings, behind the felled tree. Something dark that still lay there made him start back for a moment: but it hardly stirred. Looking closer, he saw that it was a thick black mass of cobwebs ; and, as he stirred it gingerly with his stick, several large spiders ran out of it into the grass.

There is no great difficulty in imagining the steps by which William Garrett, from being an assistant in a great library, attained to his present position of prospective owner of Bretfield Manor, now in the occupation of his mother-in-law, Mrs. Mary Simpson.

CASTING THE RUNES

April 15th, 190–.

DEAR SIR,—I am requested by the Council of the —— Association to return to you the draft of a paper on *The Truth of Alchemy,* which you have been good enough to offer to read at our forthcoming meeting, and to inform you that the Council do not see their way to including it in the programme.

I am,

Yours faithfully,

—— *Secretary.*

April 18th.

DEAR SIR,—I am sorry to say that my engagements do not permit of my affording you an interview on the subject of your proposed paper. Nor do our laws allow of your discussing the matter with a Committee of our Council, as you suggest. Please allow me to assure you that the fullest consideration was given to the draft which you submitted, and that it was not declined without having been referred to the judgment of a most competent authority. No personal question (it can hardly be necessary for me to add) can have had the slightest influence on the decision of the Council.

Believe me (*ut supra*).

April 20th.

The Secretary of the —— Association begs respect-
fully to inform Mr. Karswell that it is impossible for
him to communicate the name of any person or
persons to whom the draft of Mr. Karswell's paper
may have been submitted; and further desires to
intimate that he cannot undertake to reply to any
further letters on this subject.

" And who *is* Mr. Karswell ? " inquired the Secretary's wife. She had called at his office, and (perhaps unwarrantably) had picked up the last of these
three letters, which the typist had just brought in.

" Why, my dear, just at present Mr. Karswell
is a very angry man. But I don't know much about
him otherwise, except that he is a person of wealth,
his address is Lufford Abbey, Warwickshire, and he's
an alchemist, apparently, and wants to tell us all
about it ; and that's about all—except that I don't
want to meet him for the next week or two. Now,
if you're ready to leave this place, I am."

" What have you been doing to make him angry ? "
asked Mrs. Secretary.

" The usual thing, my dear, the usual thing :
he sent in a draft of a paper he wanted to read at he
next meeting, and we referred it to Edward Dunning
—almost the only man in England who knows about
these things—and he said it was perfectly hopeless,
so we declined it. So Karswell has been pelting me
with letters ever since. The last thing he wanted

was the name of the man we referred his nonsense to ; you saw my answer to that. But don't you say anything about it, for goodness' sake."

" I should think not, indeed. Did I ever do such a thing ? I do hope, though, he won't get to know that it was poor Mr. Dunning."

" Poor Mr. Dunning ? I don't know why you call him that ; he's a very happy man, is Dunning. Lots of hobbies and a comfortable home, and all his time to himself."

" I only meant I should be sorry for him if this man got hold of his name, and came and bothered him.'

" Oh, ah ! yes. I dare say he would be poor Mr. Dunning then."

The Secretary and his wife were lunching out, and the friends to whose house they were bound were Warwickshire people. So Mrs. Secretary had already settled it in her own mind that she would question them judiciously about Mr. Karswell. But she was saved the trouble of leading up to the subject, for the hostess said to the host, before many minutes had passed, " I saw the Abbot of Lufford this morning." The host whistled. " *Did* you ? What in the world brings him up to town ? " " Goodness knows ; he was coming out of the British Museum gate as I drove past." It was not unnatural that Mrs. Secretary should inquire whether this was a real Abbot who was being spoken of. " Oh no, my dear : only a neighbour of ours in the country who bought

Lufford Abbey a few years ago. His real name is
Karswell." "Is he a friend of yours?" asked Mr.
Secretary, with a private wink to his wife. The
question let loose a torrent of declamation. There
was really nothing to be said for Mr. Karswell.
Nobody knew what he did with himself: his servants were a horrible set of people; he had invented
a new religion for himself, and practised no one
could tell what appalling rites; he was very easily
offended, and never forgave anybody: he had a
dreadful face (so the lady insisted, her husband somewhat demurring); he never did a kind action, and
whatever influence he did exert was mischievous.
"Do the poor man justice, dear," the husband interrupted. "You forget the treat he gave the school
children." "Forget it, indeed! But I'm glad you
mentioned it, because it gives an idea of the man.
Now, Florence, listen to this. The first winter
he was at Lufford this delightful neighbour of ours
wrote to the clergyman of his parish (he's not ours,
but we know him very well) and offered to show the
school children some magic-lantern slides. He said
he had some new kinds, which he thought would
interest them. Well, the clergyman was rather surprised, because Mr. Karswell had shown himself
inclined to be unpleasant to the children—com-
plaining of their trespassing, or something of the
sort; but of course he accepted, and the evening
was fixed, and our friend went himself to see that
everything went right. He said he never had been

so thankful for anything as that his own children were all prevented from being there : they were at a children's party at our house, as a matter of fact. Because this Mr. Karswell had evidently set out with the intention of frightening these poor village children out of their wits, and I do believe, if he had been allowed to go on, he would actually have done so. He began with some comparatively mild things. Red Riding Hood was one, and even then, Mr. Farrer said, the wolf was so dreadful that several of the smaller children had to be taken out : and he said Mr. Karswell began the story by producing a noise like a wolf howling in the distance, which was the most gruesome thing he had ever heard. All the slides he showed, Mr. Farrer said, were most clever ; they were absolutely realistic, and where he had got them or how he worked them he could not imagine. Well, the show went on, and the stories kept on becoming a little more terrifying each time, and the children were mesmerized into complete silence. At last he produced a series which represented a little boy passing through his own park—Lufford, I mean —in the evening. Every child in the room could recognize the place from the pictures. And this poor boy was followed, and at last pursued and over-taken, and either torn in pieces or somehow made away with, by a horrible hopping creature in white, which you saw first dodging about among the trees, and gradually it appeared more and more plainly. Mr. Farrer said it gave him one of the worst nightmares he ever remembered, and what it must have meant to the children doesn't bear thinking of. Of course this was too much, and he spoke very sharply indeed to Mr. Karswell, and said it couldn't go on. All *he* said was : ' Oh, you think it's time to bring our little show to an end and send them home to their beds ? *Very* well ! ' And then, if you please, he switched on another slide, which showed a great mass of snakes, centipedes, and disgusting creatures with wings, and somehow or other he made it seem as if they were climbing out of the picture and getting in amongst the audience ; and this was accompanied by a sort of dry rustling noise which sent the children nearly mad, and of course they stampeded. A good many of them were rather hurt in getting out of the room, and I don't suppose one of them closed an eye that night. There was the most dreadful trouble in the village afterwards. Of course the mothers threw a good part of the blame on poor Mr. Farrer, and, if they could have got past the gates, I believe the fathers would have broken every window in the Abbey. Well, now, that's Mr. Karswell : that's the Abbot of Lufford, my dear, and you can imagine how we covet *his* society."

" Yes, I think he has all the possibilities of a distinguished criminal, has Karswell," said the host. " I should be sorry for anyone who got into his bad books."

" Is he the man, or am I mixing him up with someone else ? " asked the Secretary (who for some minutes had been wearing the frown of the man who is trying to recollect something). " Is he the man who brought out a *History of Witchcraft* some time back—ten years or more ? "

" That's the man ; do you remember the reviews of it ? "

" Certainly I do ; and what's equally to the point, I knew the author of the most incisive of the lot. So did you : you must remember John Harrington ; he was at John's in our time."

" Oh, very well indeed, though I don't think I saw or heard anything of him between the time I went down and the day I read the account of the inquest on him."

" Inquest ? " said one of the ladies. " What has happened to him ? "

" Why, what happened was that he fell out of a tree and broke his neck. But the puzzle was, what could have induced him to get up there. It was a mysterious business, I must say. Here was this man —not an athletic fellow, was he ? and with no eccentric twist about him that was ever noticed—walking home along a country road late in the evening—no tramps about—well known and liked in the place —and he suddenly begins to run like mad, loses his hat and stick, and finally shins up a tree—quite a difficult tree—growing in the hedgerow : a dead branch gives way, and he comes down with it and breaks his neck, and there he's found next morning with the most dreadful face of fear on him that could be imagined. It was pretty evident, of course, that he had been chased by something, and people talked of savage dogs, and beasts escaped out of menageries ; but there was nothing to be made of that. That was in '89, and I believe his brother Henry (whom I remember as well at Cambridge, but *you* probably don't) has been trying to get on the track of an explanation ever since. He, of course, insists there was malice in it, but I don't know. It's difficult to see how it could have come in."

After a time the talk reverted to the *History of Witchcraft*. "Did you ever look into it ?" asked the host.

"Yes, I did," said the Secretary. "I went so far as to read it."

"Was it as bad as it was made out to be ?"

"Oh, in point of style and form, quite hopeless. It deserved all the pulverizing it got. But, besides that, it was an evil book. The man believed every word of what he was saying, and I'm very much mistaken if he hadn't tried the greater part of his receipts."

"Well, I only remember Harrington's review of it, and I must say if I'd been the author it would have quenched my literary ambition for good. I should never have held up my head again."

"It hasn't had that effect in · the present case. But come, it's half-past three ; I must be off."

On the way home the Secretary's wife said, "I do hope that horrible man won't find out that Mr. Dunning had anything to do with the rejection of his paper." "I don't think there's much chance of that," said the Secretary. "Dunning won't mention it himself, for these matters are confidential, and none of us will for the same reason. Karswell won't know his name, for Dunning hasn't published anything on the same subject yet. The only danger is that Karswell might find out, if he was to ask the British Museum people who was in the habit of consulting alchemical manuscripts : I can't very well tell them not to mention Dunning, can I? It would set them talking at once. Let's hope it won't occur to him."

However, Mr. Karswell was an astute man.

This much is in the way of prologue. On an evening rather later in the same week, Mr. Edward Dunning was returning from the British Museum, where he had been engaged in Research, to the comfortable house in a suburb where he lived alone, tended by two excellent women who had been long with him. There is nothing to be added by way of description of him to what we have heard already. Let us follow him as he takes his sober course homewards.

A train took him to within a mile or two of his house, and an electric tram a stage farther. The line ended at a point some three hundred yards from his front door. He had had enough of reading when he got into the car, and indeed the light was not such as to allow him to do more than study the advertisements on the panes of glass that faced him as he sat.

As was not unnatural, the advertisements in this particular line of cars were objects of his frequent contemplation, and, with the possible exception of the brilliant and convincing dialogue between Mr. Lamplough and an eminent K.C. on the subject of Pyretic Saline, none of them afforded much scope to his imagination. I am wrong : there was one at the corner of the car farthest from him which did not seem familiar. It was in blue letters on a yellow ground, and all that he could read of it was a name —John Harrington—and something like a date. It could be of no interest to him to know more ; but for all that, as the car emptied, he was just curious enough to move along the seat until he could read it well. He felt to a slight extent repaid for his trouble ; the advertisement was *not* of the usual type. It ran thus : " In memory of John Harrington, F.S.A., of The Laurels, Ashbrooke. Died Sept. 18th, 1889. Three months were allowed."

The car stopped. Mr. Dunning, still contemplating the blue letters on the yellow ground, had to be stimulated to rise by a word from the conductor. " I beg your pardon," he said, " I was looking at that advertisement ; it's a very odd one, isn't it ? " The conductor read it slowly. " Well, my word," he said, " I never see that one before. Well, that is a cure, ain't it ? Someone bin up to their jokes 'ere, I should think." He got out a duster and applied it, not without saliva, to the pane and then to the outside. " No," he said, returning, " that ain't no

transfer; seems to me as if it was reg'lar *in* the glass,
what I mean in the substance, as you may say. Don't
you think so, sir?" Mr. Dunning examined it and
rubbed it with his glove, and agreed. "Who looks
after these advertisements, and gives leave for them
to be put up? I wish you would inquire. I will
just take a note of the words." At this moment there
came a call from the driver: "Look alive, George,
time's up." "All right, all right; there's somethink else what's up at this end. You come and
look at this 'ere glass." "What's gorn with the
glass?" said the driver, approaching. "Well, and
oo's 'Arrington? What's it all about?" "I was
just asking who was responsible for putting the
advertisements up in your cars, and saying it would
be as well to make some inquiry about this one."
"Well, sir, that's all done at the Company's orfice,
that work is: it's our Mr. Timms, I believe, looks
into that. When we put up to-night I'll leave word,
and per'aps I'll be able to tell you to-morrer if you
'appen to be coming this way."

This was all that passed that evening. Mr. Dunning did just go to the trouble of looking up Ashbrooke, and found that it was in Warwickshire.

Next day he went to town again. The car (it
was the same car) was too full in the morning to
allow of his getting a word with the conductor: he
could only be sure that the curious advertisement
had been made away with. The close of the day
brought a further element of mystery into the trans-

action. He had missed the tram, or else preferred walking home, but at a rather late hour, while he was at work in his study, one of the maids came to say that two men from the tramways was very anxious to speak to him. This was a reminder of the advertisement, which he had, he says, nearly forgotten. He had the men in—they were the conductor and driver of the car—and when the matter of refreshment had been attended to, asked what Mr. Timms had had to say about the advertisement. " Well, sir, that's what we took the liberty to step round about," said the conductor. " Mr. Timm's 'e give William 'ere the rough side of his tongue about that : 'cordin' to 'im there warn't no advertisement of that description sent in, nor ordered, nor paid for, nor put up, nor nothink, let alone not bein' there, and we was playing the fool takin' up his time. 'Well,' I says, ' if that's the case, all I ask of you, Mr. Timms,' I says, ' is to take and look at it for yourself,' I says. ' Of course if it ain't there,' I says, ' you may take and call me what you like.' ' Right,' he says, ' I will ' : and we went straight off. Now, I leave it to you, sir, if that ad., as we term 'em, with 'Arrington on it warn't as plain as ever you see anythink—blue letters on yeller glass, and as I says at the time, and you borne me out, reg'lar *in* the glass, because, if you remember, you recollect of me swabbing it with my duster." " To be sure I do, quite clearly—well ? " " You may say well, I don't think. Mr. Timms he gets in that car with a light—no, he told William

246

to 'old the light outside. ' Now,' he says, ' where's your precious ad. what we've 'eard so much about ? " ' 'Ere it is,' I says, ' Mr. Timms,' and I laid my 'and on it." The conductor paused.

" Well," said Mr. Dunning, " it was gone, I suppose. Broken ? "

" Broke !—not it. There warn't, if you'll believe me, no more trace of them letters—blue letters they was—on that piece o' glass, than—well, it's no good *me* talkin'. *I* never see such a thing. I leave it to William here if—but there, as I says, where's the benefit in me going on about it ? "

" And what did Mr. Timms say ? "

" Why 'e did what I give 'im leave to—called us pretty much anythink he liked, and I don't know as I blame him so much neither. But what we thought, William and me did, was as we seen you take down a bit of a note about that—well, that letterin'——"

" I certainly did that, and I have it now. Did you wish me to speak to Mr. Timms myself, and show it to him ? Was that what you came in about ? "

" There, didn't I say as much ? " said William. " Deal with a gent if you can get on the track of one, that's my word. Now perhaps, George, you'll allow as I ain't took you very far wrong to-night."

" Very well, William, very well ; no need for you to go on as if you'd 'ad to frog's-march me 'ere. I come quiet, didn't I ? All the same for that, we 'adn't ought to take up your time this way, sir ; but

if it so 'appened you could find time to step round
to the Company's orfice in the morning and tell Mr.
Timms what you seen for yourself, we should lay
under a very 'igh obligation to you for the trouble.
You see it ain't bein' called—well, one thing and
another, as we mind, but if they got it into their 'ead
at the orfice as we seen things as warn't there, why,
one thing leads to another, and where we should be
a twelvemunce 'ence—well, you can understand what
I mean."

Amid further elucidations of the proposition,
George, conducted by William, left the room.

The incredulity of Mr. Timms (who had a nodding acquaintance with Mr. Dunning) was greatly
modified on the following day by what the latter
could tell and show him; and any bad mark that
might have been attached to the names of William
and George was not suffered to remain on the Company's books; but explanation there was none.

Mr. Dunning's interest in the matter was kept
alive by an incident of the following afternoon.
He was walking from his club to the train, and he
noticed some way ahead a man with a handful of
leaflets such as are distributed to passers-by by agents
of enterprising firms. This agent had not chosen a
very crowded street for his operations: in fact,
Mr. Dunning did not see him get rid of a single leaflet
before he himself reached the spot. One was thrust
into his hand as he passed: the hand that gave it
touched his, and he experienced a sort of little shock

as it did so. It seemed unnaturally rough and hot.
He looked in passing at the giver, but the impression
he got was so unclear that, however much he tried
to reckon it up subsequently, nothing would come.
He was walking quickly, and as he went on glanced
at the paper. It was a blue one. The name of
Harrington in large capitals caught his eye. He
stopped, startled, and felt for his glasses. The next
instant the leaflet was twitched out of his hand by a
man who hurried past, and was irrecoverably gone.
He ran back a few paces, but where was the passer-
by? and where the distributor?

It was in a somewhat pensive frame of mind that
Mr. Dunning passed on the following day into the
Select Manuscript Room of the British Museum, and
filled up tickets for Harley 3586, and some other
volumes. After a few minutes they were brought to
him, and he was settling the one he wanted first
upon the desk, when he thought he heard his own
name whispered behind him. He turned round
hastily, and in doing so, brushed his little portfolio
of loose papers on to the floor. He saw no one he
recognized except one of the staff in charge of the
room, who nodded to him, and he proceeded to
pick up his papers. He thought he had them all,
and was turning to begin work, when a stout gentleman at the table behind him, who was just rising to
leave, and had collected his own belongings, touched
him on the shoulder, saying, " May I give you this ?
I think it should be yours," and handed him a miss-

ing quire. "It is mine, thank you," said Mr. Dunning. In another moment the man had left the room. Upon finishing his work for the afternoon, Mr. Dunning had some conversation with the assistant in charge, and took occasion to ask who the stout gentleman was. "Oh, he's a man named Karswell," said the assistant; "he was asking me a week ago who were the great authorities on alchemy, and of course I told him you were the only one in the country. I'll see if I can't catch him: he'd like to meet you, I'm sure."

"For heaven's sake don't dream of it!" said Mr. Dunning, "I'm particularly anxious to avoid him."

"Oh! very well," said the assistant, "he doesn't come here often: I dare say you won't meet him."

More than once on the way home that day Mr. Dunning confessed to himself that he did not look forward with his usual cheerfulness to a solitary evening. It seemed to him that something ill-defined and impalpable had stepped in between him and his fellow-men—had taken him in charge, as it were. He wanted to sit close up to his neighbours in the train and in the tram, but as luck would have it both train and car were markedly empty. The conductor George was thoughtful, and appeared to be absorbed in calculations as to the number of passengers. On arriving at his house he found Dr. Watson, his medical man, on his doorstep. "I've had to upset your household arrangements, I'm sorry to say, Dunning. Both your servants *hors de combat*. In fact, I've had to send them to the Nursing Home."

"Good heavens! what's the matter?"

"It's something like ptomaine poisoning, I should think: you've not suffered yourself, I can see, or you wouldn't be walking about. I think they'll pull through all right."

"Dear, dear! Have you any idea what brought it on?"

"Well, they tell me they bought some shell-fish from a hawker at their dinner-time. It's odd. I've made inquiries, but I can't find that any hawker has been to other houses in the street. I couldn't send word to you; they won't be back for a bit yet. You come and dine with me to-night, anyhow, and we can make arrangements for going on. Eight o'clock. Don't be too anxious."

The solitary evening was thus obviated; at the expense of some distress and inconvenience, it is true. Mr. Dunning spent the time pleasantly enough with the doctor (a rather recent settler), and returned to his lonely home at about 11.30. The night he passed is not one on which he looks back with any satisfaction. He was in bed and the light was out. He was wondering if the charwoman would come early enough to get him hot water next morning, when he heard the unmistakable sound of his study door opening. No step followed it on the passage floor, but the sound must mean mischief, for he knew that he had shut the door that evening after putting his papers away in his desk. It was rather shame than courage that induced him to slip out into the passage and lean over the banister in his nightgown, listening. No light was visible ; no further sound came : only a gust of warm, or even hot air played for an instant round his shins. He went back and decided to lock himself into his room. There was more unpleasantness, however. Either an economical suburban company had decided that their light would not be required in the small hours, and had stopped working, or else something was wrong with the meter ; the effect was in any case that the electric light was off. The obvious course was to find a match, and also to consult his watch : he might as well know how many hours of discomfort awaited him. So he put his hand into the well-known nook under the pillow : only, it did not get so far. What he touched was, according to his account, a mouth, with teeth, and with hair about it, and, he declares, not the mouth of a human being. I do not think it is any use to guess what he said or did ; but he was in a spare room with the door locked and his ear to it before he was clearly conscious again. And there he spent the rest of a most miserable night, looking every moment for some fumbling at the door : but nothing came.

The venturing back to his own room in the morning was attended with many listenings and quiverings. The door stood open, fortunately, and the blinds were up (the servants had been out of the house before the hour of drawing them down) ; there was, to be short, no trace of an inhabitant. The watch, too, was in its usual place ; nothing was disturbed, only the wardrobe door had swung open, in accordance with its confirmed habit. A ring at the back door now announced the charwoman, who had been ordered the night before, and nerved Mr. Dunning, after letting her in, to continue his search in other parts of the house. It was equally fruitless.

The day thus begun went on dismally enough. He dared not go to the Museum : in spite of what the assistant had said, Karswell might turn up there, and Dunning felt he could not cope with a probably hostile stranger. His own house was odious ; he hated sponging on the doctor. He spent some little time in a call at the Nursing Home, where he was slightly cheered by a good report of his housekeeper and maid. Towards lunch-time he betook himself to his club, again experiencing a gleam of satisfaction at seeing the Secretary of the Association. At luncheon Dunning told his friend the more material of his woes, but could not bring himself to speak of those that weighed most heavily on his spirits. " My poor dear man," said the Secretary, " what an upset ! Look here : we're alone at home, absolutely. You must put up with us. Yes ! no excuse : send your things in this afternoon." Dunning was unable to stand out : he was, in truth, becoming acutely anxious, as the hours went on, as to what that night might have waiting for him. He was almost happy as he hurried home to pack up.

His friends, when they had time to take stock of him, were rather shocked at his lorn appearance, and did their best to keep him up to the mark. Not altogether without success : but, when the two men were smoking alone later, Dunning became dull again. Suddenly he said, " Gayton, I believe that alchemist man knows it was I who got his paper rejected." Gayton whistled. " What makes you think that ? " he said. Dunning told of his conversation with the Museum assistant, and Gayton could only agree that the guess seemed likely to be correct. " Not that I care much," Dunning went on, " only it might be a nuisance if we were to meet. He's a bad-tempered party, I imagine." Conversation dropped again ; Gayton became more and more strongly impressed with the desolateness that came over Dunning's face and bearing, and finally—though with a considerable effort—he asked him point-blank whether something serious was not bothering him. Dunning gave an exclamation of relief. " I was perishing to get it off my mind," he said. " Do you know anything about a man named John Harrington ? " Gayton was thoroughly startled, and at the moment could only ask why. Then the complete story of Dunning's experiences came out—what had happened in the tramcar, in his own house, and in the street, the troubling of spirit that had crept over him, and still held him ; and he ended with the question he had

begun with. Gayton was at a loss how to answer
him. To tell the story of Harrington's end would
perhaps be right; only, Dunning was in a nervous
state, the story was a grim one, and he could not help
asking himself whether there were not a connecting
link between these two cases, in the person of Karswell.
It was a difficult concession for a scientific man, but it
could be eased by the phrase " hypnotic suggestion."
In the end he decided that his answer to-night should
be guarded; he would talk the situation over with
his wife. So he said that he had known Harrington
at Cambridge, and believed he had died suddenly in
1889, adding a few details about the man and his
published work. He did talk over the matter with
Mrs. Gayton, and, as he had anticipated, she leapt at
once to the conclusion which had been hovering before
him. It was she who reminded him of the surviving
brother, Henry Harrington, and she also who suggested that he might be got hold of by means of their
hosts of the day before. " He might be a hopeless
crank," objected Gayton. " That could be ascertained from the Bennetts, who knew him," Mrs.
Gayton retorted; and she undertook to see the
Bennetts the very next day.

It is not necessary to tell in further detail the steps
by which Henry Harrington and Dunning were
brought together.

The next scene that does require to be narrated is a
conversation that took place between the two.

Dunning had told Harrington of the strange ways in which the dead man's name had been brought before him, and had said something, besides, of his own subsequent experiences. Then he had asked if Harrington was disposed, in return, to recall any of the circumstances connected with his brother's death. Harrington's surprise at what he heard can be imagined : but his reply was readily given.

" John," he said, " was in a very odd state, undeniably, from time to time, during some weeks before, though not immediately before, the catastrophe. There were several things; the principal notion he had was that he thought he was being followed. No doubt he was an impressionable man, but he never had had such fancies as this before. I cannot get it out of my mind that there was ill-will at work, and what you tell me about yourself reminds me very much of my brother. Can you think of any possible connecting link ? "

" There is just one that has been taking shape vaguely in my mind. I've been told that your brother reviewed a book very severely not long before he died, and just lately I have happened to cross the path of the man who wrote that book in a way he would resent."

" Don't tell me the man was called Karswell."

" Why not ? that is exactly his name."

Henry Harrington leant back. " That is final to my mind. Now I must explain further. From something he said, I feel sure that my brother John was

beginning to believe—very much against his will—
that Karswell was at the bottom of his trouble. I
want to tell you what seems to me to have a bearing
on the situation. My brother was a great musician,
and used to run up to concerts in town. He came
back, three months before he died, from one of these,
and gave me his programme to look at—an analytical
programme : he always kept them. ' I nearly missed
this one,' he said. ' I suppose I must have dropped
it : anyhow, I was looking for it under my seat and
in my pockets and so on, and my neighbour offered
me his : said " might he give it me, he had no further
use for it," and he went away just afterwards. I don't
know who he was—a stout, clean-shaven man. I
should have been sorry to miss it ; of course I could
have bought another, but this cost me nothing.' At
another time he told me that he had been very uncomfortable both on the way to his hotel and during the
night. I piece things together now in thinking it over.
Then, not very long after, he was going over these
programmes, putting them in order to have them
bound up, and in this particular one (which by the
way I had hardly glanced at), he found quite near the
beginning a strip of paper with some very odd
writing on it in red and black—most carefully done
—it looked to me more like Runic letters than anything else. ' Why,' he said, ' this must belong to my
fat neighbour. It looks as if it might be worth
returning to him ; it may be a copy of something ;
evidently someone has taken trouble over it. How

can I find his address ? ' We talked it over for a
little and agreed that it wasn't worth advertising
about, and that my brother had better look out for
the man at the next concert, to which he was going
very soon. The paper was lying on the book and
we were both by the fire ; it was a cold, windy summer
evening. I suppose the door blew open, though I
didn't notice it : at any rate a gust—a warm gust it
was—came quite suddenly between us, took the paper
and blew it straight into the fire : it was light, thin
paper, and flared and went up the chimney in a single
ash. ' Well,' I said, ' you can't give it back now.'
He said nothing for a minute : then rather crossly,
' No, I can't ; but why you should keep on saying
so I don't know.' I remarked that I didn't say it
more than once. ' Not more than four times, you
mean,' was all he said. I remember all that very
clearly, without any good reason ; and now to come
to the point. I don't know if you looked at that
book of Karswell's which my unfortunate brother
reviewed. It's not likely that you should : but I did,
both before his death and after it. The first time
we made game of it together. It was written in no
style at all—split infinitives, and every sort of thing
that makes an Oxford gorge rise. Then there was
nothing that the man didn't swallow : mixing up
classical myths, and stories out of the *Golden Legend*
with reports of savage customs of to-day—all very
proper, no doubt, if you know how to use them,
but he didn't : he seemed to put the *Golden Legend*

and the *Golden Bough* exactly on a par, and to believe both : a pitiable exhibition, in short. Well, after the misfortune, I looked over the book again. It was no better than before, but the impression which it left this time on my mind was different. I suspected —as I told you—that Karswell had borne ill-will to my brother, even that he was in some way responsible for what had happened; and now his book seemed to me to be a very sinister performance indeed. One chapter in particular struck me, in which he spoke of ' casting the Runes ' on people, either for the purpose of gaining their affection or of getting them out of the way—perhaps more especially the latter : he spoke of all this in a way that really seemed to me to imply actual knowledge. I've not time to go into details, but the upshot is that I am pretty sure from information received that the civil man at the concert was Karswell : I suspect—I more than suspect—that the paper was of importance : and I do believe that if my brother had been able to give it back, he might have been alive now. Therefore, it occurs to me to ask you whether you have anything to put beside what I have told you."

By way of answer, Dunning had the episode in the Manuscript Room at the British Museum to relate. " Then he did actually hand you some papers ; have you examined them? No? because we must, if you'll allow it, look at them at once, and very carefully."

They went to the still empty house—empty, for the two servants were not yet able to return to work.

Dunning's portfolio of papers was gathering dust on the writing-table. In it were the quires of small-sized scribbling paper which he used for his transcripts : and from one of these, as he took it up, there slipped and fluttered out into the room with uncanny quickness, a strip of thin light paper. The window was open, but Harrington slammed it to, just in time to intercept the paper, which he caught. "I thought so," he said ; " it might be the identical thing that was given to my brother. You'll have to look out, Dunning ; this may mean something quite serious for you."

A long consultation took place. The paper was narrowly examined. As Harrington had said, the characters on it were more like Runes than anything else, but not decipherable by either man, and both hesitated to copy them, for fear, as they confessed, of perpetuating whatever evil purpose they might conceal. So it has remained impossible (if I may anticipate a little) to ascertain what was conveyed in this curious message or commission. Both Dunning and Harrington are firmly convinced that it had the effect of bringing its possessors into very undesirable company. That it must be returned to the source whence it came they were agreed, and further, that the only safe and certain way was that of personal service ; and here contrivance would be necessary, for Dunning was known by sight to Karswell. He must, for one thing, alter his appearance by shaving his beard. But then might not the blow fall first ? Harrington thought they could time it. He knew the date of the concert at which the " black spot " had been put

on his brother: it was June 18th. The death had
followed on Sept. 18th. Dunning reminded him that
three months had been mentioned on the inscription
on the car-window. "Perhaps," he added, with a
cheerless laugh, " mine may be a bill at three months
too. I believe I can fix it by my diary. Yes, April
23rd was the day at the Museum ; that brings us to
July 23rd. Now, you know, it becomes extremely
important to me to know anything you will tell me
about the progress of your brother's trouble, if it is
possible for you to speak of it." " Of course. Well,
the sense of being watched whenever he was alone
was the most distressing thing to him. After a time
I took to sleeping in his room, and he was the better
for that : still, he talked a great deal in his sleep.
What about ? Is it wise to dwell on that, at least
before things are straightened out ? I think not, but
I can tell you this : two things came for him by post
during those weeks, both with a London postmark,
and addressed in a commercial hand. One was a
woodcut of Bewick's, roughly torn out of the page :
one which shows a moonlit road and a man walking
along it, followed by an awful demon creature.
Under it were written the lines out of the ' Ancient
Mariner ' (which I suppose the cut illustrates) about
one who, having once looked round—

> ' walks on,
> And turns no more his head,
> Because he knows a frightful fiend
> Doth close behind him tread.'

The other was a calendar, such as tradesmen often

send. My brother paid no attention to this, but I looked at it after his death, and found that everything after Sept. 18 had been torn out. You may be surprised at his having gone out alone the evening he was killed, but the fact is that during the last ten days or so of his life he had been quite free from the sense of being followed or watched."

The end of the consultation was this. Harrington, who knew a neighbour of Karswell's, thought he saw a way of keeping a watch on his movements. It would be Dunning's part to be in readiness to try to cross Karswell's path at any moment, to keep the paper safe and in a place of ready access.

They parted. The next weeks were no doubt a severe strain upon Dunning's nerves : the intangible barrier which had seemed to rise about him on the day when he received the paper, gradually developed into a brooding blackness that cut him off from the means of escape to which one might have thought he might resort. No one was at hand who was likely to suggest them to him, and he seemed robbed of all initiative. He waited with inexpressible anxiety as May, June, and early July passed on, for a mandate from Harrington. But all this time Karswell remained immovable at Lufford.

At last, in less than a week before the date he had come to look upon as the end of his earthly activities, came a telegram : " Leaves Victoria by boat train Thursday night. Do not miss. I come to you to-night. Harrington."

He arrived accordingly, and they concocted plans. The train left Victoria at nine and its last stop before Dover was Croydon West. Harrington would mark down Karswell at Victoria, and look out for Dunning at Croydon, calling to him if need were by a name agreed upon. Dunning, disguised as far as might be, was to have no label or initials on any hand luggage, and must at all costs have the paper with him.

Dunning's suspense as he waited on the Croydon platform I need not attempt to describe. His sense of danger during the last days had only been sharpened by the fact that the cloud about him had perceptibly been lighter; but relief was an ominous symptom, and, if Karswell eluded him now, hope was gone : and there were so many chances of that. The rumour of the journey might be itself a device. The twenty minutes in which he paced the platform and perse- cuted every porter with inquiries as to the boat train were as bitter as any he had spent. Still, the train came, and Harrington was at the window. It was important, of course, that there should be no recog- nition : so Dunning got in at the farther end of the corridor carriage, and only gradually made his way to the compartment where Harrington and Karswell were. He was pleased, on the whole, to see that the train was far from full.

Karswell was on the alert, but gave no sign of recognition. Dunning took the seat not immediately facing him, and attempted, vainly at first, then with increasing command of his faculties, to reckon the

possibilities of making the desired transfer. Opposite
to Karswell, and next to Dunning, was a heap of
Karswell's coats on the seat. It would be of no use
to slip the paper into these—he would not be safe,
or would not feel so, unless in some way it could be
proffered by him and accepted by the other. There
was a handbag, open, and with papers in it. Could
he manage to conceal this (so that perhaps Karswell
might leave the carriage without it), and then find
and give it to him? This was the plan that suggested itself. If he could only have counselled with
Harrington! but that could not be. The minutes
went on. More than once Karswell rose and went
out into the corridor. The second time Dunning
was on the point of attempting to make the bag fall
off the seat, but he caught Harrington's eye, and read
in it a warning. Karswell, from the corridor, was
watching : probably to see if the two men recognized
each other. He returned, but was evidently restless :
and, when he rose the third time, hope dawned, for
something did slip off his seat and fall with hardly a
sound to the floor. Karswell went out once more,
and passed out of range of the corridor window.
Dunning picked up what had fallen, and saw that
the key was in his hands in the form of one of Cook's
ticket-cases, with tickets in it. These cases have a
pocket in the cover, and within very few seconds the
paper of which we have heard was in the pocket of
this one. To make the operation more secure,
Harrington stood in the doorway of the compartment

and fiddled with the blind. It was done, and done at the right time, for the train was now slowing down towards Dover.

In a moment more Karswell re-entered the compartment. As he did so, Dunning, managing, he knew not how, to suppress the tremble in his voice, handed him the ticket-case, saying, " May I give you this, sir ? I believe it is yours." After a brief glance at the ticket inside, Karswell uttered the hoped-for response, " Yes, it is ; much obliged to you, sir," and he placed it in his breast pocket.

Even in the few moments that remained—moments of tense anxiety, for they knew not to what a premature finding of the paper might lead—both men noticed that the carriage seemed to darken about them and to grow warmer ; that Karswell was fidgety and oppressed ; that he drew the heap of loose coats near to him and cast it back as if it repelled him ; and that he then sat upright and glanced anxiously at both. They, with sickening anxiety, busied themselves in collecting their belongings ; but they both thought that Karswell was on the point of speaking when the train stopped at Dover Town. It was natural that in the short space between town and pier they should both go into the corridor.

At the pier they got out, but so empty was the train that they were forced to linger on the platform until Karswell should have passed ahead of them with his porter on the way to the boat, and only then was it safe for them to exchange a pressure of

the hand and a word of concentrated congratulation.
The effect upon Dunning was to make him almost
faint. Harrington made him lean up against the
wall, while he himself went forward a few yards
within sight of the gangway to the boat, at which
Karswell had now arrived. The man at the head of
it examined his ticket, and, laden with coats, he
passed down into the boat. Suddenly the official
called after him, " You, sir, beg pardon, did the other
gentleman show his ticket ? " " What the devil do
you mean by the other gentleman ? " Karswell's
snarling voice called back from the deck. The man
bent over and looked at him. " The devil ? Well,
I don't know, I'm sure," Harrington heard him say
to himself, and then aloud, " My mistake, sir ; must
have been your rugs ! ask your pardon." And then,
to a subordinate near him, " 'Ad he got a dog with
him, or what ? Funny thing : I could 'a' swore 'e
wasn't alone. Well, whatever it was, they'll 'ave to
see to it aboard. She's off now. Another week and
we shall be gettin' the 'oliday customers." In five
minutes more there was nothing but the lessening
lights of the boat, the long line of the Dover lamps,
the night breeze, and the moon.

Long and long the two sat in their room at the
" Lord Warden." In spite of the removal of their
greatest anxiety, they were oppressed with a doubt,
not of the lightest. Had they been justified in sending
a man to his death, as they believed they had ? Ought
they not to warn him, at least ? " No," said Harring-

ton ; " if he is the murderer I think him, we have done no more than is just. Still, if you think it better—but how and where can you warn him ? " " He was booked to Abbeville only," said Dunning. " I saw that. If I wired to the hotels there in Joanne's Guide, ' Examine your ticket-case, Dunning,' I should feel happier. This is the 21st : he will have a day. But I am afraid he has gone into the dark." So telegrams were left at the hotel office.

It is not clear whether these reached their destination, or whether, if they did, they were understood. All that is known is that, on the afternoon of the 23rd, an English traveller, examining the front of St. Wulfram's Church at Abbeville, then under extensive repair, was struck on the head and instantly killed by a stone falling from the scaffold erected round the north-western tower, there being, as was clearly proved, no workman on the scaffold at that moment : and the traveller's papers identified him as Mr. Karswell.

Only one detail shall be added. At Karswell's sale a set of Bewick, sold with all faults, was acquired by Harrington. The page with the woodcut of the traveller and the demon was, as he had expected, mutilated. Also, after a judicious interval, Harrington repeated to Dunning something of what he had heard his brother say in his sleep : but it was not long before Dunning stopped him.

THE STALLS OF BARCHESTER CATHEDRAL

THIS matter began, as far as I am concerned, with the reading of a notice in the obituary section of the *Gentleman's Magazine* for an early year in the nineteenth century :

" On February 26th, at his residence in the Cathedral Close of Barchester, the Venerable John Benwell Haynes, D.D., aged 57, Archdeacon of Sowerbridge and Rector of Pickhill and Candley.   He was of —— College, Cambridge, and where, by talent and assiduity, he commanded the esteem of his seniors ; when, at the usual time, he took his first degree, his name stood high in the list of *wranglers*.   These academical honours procured for him within a short time a Fellowship of his College.   In the year 1783 he received Holy Orders, and was shortly afterwards presented to the perpetual Curacy of Ranxton-sub-Ashe by his friend and patron the late truly venerable Bishop of Lichfield. . . . His speedy preferments, first to a Prebend, and subsequently to the dignity of Precentor in the Cathedral of Barchester, form an eloquent testimony to the respect in which he was held and to his eminent qualifications.   He succeeded to the Archdeaconry upon the sudden decease of

Archdeacon Pulteney in 1810. His sermons, ever conformable to the principles of the religion and Church which he adorned, displayed in no ordinary degree, without the least trace of enthusiasm, the refinement of the scholar united with the graces of the Christian. Free from sectarian violence, and informed by the spirit of the truest charity, they will long dwell in the memories of his hearers. (Here a further omission.) The productions of his pen include an able defence of Episcopacy, which, though often perused by the author of this tribute to his memory, afford but one additional instance of the want of liberality and enterprise which is a too common characteristic of the publishers of our generation. His published works are, indeed, confined to a spirited and elegant version of the *Argonautica* of Valerius Flaccus, a volume of *Discourses upon the Several Events in the Life of Joshua*, delivered in his Cathedral, and a number of the charges which he pronounced at various visitations to the clergy of his Archdeaconry. These are distinguished by etc., etc. The urbanity and hospitality of the subject of these lines will not readily be forgotten by those who enjoyed his acquaintance. His interest in the venerable and awful pile under whose hoary vault he was so punctual an attendant, and particularly in the musical portion of its rites, might be termed filial, and formed a strong and delightful contrast to the polite indifference displayed by too many of our Cathedral dignitaries at the present time."

The final paragraph, after informing us that Dr. Haynes died a bachelor, says :

" It might have been augured that an existence so placid and benevolent would have been terminated in a ripe old age by a dissolution equally gradual and calm. But how unsearchable are the workings of Providence ! The peaceful and retired seclusion amid which the honoured evening of Dr. Haynes' life was mellowing to its close was destined to be disturbed, nay, shattered, by a tragedy as appalling as it was unexpected. The morning of the 26th of February——"

But perhaps I shall do better to keep back the remainder of the narrative until I have told the circumstances which led up to it. These, as far as they are now accessible, I have derived from another source.

I had read the obituary notice which I have been quoting, quite by chance, along with a great many others of the same period. It had excited some little speculation in my mind, but, beyond thinking that, if I ever had an opportunity of examining the local records of the period indicated, I would try to remember Dr. Haynes, I made no effort to pursue his case.

Quite lately I was cataloguing the manuscripts in the library of the college to which he belonged. I had reached the end of the numbered volumes on the shelves, and I proceeded to ask the librarian whether there were any more books which he thought I ought to include in my description. "I don't think there are," he said, "but we had better come and look at the manuscript class and make sure. Have you time to do that now?" I had time. We went to the library, checked off the manuscripts, and, at the end of our survey, arrived at a shelf of which I had seen nothing. Its contents consisted for the most part of sermons, bundles of fragmentary papers, college exercises, *Cyrus*, an epic poem in several cantos, the product of a country clergyman's leisure, mathematical tracts by a deceased professor, and other similar material of a kind with which I am only too familiar. I took brief notes of these. Lastly, there was a tin box, which was pulled out and dusted. Its label, much faded, was thus inscribed : "Papers of the Ven. Archdeacon Haynes. Bequeathed in 1834 by his sister, Miss Letitia Haynes."

I knew at once that the name was one which I had somewhere encountered, and could very soon locate it. "That must be the Archdeacon Haynes who came to a very odd end at Barchester. I've read his obituary in the *Gentleman's Magazine*. May I take the box home? Do you know if there is anything interesting in it?"

The librarian was very willing that I should take the box and examine it at leisure. "I never looked inside it myself," he said, "but I've always been meaning to. I am pretty sure that is the box which our old Master once said ought never to have been accepted by the college. He said that to Martin years ago ; and he

said also that as long as he had control over the library
it should never be opened. Martin told me about it,
and said that he wanted terribly to know what was in
it; but the Master was librarian, and always kept the
box in the lodge, so there was no getting at it in his
time, and when he died it was taken away by mistake
by his heirs, and only returned a few years ago. I
can't think why I haven't opened it; but, as I have
to go away from Cambridge this afternoon, you had
better have first go at it. I think I can trust you not
to publish anything undesirable in our catalogue."

I took the box home and examined its contents, and
thereafter consulted the librarian as to what should be
done about publication, and, since I have his leave to
make a story out of it, provided I disguise the identity
of the people concerned, I will try what can be done.

The materials are, of course, mainly journals and
letters. How much I shall quote and how much
epitomize must be determined by considerations of
space. The proper understanding of the situation
has necessitated a little—not very arduous—research,
which has been greatly facilitated by the excellent illustrations and text of the Barchester volume in Bell's
Cathedral Series.

When you enter the choir of Barchester Cathedral
now, you pass through a screen of metal and coloured
marbles, designed by Sir Gilbert Scott, and find
yourself in what I must call a very bare and odiously
furnished place. The stalls are modern, without
canopies. The places of the dignitaries and the

names of the prebends have fortunately been allowed to survive, and are inscribed on small brass plates affixed to the stalls. The organ is in the triforium, and what is seen of the case is Gothic. The reredos and its surroundings are like every other.

Careful engravings of a hundred years ago show a very different state of things. The organ is on a massive classical screen. The stalls are also classical and very massive. There is a baldacchino of wood over the altar, with urns upon its corners. Farther east is a solid altar screen, classical in design, of wood, with a pediment, in which is a triangle surrounded by rays, enclosing certain Hebrew letters in gold. Cherubs contemplate these. There is a pulpit with a great sounding-board at the eastern end of the stalls on the north side, and there is a black and white marble pavement. Two ladies and a gentleman are admiring the general effect. From other sources I gather that the archdeacon's stall then, as now, was next to the bishop's throne at the south-eastern end of the stalls. His house almost faces the west front of the church, and is a fine red-brick building of William the Third's time.

Here Dr. Haynes, already a mature man, took up his abode with his sister in the year 1810. The dignity had long been the object of his wishes, but his predecessor refused to depart until he had attained the age of ninety-two. About a week after he had held a modest festival in celebration of that ninety-second birthday, there came a morning, late in the year, when Dr. Haynes, hurrying cheerfully into his breakfast-room, rubbing his hands and humming a tune, was greeted, and checked in his genial flow of spirits, by the sight of his sister, seated, indeed, in her usual place behind the tea-urn, but bowed forward and sobbing unrestrainedly into her handkerchief. "What—what is the matter? What bad news?" he began. "Oh, Johnny, you've not heard? The poor dear archdeacon!" "The archdeacon, yes? What is it—ill, is he?" "No, no; they found him on the staircase this morning; it is so shocking." "Is it possible! Dear, dear, poor Pulteney! Had there been any seizure?" "They don't think so, and that is almost the worst thing about it. It seems to have been all the fault of that stupid maid of theirs, Jane." Dr. Haynes paused. "I don't quite understand, Letitia. How was the maid at fault?" "Why, as far as I can make out, there was a stair-rod missing, and she never mentioned it, and the poor archdeacon set his foot quite on the edge of the step—you know how slippery that oak is—and it seems he must have fallen almost the whole flight and broken his neck. It *is* so sad for poor Miss Pulteney. Of course, they will get rid of the girl at once. I never liked her." Miss Haynes's grief resumed its sway, but eventually relaxed so far as to permit of her taking some breakfast. Not so her brother, who, after standing in silence before the window for some minutes, left the room, and did not appear again that morning.

I need only add that the careless maid-servant was dismissed forthwith, but that the missing stair-rod was very shortly afterwards found *under* the stair-carpet—an additional proof, if any were needed, of extreme stupidity and carelessness on her part.

For a good many years Dr. Haynes had been marked out by his ability, which seems to have been really considerable, as the likely successor of Archdeacon Pulteney, and no disappointment was in store for him. He was duly installed, and entered with zeal upon the discharge of those functions which are appropriate to one in his position. A considerable space in his journals is occupied with exclamations upon the confusion in which Archdeacon Pulteney had left the business of his office and the documents appertaining to it. Dues upon Wringham and Barnswood have been uncollected for something like twelve years, and are largely irrecoverable; no visitation has been held for seven years; four chancels are almost past mending. The persons deputized by the archdeacon have been nearly as incapable as himself. It was almost a matter for thankfulness that this state of things had not been permitted to continue, and a letter from a friend confirms this view. " ὁ κατέχων," it says (in rather cruel allusion to the Second Epistle to the Thessalonians), " is removed at last. My poor friend! Upon what a scene of confusion will you be entering! I give you my word that, on the last occasion of my crossing his threshold, there was no single paper that he could lay hands upon, no syllable of mine that he could hear, and no fact in connection with my business that he could remember. But now, thanks to a negligent maid and a loose stair-carpet, there is some prospect that necessary business will be transacted without a complete loss alike of voice and temper." This letter was tucked into a pocket in the cover of one of the diaries.

There can be no doubt of the new archdeacon's zeal and enthusiasm. " Give me but time to reduce to some semblance of order the innumerable errors and complications with which I am confronted, and I shall gladly and sincerely join with the aged Israelite in the canticle which too many, I fear, pronounce but with their lips." This reflection I find, not in a diary, but a letter; the doctor's friends seem to have returned his correspondence to his surviving sister. He does not confine himself, however, to reflections. His investigation of the rights and duties of his office are very searching and business-like, and there is a calculation in one place that a period of three years will just suffice to set the business of the Archdeaconry upon a proper footing. The estimate appears to have been an exact one. For just three years he is occupied in reforms; but I look in vain at the end of that time for the promised *Nunc dimittis*. He has now found a new sphere of activity. Hitherto his duties have precluded him from more than an occasional attendance at the Cathedral services. Now he begins to take an interest in the fabric and the music. Upon his struggles with the organist, an old gentleman who

had been in office since 1786, I have no time to dwell ;
they were not attended with any marked success.
More to the purpose is his sudden growth of enthusiasm for the Cathedral itself and its furniture. There
is a draft of a letter to Sylvanus Urban (which I do
not think was ever sent) describing the stalls in the
choir. As I have said, these were of fairly late date
—of about the year 1700, in fact.

" The archdeacon's stall, situated at the south-east
end, west of the episcopal throne (now so worthily
occupied by the truly excellent prelate who adorns the
See of Barchester), is distinguished by some curious
ornamentation. In addition to the arms of Dean
West, by whose efforts the whole of the internal
furniture of the choir was completed, the prayer-desk
is terminated at the eastern extremity by three small
but remarkable statuettes in the grotesque manner.
One is an exquisitely modelled figure of a cat, whose
crouching posture suggests with admirable spirit the
suppleness, vigilance, and craft of the redoubted
adversary of the genus *Mus*. Opposite to this is a
figure seated upon a throne and invested with the
attributes of royalty ; but it is no earthly monarch
whom the carver has sought to portray. His feet are
studiously concealed by the long robe in which he is
draped : but neither the crown nor the cap which he
wears suffice to hide the prick-ears and curving horns
which betray his Tartarean origin ; and the hand which
rests upon his knee is armed with talons of horrifying
length and sharpness. Between these two figures

stands a shape muffled in a long mantle. This might at first sight be mistaken for a monk or 'friar of orders gray,' for the head is cowled and a knotted cord depends from somewhere about the waist. A slight inspection, however, will lead to a very different conclusion. The knotted cord is quickly seen to be a halter, held by a hand all but concealed within the draperies; while the sunken features and, horrid to relate, the rent flesh upon the cheek-bones, proclaim the King of Terrors. These figures are evidently the production of no unskilled chisel; and should it chance that any of your correspondents are able to throw light upon their origin and significance, my obligations to your valuable miscellany will be largely increased."

There is more description in the paper, and, seeing that the woodwork in question has now disappeared, it has a considerable interest. A paragraph at the end is worth quoting:

" Some late researches among the Chapter accounts have shown me that the carving of the stalls was not, as was very usually reported, the work of Dutch artists, but was executed by a native of this city or district named Austin. The timber was procured from an oak copse in the vicinity, the property of the Dean and Chapter, known as Holywood. Upon a recent visit to the parish within whose boundaries it is situated, I learned from the aged and truly respectable incumbent that traditions still lingered amongst the inhabitants of the great size and age of the oaks employed to furnish the materials of the stately structure which has been, however imperfectly, described in the above lines. Of one in particular, which stood near the centre of the grove, it is remembered that it was known as the Hanging Oak. The propriety of that title is confirmed by the fact that a quantity of human bones was found in the soil about its roots, and that at certain times of the year it was the custom for those who wished to secure a successful issue to their affairs, whether of love or the ordinary business of life, to suspend from its boughs small images or puppets rudely fashioned of straw, twigs, or the like rustic materials."

So much for the archdeacon's archæological investigations. To return to his career as it is to be gathered from his diaries. Those of his first three years of hard and careful work show him throughout in high spirits, and, doubtless, during this time, that reputation for hospitality and urbanity which is mentioned in his obituary notice was well deserved. After that, as time goes on, I see a shadow coming over him—destined to develop into utter blackness —which I cannot but think must have been reflected in his outward demeanour. He commits a good deal of his fears and troubles to his diary; there was no other outlet for them. He was unmarried, and his sister was not always with him. But I am much mistaken if he has told all that he might have told. A series of extracts shall be given:

"*Aug.* 30, 1816.—The days begin to draw in more perceptibly than ever. Now that the Archdeaconry papers are reduced to order, I must find some further employment for the evening hours of autumn and winter. It is a great blow that Letitia's health will not allow her to stay through these months. Why not go on with my *Defence of Episcopacy*? It may be useful.

"*Sept.* 15.—Letitia has left me for Brighton.

"*Oct.* 11.—Candles lit in the choir for the first time at evening prayers. It came as a shock: I find that I absolutely shrink from the dark season.

"*Nov.* 17.—Much struck by the character of the carving on my desk: I do not know that I had ever carefully noticed it before. My attention was called to it by an accident. During the *Magnificat* I was, I regret to say, almost overcome with sleep. My hand was resting on the back of the carved figure of a cat which is the nearest to me of the three figures on the end of my stall. I was not aware of this, for I was not looking in that direction, until I was startled by what seemed a softness, a feeling as of rather rough and coarse fur, and a sudden movement, as if the creature were twisting round its head to bite me. I regained complete consciousness in an instant, and I have some idea that I must have uttered a suppressed exclamation, for I noticed that Mr. Treasurer turned his head quickly in my direction. The impression of the unpleasant feeling was so strong that I found myself rubbing my hand upon my surplice. This accident led me to examine the figures after prayers more carefully than I had done before, and I realized for the first time with what skill they are executed.

"*Dec.* 6.—I do indeed miss Letitia's company. The evenings, after I have worked as long as I can at my *Defence*, are very trying. The house is too large for a lonely man, and visitors of any kind are too rare. I get an uncomfortable impression when going to my room that there *is* company of some kind. The fact is (I may as well formulate it to myself) that I hear voices. This, I am well aware, is a common symptom of incipient decay of the brain—and I believe that I should be less disquieted than I am if I had any suspicion that this was the cause. I have none—none whatever, nor is there anything in my family history to give colour to such an idea. Work, diligent work, and a punctual attention to the duties which fall to me is my best remedy, and I have little doubt that it will prove efficacious.

" *Jan.* 1.—My trouble is, I must confess it, increasing upon me. Last night, upon my return after midnight from the Deanery, I lit my candle to go upstairs. I was nearly at the top when something whispered to me, ' Let me wish you a happy New Year.' I could not be mistaken : it spoke distinctly and with a peculiar emphasis. Had I dropped my candle, as I all but did, I tremble to think what the consequences must have been. As it was, I managed to get up the last flight, and was quickly in my room with the door locked, and experienced no other disturbance.

" *Jan.* 15.—I had occasion to come downstairs last night to my workroom for my watch, which I had inadvertently left on my table when I went up to bed. I think I was at the top of the last flight when I had a sudden impression of a sharp whisper in my ear ' *Take care.*' I clutched the balusters and naturally looked round at once. Of course, there was nothing. After a moment I went on—it was no good turning back—but I had as nearly as possible fallen : a cat—a large one by the feel of it—slipped between my feet, but again, of course, I saw nothing. It *may* have been the kitchen cat, but I do not think it was.

" *Feb.* 27.—A curious thing last night, which I should like to forget. Perhaps if I put it down here I may see it in its true proportion. I worked in the library from about 9 to 10. The hall and staircase seemed to be unusually full of what I can only call movement without sound : by this I mean that there seemed to be continuous going and coming, and that whenever I ceased writing to listen, or looked out into the hall, the stillness was absolutely unbroken. Nor, in going to my room at an earlier hour than usual—about half-past ten —was I conscious of anything that I could call a noise. It so happened that I had told John to come to my room for the letter to the bishop which I wished to have delivered early in the morning at the Palace. He was to sit up, therefore, and come for it when he heard me retire. This I had for the moment forgotten, though I had remembered to carry the letter with me to my room. But when, as I was winding up my watch, I heard a light tap at the door, and a low voice saying, 'May I come in?' (which I most undoubtedly did hear), I recollected the fact, and took up the letter from my dressing-table, saying, 'Certainly: come in.' No one, however, answered my summons, and it was now that, as I strongly suspect, I committed an error: for I opened the door and held the letter out. There was certainly no one at that moment in the passage, but, in the instant of my standing there, the door at the end opened and John appeared carrying a candle. I asked him whether he had come to the door earlier; but am satisfied that he had not. I do not like the situation; but although my senses were very much on the alert, and though it was some time before I could sleep, I must allow that I perceived nothing further of an untoward character."

With the return of spring, when his sister came to live with him for some months, Dr. Haynes's entries become more cheerful, and, indeed, no symptom of depression is discernible until the early part of September, when he was again left alone. And now, indeed, there is evidence that he was incommoded again, and that more pressingly. To this matter I will return in a moment, but I digress to put in a document which, rightly or wrongly, I believe to have a bearing on the thread of the story.

The account-books of Dr. Haynes, preserved along with his other papers, show, from a date but little later than that of his institution as archdeacon, a quarterly payment of £25 to J. L. Nothing could have been made of this, had it stood by itself. But

I connect with it a very dirty and ill-written letter, which, like another that I have quoted, was in a pocket in the cover of a diary. Of date or postmark there is no vestige, and the decipherment was not easy. It appears to run :

Dr Sr.

I have bin expctin to her off you theis last wicks, and not Haveing done so must supose you have not got mine witch was saying how me and my man had met in with bad times this season all seems to go cross with us on the farm and which way to look for the rent we have no knowledge of it this been the sad case with us if you would have the great [liberality *probably, but the exact spelling defies reproduction*] to send fourty pounds otherwise steps will have to be took which I should not wish. Has you was the Means of me losing my place with Dr. Pulteney I think it is only just what I am asking and you know best what I could say if I was Put to it but I do not wish anything of that unpleasant Nature being one that always wish to have everything Pleasant about me.

Your obedt Servt,
JANE LEE.

About the time at which I suppose this letter to have been written there is, in fact, a payment of £40 to J. L.

We return to the diary :

" *Oct.* 22.—At evening prayers, during the Psalms, I had that same experience which I recollect from last year. I was resting my hand on one of the carved figures, as before (I usually avoid that of the cat now), and—I was going to have said—a change came over it, but that seems attributing too much importance to what must, after all, be due to some physical affection in myself : at any rate, the wood seemed to become chilly and soft as if made of wet linen. I can assign the moment at which I became sensible of this. The choir were singing the words (*Set thou an ungodly man to be ruler over him and*) *let Satan stand at his right hand.*

"The whispering in my house was more persistent to-night. I seemed not to be rid of it in my room. I have not noticed this before. A nervous man, which I am not, and hope I am not becoming, would have been much annoyed, if not alarmed, by it. The cat was on the stairs to-night. I think it sits there always. There *is* no kitchen cat.

"*Nov.* 15.—Here again I must note a matter I do not understand. I am much troubled in sleep. No definite image presented itself, but I was pursued by the very vivid impression that wet lips were whispering into my ear with great rapidity and emphasis for some time together. After this, I suppose, I fell asleep, but was awakened with a start by a feeling as if a hand were laid on my shoulder. To my intense alarm I found myself standing at the top of the lowest flight of the first staircase. The moon was shining brightly enough through the large window to let me see that there was a large cat on the second or third step. I can make no comment. I crept up to bed again, I do not know how. Yes, mine is a heavy burden. [Then follows a line or two which has been scratched out. I fancy I read something like 'acted for the best.'] "

Not long after this it is evident to me that the archdeacon's firmness began to give way under the pressure of these phenomena. I omit as unnecessarily painful and distressing the ejaculations and prayers which, in the months of December and January, appear for the first time and become increasingly frequent. Throughout this time, however, he is obstinate in clinging to his post. Why he did not plead ill-health and take refuge at Bath or Brighton I cannot tell; my impression is that it would have done him no good; that he was a man who, if he had confessed himself beaten by the annoyances,

would have succumbed at once, and that he was conscious of this. He did seek to palliate them by
inviting visitors to his house. The result he has
noted in this fashion :

"*Jan.* 7.—I have prevailed on my cousin Allen to give
me a few days, and he is to occupy the chamber next to mine.

"*Jan.* 8.—A still night. Allen slept well, but complained
of the wind. My own experiences were as before : still whispering and whispering : what is it that he wants to say ?

"*Jan.* 9.—Allen thinks this a very noisy house. He thinks,
too, that my cat is an unusually large and fine specimen, but
very wild.

"*Jan.* 10.—Allen and I in the library until 11. He left
me twice to see what the maids were doing in the hall : returning the second time he told me he had seen one of them passing through the door at the end of the passage, and said if his
wife were here she would soon get them into better order. I
asked him what coloured dress the maid wore ; he said grey or
white. I supposed it would be so.

"*Jan.* 11.—Allen left me to-day. I must be firm."

These words, *I must be firm*, occur again and again
on subsequent days ; sometimes they are the only
entry. In these cases they are in an unusually large
hand, and dug into the paper in a way which must
have broken the pen that wrote them.

Apparently the archdeacon's friends did not remark
any change in his behaviour, and this gives me a high
idea of his courage and determination. The diary
tells us nothing more than I have indicated of the
last days of his life. The end of it all must be told
in the polished language of the obituary notice :

"The morning of the 26th of February was cold and tempestuous. At an early hour the servants had occasion to go into the front hall of the residence occupied by the lamented subject of these lines. What was their horror upon observing the form of their beloved and respected master lying upon the landing of the principal staircase in an attitude which inspired the gravest fears. Assistance was procured, and an universal consternation was experienced upon the discovery that he had been the object of a brutal and a murderous attack. The vertebral column was fractured in more than one place. This might have been the result of a fall : it appeared that the stair-carpet was loosened at one point. But, in addition to this, there were injuries inflicted upon the eyes, nose and mouth, as if by the agency of some savage animal, which, dreadful to relate, rendered those features unrecognizable. The vital spark was, it is needless to add, completely extinct, and had been so, upon the testimony of respectable medical authorities, for several hours. The author or authors of this mysterious outrage are alike buried in mystery, and the most active conjecture has hitherto failed to suggest a solution of the melancholy problem afforded by this appalling occurrence."

The writer goes on to reflect upon the probability that the writings of Mr. Shelley, Lord Byron, and M. Voltaire may have been instrumental in bringing about the disaster, and concludes by hoping, somewhat vaguely, that this event may " operate as an example to the rising generation " ; but this portion of his remarks need not be quoted in full.

I had already formed the conclusion that Dr. Haynes was responsible for the death of Dr. Pulteney. But the incident connected with the carved figure of death upon the archdeacon's stall was a very perplexing feature. The conjecture that it had been cut out of the wood of the Hanging Oak was not difficult, but seemed impossible to substantiate. However, I paid a visit to Barchester, partly with the view of finding out whether there were any relics of the wood-work to be heard of. I was introduced by one of the canons to the curator of the local museum, who was, my friend said, more likely to be able to give me information on the point than anyone else. I told this gentleman of the description of certain carved figures and arms formerly on the stalls, and asked whether any had survived. He was able to show me the arms of Dean West and some other fragments. These, he said, had been got from an old resident, who had also once owned a figure—perhaps one of those which I was inquiring for. There was a very odd thing about that figure, he said. " The old man who had it told me that he picked it up in a wood-yard, whence he had obtained the still extant pieces, and had taken it home for his children. On the way home he was fiddling about with it and it came in two in his hands, and a bit of paper dropped out. This he picked up and, just noticing that there was writing on it, put it into his pocket, and subsequently into a vase on his mantelpiece. I was at his house not very long ago, and happened to pick up the vase and turn it over to see whether there were any marks on it, and the paper fell into my hand. The old man, on my handing it to him, told me the story I have told you, and said I might keep the paper. It was crumpled and rather torn, so I have mounted it on a card, which I have here. If you can tell me what it means I shall be very glad, and also, I may say, a good deal surprised."

He gave me the card. The paper was quite legibly inscribed in an old hand, and this is what was on it :

> " When I grew in the Wood
> I was water'd wth Blood
> Now in the Church I stand
> Who that touches me with his Hand
> If a Bloody hand he bear
> I councell him to be ware
> Lest he be fetcht away
> Whether by night or day,
> But chiefly when the wind blows high
> In a night of February."

" This I drempt, 26 Febr. A⁰ 1699. JOHN AUSTIN."

" I suppose it is a charm or a spell : wouldn't you call it something of that kind ? " said the curator.

" Yes," I said, " I suppose one might. What became of the figure in which it was concealed ? "

" Oh, I forgot," said he. " The old man told me it was so ugly and frightened his children so much that he burnt it."

MARTIN'S CLOSE

Some few years back I was staying with the rector of a parish in the West, where the society to which I belong owns property. I was to go over some of this land : and, on the first morning of my visit, soon after breakfast, the estate carpenter and general handy man, John Hill, was announced as in readiness to accompany us. The rector asked which part of the parish we were to visit that morning. The estate map was produced, and when we had showed him our round, he put his finger on a particular spot. "Don't forget," he said, "to ask John Hill about Martin's Close when you get there. I should like to hear what he tells you." "What ought he to tell us ? " I said. "I haven't the slightest idea," said the rector, "or, if that is not exactly true, it will do till lunch-time." And here he was called away.

We set out ; John Hill is not a man to withhold such information as he possesses on any point, and you may gather from him much that is of interest about the people of the place and their talk. An unfamiliar word, or one that he thinks ought to be unfamiliar to you, he will usually spell—as c-o-b cob, and the like. It is not, however, relevant to my purpose to record his conversation before the moment when we reached Martin's Close. The bit of land is noticeable, for it is one of the smallest enclosures you are likely to see—a very few square yards, hedged in with quickset on all sides, and without any gate or gap leading into it. You might take it for a small cottage garden long deserted, but that it lies away from the village and bears no trace of cultivation. It is at no great distance from the road, and is part of what is there called a moor, in other words, a rough upland pasture cut up into largish fields.

"Why is this little bit hedged off so?" I asked, and John Hill (whose answer I cannot represent as perfectly as I should like) was not at fault. "That's what we call Martin's Close, sir: 'tes a curious thing 'bout that bit of land, sir: goes by the name of Martin's Close, sir. M-a-r-t-i-n Martin. Beg pardon, sir, did Rector tell you to make inquiry of me 'bout that, sir?" "Yes, he did." "Ah, I thought so much, sir. I was tell'n Rector 'bout that last week, and he was very much interested. It 'pears there's a murderer buried there, sir, by the name of Martin. Old Samuel Saunders, that formerly lived yurr at what we call South-town, sir, he had a long tale 'bout that, sir: terrible murder done 'pon a young woman, sir. Cut her throat and cast her in the water down yurr." "Was he hung for it?" "Yes, sir, he was hung just up yurr on the roadway, by what I've 'eard, on the Holy Innocents' Day, many 'undred years ago, by the man that went by the name of the bloody judge: terrible red and bloody, I've 'eard." "Was his name Jeffreys, do you think?" "Might be possible 'twas—Jeffreys—J-e-f—Jeffreys. I reckon 'twas, and the tale I've 'eard many times from Mr. Saunders,—how this young man Martin—George Martin—was troubled before his crule action come to light by the young woman's sperit." "How was that, do you know?" "No, sir, I don't exactly know how 'twas with it : but by what I've 'eard he was fairly tormented ; and rightly tu. Old Mr. Saunders, he told a history regarding a cupboard down yurr in the New Inn. According to what he related, this young woman's sperit come out of this cupboard : but I don't racollact the matter."

This was the sum of John Hill's information. We passed on, and in due time I reported what I had heard to the Rector. He was able to show me from the parish account-books that a gibbet had been paid for in 1684, and a grave dug in the following year, both for the benefit of George Martin ; but he was unable to suggest anyone in the parish, Saunders being now gone, who was likely to throw any further light on the story.

Naturally, upon my return to the neighbourhood of libraries, I made search in the more obvious places. The trial seemed to be nowhere reported. A newspaper of the time, and one or more news-letters, however, had some short notices, from which I learnt that, on the ground of local prejudice against the prisoner (he was described as a young gentleman of a good estate), the venue had been moved from Exeter

to London; that Jeffreys had been the judge, and
death the sentence, and that there had been some
" singular passages " in the evidence. Nothing
further transpired till September of this year. A
friend who knew me to be interested in Jeffreys then
sent me a leaf torn out of a second-hand bookseller's
catalogue with the entry : JEFFREYS, JUDGE : *Interesting old MS. trial for murder*, and so forth, from which
I gathered, to my delight, that I could become possessed, for a very few shillings, of what seemed to be
a verbatim report, in shorthand, of the Martin trial.
I telegraphed for the manuscript and got it. It was
a thin bound volume, provided with a title written
in longhand by someone in the eighteenth century,
who had also added this note : " My father, who took
these notes in court, told me that the prisoner's friends
had made interest with Judge Jeffreys that no report
should be put out : he had intended doing this himself when times were better, and had shew'd it to the
Revd. Mr. Glanvil, who incourag'd his design very
warmly, but death surpriz'd them both before it could
be brought to an accomplishment."

The initials W. G. are appended ; I am advised
that the original reporter may have been T. Gurney,
who appears in that capacity in more than one State
trial.

This was all that I could read for myself. After
no long delay I heard of someone who was capable
of deciphering the shorthand of the seventeenth century, and a little time ago the typewritten copy of

the whole manuscript was laid before me. The portions which I shall communicate here help to fill in the very imperfect outline which subsists in the memories of John Hill and, I suppose, one or two others who live on the scene of the events.

The report begins with a species of preface, the general effect of which is that the copy is not that actually taken in court, though it is a true copy in regard to the notes of what was said; but that the writer has added to it some "remarkable passages" that took place during the trial, and has made this present fair copy of the whole, intending at some favourable time to publish it; but has not put it into longhand, lest it should fall into the possession of unauthorized persons, and he or his family be deprived of the profit.

The report then begins:

This case came on to be tried on Wednesday, the 19th of November, between our sovereign lord the King, and George Martin Esquire, of (I take leave to omit some of the place-names), at a sessions of oyer and terminer and gaol delivery, at the Old Bailey, and the prisoner, being in Newgate, was brought to the bar.

Clerk of the Crown. George Martin, hold up thy hand (which he did).

Then the indictment was read, which set forth that the prisoner "not having the fear of God before his eyes, but being moved and seduced by the instigation of the devil, upon the 15th day of May, in the 36th year of our sovereign lord King Charles the Second, with force and arms in the parish aforesaid, in and upon Ann Clark, spinster, of the same place, in the peace of God and of our said sovereign lord the King then and there being, feloniously, wilfully, and of your malice aforethought did make an assault and with a certain knife value a penny the throat of the said Ann Clark then and there did cut, of the which wound the said Ann Clark then and there did die, and the body of the said Ann Clark did cast into a certain pond of water situate in the same parish (with more that is not material to our purpose) against the peace of our sovereign lord the King, his crown and dignity."

Then the prisoner prayed a copy of the indictment.

L. C. J. (Sir George Jeffreys). What is this? Sure you know that is never allowed. Besides, here is a plain indictment as ever I heard; you have nothing to do but to plead to it.

Pris. My lord, I apprehend there may be matter of law arising out of the indictment, and I would humbly beg the court to assign me counsel to consider of it. Besides, my lord, I believe it was done in another case : copy of the indictment was allowed.

L. C. J. What case was that?

Pris. Truly, my lord, I have been kept close prisoner ever since I came up from Exeter Castle, and no one allowed to come at me and no one to advise with.

L. C. J. But I say, what was that case you allege?

Pris. My lord, I cannot tell your lordship precisely the name of the case, but it is in my mind that there was such an one, and I would humbly desire——

L. C. J. All this is nothing. Name your case, and we will tell you whether there be any matter for you in it. God forbid but you should have anything that may be allowed you by law: but this is against law, and we must keep the course of the court.

Att.-Gen. (Sir Robert Sawyer). My lord, we pray for the King that he may be asked to plead.

Cl. of Ct. Are you guilty of the murder whereof you stand indicted, or not guilty?

Pris. My lord, I would humbly offer this to the court. If I plead now, shall I have an opportunity after to except against the indictment?

L. C. J. Yes, yes, that comes after verdict: that will be saved to you, and counsel assigned if there be matter of law: but that which you have now to do is to plead.

Then after some little parleying with the court (which seemed strange upon such a plain indictment) the prisoner pleaded *Not Guilty*.

Cl. of Ct. Cul-prit. How wilt thou be tried?

Pris. By God and my country.

Cl. of Ct. God send thee a good deliverance.

L. C. J. Why, how is this? Here has been a great to-do that you should not be tried at Exeter by your country, but be brought here to London,

and now you ask to be tried by your country. Must
we send you to Exeter again?

Pris. My lord, I understood it was the form.

L. C. J. So it is, man : we spoke only in the way
of pleasantness. Well, go on and swear the jury.

So they were sworn. I omit the names. There
was no challenging on the prisoner's part, for, as he
said, he did not know any of the persons called.
Thereupon the prisoner asked for the use of pen, ink,
and paper, to which the L. C. J. replied : " Ay, ay,
in God's name let him have it." Then the usual
charge was delivered to the jury, and the case opened
by the junior counsel for the King, Mr. Dolben.

The Attorney-General followed :

May it please your lordship, and you gentlemen of
the jury, I am of counsel for the King against the
prisoner at the bar. You have heard that he stands
indicted for a murder done upon the person of a
young girl. Such crimes as this you may perhaps
reckon to be not uncommon, and, indeed, in these
times, I am sorry to say it, there is scarce any fact
so barbarous and unnatural but what we may hear
almost daily instances of it. But I must confess that
in this murder that is charged upon the prisoner there
are some particular features that mark it out to be
such as I hope has but seldom if ever been perpetrated
upon English ground. For as we shall make it
appear, the person murdered was a poor country girl
(whereas the prisoner is a gentleman of a proper

estate) and, besides that, was one to whom Providence
had not given the full use of her intellects, but was
what is termed among us commonly an innocent or
natural : such an one, therefore, as one would have
supposed a gentleman of the prisoner's quality more
likely to overlook, or, if he did notice her, to be moved
to compassion for her unhappy condition, than to lift
up his hand against her in the very horrid and barbarous manner which we shall show you he used.

Now to begin at the beginning and open the matter
to you orderly : About Christmas of last year, that
is the year 1683, this gentleman, Mr. Martin, having
newly come back into his own country from the
University of Cambridge, some of his neighbours, to
show him what civility they could (for his family is
one that stands in very good repute all over that
country), entertained him here and there at their
Christmas merrymakings, so that he was constantly
riding to and fro, from one house to another, and
sometimes, when the place of his destination was
distant, or for other reason, as the unsafeness of the
roads, he would be constrained to lie the night at an
inn. In this way it happened that he came, a day or
two after the Christmas, to the place where this young
girl lived with her parents, and put up at the inn
there, called the New Inn, which is, as I am informed,
a house of good repute. Here was some dancing
going on among the people of the place, and Ann
Clark had been brought in, it seems, by her elder sister
to look on ; but being, as I have said, of weak under-

standing, and, besides that, very uncomely in her appearance, it was not likely she should take much part in the merriment; and accordingly was but standing by in a corner of the room. The prisoner at the bar, seeing her, one must suppose by way of a jest, asked her would she dance with him. And in spite of what her sister and others could say to prevent it and to dissuade her——

L. C. J. Come, Mr. Attorney, we are not set here to listen to tales of Christmas parties in taverns. I would not interrupt you, but sure you have more weighty matters than this. You will be telling us next what tune they danced to.

Att. My lord, I would not take up the time of the court with what is not material: but we reckon it to be material to show how this unlikely acquaintance begun: and as for the tune, I believe, indeed, our evidence will show that even that hath a bearing on the matter in hand.

L. C. J. Go on, go on, in God's name: but give us nothing that is impertinent.

Att. Indeed, my lord, I will keep to my matter. But, gentlemen, having now shown you, as I think, enough of this first meeting between the murdered person and the prisoner, I will shorten my tale so far as to say that from then on there were frequent meetings of the two: for the young woman was greatly tickled with having got hold (as she conceived it) of so likely a sweetheart, and he being once a week at least in the habit of passing through the street where

she lived, she would be always on the watch for him ;
and it seems they had a signal arranged : he should
whistle the tune that was played at the tavern : it is
a tune, as I am informed, well known in that country,
and has a burden, " *Madam, will you walk, will you talk
with me ?* "

L. C. J. Ay, I remember it in my own country,
in Shropshire. It runs somehow thus, doth it not ?
[Here his lordship whistled a part of a tune, which
was very observable, and seemed below the dignity
of the court. And it appears he felt it so himself, for
he said :] But this is by the mark, and I doubt it is
the first time we have had dance-tunes in this court.
The most part of the dancing we give occasion for
is done at Tyburn. [Looking at the prisoner, who
appeared very much disordered.] You said the tune
was material to your case, Mr. Attorney, and upon
my life I think Mr. Martin agrees with you. What
ails you, man ? staring like a player that sees a ghost !

Pris. My lord, I was amazed at hearing such
trivial, foolish things as they bring against me.

L. C. J. Well, well, it lies upon Mr. Attorney to
show whether they be trivial or not : but I must say,
if he has nothing worse than this he has said, you
have no great cause to be in amaze. Doth it not lie
something deeper ? But go on, Mr. Attorney.

Att. My lord and gentlemen—all that I have said
so far you may indeed very reasonably reckon as
having an appearance of triviality. And, to be sure,
had the matter gone no further than the humouring

of a poor silly girl by a young gentleman of quality,
it had been very well. But to proceed. We shall
make it appear that after three or four weeks the
prisoner became contracted to a young gentlewoman
of that country, one suitable every way to his own
condition, and such an arrangement was on foot that
seemed to promise him a happy and a reputable living.
But within no very long time it seems that this young
gentlewoman, hearing of the jest that was going about
that countryside with regard to the prisoner and Ann
Clark, conceived that it was not only an unworthy
carriage on the part of her lover, but a derogation to
herself that he should suffer his name to be sport for
tavern company : and so without more ado she, with
the consent of her parents, signified to the prisoner
that the match between them was at an end. We
shall show you that upon the receipt of this intelligence the prisoner was greatly enraged against Ann
Clark as being the cause of his misfortune (though
indeed there was nobody answerable for it but himself), and that he made use of many outrageous
expressions and threatenings against her, and subsequently upon meeting with her both abused her and
struck at her with his whip : but she, being but a
poor innocent, could not be persuaded to desist from
her attachment to him, but would often run after him
testifying with gestures and broken words the affection she had to him : until she was become, as he
said, the very plague of his life. Yet, being that
affairs in which he was now engaged necessarily took

him by the house in which she lived, he could not
(as I am willing to believe he would otherwise have
done) avoid meeting with her from time to time. We
shall further show you that this was the posture of
things up to the 15th day of May in this present year.
Upon that day the prisoner comes riding through the
village, as of custom, and met with the young woman :
but in place of passing her by, as he had lately done,
he stopped, and said some words to her with which
she appeared wonderfully pleased, and so left her ;
and after that day she was nowhere to be found,
notwithstanding a strict search was made for her.
The next time of the prisoner's passing through the
place, her relations inquired of him whether he should
know anything of her whereabouts ; which he totally
denied. They expressed to him their fears lest her
weak intellects should have been upset by the attention he had showed her, and so she might have
committed some rash act against her own life, calling
him to witness the same time how often they had
beseeched him to desist from taking notice of her, as
fearing trouble might come of it : but this, too, he
easily laughed away. But in spite of this light behaviour, it was noticeable in him that about this time
his carriage and demeanour changed, and it was said
of him that he seemed a troubled man. And here I
come to a passage to which I should not dare to ask
your attention, but that it appears to me to be founded
in truth, and is supported by testimony deserving of
credit. And, gentlemen, to my judgment it doth

afford a great instance of God's revenge against
murder, and that He will require the blood of the
innocent.

[Here Mr. Attorney made a pause, and shifted with
his papers : and it was thought remarkable by me
and others, because he was a man not easily dashed.]

L. C. J. Well, Mr. Attorney, what is your
instance ?

Att. My lord, it is a strange one, and the truth
is that, of all the cases I have been concerned in, I
cannot call to mind the like of it. But to be short,
gentlemen, we shall bring you testimony that Ann
Clark was seen after this 15th of May, and that, at
such time as she was so seen, it was impossible she
could have been a living person.

[Here the people made a hum, and a good deal of
laughter, and the Court called for silence, and when
it was made]——

L. C. J. Why, Mr. Attorney, you might save up
this tale for a week ; it will be Christmas by that time,
and you can frighten your cook-maids with it [at
which the people laughed again, and the prisoner also,
as it seemed]. God, man, what are you prating of
—ghosts and Christmas jigs and tavern company—
and here is a man's life at stake ! (To the prisoner) :
And you, sir, I would have you know there is not
so much occasion for you to make merry neither.
You were not brought here for that, and if I know

Mr. Attorney, he has more in his brief than he has shown yet. Go on, Mr. Attorney. I need not, mayhap, have spoken so sharply, but you must confess your course is something unusual.

Att. Nobody knows it better than I, my lord : but I shall bring it to an end with a round turn. I shall show you, gentlemen, that Ann Clark's body was found in the month of June, in a pond of water, with the throat cut : that a knife belonging to the prisoner was found in the same water : that he made efforts to recover the said knife from the water : that the coroner's quest brought in a verdict against the prisoner at the bar, and that therefore he should by course have been tried at Exeter : but that, suit being made on his behalf, on account that an impartial jury could not be found to try him in his own country, he hath had that singular favour shown him that he should be tried here in London. And so we will proceed to call our evidence.

Then the facts of the acquaintance between the prisoner and Ann Clark were proved, and also the coroner's inquest. I pass over this portion of the trial, for it offers nothing of special interest.

Sarah Arscott was next called and sworn.

Att. What is your occupation ?

S. I keep the New Inn at ——.

Att. Do you know the prisoner at the bar ?

S. Yes : he was often at our house since he come first at Christmas of last year.

Att. Did you know Ann Clark?

S. Yes, very well.

Att. Pray, what manner of person was she in her appearance?

S. She was a very short thick-made woman: I do not know what else you would have me say.

Att. Was she comely?

S. No, not by no manner of means: she was very uncomely, poor child! She had a great face and hanging chops and a very bad colour like a puddock.

L. C. J. What is that, mistress? What say you she was like?

S. My lord, I ask pardon; I heard Esquire Martin say she looked like a puddock in the face; and so she did.

L. C. J. Did you that? Can you interpret her, Mr. Attorney?

Att. My lord, I apprehend it is the country word for a toad.

L. C. J. Oh, a hop-toad! Ay, go on.

Att. Will you give an account to the jury of what passed between you and the prisoner at the bar in May last?

S. Sir, it was this. It was about nine o'clock the evening after that Ann did not come home, and I was about my work in the house; there was no company there only Thomas Snell, and it was foul weather. Esquire Martin came in and called for some drink, and I, by way of pleasantry, I said to him, " Squire, have you been looking after your

sweetheart ? " and he flew out at me in a passion and
desired I would not use such expressions. I was
amazed at that, because we were accustomed to joke
with him about her.

L. C. J. Who, her ?

S. Ann Clark, my lord. And we had not heard
the news of his being contracted to a young gentlewoman elsewhere, or I am sure I should have used
better manners. So I said nothing, but being I was
a little put out, I begun singing, to myself as it were,
the song they danced to the first time they met, for
I thought it would prick him. It was the same that
he was used to sing when he came down the street ;
I have heard it very often : " *Madam, will you walk,
will you talk with me ?* " And it fell out that I needed
something that was in the kitchen. So I went out
to get it, and all the time I went on singing, something louder and more bold-like. And as I was there
all of a sudden I thought I heard someone answering
outside the house, but I could not be sure because
of the wind blowing so high. So then I stopped
singing, and now I heard it plain, saying, " *Yes, sir,
I will walk, I will talk with you,*" and I knew the voice
for Ann Clark's voice.

Att. How did you know it to be her voice ?

S. It was impossible I could be mistaken. She
had a dreadful voice, a kind of a squalling voice, in
particular if she tried to sing. And there was nobody
in the village that could counterfeit it, for they often
tried. So, hearing that, I was glad, because we were

all in an anxiety to know what was gone with her : for though she was a natural, she had a good disposition and was very tractable : and says I to myself, " What, child ! are you returned, then ? " and I ran into the front room, and said to Squire Martin as I passed by, " Squire, here is your sweetheart back again : shall I call her in ? " and with that I went to open the door ; but Squire Martin he caught hold of me, and it seemed to me he was out of his wits, or near upon. " Hold, woman," says he, " in God's name ! " and I know not what else : he was all of a shake. Then I was angry, and said I, " What ! are you not glad that poor child is found ? " and I called to Thomas Snell and said, " If the Squire will not let me, do you open the door and call her in." So Thomas Snell went and opened the door, and the wind setting that way blew in and overset the two candles that was all we had lighted : and Esquire Martin fell away from holding me ; I think he fell down on the floor, but we were wholly in the dark, and it was a minute or two before I got a light again : and while I was feeling for the fire-box, I am not certain but I heard someone step 'cross the floor, and I am sure I heard the door of the great cupboard that stands in the room open and shut to. Then, when I had a light again, I see Esquire Martin on the settle, all white and sweaty as if he had swounded away, and his arms hanging down ; and I was going to help him ; but just then it caught my eye that there was something like a bit of a dress shut into the cupboard door, and it came

to my mind I had heard that door shut. So I thought
it might be some person had run in when the light
was quenched, and was hiding in the cupboard. So
I went up closer and looked : and there was a bit of
a black stuff cloak, and just below it an edge of a
brown stuff dress, both sticking out of the shut of
the door : and both of them was low down, as if the
person that had them on might be crouched down
inside.

Att. What did you take it to be ?

S. I took it to be a woman's dress.

Att. Could you make any guess whom it belonged
to ? Did you know anyone who wore such a dress ?

S. It was a common stuff, by what I could see.
I have seen many women wearing such a stuff in our
parish.

Att. Was it like Ann Clark's dress ?

S. She used to wear just such a dress : but I could
not say on my oath it was hers.

Att. Did you observe anything else about it ?

S. I did notice that it looked very wet : but it
was foul weather outside.

L. C. J. Did you feel of it, mistress ?

S. No, my lord, I did not like to touch it.

L. C. J. Not like ? Why that ? Are you so
nice that you scruple to feel of a wet dress ?

S. Indeed, my lord, I cannot very well tell why :
only it had a nasty ugly look about it.

L. C. J. Well, go on.

S. Then I called again to Thomas Snell, and bid

him come to me and catch anyone that come out
when I should open the cupboard door, "for," says
I, "there is someone hiding within, and I would know
what she wants." And with that Squire Martin gave
a sort of a cry or a shout and ran out of the house
into the dark, and I felt the cupboard door pushed
out against me while I held it, and Thomas Snell
helped me : but for all we pressed to keep it shut as
hard as we could, it was forced out against us, and
we had to fall back.

L. C. J. And pray what came out—a mouse ?

S. No, my lord, it was greater than a mouse, but
I could not see what it was : it fleeted very swift over
the floor and out at the door.

L. C. J. But come ; what did it look like ? Was
it a person ?

S. My lord, I cannot tell what it was, but it ran
very low, and it was of a dark colour. We were
both daunted by it, Thomas Snell and I, but we made
all the haste we could after it to the door that stood
open. And we looked out, but it was dark and we
could see nothing.

L. C. J. Was there no tracks of it on the floor ?
What floor have you there ?

S. It is a flagged floor and sanded, my lord, and
there was an appearance of a wet track on the floor,
but we could make nothing of it, neither Thomas
Snell nor me, and besides, as I said, it was a foul
night.

L. C. J. Well, for my part, I see not—though to

be sure it is an odd tale she tells—what you would do with this evidence.

Att. My lord, we bring it to show the suspicious carriage of the prisoner immediately after the disappearance of the murdered person : and we ask the jury's consideration of that ; and also to the matter of the voice heard without the house.

Then the prisoner asked some questions not very material, and Thomas Snell was next called, who gave evidence to the same effect as Mrs. Arscott, and added the following :

Att. Did anything pass between you and the prisoner during the time Mrs. Arscott was out of the room ?

Th. I had a piece of twist in my pocket.

Att. Twist of what ?

Th. Twist of tobacco, sir, and I felt a disposition to take a pipe of tobacco. So I found a pipe on the chimney-piece, and being it was twist, and in regard of me having by an oversight left my knife at my house, and me not having over many teeth to pluck at it, as your lordship or anyone else may have a view by their own eyesight——

L. C. J. What is the man talking about ? Come to the matter, fellow ! Do you think we sit here to look at your teeth ?

Th. No, my lord, nor I would not you should do, God forbid ! I know your honours have better employment, and better teeth, I would not wonder.

L. C. J. Good God, what a man is this! Yes, I *have* better teeth, and that you shall find if you keep not to the purpose.

Th. I humbly ask pardon, my lord, but so it was. And I took upon me, thinking no harm, to ask Squire Martin to lend me his knife to cut my tobacco. And he felt first of one pocket and then of another and it was not there at all. And says I, "What! have you lost your knife, Squire?" And up he gets and feels again and he sat down, and such a groan as he gave. "Good God!" he says, "I must have left it there." "But," says I, "Squire, by all appearance it is *not* there. Did you set a value on it," says I, "you might have it cried." But he sat there and put his head between his hands and seemed to take no notice to what I said. And then it was Mistress Arscott come tracking back out of the kitchen place.

Asked if he heard the voice singing outside the house, he said "No," but the door into the kitchen was shut, and there was a high wind: but says that no one could mistake Ann Clark's voice.

Then a boy, William Reddaway, about thirteen years of age, was called, and by the usual questions, put by the Lord Chief Justice, it was ascertained that he knew the nature of an oath. And so he was sworn. His evidence referred to a time about a week later.

Att. Now, child, don't be frighted: there is no one here will hurt you if you speak the truth.

L. C. J. Ay, if he speak the truth. But remem-

ber, child, thou art in the presence of the great God
of heaven and earth, that hath the keys of hell, and
of us that are the king's officers, and have the keys
of Newgate; and remember, too, there is a man's
life in question; and if thou tellest a lie, and by that
means he comes to an ill end, thou art no better than
his murderer; and so speak the truth.

Att.   Tell the jury what you know, and speak out.
Where were you on the evening of the 23rd of May
last?

L. C. J.   Why, what does such a boy as this know
of days.   Can you mark the day, boy?

W.   Yes, my lord, it was the day before our feast,
and I was to spend sixpence there, and that falls a
month before Midsummer Day.

One of the Jury.   My lord, we cannot hear what he
says.

L. C. J.   He says he remembers the day because
it was the day before the feast they had there, and
he had sixpence to lay out.   Set him up on the table
there.   Well, child, and where wast thou then?

W.   Keeping cows on the moor, my lord.

But, the boy using the country speech, my lord
could not well apprehend him, and so asked if there
was anyone that could interpret him, and it was
answered the parson of the parish was there, and he
was accordingly sworn and so the evidence given.
The boy said:

" I was on the moor about six o'clock, and sitting

behind a bush of furze near a pond of water: and
the prisoner came very cautiously and looking about
him, having something like a long pole in his hand,
and stopped a good while as if he would be listening,
and then began to feel in the water with the pole:
and I being very near the water—not above five
yards—heard as if the pole struck up against something that made a wallowing sound, and the prisoner
dropped the pole and threw himself on the ground,
and rolled himself about very strangely with his hands
to his ears, and so after a while got up and went
creeping away."

Asked if he had had any communication with the
prisoner, "Yes, a day or two before, the prisoner,
hearing I was used to be on the moor, he asked me
if I had seen a knife laying about, and said he would
give sixpence to find it. And I said I had not seen
any such thing, but I would ask about. Then he said
he would give me sixpence to say nothing, and so
he did.

L. C. J. And was that the sixpence you were to
lay out at the feast?
W. Yes, if you please, my lord.

Asked if he had observed anything particular as to
the pond of water, he said, " No, except that it begun
to have a very ill smell and the cows would not drink
of it for some days before."

Asked if he had ever seen the prisoner and Ann
Clark in company together, he began to cry very

much, and it was a long time before they could get him to speak intelligibly. At last the parson of the parish, Mr. Matthews, got him to be quiet, and the question being put to him again, he said he had seen Ann Clark waiting on the moor for the prisoner at some way off, several times since last Christmas.

Att. Did you see her close, so as to be sure it was she?

W. Yes, quite sure.

L. C. J. How quite sure, child?

W. Because she would stand and jump up and down and clap her arms like a goose (which he called by some country name: but the parson explained it to be a goose). And then she was of such a shape that it could not be no one else.

Att. What was the last time that you so saw her?

Then the witness began to cry again and clung very much to Mr. Matthews, who bid him not be frightened. And so at last he told this story: that on the day before their feast (being the same evening that he had before spoken of) after the prisoner had gone away, it being then twilight and he very desirous to get home, but afraid for the present to stir from where he was lest the prisoner should see him, remained some few minutes behind the bush, looking on the pond, and saw something dark come up out of the water at the edge of the pond farthest away from him, and so up the bank. And when it got to the top where he could see it plain against the sky,

it stood up and flapped the arms up and down, and
then run off very swiftly in the same direction the
prisoner had taken : and being asked very strictly
who he took it to be, he said upon his oath that it
could be nobody but Ann Clark.

Thereafter his master was called, and gave evidence
that the boy had come home very late that evening
and been chided for it, and that he seemed very much
amazed, but could give no account of the reason.

Att. My lord, we have done with our evidence
for the King.

Then the Lord Chief Justice called upon the
prisoner to make his defence ; which he did, though
at no great length, and in a very halting way, saying
that he hoped the jury would not go about to take
his life on the evidence of a parcel of country people
and children that would believe any idle tale ; and
that he had been very much prejudiced in his trial ;
at which the L. C. J. interrupted him, saying that he
had had singular favour shown to him in having his
trial removed from Exeter, which the prisoner acknowledging, said that he meant rather that since he
was brought to London there had not been care taken
to keep him secured from interruption and disturbance. Upon which the L. C. J. ordered the Marshal
to be called, and questioned him about the safe keeping of the prisoner, but could find nothing : except
the Marshal said that he had been informed by the
underkeeper that they had seen a person outside his

door or going up the stairs to it : but there was no
possibility the person should have got in. And it
being inquired further what sort of person this might
be, the Marshal could not speak to it save by hearsay,
which was not allowed. And the prisoner, being
asked if this was what he meant, said no, he knew
nothing of that, but it was very hard that a man should
not be suffered to be at quiet when his life stood on
it. But it was observed he was very hasty in his
denial. And so he said no more, and called no witnesses. Whereupon the Attorney-General spoke to
the jury. [A full report of what he said is given,
and, if time allowed, I would extract that portion in
which he dwells on the alleged appearance of the
murdered person : he quotes some authorities of
ancient date, as St. Augustine *de cura pro mortuis
gerenda* (a favourite book of reference with the old
writers on the supernatural) and also cites some cases
which may be seen in Glanvil's, but more conveniently
in Mr. Lang's books. He does not, however, tell us
more of those cases than is to be found in print.]

The Lord Chief Justice then summed up the
evidence for the jury. His speech, again, contains
nothing that I find worth copying out : but he was
naturally impressed with the singular character of
the evidence, saying that he had never heard such
given in his experience ; but that there was nothing
in law to set it aside, and that the jury must consider
whether they believed these witnesses or not.

And the jury after a very short consultation brought the prisoner in Guilty.

So he was asked whether he had anything to say in arrest of judgment, and pleaded that his name was spelt wrong in the indictment, being Martin with an I, whereas it should be with a Y. But this was overruled as not material, Mr. Attorney saying, moreover, that he could bring evidence to show that the prisoner by times wrote it as it was laid in the indictment. And, the prisoner having nothing further to offer, sentence of death was passed upon him, and that he should be hanged in chains upon a gibbet near the place where the fact was committed, and that execution should take place upon the 28th December next ensuing, being Innocents' Day.

Thereafter the prisoner being to all appearance in a state of desperation, made shift to ask the L. C. J. that his relations might be allowed to come to him during the short time he had to live.

L. C. J. Ay, with all my heart, so it be in the presence of the keeper; and Ann Clark may come to you as well, for what I care.

At which the prisoner broke out and cried to his lordship not to use such words to him, and his lordship very angrily told him he deserved no tenderness at any man's hands for a cowardly butcherly murderer that had not the stomach to take the reward of his deeds : " and I hope to God," said he, " that she *will* be with you by day and by night till an end is

made of you." Then the prisoner was removed,
and, so far as I saw, he was in a swound, and the
Court broke up.

I cannot refrain from observing that the prisoner
during all the time of the trial seemed to be more
uneasy than is commonly the case even in capital
causes : that, for example, he was looking narrowly
among the people and often turning round very
sharply, as if some person might be at his ear. It
was also very noticeable at this trial what a silence
the people kept, and further (though this might
not be otherwise than natural in that season of the
year), what a darkness and obscurity there was in
the court room, lights being brought in not long
after two o'clock in the day, and yet no fog in the
town.

It was not without interest that I heard lately from
some young men who had been giving a concert in
the village I speak of, that a very cold reception was
accorded to the song which has been mentioned in
this narrative : " *Madam, will you walk ?* " It came
out in some talk they had next morning with some
of the local people that that song was regarded with
an invincible repugnance ; it was not so, they believed,
at North Tawton, but here it was reckoned to be
unlucky. However, why that view was taken no
one had the shadow of an idea.

MR. HUMPHREYS AND HIS INHERITANCE

ABOUT fifteen years ago, on a date late in August or early in September, a train drew up at Wilsthorpe, a country station in Eastern England. Out of it stepped (with other passengers) a rather tall and reasonably good-looking young man, carrying a handbag and some papers tied up in a packet. He was expecting to be met, one would say, from the way in which he looked about him : and he was, as obviously, expected. The stationmaster ran forward a step or two, and then, seeming to recollect himself, turned and beckoned to a stout and consequential person with a short round beard who was scanning the train with some appearance of bewilderment. "Mr. Cooper," he called out,—"Mr. Cooper, I think this is your gentleman"; and then to the passenger who had just alighted, "Mr. Humphreys, sir? Glad to bid you welcome to Wilsthorpe. There's a cart from the Hall for your luggage, and here's Mr. Cooper, what I think you know." Mr. Cooper had hurried up, and now raised his hat and shook hands. "Very pleased, I'm sure," he said, "to give the echo to Mr. Palmer's kind words. I should have been the first to render expression to them but for the face not being familiar to me, Mr.

Humphreys. May your residence among us be marked as a red-letter day, sir." "Thank you very much, Mr. Cooper," said Humphreys, "for your good wishes, and Mr. Palmer also. I do hope very much that this change of—er—tenancy—which you must all regret, I am sure—will not be to the detriment of those with whom I shall be brought in contact." He stopped, feeling that the words were not fitting themselves together in the happiest way, and Mr. Cooper cut in, "Oh, you may rest satisfied of that, Mr. Humphreys. I'll take it upon myself to assure you, sir, that a warm welcome awaits you on all sides. And as to any change of propriety turning out detrimental to the neighbourhood, well, your late uncle——" And here Mr. Cooper also stopped, possibly in obedience to an inner monitor, possibly because Mr. Palmer, clearing his throat loudly, asked Humphreys for his ticket. The two men left the little station, and—at Humphreys' suggestion—decided to walk to Mr. Cooper's house, where luncheon was awaiting them.

The relation in which these personages stood to each other can be explained in a very few lines. Humphreys had inherited—quite unexpectedly—a property from an uncle : neither the property nor the uncle had he ever seen. He was alone in the world—a man of good ability and kindly nature, whose employment in a Government office for the last four or five years had not gone far to fit him for the life of a country gentleman. He was studious

and rather diffident, and had few out-of-door pursuits
except golf and gardening. To-day he had come
down for the first time to visit Wilsthorpe and confer
with Mr. Cooper, the bailiff, as to the matters which
needed immediate attention. It may be asked how
this came to be his first visit? Ought he not in
decency to have attended his uncle's funeral? The
answer is not far to seek: he had been abroad at the
time of the death, and his address had not been at once
procurable. So he had put off coming to Wilsthorpe
till he heard that all things were ready for him. And
now we find him arrived at Mr. Cooper's comfortable
house, facing the parsonage, and having just shaken
hands with the smiling Mrs. and Miss Cooper.

During the minutes that preceded the announcement of luncheon the party settled themselves on
elaborate chairs in the drawing-room, Humphreys,
for his part, perspiring quietly in the consciousness
that stock was being taken of him.

" I was just saying to Mr. Humphreys, my dear,"
said Mr. Cooper, " that I hope and trust that his
residence among us here in Wilsthorpe will be marked
as a red-letter day."

" Yes, indeed, I'm sure," said Mrs. Cooper heartily,
" and many, many of them."

Miss Cooper murmured words to the same effect,
and Humphreys attempted a pleasantry about painting
the whole calendar red, which, though greeted with
shrill laughter, was evidently not fully understood.
At this point they proceeded to luncheon.

"Do you know this part of the country at all, Mr. Humphreys?" said Mrs. Cooper, after a short interval. This was a better opening.

"No, I'm sorry to say I do *not*," said Humphreys. "It seems very pleasant, what I could see of it coming down in the train."

"Oh, it *is* a pleasant part. Really, I sometimes say I don't know a nicer district, for the country; and the people round, too: such a quantity always going on. But I'm afraid you've come a little late for some of the better garden parties, Mr. Humphreys."

"I suppose I have; dear me, what a pity!" said Humphreys, with a gleam of relief; and then, feeling that something more could be got out of this topic, "But after all, you see, Mrs. Cooper, even if I could have been here earlier, I should have been cut off from them, should I not? My poor uncle's recent death, you know——"

"Oh dear, Mr. Humphreys, to be sure; what a dreadful thing of me to say!" (And Mr. and Miss Cooper seconded the proposition inarticulately.) "What must you have thought? I *am* so sorry: you must really forgive me."

"Not at all, Mrs. Cooper, I assure you. I can't honestly assert that my uncle's death was a great grief to me, for I had never seen him. All I meant was that I supposed I shouldn't be expected to take part for some little time in festivities of that kind."

"Now, really it's very kind of you to take it in that way, Mr. Humphreys, isn't it, George? And you *do* forgive me? But only fancy! You never saw poor old Mr. Wilson!"

"Never in my life; nor did I ever have a letter from him. But, by the way, you have something to forgive *me* for. I've never thanked you, except by letter, for all the trouble you've taken to find people to look after me at the Hall."

"Oh, I'm sure that was nothing, Mr. Humphreys; but I really do think that you'll find them give satisfaction. The man and his wife whom we've got for the butler and housekeeper we've known for a number of years: such a nice respectable couple, and Mr. Cooper, I'm sure, can answer for the men in the stables and gardens."

"Yes, Mr. Humphreys, they're a good lot. The head gardener's the only one who's stopped on from Mr. Wilson's time. The major part of the employees, as you no doubt saw by the will, received legacies from the old gentleman and retired from their posts, and as the wife says, your housekeeper and butler are calculated to render you every satisfaction."

"So everything, Mr. Humphreys, is ready for you to step in this very day, according to what I understood you to wish," said Mrs. Cooper. "Everything, that is, except company, and there I'm afraid you'll find yourself quite at a standstill. Only we did understand it was your intention to move in at once. If not, I'm sure you know we should have been only too pleased for you to stay here."

"I'm quite sure you would, Mrs. Cooper, and I'm

very grateful to you. But I thought I had really
better make the plunge at once. I'm accustomed to
living alone, and there will be quite enough to occupy
my evenings—looking over papers and books and
so on—for some time to come. I thought if Mr.
Cooper could spare the time this afternoon to go
over the house and grounds with me——"

"Certainly, certainly, Mr. Humphreys. My time
is your own, up to any hour you please."

"Till dinner-time, father, you mean," said Miss
Cooper. "Don't forget we're going over to the
Brasnetts'. And have you got all the garden keys?"

"Are you a great gardener, Miss Cooper?" said
Mr. Humphreys. "I wish you would tell me what
I'm to expect at the Hall."

"Oh, I don't know about a *great* gardener, Mr.
Humphreys: I'm very fond of flowers—but the Hall
garden might be made quite lovely, I often say. It's
very old-fashioned as it is: and a great deal of shrubbery. There's an old temple, besides, and a maze."

"Really? Have you explored it ever?"

"No-o," said Miss Cooper, drawing in her lips
and shaking her head. "I've often longed to try,
but old Mr. Wilson always kept it locked. He
wouldn't even let Lady Wardrop into it. (She lives
near here, at Bentley, you know, and she's a *great*
gardener, if you like.) That's why I asked father if
he had all the keys."

"I see. Well, I must evidently look into that,
and show you over it when I've learnt the way."

"Oh, thank you so much, Mr. Humphreys! Now I shall have the laugh of Miss Foster (that's our rector's daughter, you know; they're away on their holiday now—such nice people). We always had a joke between us which should be the first to get into the maze."

"I think the garden keys must be up at the house," said Mr. Cooper, who had been looking over a large bunch. "There is a number there in the library. Now, Mr. Humphreys, if you're prepared, we might bid good-bye to these ladies and set forward on our little tour of exploration."

As they came out of Mr. Cooper's front gate, Humphreys had to run the gauntlet—not of an organized demonstration, but of a good deal of touching of hats and careful contemplation from the men and women who had gathered in somewhat unusual numbers in the village street. He had, further, to exchange some remarks with the wife of the lodge-keeper as they passed the park gates, and with the lodge-keeper himself, who was attending to the park road. I cannot, however, spare the time to report the progress fully. As they traversed the half-mile or so between the lodge and the house, Humphreys took occasion to ask his companion some question which brought up the topic of his late uncle, and it did not take long before Mr. Cooper was embarked upon a disquisition.

"It is singular to think, as the wife was saying

just now, that you should never have seen the old
gentleman. And yet—you won't misunderstand me,
Mr. Humphreys, I feel confident, when I say that in
my opinion there would have been but little con-
geniality betwixt yourself and him. Not that I have
a word to say in deprecation—not a single word.
I can tell you what he was," said Mr. Cooper, pulling
up suddenly and fixing Humphreys with his eye.
" Can tell you what he was in a nutshell, as the saying
goes. He was a complete, thorough valentudinarian.
That describes him to a T. That's what he was,
sir, a complete valentudinarian. No participation
in what went on around him. I did venture, I think,
to send you a few words of cutting from our local
paper, which I took the occasion to contribute on
his decease. If I recollect myself aright, such is
very much the ghist of them. But don't, Mr.
Humphreys," continued Cooper, tapping him im-
pressively on the chest,—" don't you run away with
the impression that I wish to say aught but what is
most creditable—*most* creditable—of your respected
uncle and my late employer. Upright, Mr.
Humphreys—open as the day ; liberal to all in his
dealings. He had the heart to feel and the hand
to accommodate. But there it was : there was
the stumbling-block—his unfortunate health—or, as
I might more truly phrase it, his *want* of health."

" Yes, poor man. Did he suffer from any special
disorder before his last illness—which, I take it,
was little more than old age ? "

" Just that, Mr. Humphreys—just that. The flash flickering slowly away in the pan," said Cooper, with what he considered an appropriate gesture,—" the golden bowl gradually ceasing to vibrate. But as to your other question I should return a negative answer. General absence of vitality ? yes : special complaint ? no, unless you reckon a nasty cough he had with him. Why, here we are pretty much at the house. A handsome mansion, Mr. Humphreys, don't you consider ? "

It deserved the epithet, on the whole : but it was oddly proportioned—a very tall red-brick house, with a plain parapet concealing the roof almost entirely. It gave the impression of a town house set down in the country ; there was a basement, and a rather imposing flight of steps leading up to the front door. It seemed also, owing to its height, to desiderate wings, but there were none. The stables and other offices were concealed by trees. Humphreys guessed its probable date as 1770 or thereabouts.

The mature couple who had been engaged to act as butler and cook-housekeeper were waiting inside the front door, and opened it as their new master approached. Their name, Humphreys already knew, was Calton ; of their appearance and manner he formed a favourable impression in the few minutes' talk he had with them. It was agreed that he should go through the plate and the cellar next day with Mr. Calton, and that Mrs. C. should have a talk with him about linen, bedding, and so on—what there

was, and what there ought to be. Then he and
Cooper, dismissing the Caltons for the present, began
their view of the house. Its topography is not of
importance to this story. The large rooms on the
ground floor were satisfactory, especially the library,
which was as large as the dining-room, and had
three tall windows facing east. The bedroom prepared for Humphreys was immediately above it.
There were many pleasant, and a few really interesting, old pictures. None of the furniture was new,
and hardly any of the books were later than the
seventies. After hearing of and seeing the few
changes his uncle had made in the house, and contemplating a shiny portrait of him which adorned
the drawing-room, Humphreys was forced to agree
with Cooper that in all probability there would have
been little to attract him in his predecessor. It made
him rather sad that he could not be sorry—*dolebat se
dolere non posse*—for the man who, whether with or
without some feeling of kindliness towards his
unknown nephew, had contributed so much to his
well-being; for he felt that Wilsthorpe was a place
in which he could be happy, and especially happy,
it might be, in its library.

And now it was time to go over the garden: the
empty stables could wait, and so could the laundry.
So to the garden they addressed themselves, and it
was soon evident that Miss Cooper had been right
in thinking that there were possibilities. Also that
Mr. Cooper had done well in keeping on the gardener.

The deceased Mr. Wilson might not have, indeed plainly had not, been imbued with the latest views on gardening, but whatever had been done here had been done under the eye of a knowledgeable man, and the equipment and stock were excellent. Cooper was delighted with the pleasure Humphreys showed, and with the suggestions he let fall from time to time. "I can see," he said, "that you've found your meatear here, Mr. Humphreys : you'll make this place a regular signosier before very many seasons have passed over our heads. I wish Clutterham had been here—that's the head gardener—and here he would have been of course, as I told you, but for his son's being horse doover with a fever, poor fellow ! I should like him to have heard how the place strikes you."

"Yes, you told me he couldn't be here to-day, and I was very sorry to hear the reason, but it will be time enough to-morrow. What is that white building on the mound at the end of the grass ride ? Is it the temple Miss Cooper mentioned ? "

" That it is, Mr. Humphreys—the Temple of Friendship. Constructed of marble brought out of Italy for the purpose, by your late uncle's grandfather. Would it interest you perhaps to take a turn there ? You get a very sweet prospect of the park."

The general lines of the temple were those of the Sibyl's Temple at Tivoli, helped out by a dome, only the whole was a good deal smaller. Some ancient sepulchral reliefs were built into the wall, and about it all was a pleasant flavour of the grand tour. Cooper produced the key, and with some difficulty opened the heavy door. Inside there was a handsome ceiling, but little furniture. Most of the floor was occupied by a pile of thick circular blocks of stone, each of which had a single letter deeply cut on its slightly convex upper surface. "What is the meaning of these?" Humphreys inquired.

"Meaning? Well, all things, we're told, have their purpose, Mr. Humphreys, and I suppose these blocks have had theirs as well as another. But what that purpose is or was (Mr. Cooper assumed a didactic attitude here), I, for one, should be at a loss to point out to you, sir. All I know of them—and it's summed up in a very few words—is just this: that they're stated to have been removed by your late uncle, at a period before I entered on the scene, from the maze. That, Mr. Humphreys, is——"

"Oh, the maze!" exclaimed Humphreys. "I'd forgotten that: we must have a look at it. Where is it?"

Cooper drew him to the door of the temple, and pointed with his stick. "Guide your eye," he said (somewhat in the manner of the Second Elder in Handel's "Susanna"—

"Far to the west direct your straining eyes
Where yon tall holm-tree rises to the skies.")

"Guide your eye by my stick here, and follow out the line directly opposite to the spot where we're standing now, and I'll engage, Mr. Humphreys, that you'll catch the archway over the entrance. You'll see it just at the end of the walk answering to the one that leads up to this very building. Did you think of going there at once? because if that be the case, I must go to the house and procure the key. If you would walk on there, I'll rejoin you in a few moments' time."

Accordingly Humphreys strolled down the ride leading to the temple, past the garden-front of the house, and up the turfy approach to the archway which Cooper had pointed out to him. He was surprised to find that the whole maze was surrounded by a high wall, and that the archway was provided with a padlocked iron gate; but then he remembered that Miss Cooper had spoken of his uncle's objection to letting anyone enter this part of the garden. He was now at the gate, and still Cooper came not. For a few minutes he occupied himself in reading the motto cut over the entrance, " *Secretum meum mihi et filiis domus meae*," and in trying to recollect the source of it. Then he became impatient and considered the possibility of scaling the wall. This was clearly not worth while; it might have been done if he had been wearing an older suit: or could the padlock—a very old one—be forced? No, apparently not: and yet, as he gave a final irritated kick at the gate, something gave way, and the lock fell at his feet. He pushed the gate open, inconveniencing a number of nettles as he did so, and stepped into the enclosure.

It was a yew maze, of circular form, and the hedges,

long untrimmed, had grown out and upwards to a most unorthodox breadth and height. The walks, too, were next door to impassable. Only by entirely disregarding scratches, nettle-stings, and wet, could Humphreys force his way along them; but at any rate this condition of things, he reflected, would make it easier for him to find his way out again, for he left a very visible track. So far as he could remember, he had never been in a maze before, nor did it seem to him now that he had missed much. The dankness and darkness, and smell of crushed goosegrass and nettles were anything but cheerful. Still, it did not seem to be a very intricate specimen of its kind. Here he was (by the way, was that Cooper arrived at last? No!) very nearly at the heart of it, without having taken much thought as to what path he was following. Ah! there at last was the centre, easily gained. And there was something to reward him. His first impression was that the central ornament was a sundial; but when he had switched away some portion of the thick growth of brambles and bindweed that had formed over it, he saw that it was a less ordinary decoration. A stone column about four feet high, and on the top of it a metal globe—copper, to judge by the green patina —engraved, and finely engraved too, with figures in outline, and letters. That was what Humphreys saw, and a brief glance at the figures convinced him that it was one of those mysterious things called celestial globes, from which, one would suppose, no one ever yet derived any information about the heavens. However, it was too dark—at least in the maze—for him to examine this curiosity at all closely, and besides, he now heard Cooper's voice, and sounds as of an elephant in the jungle. Humphreys called to him to follow the track he had beaten out, and soon Cooper emerged panting into the central circle. He was full of apologies for his delay; he had not been able, after all, to find the key. "But there!" he said, "you've penetrated into the heart of the mystery unaided and unannealed, as the saying goes. Well! I suppose it's a matter of thirty to forty years since any human foot has trod these precincts. Certain it is that I've never set foot in them before. Well, well! what's the old proverb about angels fearing to tread? It's proved true once again in this case." Humphreys' acquaintance with Cooper, though it had been short, was sufficient to assure him that there was no guile in this allusion, and he forbore the obvious remark, merely suggesting that it was fully time to get back to the house for a late cup of tea, and to release Cooper for his evening engagement. They left the maze accordingly, experiencing well-nigh the same ease in retracing their path as they had in coming in.

"Have you any idea," Humphreys asked, as they went towards the house, "why my uncle kept that place so carefully locked?"

Cooper pulled up, and Humphreys felt that he must be on the brink of a revelation.

"I should merely be deceiving you, Mr. Humphreys, and that to no good purpose, if I laid claim to possess any information whatsoever on that topic. When I first entered upon my duties here, some eighteen years back, that maze was word for word in the condition you see it now, and the one and only occasion on which the question ever arose within my knowledge was that of which my girl made mention in your hearing. Lady Wardrop—I've not a word to say against her—wrote applying for admission to the maze. Your uncle showed me the note—a most civil note—everything that could be expected from such a quarter. 'Cooper,' he said, 'I wish you'd reply to that note on my behalf.' 'Certainly, Mr. Wilson,' I said, for I was quite inured to acting as his secretary, 'what answer shall I return to it?' 'Well,' he said, 'give Lady Wardrop my compliments, and tell her that if ever that portion of the grounds is taken in hand I shall be happy to give her the first opportunity of viewing it, but that it has been shut up now for a number of years, and I shall be grateful to her if she kindly won't press the matter.' That, Mr. Humphreys, was your good uncle's last word on the subject, and I don't think I can add anything to it. Unless," added Cooper, after a pause, "it might be just this : that, so far as I could form a judgment, he had a dislike (as people often will for one reason or another) to the memory of his grandfather, who, as I mentioned to you, had that maze laid out. A man of peculiar teenets, Mr. Humphreys, and a great

333

traveller. You'll have the opportunity, on the coming Sabbath, of seeing the tablet to him in our little parish church; put up it was some long time after his death."

"Oh! I should have expected a man who had such a taste for building to have designed a mausoleum for himself."

"Well, I've never noticed anything of the kind you mention; and, in fact, come to think of it, I'm not at all sure that his resting-place is within our boundaries at all : that he lays in the vault I'm pretty confident is not the case. Curious now that I shouldn't be in a position to inform you on that heading! Still, after all, we can't say, can we, Mr. Humphreys, that it's a point of crucial importance where the pore mortal coils are bestowed?"

At this point they entered the house, and Cooper's speculations were interrupted.

Tea was laid in the library, where Mr. Cooper fell upon subjects appropriate to the scene. "A fine collection of books! One of the finest, I've understood from connoisseurs, in this part of the country; splendid plates, too, in some of these works. I recollect your uncle showing me one with views of foreign towns—most absorbing it was : got up in first-rate style. And another all done by hand, with the ink as fresh as if it had been laid on yesterday, and yet, he told me, it was the work of some old monk hundreds of years back. I've always taken a keen interest in literature myself. Hardly anything to my mind can compare with a good hour's reading after a hard day's work ; far better than wasting the whole evening at a friend's house—and that reminds me, to be sure. I shall be getting into trouble with the wife if I don't make the best of my way home and get ready to squander away one of these same evenings ! I must be off, Mr. Humphreys."

" And that reminds *me*," said Humphreys, " if I'm to show Miss Cooper the maze to-morrow we must have it cleared out a bit. Could you say a word about that to the proper person ? "

" Why, to be sure. A couple of men with scythes could cut out a track to-morrow morning. I'll leave word as I pass the lodge, and I'll tell them, what'll save you the trouble, perhaps, Mr. Humphreys, of having to go up and extract them yourself : that they'd better have some sticks or a tape to mark out their way with as they go on."

" A very good idea ! Yes, do that ; and I'll expect Mrs. and Miss Cooper in the afternoon, and yourself about half-past ten in the morning."

" It'll be a pleasure, I'm sure, both to them and to myself, Mr. Humphreys. Good night ! "

Humphreys dined at eight. But for the fact that it was his first evening, and that Calton was evidently inclined for occasional conversation, he would have finished the novel he had bought for his journey. As it was, he had to listen and reply to some of Calton's impressions of the neighbourhood and the season :

the latter, it appeared, was seasonable, and the former
had changed considerably—and not altogether for
the worse—since Calton's boyhood (which had been
spent there). The village shop in particular had
greatly improved since the year 1870. It was now
possible to procure there pretty much anything you
liked in reason : which was a conveniency, because
suppose anythink was required of a suddent (and he
had known such things before now), he (Calton)
could step down there (supposing the shop to be
still open), and order it in, without he borrered it
of the Rectory, whereas in earlier days it would have
been useless to pursue such a course in respect of
anything but candles, or soap, or treacle, or perhaps a
penny child's picture-book, and nine times out of ten
it'd be something more in the nature of a bottle of
whisky *you'd* be requiring ; leastways—— On the
whole Humphreys thought he would be prepared
with a book in future.

The library was the obvious place for the after-
dinner hours. Candle in hand and pipe in mouth,
he moved round the room for some time, taking
stock of the titles of the books. He had all the
predisposition to take interest in an old library, and
there was every opportunity for him here to make
systematic acquaintance with one, for he had learned
from Cooper that there was no catalogue save the
very superficial one made for purposes of probate.
The drawing up of a *catalogue raisonné* would be a
delicious occupation for winter. There were prob-

ably treasures to be found, too : even manuscripts,
if Cooper might be trusted.

As he pursued his round the sense came upon
him (as it does upon most of us in similar places)
of the extreme unreadableness of a great portion of
the collection. " Editions of Classics and Fathers,
and Picart's *Religious Ceremonies*, and the *Harleian
Miscellany*, I suppose are all very well, but who is
ever going to read Tostatus Abulensis, or Pineda on
Job, or a book like this ? " He picked out a small
quarto, loose in the binding, and from which the
lettered label had fallen off ; and observing that coffee
was waiting for him, retired to a chair. Eventually
he opened the book. It will be observed that his
condemnation of it rested wholly on external grounds.
For all he knew it might have been a collection of
unique plays, but undeniably the outside was blank
and forbidding. As a matter of fact, it was a collection of sermons or meditations, and mutilated
at that, for the first sheet was gone. It seemed to
belong to the latter end of the seventeenth century.
He turned over the pages till his eye was caught
by a marginal note : " *A Parable of this Unhappy
Condition*," and he thought he would see what apti-
tudes the author might have for imaginative composition. " I have heard or read," so ran the passage,
" whether in the way of *Parable* or true *Relation* I
leave my Reader to judge, of a Man who, like *Theseus*,
in the *Attick Tale*, should adventure himself, into a
Labyrinth or *Maze* : and such an one indeed as was

not laid out in the Fashion of our *Topiary* artists of
this Age, but of a wide compass, in which, moreover,
such unknown Pitfalls and Snares, nay, such ill
omened Inhabitants were commonly thought to lurk
as could only be encountered at the Hazard of one's
very life. Now you may be sure that in such a Case
the Disswasions of Friends were not wanting. ' Consider of such-an-one ' says a Brother ' how he went
the way you wot of, and was never seen more.' ' Or
of such another ' says the Mother ' that adventured
himself but a little way in, and from that day forth
is so troubled in his Wits that he cannot tell what
he saw, nor hath passed one good Night.' ' And
have you never heard ' cries a Neighbour ' of what
Faces have been seen to look out over the *Palisadoes*
and betwixt the Bars of the Gate ? ' But all would
not do : the Man was set upon his Purpose : for it
seems it was the common fireside Talk of that Country
that at the Heart and Centre of this *Labyrinth* there
was a Jewel of such Price and Rarity that would
enrich the Finder thereof for his life : and this should
be his by right that could persever to come at it.
What then ? *Quid multa ?* The Adventurer pass'd
the Gates, and for a whole day's space his Friends
without had no news of him, except it might be by
some indistinct Cries heard afar off in the Night,
such as made them turn in their restless Beds and
sweat for very Fear, not doubting but that their Son
and Brother had put one more to the *Catalogue* of
those unfortunates that had suffer'd shipwreck on

that Voyage. So the next day they went with weep-
ing Tears to the Clark of the Parish to order the Bell
to be toll'd. And their Way took them hard by the
gate of the *Labyrinth*: which they would have
hastened by, from the Horrour they had of it, but
that they caught sight of a sudden of a Man's Body
lying in the Roadway, and going up to it (with what
Anticipations may be easily figured) found it to be
him whom they reckoned as lost: and not dead,
though he were in a Swound most like Death. They
then, who had gone forth as Mourners came back
rejoycing, and set to by all means to revive their
Prodigal. Who, being come to himself, and hearing
of their Anxieties and their Errand of that Morning,
'Ay' says he 'you may as well finish what you were
about: for, for all I have brought back the Jewel
(which he shew'd them, and 'twas indeed a rare Piece)
I have brought back that with it that will leave me
neither Rest at Night nor Pleasure by Day.' Whereupon they were instant with him to learn his Meaning,
and where his Company should be that went so sore
against his Stomach. 'O' says he ''tis here in my
Breast: I cannot flee from it, do what I may.' So
it needed no Wizard to help them to a guess that it
was the Recollection of what he had seen that troubled
him so wonderfully. But they could get no more
of him for a long Time but by Fits and Starts. However at long and at last they made shift to collect
somewhat of this kind: that at first, while the Sun
was bright, he went merrily on, and without any

Difficulty reached the Heart of the *Labyrinth* and got the Jewel, and so set out on his way back rejoycing : but as the Night fell, *wherein all the Beasts of the Forest do move*, he begun to be sensible of some Creature keeping Pace with him and, as he thought, *peering and looking upon him* from the next Alley to that he was in ; and that when he should stop, this Companion should stop also, which put him in some Disorder of his Spirits. And, indeed, as the Darkness increas'd, it seemed to him that there was more than one, and, it might be, even a whole Band of such Followers : at least so he judg'd by the Rustling and Cracking that they kept among the Thickets ; besides that there would be at a Time a Sound of Whispering, which seem'd to import a Conference among them. But in regard of who they were or what Form they were of, he would not be persuaded to say what he thought. Upon his Hearers asking him what the Cries were which they heard in the Night (as was observ'd above) he gave them this Account : That about Midnight (so far as he could judge) he heard his Name call'd from a long way off, and he would have been sworn it was his Brother that so call'd him. So he stood still and hilloo'd at the Pitch of his Voice, and he suppos'd that the *Echo*, or the Noyse of his Shouting, disguis'd for the Moment any lesser sound ; because, when there fell a Stillness again, he distinguish'd a Trampling (not loud) of running Feet coming very close behind him, wherewith he was so daunted that himself set off to run, and that he con-

tinued till the Dawn broke. Sometimes when his
Breath fail'd him, he would cast himself flat on his
Face, and hope that his Pursuers might over-run him
in the Darkness, but at such a Time they would
regularly make a Pause, and he could hear them pant
and snuff as it had been a Hound at Fault : which
wrought in him so extream an Horrour of mind,
that he would be forc'd to betake himself again to
turning and doubling, if by any Means he might
throw them off the Scent. And, as if this Exertion
was in itself not terrible enough, he had before him
the constant Fear of falling into some Pit or Trap,
of which he had heard, and indeed seen with his own
Eyes that there were several, some at the sides and
other in the Midst of the Alleys. So that in fine
(he said) a more dreadful Night was never spent by
Mortal Creature than that he had endur'd in that
Labyrinth ; and not that Jewel which he had in his
Wallet, nor the richest that was ever brought out of
the *Indies*, could be a sufficient Recompence to him
for the Pains he had suffered.

"I will spare to set down the further Recital of
this Man's Troubles, inasmuch as I am confident my
Reader's Intelligence will hit the *Parallel* I desire to
draw. For is not this Jewel a just Emblem of the
Satisfaction which a Man may bring back with him
from a Course of this World's Pleasures ? and will
not the *Labyrinth* serve for an Image of the World
itself wherein such a Treasure (if we may believe
the common Voice) is stored up ? "

At about this point Humphreys thought that a little Patience would be an agreeable change, and that the writer's "improvement" of his Parable might be left to itself. So he put the book back in its former place, wondering as he did so whether his uncle had ever stumbled across that passage; and if so, whether it had worked on his fancy so much as to make him dislike the idea of a maze, and determine to shut up the one in the garden. Not long afterwards he went to bed.

The next day brought a morning's hard work with Mr. Cooper, who, if exuberant in language, had the business of the estate at his fingers' ends. He was very breezy this morning, Mr. Cooper was: had not forgotten the order to clear out the maze—the work was going on at that moment: his girl was on the tentacles of expectation about it. He also hoped that Humphreys had slept the sleep of the just, and that we should be favoured with a continuance of this congenial weather. At luncheon he enlarged on the pictures in the dining-room, and pointed out the portrait of the constructor of the temple and the maze. Humphreys examined this with considerable interest. It was the work of an Italian, and had been painted when old Mr. Wilson was visiting Rome as a young man. (There was, indeed, a view of the Colosseum in the background.) A pale thin face and large eyes were the characteristic features. In the hand was a partially unfolded roll of paper, on

which could be distinguished the plan of a circular
building, very probably the temple, and also part of
that of a labyrinth. Humphreys got up on a chair
to examine it, but it was not painted with sufficient
clearness to be worth copying. It suggested to him,
however, that he might as well make a plan of his
own maze and hang it in the hall for the use of visitors.

This determination of his was confirmed that same
afternoon ; for when Mrs. and Miss Cooper arrived,
eager to be inducted into the maze, he found that he
was wholly unable to lead them to the centre. The
gardeners had removed the guide-marks they had
been using, and even Clutterham, when summoned
to assist, was as helpless as the rest. " The point
is, you see, Mr. Wilson—I should say 'Umphreys—
these mazes is purposely constructed so much alike,
with a view to mislead. Still, if you'll foller me, I
think I can put you right. I'll just put my 'at down
'ere as a starting-point." He stumped off, and after
five minutes brought the party safe to the hat again.
" Now that's a very peculiar thing," he said, with a
sheepish laugh. " I made sure I'd left that 'at just
over against a bramble-bush, and you can see for
yourself there ain't no bramble-bush not in this walk
at all. If you'll allow me, Mr. Humphreys—that's
the name, ain't it, sir ?—I'll just call one of the men
in to mark the place like."

William Crack arrived, in answer to repeated
shouts. He had some difficulty in making his way
to the party. First he was seen or heard in an inside

alley, then, almost at the same moment, in an outer one. However, he joined them at last, and was first consulted without effect and then stationed by the hat, which Clutterham still considered it necessary to leave on the ground. In spite of this strategy, they spent the best part of three-quarters of an hour in quite fruitless wanderings, and Humphreys was obliged at last, seeing how tired Mrs. Cooper was becoming, to suggest a retreat to tea, with profuse apologies to Miss Cooper. "At any rate you've won your bet with Miss Foster," he said; "you have been inside the maze; and I promise you the first thing I do shall be to make a proper plan of it with the lines marked out for you to go by." "That's what's wanted, sir," said Clutterham, "someone to draw out a plan and keep it by them. It might be very awkward, you see, anyone getting into that place and a shower of rain come on, and them not able to find their way out again; it might be hours before they could be got out, without you'd permit of me makin' a short cut to the middle: what my meanin' is, takin' down a couple of trees in each 'edge in a straight line so as you could git a clear view right through. Of course that'd do away with it as a maze, but I don't know as you'd approve of that."

"No, I won't have that done yet: I'll make a plan first, and let you have a copy. Later on, if we find occasion, I'll think of what you say."

Humphreys was vexed and ashamed at the fiasco of the afternoon, and could not be satisfied without making another effort that evening to reach the centre of the maze. His irritation was increased by finding it without a single false step. He had thoughts of beginning his plan at once; but the light was fading, and he felt that by the time he had got the necessary materials together, work would be impossible.

Next morning accordingly, carrying a drawing-board, pencils, compasses, cartridge paper, and so forth (some of which had been borrowed from the Coopers and some found in the library cupboards), he went to the middle of the maze (again without any hesitation), and set out his materials. He was, however, delayed in making a start. The brambles and weeds that had obscured the column and globe were now all cleared away, and it was for the first time possible to see clearly what these were like. The column was featureless, resembling those on which sundials are usually placed. Not so the globe. I have said that it was finely engraved with figures and inscriptions, and that on a first glance Humphreys had taken it for a celestial globe : but he soon found that it did not answer to his recollection of such things. One feature seemed familiar; a winged serpent—*Draco*—encircled it about the place which, on a terrestrial globe, is occupied by the equator : but on the other hand, a good part of the upper hemisphere was covered by the outspread wings of a large figure whose head was concealed by a ring at the pole or summit of the whole. Around the place of the head the words *princeps tenebrarum* could be deciphered. In the lower hemisphere there was a space hatched all over with cross-lines and marked as *umbra mortis*. Near it was a range of mountains, and among them a valley with flames rising from it. This was lettered (will you be surprised to learn it?) *vallis filiorum Hinnom*. Above and below *Draco* were outlined various figures not unlike the pictures of the ordinary constellations, but not the same. Thus, a nude man with a raised club was described, not as *Hercules* but as *Cain*. Another, plunged up to his middle in earth and stretching out despairing arms, was *Chore*, not *Ophiuchus*, and a third, hung by his hair to a snaky tree, was *Absolon*. Near the last, a man in long robes and high cap, standing in a circle and addressing two shaggy demons who hovered outside, was described as *Hostanes magus* (a character unfamiliar to Humphreys). The scheme of the whole, indeed, seemed to be an assemblage of the patriarchs of evil, perhaps not uninfluenced by a study of Dante. Humphreys thought it an unusual exhibition of his great-grandfather's taste, but reflected that he had probably picked it up in Italy and had never taken the trouble to examine it closely: certainly, had he set much store by it, he would not have exposed it to wind and weather. He tapped the metal—it seemed hollow and not very thick— and, turning from it, addressed himself to his plan. After half an hour's work he found it was impossible to get on without using a clue: so he procured a roll of twine from Clutterham, and laid it out along the alleys from the entrance to the centre, tying the end to the ring at the top of the globe. This expedient helped him to set out a rough plan before luncheon, and in the afternoon he was able to draw it in more neatly. Towards tea-time Mr. Cooper joined him, and was much interested in his progress. " Now this——" said Mr. Cooper, laying his hand on the globe, and then drawing it away hastily. " Whew! Holds the heat, doesn't it, to a surprising degree, Mr. Humphreys. I suppose this metal— copper, isn't it?—would be an insulator or con- ductor, or whatever they call it."

" The sun has been pretty strong this afternoon," said Humphreys, evading the scientific point, " but I didn't notice the globe had got hot. No—it doesn't seem very hot to me," he added.

" Odd! " said Mr. Cooper. " Now I can't hardly bear my hand on it. Something in the difference of temperament between us, I suppose. I dare say you're a chilly subject, Mr. Humphreys : I'm not : and there's where the distinction lies. All this summer I've slept, if you'll believe me, practically *in statu quo*, and had my morning tub as cold as I could get it. Day out and day in—let me assist you with that string."

" It's all right, thanks ; but if you'll collect some of these pencils and things that are lying about I shall be much obliged. Now I think we've got everything, and we might get back to the house."

They left the maze, Humphreys rolling up the clue as they went.

The night was rainy.

Most unfortunately it turned out that, whether by Cooper's fault or not, the plan had been the one thing forgotten the evening before. As was to be expected, it was ruined by the wet. There was nothing for it but to begin again (the job would not be a long one this time). The clue therefore was put in place once more and a fresh start made. But Humphreys had not done much before an interruption came in the shape of Calton with a telegram. His late chief in London wanted to consult him. Only a brief interview was wanted, but the summons was urgent. This was annoying, yet it was not really upsetting; there was a train available in half an hour, and, unless things went very cross, he could be back, possibly by five o'clock, certainly by eight. He gave the plan to Calton to take to the house, but it was not worth while to remove the clue.

All went as he had hoped. He spent a rather exciting evening in the library, for he lighted to-night upon a cupboard where some of the rarer books were kept. When he went up to bed he was glad to find that the servant had remembered to leave his curtains undrawn and his windows open. He put down his light, and went to the window which commanded a view of the garden and the park. It was a brilliant moonlight night. In a few weeks' time the sonorous winds of autumn would break up all this calm. But now the distant woods were in a deep stillness ; the slopes of the lawns were shining with dew ; the colours of some of the flowers could almost be guessed. The light of the moon just caught the cornice of the temple and the curve of its leaden dome, and Humphreys had to own that, so seen, these conceits of a past age have a real beauty. In short, the light, the perfume of the woods, and the absolute quiet called up such kind old associations in his mind that he went on ruminating them for a long, long time. As he turned from the window he felt he had never seen anything more complete of its sort. The one feature that struck him with a sense of incongruity was a small Irish yew, thin and black, which stood out like an outpost of the shrubbery, through which the maze was approached. That, he thought, might as well be away : the wonder was that anyone should have thought it would look well in that position.

However, next morning, in the press of answering letters and going over books with Mr. Cooper, the Irish yew was forgotten. One letter, by the way, arrived this day which has to be mentioned. It was from that Lady Wardrop whom Miss Cooper had mentioned, and it renewed the application which she had addressed to Mr. Wilson. She pleaded, in the first place, that she was about to publish a Book of Mazes, and earnestly desired to include the plan of the Wilsthorpe Maze, and also that it would be a great kindness if Mr. Humphreys could let her see it (if at all) at an early date, since she would soon have to go abroad for the winter months. Her house at Bentley was not far distant, so Humphreys was able to send a note by hand to her suggesting the very next day or the day after for her visit; it may be said at once that the messenger brought back a most grateful answer, to the effect that the morrow would suit her admirably.

The only other event of the day was that the plan of the maze was successfully finished.

This night again was fair and brilliant and calm, and Humphreys lingered almost as long at his window. The Irish yew came to his mind again as he was on the point of drawing his curtains : but either he had been misled by a shadow the night before, or else the shrub was not really so obtrusive as he had fancied. Anyhow, he saw no reason for interfering with it. What he *would* do away with, however, was a clump of dark growth which had usurped a place against the house wall, and was threatening to obscure one of the lower range of windows. It did not look as if it could possibly be worth keeping; he fancied it dank and unhealthy, little as he could see of it.

Next day (it was a Friday—he had arrived at Wilsthorpe on a Monday) Lady Wardrop came over in her car soon after luncheon. She was a stout elderly person, very full of talk of all sorts and particularly inclined to make herself agreeable to Humphreys, who had gratified her very much by his ready granting of her request. They made a thorough exploration of the place together; and Lady Wardrop's opinion of her host obviously rose sky-high when she found that he really knew something of gardening. She entered enthusiastically into all his plans for improvement, but agreed that it would be a vandalism to interfere with the characteristic laying-out of the ground near the house. With the temple she was particularly delighted, and, said she, " Do you know, Mr. Humphreys, I think your bailiff must be right about those lettered blocks of stone. One of my mazes—I'm sorry to say the stupid people have destroyed it now—it was at a place in Hampshire—had the track marked out in that way. They were tiles there, but lettered just like yours, and the letters, taken in the right order, formed an inscription —what it was I forget—something about Theseus and Ariadne. I have a copy of it, as well as the plan of the maze where it was. How people can do such things! I shall never forgive you if you injure *your* maze. Do you know, they're becoming very uncommon? Almost every year I hear of one being grubbed up. Now, do let's get straight to it: or, if you're too busy, I know my way there perfectly, and I'm not afraid of getting lost in it; I know too much about mazes for that. Though I remember missing my lunch—not so very long ago either— through getting entangled in the one at Busbury. Well, of course, if you *can* manage to come with me, that will be all the nicer."

After this confident prelude justice would seem to require that Lady Wardrop should have been hopelessly muddled by the Wilsthorpe maze. Nothing of that kind happened : yet it is to be doubted whether she got all the enjoyment from her new specimen that she expected. She was interested—keenly interested —to be sure, and pointed out to Humphreys a series of little depressions in the ground which, she thought, marked the places of the lettered blocks. She told him, too, what other mazes resembled his most closely in arrangement, and explained how it was usually possible to date a maze to within twenty years by means of its plan. This one, she already knew, must be about as old as 1780, and its features were just what might be expected. The globe, furthermore, completely absorbed her. It was unique in her experience, and she pored over it for long. " I should like a rubbing of that," she said, " if it could possibly be made. Yes, I am sure you would be most kind about it, Mr. Humphreys, but I trust you won't attempt it on my account, I do indeed ; I shouldn't like to take any liberties here. I have the feeling that it might be resented. Now, confess," she went on, turning and facing Humphreys, " don't you feel —haven't you felt ever since you came in here—that a watch is being kept on us, and that if we overstepped the mark in any way there would be a—well, a pounce ? No ? *I* do ; and I don't care how soon we are outside the gate.

" After all," she said, when they were once more

on their way to the house, " it may have been only the airlessness and the dull heat of that place that pressed on my brain. Still, I'll take back one thing I said. I'm not sure that I shan't forgive you after all, if I find next spring that that maze has been grubbed up."

" Whether or no that's done, you shall have the plan, Lady Wardrop. I have made one, and no later than to-night I can trace you a copy."

" Admirable : a pencil tracing will be all I want, with an indication of the scale. I can easily have it brought into line with the rest of my plates. Many, many thanks."

" Very well, you shall have that to-morrow. I wish you could help me to a solution of my block-puzzle."

" What, those stones in the summer-house ? That *is* a puzzle ; they are in no sort of order ? Of course not. But the men who put them down must have had some directions—perhaps you'll find a paper about it among your uncle's things. If not, you'll have to call in somebody who's an expert in cyphers."

" Advise me about something else, please," said Humphreys. " That bush-thing under the library window : you would have that away, wouldn't you ? "

" Which ? That ? Oh, I think not," said Lady Wardrop. " I can't see it very well from this distance, but it's not unsightly."

" Perhaps you're right ; only, looking out of my

window, just above it, last night, I thought it took up too much room. It doesn't seem to, as one sees it from here, certainly. Very well, I'll leave it alone for a bit."

Tea was the next business, soon after which Lady Wardrop drove off; but, half-way down the drive, she stopped the car and beckoned to Humphreys, who was still on the front-door steps. He ran to glean her parting words, which were : " It just occurs to me, it might be worth your while to look at the underside of those stones. They *must* have been numbered, mustn't they ? *Good*-bye again. Home, please."

The main occupation of this evening at any rate was settled. The tracing of the plan for Lady Wardrop and the careful collation of it with the original meant a couple of hours' work at least. Accordingly, soon after nine Humphreys had his materials put out in the library and began. It was a still, stuffy evening; windows had to stand open, and he had more than one grisly encounter with a bat. These unnerving episodes made him keep the tail of his eye on the window. Once or twice it was a question whether there was—not a bat, but something more considerable—that had a mind to join him. How unpleasant it would be if someone had slipped noiselessly over the sill and was crouching on the floor !

The tracing of the plan was done : it remained

to compare it with the original, and to see whether
any paths had been wrongly closed or left open.
With one finger on each paper, he traced out the
course that must be followed from the entrance.
There were one or two slight mistakes, but here,
near the centre, was a bad confusion, probably due
to the entry of the Second or Third Bat. Before
correcting the copy he followed out carefully the
last turnings of the path on the original. These, at
least, were right; they led without a hitch to the
middle space. Here was a feature which need not
be repeated on the copy—an ugly black spot about
the size of a shilling. Ink? No. It resembled a
hole, but how should a hole be there? He stared at
it with tired eyes : the work of tracing had been very
laborious, and he was drowsy and oppressed. . . .
But surely this was a very odd hole. It seemed to
go not only through the paper, but through the table
on which it lay. Yes, and through the floor below
that, down, and still down, even into infinite depths.
He craned over it, utterly bewildered. Just as, when
you were a child, you may have pored over a square
inch of counterpane until it became a landscape with
wooded hills, and perhaps even churches and houses,
and you lost all thought of the true size of yourself
and it, so this hole seemed to Humphreys for the
moment the only thing in the world. For some
reason it was hateful to him from the first, but he had
gazed at it for some moments before any feeling of
anxiety came upon him; and then it did come,

stronger and stronger—a horror lest something might emerge from it, and a really agonizing conviction that a terror was on its way, from the sight of which he would not be able to escape. Oh yes, far, far down there was a movement, and the movement was upwards—towards the surface. Nearer and nearer it came, and it was of a blackish-grey colour with more than one dark hole. It took shape as a face—a human face—a *burnt* human face : and with the odious writhings of a wasp creeping out of a rotten apple there clambered forth an appearance of a form, waving black arms prepared to clasp the head that was bending over them. With a convulsion of despair Humphreys threw himself back, struck his head against a hanging lamp, and fell.

There was concussion of the brain, shock to the system, and a long confinement to bed. The doctor was badly puzzled, not by the symptoms, but by a request which Humphreys made to him as soon as he was able to say anything. " I wish you would open the ball in the maze." " Hardly room enough there, I should have thought," was the best answer he could summon up ; " but it's more in your way than mine ; my dancing days are over." At which Humphreys muttered and turned over to sleep, and the doctor intimated to the nurses that the patient was not out of the wood yet. When he was better able to express his views, Humphreys made his meaning clear, and received a promise that the thing should be done at once. He was so anxious to learn the result that the doctor, who seemed a little pensive next morning, saw that more harm than good would be done by saving up his report. "Well," he said, "I am afraid the ball is done for; the metal must have worn thin, I suppose. Anyhow, it went all to bits with the first blow of the chisel." "Well? go on, do!" said Humphreys impatiently. "Oh! you want to know what we found in it, of course. Well, it was half full of stuff like ashes." "Ashes? What did you make of them?" "I haven't thoroughly examined them yet; there's hardly been time: but Cooper's made up his mind—I dare say from something I said—that it's a case of cremation. . . . Now don't excite yourself, my good sir: yes, I must allow I think he's probably right."

The maze is gone, and Lady Wardrop has forgiven Humphreys; in fact, I believe he married her niece. She was right, too, in her conjecture that the stones in the temple were numbered. There had been a numeral painted on the bottom of each. Some few of these had rubbed off, but enough remained to enable Humphreys to reconstruct the inscription. It ran thus:

"PENETRANS AD INTERIORA MORTIS."

Grateful as Humphreys was to the memory of his uncle, he could not quite forgive him for having burnt the journals and letters of the James Wilson who had gifted Wilsthorpe with the maze and the temple.

As to the circumstances of that ancestor's death and burial no tradition survived ; but his will, which was almost the only record of him accessible, assigned an unusually generous legacy to a servant who bore an Italian name.

Mr. Cooper's view is that, humanly speaking, all these many solemn events have a meaning for us, if our limited intelligence permitted of our disintegrating it, while Mr. Calton has been reminded of an aunt now gone from us, who, about the year 1866, had been lost for upwards of an hour and a half in the maze at Covent Gardens, or it might be Hampton Court.

One of the oddest things in the whole series of transactions is that the book which contained the Parable has entirely disappeared. Humphreys has never been able to find it since he copied out the passage to send to Lady Wardrop.

THE RESIDENCE AT WHITMINSTER

DR. ASHTON—Thomas Ashton, Doctor of Divinity
—sat in his study, habited in a dressing-gown, and
with a silk cap on his shaven head—his wig being
for the time taken off and placed on its block on a
side table. He was a man of some fifty-five years,
strongly made, of a sanguine complexion, an angry
eye, and a long upper lip. Face and eye were lighted
up at the moment when I picture him by the level ray
of an afternoon sun that shone in upon him through
a tall sash window, giving on the west. The room
into which it shone was also tall, lined with book-
cases, and, where the wall showed between them,
panelled. On the table near the doctor's elbow was
a green cloth, and upon it what he would have called
a silver standish—a tray with inkstands—quill pens,
a calf-bound book or two, some papers, a church-
warden pipe and brass tobacco-box, a flask cased in
plaited straw, and a liqueur glass. The year was
1730, the month December, the hour somewhat past
three in the afternoon.

I have described in these lines pretty much all that
a superficial observer would have noted when he
looked into the room. What met Dr. Ashton's eye
when he looked out of it, sitting in his leather arm-

chair ? Little more than the tops of the shrubs and fruit-trees of his garden could be seen from that point, but the red-brick wall of it was visible in almost all the length of its western side. In the middle of that was a gate—a double gate of rather elaborate iron scroll-work, which allowed something of a view beyond. Through it he could see that the ground sloped away almost at once to a bottom, along which a stream must run, and rose steeply from it on the other side, up to a field that was park-like in character, and thickly studded with oaks, now, of course, leafless. They did not stand so thick together but that some glimpse of sky and horizon could be seen between their stems. The sky was now golden and the horizon, a horizon of distant woods, it seemed, was purple.

But all that Dr. Ashton could find to say, after contemplating this prospect for many minutes, was : " Abominable ! "

A listener would have been aware, immediately upon this, of the sound of footsteps coming somewhat hurriedly in the direction of the study : by the resonance he could have told that they were traversing a much larger room. Dr. Ashton turned round in his chair as the door opened, and looked expectant. The incomer was a lady—a stout lady in the dress of the time : though I have made some attempt at indicating the doctor's costume, I will not enterprise that of his wife—for it was Mrs. Ashton who now entered. She had an anxious, even a sorely distracted, look, and it was in a very disturbed voice that she almost whispered to Dr. Ashton, putting her head close to his, "He's in a very sad way, love, worse, I'm afraid." "Tt—tt, is he really?" and he leaned back and looked in her face. She nodded. Two solemn bells, high up, and not far away, rang out the half-hour at this moment. Mrs. Ashton started. "Oh, do you think you can give order that the minster clock be stopped chiming to-night? 'Tis just over his chamber, and will keep him from sleeping, and to sleep is the only chance for him, that's certain." "Why, to be sure, if there were need, real need, it could be done, but not upon any light occasion. This Frank, now, do you assure me that his recovery stands upon it?" said Dr. Ashton: his voice was loud and rather hard. "I do verily believe it," said his wife. "Then, if it must be, bid Molly run across to Simpkins and say on my authority that he is to stop the clock chimes at sunset: and—yes—she is after that to say to my lord Saul that I wish to see him presently in this room." Mrs. Ashton hurried off.

Before any other visitor enters, it will be well to explain the situation.

Dr. Ashton was the holder, among other preferments, of a prebend in the rich collegiate church of Whitminster, one of the foundations which, though not a cathedral, survived Dissolution and Reformation, and retained its constitution and endowments for a hundred years after the time of which I write. The great church, the residences of the dean and the two prebendaries, the choir and its appurtenances, were all intact and in working order. A dean who flourished soon after 1500 had been a great builder, and had erected a spacious quadrangle of red brick adjoining the church for the residence of the officials. Some of these persons were no longer required: their offices had dwindled down to mere titles, borne by clergy or lawyers in the town and neighbourhood; and so the houses that had been meant to accommodate eight or ten people were now shared among three—the dean and the two prebendaries. Dr. Ashton's included what had been the common parlour and the dining-hall of the whole body. It occupied a whole side of the court, and at one end had a private door into the minster. The other end, as we have seen, looked out over the country.

So much for the house. As for the inmates, Dr. Ashton was a wealthy man and childless, and he had adopted, or rather undertaken to bring up, the orphan son of his wife's sister. Frank Sydall was the lad's name: he had been a good many months in the house. Then one day came a letter from an Irish peer, the Earl of Kildonan (who had known Dr. Ashton at college), putting it to the doctor whether he would consider taking into his family the Viscount Saul, the Earl's heir, and acting in some sort as his tutor. Lord Kildonan was shortly to take up a post in the Lisbon Embassy, and the boy was unfit to make the voyage: "not that he is sickly," the Earl wrote, "though you'll find him whimsical, or of late I've thought him so, and to confirm this, 'twas only to-day his old nurse came expressly to tell me he was possess'd : but let that pass ; I'll warrant you can find a spell to make all straight. Your arm was stout enough in old days, and I give you plenary authority to use it as you see fit. The truth is, he has here no boys of his age or quality to consort with, and is given to moping about in our raths and graveyards : and he brings home romances that fright my servants out of their wits. So there are you and your lady fore-warned." It was perhaps with half an eye open to the possibility of an Irish bishopric (at which another sentence in the Earl's letter seemed to hint) that Dr. Ashton accepted the charge of my Lord Viscount Saul and of the 200 guineas a year that were to come with him.

So he came, one night in September. When he got out of the chaise that brought him, he went first and spoke to the postboy and gave him some money, and patted the neck of his horse. Whether he made some movement that scared it or not, there was very nearly a nasty accident, for the beast started violently, and the postilion being unready was thrown and lost his fee, as he found afterwards, and the chaise lost some paint on the gateposts, and the wheel went over the man's foot who was taking out the baggage. When Lord Saul came up the steps into the light of the lamp in the porch to be greeted by Dr. Ashton, he was seen to be a thin youth of, say, sixteen years

old, with straight black hair and the pale colouring
that is common to such a figure. He took the accident and commotion calmly enough, and expressed
a proper anxiety for the people who had been, or
might have been, hurt : his voice was smooth and
pleasant, and without any trace, curiously, of an
Irish brogue.

Frank Sydall was a younger boy, perhaps of eleven
or twelve, but Lord Saul did not for that reject his
company. Frank was able to teach him various
games he had not known in Ireland, and he was apt
at learning them ; apt, too, at his books, though he
had had little or no regular teaching at home. It
was not long before he was making a shift to puzzle
out the inscriptions on the tombs in the minster, and
he would often put a question to the doctor about
the old books in the library that required some thought
to answer. It is to be supposed that he made himself
very agreeable to the servants, for within ten days
of his coming they were almost falling over each
other in their efforts to oblige him. At the same
time, Mrs. Ashton was rather put to it to find new
maidservants ; for there were several changes, and
some of the families in the town from which she had
been accustomed to draw seemed to have no one
available. She was forced to go farther afield than
was usual.

These generalities I gather from the doctor's notes
in his diary and from letters. They are generalities,
and we should like, in view of what has to be told,

something sharper and more detailed. We get it in entries which begin late in the year, and, I think, were posted up all together after the final incident; but they cover so few days in all that there is no need to doubt that the writer could remember the course of things accurately.

On a Friday morning it was that a fox, or perhaps a cat, made away with Mrs. Ashton's most prized black cockerel, a bird without a single white feather on its body. Her husband had told her often enough that it would make a suitable sacrifice to Æsculapius; that had discomfited her much, and now she would hardly be consoled. The boys looked everywhere for traces of it : Lord Saul brought in a few feathers, which seemed to have been partially burnt on the garden rubbish-heap. It was on the same day that Dr. Ashton, looking out of an upper window, saw the two boys playing in the corner of the garden at a game he did not understand. Frank was looking earnestly at something in the palm of his hand. Saul stood behind him and seemed to be listening. After some minutes he very gently laid his hand on Frank's head, and almost instantly thereupon, Frank suddenly dropped whatever it was that he was holding, clapped his hands to his eyes, and sank down on the grass. Saul, whose face expressed great anger, hastily picked the object up, of which it could only be seen that it was glittering, put it in his pocket, and turned away, leaving Frank huddled up on the grass. Dr. Ashton rapped on the window to attract their attention, and

Saul looked up as if in alarm, and then springing to Frank, pulled him up by the arm and led him away. When they came in to dinner, Saul explained that they had been acting a part of the tragedy of Radamistus, in which the heroine reads the future fate of her father's kingdom by means of a glass ball held in her hand, and is overcome by the terrible events she has seen. During this explanation Frank said nothing, only looked rather bewilderedly at Saul. He must, Mrs. Ashton thought, have contracted a chill from the wet of the grass, for that evening he was certainly feverish and disordered; and the disorder was of the mind as well as the body, for he seemed to have something he wished to say to Mrs. Ashton, only a press of household affairs prevented her from paying attention to him; and when she went, according to her habit, to see that the light in the boys' chamber had been taken away, and to bid them good night, he seemed to be sleeping, though his face was unnaturally flushed, to her thinking: Lord Saul, however, was pale and quiet, and smiling in his slumber.

Next morning it happened that Dr. Ashton was occupied in church and other business, and unable to take the boys' lessons. He therefore set them tasks to be written and brought to him. Three times, if not oftener, Frank knocked at the study door, and each time the doctor chanced to be engaged with some visitor, and sent the boy off rather roughly, which he later regretted. Two clergymen were at dinner this day, and both remarked—being fathers of families—that the lad seemed sickening for a fever, in which they were too near the truth, and it had been better if he had been put to bed forthwith : for a couple of hours later in the afternoon he came running into the house, crying out in a way that was really terrifying, and rushing to Mrs. Ashton, clung about her, begging her to protect him, and saying, " Keep them off ! keep them off ! " without intermission. And it was now evident that some sickness had taken strong hold of him. He was therefore got to bed in another chamber from that in which he commonly lay, and the physician brought to him : who pronounced the disorder to be grave and affecting the lad's brain, and prognosticated a fatal end to it if strict quiet were not observed, and those sedative remedies used which he should prescribe.

We are now come by another way to the point we had reached before. The minster clock has been stopped from striking, and Lord Saul is on the threshold of the study.

" What account can you give of this poor lad's state ? " was Dr. Ashton's first question. " Why, sir, little more than you know already, I fancy. I must blame myself, though, for giving him a fright yesterday when we were acting that silly play you saw. I fear I made him take it more to heart than I meant." " How so ? " " Well, by telling him foolish tales I had picked up in Ireland of what we call the second sight." " *Second* sight ! What kind of sight might that be?" "Why, you know our ignorant people pretend that some are able to foresee what is to come—sometimes in a glass, or in the air, maybe, and at Kildonan we had an old woman that pretended to such a power. And I dare say I coloured the matter more highly than I should: but I never dreamed Frank would take it so near as he did." "You were wrong, my lord, very wrong, in meddling with such superstitious matters at all, and you should have considered whose house you were in, and how little becoming such actions are to my character and person or to your own: but pray how came it that you, acting, as you say, a play, should fall upon anything that could so alarm Frank?" "That is what I can hardly tell, sir: he passed all in a moment from rant about battles and lovers and Cleodora and Antigenes to something I could not follow at all, and then dropped down as you saw." "Yes: was that at the moment when you laid your hand on the top of his head?" Lord Saul gave a quick look at his questioner—quick and spiteful—and for the first time seemed unready with an answer. "About that time it may have been," he said. "I have tried to recollect myself, but I am not sure. There was, at any rate, no significance in what I did then." "Ah!" said Dr. Ashton, "well, my lord, I should do wrong were I not to tell you that this fright of my poor nephew may have very ill consequences to him. The doctor speaks very despondingly of his state." Lord Saul pressed his hands together and looked earnestly upon Dr. Ashton. "I am willing to believe you had no bad intention, as assuredly you could have no reason to bear the poor boy malice : but I cannot wholly free you from blame in the affair." As he spoke, the hurrying steps were heard again, and Mrs. Ashton came quickly into the room, carrying a candle, for the evening had by this time closed in. She was greatly agitated. "O come!" she cried, "come directly. I'm sure he is going." "Going? Frank? Is it possible? Already?" With some such incoherent words the doctor caught up a book of prayers from the table and ran out after his wife. Lord Saul stopped for a moment where he was. Molly, the maid, saw him bend over and put both hands to his face. If it were the last words she had to speak, she said afterwards, he was striving to keep back a fit of laughing. Then he went out softly, following the others.

Mrs. Ashton was sadly right in her forecast. I have no inclination to imagine the last scene in detail. What Dr. Ashton records is, or may be taken to be, important to the story. They asked Frank if he would like to see his companion, Lord Saul, once again. The boy was quite collected, it appears, in these moments. "No," he said, "I do not want to see him ; but you should tell him I am afraid he will be very cold." "What do you mean, my dear?" said Mrs. Ashton. "Only that," said Frank ; "but say to him besides that I am free of them now, but he should take care. And I am sorry about your black cockerel, Aunt

Ashton ; but he said we must use it so, if we were to see all that could be seen."

Not many minutes after, he was gone. Both the Ashtons were grieved, she naturally most ; but the doctor, though not an emotional man, felt the pathos of the early death : and, besides, there was the growing suspicion that all had not been told him by Saul, and that there was something here which was out of his beaten track. When he left the chamber of death, it was to walk across the quadrangle of the residence to the sexton's house. A passing bell, the greatest of the minster bells, must be rung, a grave must be dug in the minster yard, and there was now no need to silence the chiming of the minster clock. As he came slowly back in the dark, he thought he must see Lord Saul again. That matter of the black cockerel —trifling as it might seem—would have to be cleared up. It might be merely a fancy of the sick boy, but if not, was there not a witch-trial he had read, in which some grim little rite of sacrifice had played a part ? Yes, he must see Saul.

I rather guess these thoughts of his than find written authority for them. That there was another inter-view is certain : certain also that Saul would (or, as he said, could) throw no light on Frank's words : though the message, or some part of it, appeared to affect him horribly. But there is no record of the talk in detail. It is only said that Saul sat all that evening in the study, and when he bid good night, which he did most reluctantly, asked for the doctor's prayers.

The month of January was near its end when
Lord Kildonan, in the Embassy at Lisbon, received a
letter that for once gravely disturbed that vain man
and neglectful father. Saul was dead. The scene
at Frank's burial had been very distressing. The day
was awful in blackness and wind : the bearers, stag-
gering blindly along under the flapping black pall,
found it a hard job, when they emerged from the
porch of the minster, to make their way to the grave.
Mrs. Ashton was in her room—women did not then
go to their kinsfolk's funerals—but Saul was there,
draped in the mourning cloak of the time, and his
face was white and fixed as that of one dead, except
when, as was noticed three or four times, he suddenly
turned his head to the left and looked over his shoulder.
It was then alive with a terrible expression of listening
fear. No one saw him go away : and no one could
find him that evening. All night the gale buffeted
the high windows of the church, and howled over
the upland and roared through the woodland. It
was useless to search in the open : no voice of shouting or cry for help could possibly be heard. All that
Dr. Ashton could do was to warn the people about
the college, and the town constables, and to sit up,
on the alert for any news, and this he did. News came
early next morning, brought by the sexton, whose
business it was to open the church for early prayers
at seven, and who sent the maid rushing upstairs with
wild eyes and flying hair to summon her master.
The two men dashed across to the south door of the

minster, there to find Lord Saul clinging desperately
to the great ring of the door, his head sunk between
his shoulders, his stockings in rags, his shoes gone,
his legs torn and bloody.

This was what had to be told to Lord Kildonan,
and this really ends the first part of the story. The
tomb of Frank Sydall and of the Lord Viscount Saul,
only child and heir to William Earl of Kildonan, is
one : a stone altar tomb in Whitminster churchyard.

Dr. Ashton lived on for over thirty years in his
prebendal house, I do not know how quietly, but
without visible disturbance. His successor preferred
a house he already owned in the town, and left that
of the senior prebendary vacant. Between them
these two men saw the eighteenth century out and
the nineteenth in ; for Mr. Hindes, the successor of
Ashton, became prebendary at nine-and-twenty and
died at nine-and-eighty. So that it was not till 1823
or 1824 that anyone succeeded to the post who intended to make the house his home. The man who did
so was Dr. Henry Oldys, whose name may be known
to some of my readers as that of the author of a row
of volumes labelled *Oldys's Works,* which occupy a
place that must be honoured, since it is so rarely
touched, upon the shelves of many a substantial
library.

Dr. Oldys, his niece, and his servants took some
months to transfer furniture and books from his
Dorsetshire parsonage to the quadrangle of Whitminster, and to get everything into place. But

eventually the work was done, and the house (which, though untenanted, had always been kept sound and weather-tight) woke up, and like Monte Cristo's mansion at Auteuil, lived, sang, and bloomed once more. On a certain morning in June it looked especially fair, as Dr. Oldys strolled in his garden before breakfast and gazed over the red roof at the minster tower with its four gold vanes, backed by a very blue sky, and very white little clouds.

"Mary," he said, as he seated himself at the breakfast-table and laid down something hard and shiny on the cloth, "here's a find which the boy made just now. You'll be sharper than I if you can guess what it's meant for." It was a round and perfectly smooth tablet—as much as an inch thick—of what seemed clear glass. "It is rather attractive, at all events," said Mary: she was a fair woman, with light hair and large eyes, rather a devotee of literature. "Yes," said her uncle, "I thought you'd be pleased with it. I presume it came from the house: it turned up in the rubbish-heap in the corner." "I'm not sure that I do like it, after all," said Mary, some minutes later. "Why in the world not, my dear?" "I don't know, I'm sure. Perhaps it's only fancy." "Yes, only fancy and romance, of course. What's that book, now—the name of that book, I mean, that you had your head in all yesterday?" "*The Talisman*, Uncle. Oh, if this should turn out to be a talisman, how enchanting it would be!" "Yes, *The Talisman*: ah, well, you're welcome to it, what-

ever it is : I must be off about my business. Is
all well in the house ? Does it suit you ? Any
complaints from the servants' hall ? " " No, indeed,
nothing could be more charming. The only *soupçon*
of a complaint besides the lock of the linen closet,
which I told you of, is that Mrs. Maple says she
cannot get rid of the sawflies out of that room you
pass through at the other end of the hall. By
the way, are you sure you like your bedroom ? It
is a long way off from anyone else, you know."
" Like it ? To be sure I do ; the farther off from you,
my dear, the better. There, don't think it necessary
to beat me : accept my apologies. But what are
sawflies ? Will they eat my coats ? If not, they may
have the room to themselves for what I care. We
are not likely to be using it." " No, of course not.
Well, what she calls sawflies are those reddish things
like a daddy-long-legs, but smaller,[1] and there are a
great many of them perching about that room, certainly. I don't like them, but I don't fancy they are
mischievous." " There seem to be several things you
don't like this fine morning," said her uncle, as he
closed the door. Miss Oldys remained in her chair
looking at the tablet, which she was holding in the
palm of her hand. The smile that had been on her
face faded slowly from it and gave place to an expression of curiosity and almost strained attention. Her
reverie was broken by the entrance of Mrs. Maple,

[1] Apparently the ichneumon fly (*Ophion obscurum*), and not
the true sawfly, is meant.

and her invariable opening, " Oh, Miss, could I speak to you a minute ? "

A letter from Miss Oldys to a friend in Lichfield, begun a day or two before, is the next source for this story. It is not devoid of traces of the influence of that leader of female thought in her day, Miss Anna Seward, known to some as the Swan of Lichfield.

" My sweetest Emily will be rejoiced to hear that we are at length—my beloved uncle and myself—settled in the house that now calls us master—nay, master and mistress—as in past ages it has called so many others. Here we taste a mingling of modern elegance and hoary antiquity, such as has never ere now graced life for either of us. The town, small as it is, affords us some reflection, pale indeed, but veritable, of the sweets of polite intercourse : the adjacent country numbers amid the occupants of its scattered mansions some whose polish is annually refreshed by contact with metropolitan splendour, and others whose robust and homely geniality is, at times, and by way of contrast, not less cheering and acceptable. Tired of the parlours and drawing-rooms of our friends, we have ready to hand a refuge from the clash of wits or the small talk of the day amid the solemn beauties of our venerable minster, whose silver chimes daily ' knoll us to prayer,' and in the shady walks of whose tranquil graveyard we muse with softened heart, and ever and anon with moistened eye, upon the memorials of the young, the beautiful, the aged, the wise, and the good."

Here there is an abrupt break both in the writing and the style.

" But my dearest Emily, I can no longer write with the care which you deserve, and in which we both take pleasure. What I have to tell you is wholly foreign to what has gone before. This morning my uncle brought in to breakfast an object which had been found in the garden ; it was a glass or crystal tablet of this shape (a little sketch is given), which he handed to me, and which, after he left the room, remained on the table by me. I gazed at it, I know not why, for some minutes, till called away by the day's duties ; and you will smile incredulously when I say that I seemed to myself to begin to descry reflected in it objects and scenes which were not in the room where I was. You will not, however, think it strange that after such an experience I took the first opportunity to seclude myself in my room with what I now half believed to be a talisman of mickle might. I was not disappointed. I assure you, Emily, by that memory which is dearest to both of us, that what I went through this afternoon transcends the limits of what I had before deemed credible. In brief, what I saw, seated in my bedroom, in the broad daylight of summer, and looking into the crystal depth of that small round tablet, was this. First, a prospect, strange to me, of an enclosure of rough and hillocky grass, with a grey stone ruin in the midst, and a wall of rough stones about it. In this stood an old, and very ugly, woman in a red cloak and ragged skirt, talking to a boy dressed in the fashion of maybe a hundred years ago. She put something which glittered into his hand, and he something into hers, which I saw to be money, for a single coin fell from her trembling hand into the grass. The scene passed: I should have remarked, by the way, that on the rough walls of the enclosure I could distinguish bones, and even a skull, lying in a disorderly fashion. Next, I was looking upon two boys; one the figure of the former vision, the other younger. They were in a plot of garden, walled round, and this garden, in spite of the difference in arrangement, and the small size of the trees, I could clearly recognize as being that upon which I now look from my window. The boys were engaged in some curious play, it seemed. Something was smouldering on the ground. The elder placed his hands upon it, and then raised them in what I took to be an attitude of prayer: and I saw, and started at seeing, that on them were deep stains of blood. The sky above was overcast. The same boy now turned his face towards the wall of the garden, and beckoned with both his raised hands, and as he did so I was conscious that some moving objects were becoming visible over the top of the wall—whether heads or other parts of some animal or human forms I could not tell. Upon the instant the elder boy turned sharply, seized the arm of the younger (who all this time had been poring over what lay on the ground), and both hurried off. I then saw blood upon the grass, a little pile of bricks, and what I thought were black feathers scattered about. That scene closed, and the next was so dark that perhaps the full meaning of it escaped me. But what I seemed to see was a form, at first crouching low among trees or bushes that were being threshed by a violent wind, then running very swiftly, and constantly turning a pale face to look behind him, as if he feared a pursuer : and, indeed, pursuers were following hard after him. Their shapes were but dimly seen, their number—three or four, perhaps—only guessed. I suppose they were on the whole more like dogs than anything else, but dogs such as we have seen they assuredly were not. Could I have closed my eyes to this horror, I would have done so at once, but I was helpless. The last I saw was the victim darting beneath an arch and clutching at some object to which he clung : and those that were pursuing him overtook him, and I seemed to hear the echo of a cry of despair. It may be that I became unconscious : certainly I had the sensation of awaking to the light of day after an interval of darkness. Such, in literal truth, Emily, was my vision —I can call it by no other name—of this afternoon. Tell me, have I not been the unwilling witness of some episode of a tragedy connected with this very house ? "

The letter is continued next day. " The tale of yesterday was not completed when I laid down my pen. I said nothing of my experiences to my uncle —you know, yourself, how little his robust common sense would be prepared to allow of them, and how in his eyes the specific remedy would be a black draught or a glass of port. After a silent evening, then—silent, not sullen—I retired to rest. Judge of my terror, when, not yet in bed, I heard what I can only describe as a distant bellow, and knew it for my uncle's voice, though never in my hearing so exerted before. His sleeping-room is at the farther extremity of this large house, and to gain access to it one must traverse an antique hall some eighty feet long, a lofty panelled chamber, and two unoccupied bedrooms. In the second of these— a room almost devoid of furniture—I found him, in the dark, his candle lying smashed on the floor. As I ran in, bearing a light, he clasped me in arms that trembled for the first time since I have known him, thanked God, and hurried me out of the room. He would say nothing of what had alarmed him. ' To-morrow, to-morrow,' was all I could get from him. A bed was hastily improvised for him in the room next to my own. I doubt if his night was more restful than mine. I could only get to sleep in the small hours, when daylight was already strong, and then my dreams were of the grimmest—particularly one which stamped itself on my brain, and which I must set down on the chance of dispersing the impression it has made. It was that I came up to my room with a heavy foreboding of evil oppressing me, and went with a hesitation and reluctance I could not explain to my chest of drawers. I opened the top drawer, in which was nothing but ribbons and hand-kerchiefs, and then the second, where was as little to alarm, and then, O heavens, the third and last : and there was a mass of linen neatly folded : upon which, as I looked with a curiosity that began to be tinged with horror, I perceived a movement in it, and a pink hand was thrust out of the folds and began to grope feebly in the air. I could bear it no more, and rushed from the room, clapping the door after me, and strove with all my force to lock it. But the key would not turn in the wards, and from within the room came a sound of rustling and bumping, drawing nearer and nearer to the door. Why I did not flee down the stairs I know not. I continued grasping the handle, and mercifully, as the door was plucked from my hand with an irresistible force, I awoke. You may not think this very alarming, but I assure you it was so to me.

" At breakfast to-day my uncle was very uncommunicative, and I think ashamed of the fright he had given us ; but afterwards he inquired of me whether Mr. Spearman was still in town, adding that he thought that was a young man who had some sense left in his head. I think you know, my dear Emily, that I am not inclined to disagree with him there, and also that I was not unlikely to be able to answer his question. To Mr. Spearman he accordingly went, and I have not seen him since. I must send this strange budget of news to you now, or it may have to wait over more than one post."

The reader will not be far out if he guesses that Miss Mary and Mr. Spearman made a match of it not very long after this month of June. Mr. Spearman was a young spark, who had a good property in the neighbourhood of Whitminster, and not unfrequently about this time spent a few days at the " King's Head," ostensibly on business. But he must have had some leisure, for his diary is copious, especially for the days of which I am telling the story. It is probable to me that he wrote this episode as fully as he could at the bidding of Miss Mary.

" Uncle Oldys (how I hope I may have the right to call him so before long!) called this morning. After throwing out a good many short remarks on indifferent topics, he said, ' I wish, Spearman, you'd listen to an odd story and keep a close tongue about it just for a bit, till I get more light on it.' ' To be sure,' said I, ' you may count on me.' ' I don't know what to make of it,' he said. ' You know my bed-room. It is well away from everyone else's, and I pass through the great hall and two or three other rooms to get to it.' ' Is it at the end next the minster, then ? ' I asked. ' Yes, it is : well, now, yesterday morning my Mary told me that the room next before it was infested with some sort of fly that the house-keeper couldn't get rid of. That may be the explana-tion, or it may not. What do you think ? ' ' Why,' said I, ' you've not yet told me what has to be ex-plained.' ' True enough, I don't believe I have ; but by the by, what are these saw flies ? What's the size of them ? ' I began to wonder if he was touched in the head. ' What I call a sawfly,' I said very patiently, ' is a red animal, like a daddy-long-legs, but not so big, perhaps an inch long, perhaps less. It is very hard in the body, and to me '—I was going to say ' particularly offensive,' but he broke in, ' Come, come; an inch or less. That won't do.' ' I can only tell you,' I said, ' what I know. Would it not be better if you told me from first to last what it is that has puzzled you, and then I may be able to give you some kind of an opinion.' He gazed at me meditatively. ' Perhaps it would,' he said. ' I told Mary only to-day that I thought you had some vestiges of sense in your head.' (I bowed my acknowledgments.) ' The thing is, I've an odd kind of shyness about talking of it. Nothing of the sort has happened to me before. Well, about eleven o'clock last night, or after, I took my candle and set out for my room. I had a book in my other hand—I always read something for a few minutes before I drop off to sleep. A dangerous habit: I don't recommend it: but *I* know how to manage my light and my bed curtains. Now then, first, as I stepped out of my study into the great hall that's next to it, and shut the door, my candle went out. I supposed I had clapped the door behind me too quick, and made a draught, and I was annoyed, for I'd no tinder-box nearer than my bedroom. But I knew my way well enough, and went on. The next thing was that my book was struck out of my hand in the dark : if I said twitched out of my hand it would better express the sensation. It fell on the floor. I picked it up, and went on, more annoyed than before, and a little startled. But as you know, that hall has many windows without curtains, and in summer nights like these it's easy to see not only where the furniture is, but whether there's anyone or anything moving: and there was no one —nothing of the kind. So on I went through the hall and through the audit chamber next to it, which also has big windows, and then into the bedrooms which lead to my own, where the curtains were drawn, and I had to go slower because of steps here and there. It was in the second of those rooms that I nearly got my *quietus*. The moment I opened the door of it I felt there was something wrong. I thought twice, I confess, whether I shouldn't turn back and find another way there is to my room rather than go through that one. Then I was ashamed of myself, and thought what people call better of it, though I don't know about " better " in this case. If I was to describe my experience exactly, I should say this: there was a dry, light, rustling sound all over the room as I went in, and then (you remember it was perfectly dark) something seemed to rush at me, and there was —I don't know how to put it—a sensation of long thin arms, or legs, or feelers, all about my face, and neck, and body. Very little strength in them, there seemed to be, but, Spearman, I don't think I was ever more horrified or disgusted in all my life, that I remember: and it does take something to put me out. I roared out as loud as I could, and flung away my candle at random, and, knowing I was near the

window, I tore at the curtain and somehow let in
enough light to be able to see something waving
which I knew was an insect's leg, by the shape of it :
but, Lord, what a size ! Why, the beast must have
been as tall as I am. And now you tell me sawflies
are an inch long or less. What do you make of it,
Spearman ? '

" ' For goodness' sake finish your story first,' I said.
' I never heard anything like it.' ' Oh,' said he,
' there's no more to tell. Mary ran in with a light,
and there was nothing there. I didn't tell her what
was the matter. I changed my room for last night,
and I expect for good.' ' Have you searched this odd
room of yours ? ' I said. ' What do you keep in it ? '
' We don't use it,' he answered. ' There's an old
press there, and some little other furniture.' ' And
in the press ? ' said I. ' I don't know ; I never saw it
opened, but I do know that it's locked.' ' Well, I
should have it looked into, and, if you had time, I
own to having some curiosity to see the place myself.'
' I didn't exactly like to ask you, but that's rather what
I hoped you'd say. Name your time and I'll take
you there.' ' No time like the present,' I said at once,
for I saw he would never settle down to anything while
this affair was in suspense. He got up with great
alacrity, and looked at me, I am tempted to think,
with marked approval. ' Come along,' was all he
said, however ; and was pretty silent all the way to
his house. My Mary (as he calls her in public, and I
in private) was summoned, and we proceeded to the

room. The Doctor had gone so far as to tell her
that he had had something of a fright there last night,
of what nature he had not yet divulged ; but now he
pointed out and described, very briefly, the incidents
of his progress. When we were near the important
spot, he pulled up, and allowed me to pass on.
' There's the room,' he said. ' Go in, Spearman, and
tell us what you find.' Whatever I might have felt
at midnight, noonday I was sure would keep back
anything sinister, and I flung the door open with an
air and stepped in. It was a well-lighted room, with
its large window on the right, though not, I thought,
a very airy one. The principal piece of furniture was
the gaunt old press of dark wood. There was, too,
a four-post bedstead, a mere skeleton which could
hide nothing, and there was a chest of drawers. On
the window-sill and the floor near it were the dead
bodies of many hundred sawflies, and one torpid one
which I had some satisfaction in killing. I tried the
door of the press, but could not open it : the drawers,
too, were locked. Somewhere, I was conscious, there
was a faint rustling sound, but I could not locate it,
and when I made my report to those outside, I said
nothing of it. But, I said, clearly the next thing was
to see what was in those locked receptacles. Uncle
Oldys turned to Mary. ' Mrs. Maple,' he said, and
Mary ran off—no one, I am sure, steps like her—and
soon came back at a soberer pace, with an elderly
lady of discreet aspect.

" ' Have you the keys of these things, Mrs. Maple ? '

said Uncle Oldys. His simple words let loose a
torrent (not violent, but copious) of speech : had she
been a shade or two higher in the social scale, Mrs.
Maple might have stood as the model for Miss Bates.

" ' Oh, Doctor, and Miss, and you too, sir,' she
said, acknowledging my presence with a bend, ' them
keys ! who was that again that come when first we
took over things in this house—a gentleman in business it was, and I gave him his luncheon in the small
parlour on account of us not having everything as
we should like to see it in the large one—chicken,
and apple-pie, and a glass of madeira—dear, dear,
you'll say I'm running on, Miss Mary ; but I only
mention it to bring back my recollection ; and there
it comes—Gardner, just the same as it did last week
with the artichokes and the text of the sermon. Now
that Mr. Gardner, every key I got from him were
labelled to itself, and each and every one was a key
of some door or another in this house, and sometimes
two ; and when I say door, my meaning is door of a
room, not like such a press as this is. Yes, Miss Mary,
I know full well, and I'm just making it clear to your
uncle and you too, sir. But now there *was* a box
which this same gentleman he give over into my
charge, and thinking no harm after he was gone I
took the liberty, knowing it was your uncle's property,
to rattle it : and unless I'm most surprisingly deceived,
in that box there was keys, but what keys, that,
Doctor, is known Elsewhere, for open the box, no
that I would not do.'

" I wondered that Uncle Oldys remained as quiet as he did under this address. Mary, I knew, was amused by it, and he probably had been taught by experience that it was useless to break in upon it. At any rate he did not, but merely said at the end, ' Have you that box handy, Mrs. Maple? If so, you might bring it here.' Mrs. Maple pointed her finger at him, either in accusation or in gloomy triumph. ' There,' she said, ' was I to choose out the very words out of your mouth, Doctor, them would be the ones. And if I've took it to my own rebuke one half a dozen times, it's been nearer fifty. Laid awake I have in my bed, sat down in my chair I have, the same you and Miss Mary gave me the day I was twenty year in your service, and no person could desire a better—yes, Miss Mary, but it *is* the truth, and well we know who it is would have it different if he could. " All very well," says I to myself, " but pray, when the Doctor calls you to account for that box, what are you going to say? " No, Doctor, if you was some masters I've heard of and I was some servants I could name, I should have an easy task before me, but things being, humanly speaking, what they are, the one course open to me is just to say to you that without Miss Mary comes to my room and helps me to my recollection, which her wits *may* manage what's slipped beyond mine, no such box as that, small though it be, will cross your eyes this many a day to come.'

" ' Why, dear Mrs. Maple, why didn't you tell me

before that you wanted me to help you to find it?' said my Mary. 'No, never mind telling me why it was: let us come at once and look for it.' They hastened off together. I could hear Mrs. Maple beginning an explanation which, I doubt not, lasted into the farthest recesses of the housekeeper's department. Uncle Oldys and I were left alone. 'A valuable servant,' he said, nodding towards the door. 'Nothing goes wrong under her: the speeches are seldom over three minutes.' 'How will Miss Oldys manage to make her remember about the box?' I asked.

"'Mary? Oh, she'll make her sit down and ask her about her aunt's last illness, or who gave her the china dog on the mantelpiece—something quite off the point. Then, as Maple says, one thing brings up another, and the right one will come round sooner than you could suppose. There! I believe I hear them coming back already.'

"It was indeed so, and Mrs. Maple was hurrying on ahead of Mary with the box in her outstretched hand, and a beaming face. 'What was it,' she cried as she drew near, 'what was it as I said, before ever I come out of Dorsetshire to this place? Not that I'm a Dorset woman myself, nor had need to be. "Safe bind, safe find," and there it was in the place where I'd put it—what?—two months back, I dare say.' She handed it to Uncle Oldys, and he and I examined it with some interest, so that I ceased to pay attention to Mrs. Ann Maple for the moment, though I know that she went on to expound exactly where the box had been, and in what way Mary had helped to refresh her memory on the subject.

"It was an oldish box, tied with pink tape and sealed, and on the lid was pasted a label inscribed in old ink, 'The Senior Prebendary's House, Whitminster.' On being opened it was found to contain two keys of moderate size, and a paper, on which, in the same hand as the label, was 'Keys of the Press and Box of Drawers standing in the disused Chamber.' Also this : 'The Effects in this Press and Box are held by me, and to be held by my successors in the Residence, in trust for the noble Family of Kildonan, if claim be made by any survivor of it. I having made all the Enquiry possible to myself am of the opinion that that noble House is wholly extinct : the last Earl having been, as is notorious, cast away at sea, and his only Child and Heire deceas'd in my House (the Papers as to which melancholy Casualty were by me repos'd in the same Press in this year of our Lord 1753, 21 March). I am further of opinion that unless grave discomfort arise, such persons, not being of the Family of Kildonan, as shall become possess'd of these keys, will be well advised to leave matters as they are : which opinion I do not express without weighty and sufficient reason ; and am Happy to have my Judgment confirm'd by the other Members of this College and Church who are conversant with the Events referr'd to in this Paper. Tho. Ashton, *S.T.P.*, *Præb. senr.* Will. Blake, *S.T.P.*, *Decanus.* Hen. Goodman, *S.T.B.*, *Præb. junr.*'

" ' Ah ! ' said Uncle Oldys, ' grave discomfort !
So he thought there might be something. I suspect
it was that young man,' he went on, pointing with
the key to the line about the ' only Child and Heire.'
' Eh, Mary ? The viscounty of Kildonan was Saul.'
' How *do* you know that, Uncle ? ' said Mary. ' Oh,
why not ? it's all in Debrett—two little fat books.
But I meant the tomb by the lime walk. He's there.
What's the story, I wonder ? Do you know it, Mrs.
Maple ? and, by the way, look at your sawflies by the
window there.'

" Mrs. Maple, thus confronted with two subjects
at once, was a little put to it to do justice to both.
It was no doubt rash in Uncle Oldys to give her the
opportunity. I could only guess that he had some
slight hesitation about using the key he held in his
hand.

" ' Oh them flies, how bad they was, Doctor and
Miss, this three or four days : and you, too, sir, you
wouldn't guess, none of you ! And how they come,
too ! First we took the room in hand, the shutters
was up, and had been, I dare say, years upon years, and
not a fly to be seen. Then we got the shutter bars
down with a deal of trouble and left it so for the day,
and next day I sent Susan in with the broom to sweep
about, and not two minutes hadn't passed when out
she come into the hall like a blind thing, and we had
regular to beat them off her. Why, her cap and her
hair, you couldn't see the colour of it, I do assure you,
and all clustering round her eyes, too. Fortunate

enough she's not a girl with fancies, else if it had been
me, why only the tickling of the nasty things would
have drove me out of my wits. And now there they
lay like so many dead things. Well, they was lively
enough on the Monday, and now here's Thursday,
is it, or no, Friday. Only to come near the door and
you'd hear them pattering up against it, and once you
opened it, dash at you, they would, as if they'd eat
you. I couldn't help thinking to myself, " If you was
bats, where should we be this night ? " Nor you
can't cresh 'em, not like a usual kind of a fly. Well,
there's something to be thankful for, if we could but
learn by it. And then this tomb, too,' she said,
hastening on to her second point to elude any chance
of interruption, ' of them two poor young lads. I
say poor, and yet when I recollect myself, I was at
tea with Mrs. Simpkins, the sexton's wife, before you
come, Doctor and Miss Mary, and that's a family has
been in the place, what ? I dare say a hundred years
in that very house, and could put their hand on any
tomb or yet grave in all the yard and give you name
and age. And his account of that young man, Mr.
Simpkins's I mean to say—*well !* " She compressed
her lips and nodded several times. ' Tell us, Mrs.
Maple,' said Mary. ' Go on,' said Uncle Oldys.
' What about him ? ' said I. ' Never was such a
thing seen in this place, not since Queen Mary's
times and the Pope and all,' said Mrs. Maple. ' Why,
do you know he lived in this very house, him and
them that was with him, and for all I can tell in this

identical room' (she shifted her feet uneasily on the floor). 'Who was with him? Do you mean the people of the house?' said Uncle Oldys suspiciously. 'Not to call people, Doctor, dear no,' was the answer; 'more what he brought with him from Ireland, I believe it was. No, the people in the house was the last to hear anything of his goings-on. But in the town not a family but knew how he stopped out at night: and them that was with him, why, they were such as would strip the skin from the child in its grave; and a withered heart makes an ugly thin ghost, says Mr. Simpkins. But they turned on him at the last, he says, and there's the mark still to be seen on the minster door where they run him down. And that's no more than the truth, for I got him to show it to myself, and that's what he said. A lord he was, with a Bible name of a wicked king, whatever his god-fathers could have been thinking of.' 'Saul was the name,' said Uncle Oldys. 'To be sure it was Saul, Doctor, and thank you; and now isn't it King Saul that we read of raising up the dead ghost that was slumbering in its tomb till he disturbed it, and isn't that a strange thing, this young lord to have such a name, and Mr. Simpkins's grandfather to see him out of his window of a dark night going about from one grave to another in the yard with a candle, and them that was with him following through the grass at his heels: and one night him to come right up to old Mr. Simpkins's window that gives on the yard and press his face up against it to find out if there was anyone in the room that could see him : and only just time there was for old Mr. Simpkins to drop down like, quiet, just under the window and hold his breath, and not stir till he heard him stepping away again, and this rustling-like in the grass after him as he went, and then when he looked out of his window in the morning there was treadings in the grass and a dead man's bone. Oh, he was a cruel child for certain, but he had to pay in the end, and after.' 'After ? ' said Uncle Oldys, with a frown. ' Oh yes, Doctor, night after night in old Mr. Simpkins's time, and his son, that's our Mr. Simpkins's father, yes, and our own Mr. Simpkins too. Up against that same window, particular when they've had a fire of a chilly evening, with his face right on the panes, and his hands fluttering out, and his mouth open and shut, open and shut, for a minute or more, and then gone off in the dark yard. But open the window at such times, no, that they dare not do, though they could find it in their heart to pity the poor thing, that pinched up with the cold, and seemingly fading away to a nothink as the years passed on. Well, indeed, I believe it is no more than the truth what our Mr. Simpkins says on his own grandfather's word, " A withered heart makes an ugly thin ghost." ' ' I dare say,' said Uncle Oldys suddenly : so suddenly that Mrs. Maple stopped short. ' Thank you. Come away, all of you.' ' Why, *Uncle*,' said Mary, ' are you not going to open the press after all ? ' Uncle Oldys blushed, actually blushed. ' My dear,' he said, ' you are at liberty to call me a coward, or applaud me as a prudent man, whichever you please. But I am neither going to open that press nor that chest of drawers myself, nor am I going to hand over the keys to you or to any other person. Mrs. Maple, will you kindly see about getting a man or two to move those pieces of furniture into the garret?' 'And when they do it, Mrs. Maple,' said Mary, who seemed to me—I did not then know why—more relieved than disappointed by her uncle's decision, 'I have something that I want put with the rest; only quite a small packet.'

"We left that curious room not unwillingly, I think. Uncle Oldys's orders were carried out that same day. And so," concludes Mr. Spearman, "Whitminster has a Bluebeard's chamber, and, I am rather inclined to suspect, a Jack-in-the-box, awaiting some future occupant of the residence of the senior prebendary."